THE WORKS OF
VICTOR HUGO

IN TWENTY VOLUMES

L IMITED TO FIVE HUNDRED
REGISTERED SETS, OF WHICH
THIS IS NUMBER.............................

THE WORKS OF
VICTOR HUGO

VOLUME TEN

TOILERS OF THE SEA

PART TWO

BUG-JARGAL

THE JENSON SOCIETY
PRINTED FOR MEMBERS ONLY
MCMVII

CONTENTS

LIST OF ILLUSTRATIONS

CONTENTS

Vol. II.

PART II.— MALICIOUS GILLIATT.

BOOK I.— The Reef.

BOOK II.— The Task.

BOOK III.— The Struggle.

TOILERS OF THE SEA

TOILERS OF THE SEA

PART II

MALICIOUS GILLIATT

BOOK I

THE REEF

CHAPTER I

EASY TO REACH, BUT DIFFICULT TO LEAVE

THE bark which had been seen by so many persons on the coast of Guernsey the previous evening was, as the reader has probably suspected, the old Dutch barge or sloop. Gilliatt had chosen the channel between the rocks along the coast. It was the most dangerous route, but it was also the most direct. To reach his destination as soon as possible was his only thought. Shipwrecks will not wait; the sea is an urgent creditor; an hour's delay may be irreparable. He was anxious to go to the rescue of the machinery immediately.

One of his objects in leaving Guernsey at night was to avoid notice.

1

He set out like one fleeing from justice, and anxious to hide from human eyes. He shunned the eastern coast, as if he did not care to pass within sight of St. Sampson and St. Peter's Port, and glided silently along the opposite coast, which is comparatively uninhabited. It was necessary to ply the oars among the breakers; but Gilliatt managed them on scientific principles. Taking the water quietly, and dropping it with perfect regularity, he was able to move on in the darkness with very little noise and great rapidity. So stealthy were his movements that one might have supposed him bent upon some evil deed.

The fact is, though he was embarking in an enterprise which might well be called impossible, and was risking his life with every chance against him, his greatest fear was of some possible rival.

As day began to break, those unseen eyes which look down on the world from boundless space might have beheld, in one of the most dangerous and lonely places in the channel, two objects, the distance between which gradually decreased as one approached the other. One which was almost imperceptible in the general movement of the waters, was a sailboat. In this sailboat was a man. It was Gilliatt's sloop.

The other, black, motionless, colossal, rose high above the waves. It was of singular form. Two tall pillars emerging from the sea bore aloft a sort of cross-beam that strongly resembled a bridge between them. This bridge, so singular in shape that it was impossible to imagine what it really was, from a distance, touched each of the two pillars. The whole thing looked like a vast portal. Of what use could such a structure be in the open sea, which stretched far and wide around it? It might have been a Titanic Dolmen, planted there in mid-ocean by an imperious whim, and built by hands accustomed to proportion their labours to the mighty deep. Its huge outlines stood out in bold relief against the clear sky.

The morning light was growing stronger in the east; the

whiteness in the horizon made the water look still darker. In the western sky the moon was sinking.

The two tall perpendicular rocks were the Douvres. The huge mass held fast between them, like an architrave between two pillars, was the wreck of the Durande.

The rocks, thus holding fast and exhibiting their prey, were terrible to behold. Inanimate things sometimes look as if they were endowed with a grim and hostile spirit towards man. There was a menace in the attitude of these rocks. They seemed to be biding their time.

Their whole appearance was highly suggestive of haughtiness and arrogance.

The two rocks, still dripping from the tempest of the day before, were like two wrestlers sweating from a recent contest. The wind had subsided; the sea rippled gently, but the presence of breakers might be detected here and there in light streaks of foam upon the surface of the waters. A sound like the murmuring of bees arose from the sea.

Up to a certain height the Douvres were thickly covered with sea-weed; above this, their steep haunches glittered in places like polished armour. They seemed ready to commence the strife anew. The beholder felt that they were rooted deep in mountains whose summits were beneath the sea. Their aspect was full of tragic power.

Ordinarily the sea conceals her crimes. She delights in secrecy. Her unfathomable depths maintain a rigorous silence. She envelops herself in mystery and very rarely consents to disclose secrets. We know her savage nature, but who knows the extent of her evil deeds? She is at once open and secretive. She wrecks a vessel, and covering it with the waves, ingulfs it deep, as if conscious of her guilt. One of her worst crimes is hypocrisy. She slays and steals, then she conceals her booty, assumes an air of unconsciousness, and smiles. She roars like a lion one minute, and bleats like a lamb the next. There was nothing of that kind here, however. The Douvres, lifting above the level of the waters the shattered hull of the Durande, wore an air of triumph. One might have fancied they were two monstrous arms, reaching upwards from the gulf, and exhibiting to the tempest the lifeless body of the ship.   Their aspect was like that of an assassin boasting of his evil deeds.

The hour contributed not a little to the solemnity of the scene.   There is a mysterious grandeur in the dawn as of the border-land between the region of consciousness and the world of our dreams.   There is something almost ghastly about this transition period.   The immense form of the two Douvres, like a capital letter H, the Durande forming its cross-stroke, stood out against the horizon in a sort of gruesome majesty.

Gilliatt was attired in his seaman's rig,— a woollen shirt, woollen stockings, thick shoes, a knitted jacket, trousers of thick stuff, with pockets, and upon his head a cap of red worsted, of the kind then in use among sailors, and known in the last century as a *galérienne*.

He recognized the rocks, and steered towards them.

The situation of the Durande was exactly the contrary of that of a vessel gone to the bottom: it was a vessel suspended in mid-air.

No stranger instance of salvage as ever seen.

It was broad daylight when Gilliatt neared the Douvres.

As we have said, there was very little sea.   The slight agitation of the water was due almost entirely to its confinement among the rocks.   Every passage, small or large, is subject to this chopping movement.   The inside of a channel is always more or less white with foam.

Gilliatt did not approach the Douvres without caution.

He cast the sounding-lead several times.

He had a cargo to land.

Accustomed to long absences, he had a number of necessaries always ready at home.   He had brought with him a sack of biscuit, another of rye-meal, a basket of salt fish and smoked beef, a large can of fresh water; a gaily painted Norwegian chest, containing several coarse woollen shirts, his tarpaulin and waterproof overalls, and a sheepskin which he was accustomed to throw over him at night.   On leaving the

Bu de la Rue he had put all these things into the barge, with the addition of a large loaf of bread. In his haste, he had brought no other tools but his huge forge-hammer, his axe and hatchet, and saw, and a knotted rope, fastened to a grappling-iron. With a ladder of that sort, provided one knows how to use it, the steepest rocks become accessible, and a good sailor will find it possible to scale the highest escarpment. In the island of Sark the visitor can see what feats the fishermen of the Havre Gosselin manage to accomplish with a knotted rope.

His nets and lines and all his fishing tackle were in the sloop. He had placed them there mechanically and rather from force of habit than otherwise; for he intended, if his enterprise succeeded, to remain for some time in a region of breakers, where fishing nets and tackle are of very little use.

When Gilliatt approached the great rock the sea was retiring; a circumstance favourable to his purpose, for the ebbing tide left bare one or two table-rocks, horizontal, or only slightly inclined, at the foot of the smaller Douvre. These table-rocks which varied considerably in breadth, some being narrow and some very wide, and which stood at unequal distances along the side of the great perpendicular column, were continued in the form of a thin cornice up to a spot just beneath the Durande, which was held fast between the two rocks as in a vice.

This series of platforms would be convenient for approaching and surveying the position. It was convenient also for disembarking the contents of the barge provisionally; but it was necessary to make haste, for it was only above water for a few hours. With the rising tide the table-rocks would be again covered with foam.

It was in front of these table-rocks that Gilliatt pushed in and brought the boat to a standstill.

A thick mass of wet and slippery sea-wrack covered them, rendered more slippery here and there by their sloping surface.

Gilliatt pulled off his shoes, sprang bare-footed on to the slimy weeds, and made the sloop fast to a point of rock.

Then he advanced as far as he could along the granite cornice, reached the rock immediately beneath the wreck, looked up, and examined it.

The Durande had been caught between the two rocks, about twenty feet above the water. It must have been a huge billow that had carried her there.

Such effects from furious seas are not surprising to those who are familiar with the ocean. To cite one example only: — On the 25th of January, 1840, in the Gulf of Stora, a tempest struck a brig, and carried it intact over the broken wreck of the corvette " La Marne," and fixed it immovably, bowsprit first, in a gap between the cliffs.

The Douvres, however, held only a part of the Durande.

The vessel had been, as it were, uprooted from the waters by the hurricane. A whirlwind had hurled it against the counteracting force of the rolling waves, and the vessel thus caught in contrary directions by the two claws of the tempest had snapped like a lath. The afterpart, with the engine and the paddles, lifted out of the foam and driven by the fury of the cyclone into passage between the Douvres, had plunged in up to her midship beam, and remained wedged there.

The blow that had driven it in this fashion between the two rocks, had been as accurately directed as if dealt with a hammer. The forecastle, carried away by the sea, had fallen in fragments among the breakers.

The hold, broken in, had scattered the bodies of the drowned cattle upon the sea.

A large portion of the forward side and bulwarks still hung to the riders by the larboard paddle-box, and by some shattered braces that could be severed with the blow from a hatchet.

Beams, planks, bits of canvas, pieces of chain, and other fragments of wreck were lying around here and there on the rugged rocks.

Gilliatt examined the Durande attentively. The keel formed a roof over his head.

A cloudless sky stretched far and wide over the motionless waters. The sun rose gloriously above the vast azure circle.

Now and then a drop of water oozed from the wreck and fell into the sea below.

CHAPTER II

THE CATALOGUE OF DISASTERS

THE Douvres differed in shape as well as in height. Upon the Little Douvre, which was curved and pointed, long veins of reddish rock, of a comparatively soft texture, could be seen running through the granite. At the edges of these red veins were fractures which would be of great service in climbing. One of these openings, a little above the wreck, had been so worn and scooped out by the action of the waves that it had become a sort of niche, in which it would have been quite possible to place a statue. The granite of the Little Douvre was rounded at the surface, and as soft as the touchstone; but this peculiarity did not impair its durability. The Little Douvre terminated in a point like a horn. The Great Douvre, polished, smooth, glossy, perpendicular, and looking as if it had been cut out by the builder's square, was in one piece, and seemed made of black ivory. There was not a hole or a break in its smooth surface. The place looked inhospitable enough. A convict could not have used it for a refuge, nor a bird for its nest. True, there was a horizontal space on its summit as upon " The Man " rock; but the summit of the Great Douvre was inaccessible.

It was possible to scale the Little Douvre, but not to remain on the summit; it would have been possible to remain on the summit of the Great Douvre, but not to scale it.

Gilliatt, having rapidly taken in the situation of affairs, returned to the sloop, landed its contents upon the largest of the horizontal rocks, made the whole mass into a sort of bale, which he rolled up in tarpaulin, made a slip-noose around it with his rope, pushed the package into a nook in the rocks where the waves could not reach it, and then clutching the Little Douvre with his hands, and holding on with his naked feet, he clambered from projection to projection, and from niche to niche, until he found himself on a level with the wrecked vessel.

Having reached the height of the paddle-wheels, he leaped on deck.

The interior of the wreck presented a terrible aspect.

Traces of a frightful struggle were everywhere visible. The ravages of the wind and waves could be seen on every side. The action of the tempest resembles the violence of a band of pirates. The storm-cloud, the thunder, the rain, the squall, the waves, and the breakers are a formidable band of destroyers.

Standing upon the dismantled deck, it was easy to picture the orgy that had been held there by spirits of the storm. All around were traces of their rage. The strange distortion of many parts of the iron-work testified to the terrific force of the gale.

No wild beast can compare with the sea for mangling its prey. Each wave has its talons. The north wind rends, the billows shatter, the waves are like hungry jaws. The ocean strikes as a lion strikes with its heavy paw, tearing and dismembering at the same time.

The destruction everywhere apparent in the Durande had the peculiarity of being detailed and minute. It was a sort of horrible stripping and plucking. Much of it seemed to have been done designedly. The beholder was tempted to exclaim, " What wanton mischief! "

The planking was jagged here and there artistically. This peculiarity is common in the ravages made by a cyclone. To chip and tear away is one of the whims of that great devastator. Its ways resemble those of the professional torturer. The damages which it causes appear like ingenious punishments. One might fancy it actuated by the worst passions of man. It has the refined cruelty of a savage. While it is exterminating, it dissects bone by bone. It tortures its victim, revenges itself, and appears to take delight in its work. It even seems to stoop to petty acts of malice.

Cyclones are rare in our latitudes, and are for that reason the more dangerous, being generally unexpected. A rock in the pathway of a heavy wind may become the pivot of a storm. It is probable that the squall had rotated around the Douvres, and been suddenly turned into a waterspout by its encounter with the rocks,— a fact which explained the casting of a vessel so high between them. In a cyclone the wind drives the largest vessel onward as swiftly and easily as a stone is hurled from a sling.

The injury which the Durande had received was like the wound of a man cut in twain. It was a divided trunk from which depended a mass of *débris* like the entrails of a human body. Various kinds of cordage hung floating and trembling, chains swung clattering; the fibres and nerves of the vessel hung there naked and exposed. Everything that was not shattered was disjointed. Some fragments of the sheething resembled currycombs bristling with nails; a hand-spike had become nothing but a piece of iron; a sounding-lead, nothing but a lump of metal; a dead-eye had become a mere piece of wood; a halliard, an end of rope; a strand of rope, a tangled skein. Naught remained that was not unhooked, unnailed, cracked, torn, warped and pierced with holes. Nothing hung together in the dreadful mass, everything was torn, dislocated or broken. Upon every side reigned that wild disorder which characterizes the scene of all struggles,— from the *melées* of men, which are called battles, to the *melées* of the elements, to which we give the name of chaos. Everything was hanging lose and dropping off. A rolling mass of planks, panelling, iron-work, cables, and beams had stopped just at one edge of the big rent in the hull, where the least additional shock would have precipitated it into the water below.

This remnant of her once powerful frame, suspended here between the two Douvres and in imminent danger of falling at any moment, was cracked here and there, showing through big apertures the dismal gloom within.

———·—·—·—·—

CHAPTER III

SOUND, BUT NOT SAFE

GILLIATT had not expected to find only a part of the ship left. Nothing in the account given by the captain of the " Shealtiel " had led him to anticipate this division of the vessel in the center. It was probable that the " frightful crash " heard by the captain of the " Shealtiel " had marked the moment when this destruction had taken place under the blows of a tremendous sea. The captain had borne off a little doubtless just before this last heavy squall; and what he had taken for a huge wave was probably a waterspout. Later, when he drew near again to observe the wreck, he had only been able to see the stern of the vessel, the remainder,— that is to say, the large opening where the forepart had given way, — having been concealed from him by huge masses of rock.

With that exception, the information given by the captain of the " Shealtiel " was strictly correct. The hull was useless, but the engine remained intact.

Such cases are common in the history of shipwrecks. The logic of disaster at sea is beyond human science.

The masts, having snapped off short, had fallen over the side; the smoke-stack was not even bent. The thick iron plating which supported the machinery had kept it together. The planks of the paddle-boxes were disjointed, like the slats of wooden shutters; but through the apertures thus made the paddles themselves could be seen in good condition. A few of their floats only were missing.

The huge stern capstan had escaped destruction as well as the machinery. Its chain was there, and, thanks to its firm fixture in a frame of joists, might still be of service, unless the strain of the voyal should break away the planking. The floor of the deck bent at almost every point, and seemed unsafe throughout.

On the other hand, the trunk of the hull, wedged between the Douvres, held together, as we have already said, and appeared strong.

There was something like derision in this preservation of the machinery; something which imparted an air of irony to the misfortune. The grim malice of the unseen powers of mischief displays itself sometimes in such bitter mockeries. The machinery was safe, but its preservation did not make it any the less lost. The ocean seemed to have kept it only to demolish it at her leisure, as a cat toys with her prey.

To suffer there and to be dismembered day by day seemed its inevitable fate. It seemed doomed to be the plaything of the cruel, relentless sea, and slowly to dwindle away until it disappeared altogether. For what could be done? That this huge mass of machinery and gearing, so ponderous and yet so delicate in its construction, thus hopelessly imprisoned here, could escape slow, but none the less sure, destruction in this lonely, inaccessible spot, seemed an utter impossibility.

The Durande was the captive of the Douvres.

How could she be extricated from that position?

How could she be delivered from her bondage?

This was, indeed, a perplexing problem!

CHAPTER IV

A PRELIMINARY SURVEY

GILLIATT was beset on every side with urgent demands upon his attention. The most pressing, however, was to find a safe harbour for the sloop; then, a shelter for himself.

The Durande having settled down more on the larboard than on the starboard side, the right paddle-box was much higher than the left.

Gilliatt climbed upon the right paddle-box. From that position, although the cleft extending at an acute angle behind the Douvres had several elbows, he was able to study the ground-plan of the group.

This survey was the preliminary step of his operations.

The Douvres, as we have already described them, were like two high-gable ends, forming the narrow entrance to a straggling alley of small cliffs with perpendicular sides. It is not unusual to find in primitive submarine formations these singular passages, which seem to have been cut with a hatchet.

This defile was extremely winding, and never dry even at low water. A turbulent current traversed it from end to end at all times. The sharpness of its turnings was favourable or unfavourable, according to the nature of the prevailing wind; sometimes it broke the swell and caused it to subside; sometimes it augmented it. This latter effect was the most frequent. An obstacle arouses the anger of the sea, and leads it into excesses.

Stormy winds are subjected to similar compression in these narrow, winding passages between the rocks, and acquire the same malevolent character. The tempest chafes against its sudden imprisonment. Its bulk is still immense, but sharpened and contracted. It is both ponderous and keen. It pierces even while it fells. It is a hurricane contracted, like the draught through the crevice of a door.

The two ridges of rock, leaving this passage-way between them, were much lower than the Douvres, and gradually decreased until they finally disappeared altogether beneath the waves.

There was another, but much narrower inlet, which formed the eastern entrance of the defile. It was evident that the double prolongation of the ridge of rocks continued under water as far as " The Man " rock which stood like a square citadel at the extremity of the group.

At low water, indeed, which was the time when Gilliatt was observing them, the two rows of rock showed their tops, some high and dry, all visible, and maintaining an unbroken line.

" The Man " formed one boundary, and buttressed on the eastern side the entire mass, which was protected on the opposite side by the two Douvres.

The whole looked like a winding chaplet of rocks, having the Douvres at one extremity and " The Man " at the other.

The Douvres themselves were merely two gigantic shafts of granite which rose perpendicularly out of the water almost touching each other, and forming the crest of one of the mountain ranges lying beneath the ocean. The surf and the squall had broken them up and divided them like the teeth of a saw. Only the highest part of the ridge was visible; this was the group of rocks. The base, which was concealed by the waves, must have been enormous. The passage in which the storm had wedged the Durande was between these two colossal shafts.

This passage, which was as zig-zag in form as forked lightning, was of the same width throughout. The ocean had so fashioned it. Its eternal commotion sometimes produces singular regularities. There is a sort of geometry in the action of the sea.

From one extremity of the defile to the other, the two granite walls confronted each other at a distance in which

the midship frame of the Durande exactly fitted. Between
the two Douvres, the widening of the Little Douvre, curved
and turned back as it was, had left space enough for the paddles. Any where else they would have been hopelessly shattered.

The high double façade of rock within the passage was
hideous to behold. When in the exploration of the watery
waste we call the ocean, we encounter the unknown world of
the sea, all is uncouth and shapeless. All of the defile that
Gilliatt could see from the deck, was appalling. In the rocky
gorges of ocean we can often trace a forcible representation
of shipwreck. The defile of the Douvres was one of these
gorges, and its effect was exciting to the imagination. The
oxides in the rock showed on the escarpment here and there in
red splotches, like marks of clotted blood; it resembled the
splashes on the walls of an abattoir. Associations of the
charnel-house haunted the place. The rough marine stones,
diversely tinted, here by the decomposition of metallic amal-
gams, there by mould causing purple scales, hideous green
blotches, and lurid splashes, aroused ideas of murder and ex-
termination. It was like the unwashed walls of a chamber
which had been the scene of an assassination; or it might have
been imagined that men had been crushed to death there,
leaving traces of their wretched fate. Some spots seemed to
be still dripping with carnage; here the wall was wet, and it
seemed impossible to touch it without making one's fingers
bloody. The blight of massacre seemed everywhere. At the
base of the double escarpment, scattered along the water's
edge, or just below the waves, or in the worn hollows of the
rocks, were monstrous rounded masses of shingle, some scarlet, others black or purple, which bore a strange resemblance to
the internal organs of the body; they might have been taken
for fresh lungs, or decaying livers. Giants might have been
disembowelled there. From the top to the bottom of the cliff,
ran long red lines, which might have been mistaken for oozings
from a funeral bier.

Such sights are frequent in marine caverns.

CHAPTER V

A WORD UPON THE SECRET CO-OPERATIONS OF THE ELEMENTS

THOSE who, by the disastrous chances of sea-voyages, happen to be condemned to a temporary sojourn upon a rock in mid-ocean, find that the shape of their inhospitable refuge is by no means a matter of indifference. There is the pyramidal-shaped rock,— a single peak rising out of the water; there is the round rock somewhat resembling a circle of big stones; and there is the corridor-rock. The latter is the most alarming of all. It is not only the incessant agony of the waves between its walls, or the tumult of the imprisoned sea; there are also certain obscure meteorological characteristics which seem to result from the parallelism of two rocks in mid-ocean. The two straight sides seem to form a genuine galvanic battery.

The first result of the peculiar position of these corridor-rocks is an action upon the air and the water. The corridor-rock acts upon the waves and the wind mechanically by its form; galvanically, by the different magnetic action rendered possible by its vertical sides and by the masses in juxtaposition and opposite to each other.

This kind of rock attracts to itself all the forces scattered in the winds, and exercises a singular power of concentration over the tempest.

Hence there is an increased violence in storms that occur in the immediate neighbourhood of such rocks.

It must be borne in mind that the wind is composite in character. The wind is believed to be simple; but it is by no means simple. Its power is not merely chemical, but also magnetic. Its effects are often inexplicable. The wind is as much electrical as aerial. Certain winds coincide with the *auroræ boreales*. The wind blowing from the bank of the Aiguilles heaps up waves one hundred feet high, a fact noticed with astonishment by Dumont-d'Urville. " The corvette," he says, " knew not what to make of it."

In southern seas the waters often become inflated like an immense tumour ; and at such times the ocean becomes so terrible that the savages flee from the sight of it. The storms in polar seas are different. The air is filled with tiny bits of ice ; and the fierce gusts of wind blow the sledges of the Esquimaux backwards on the snow. Other winds burn. The simoon of Africa is the typhoon of China and the samiel of India. Simoon, typhoon, and samiel are believed to be the names of demons. These storms come down from the mountains. A storm vitrified the volcano of Toulucca. This hot wind, a whirlwind of inky blackness, rushing upon red clouds, is alluded to in the Vedas : " Behold the black god, who comes to steal the red cows." In all these facts we trace the presence of the electric mystery.

The air is full of it ; so are the waves. The sea, too, is composite in its nature. Beneath the waves of water which we see, it has its waves of force, which are invisible. Its constituents are innumerable. Of all the elements the ocean is the most indivisible and the most profound.

Think of this chaos, so enormous that it reduces all other things to one level. It is the universal recipient, the reservoir of germs of life, and the crucible of transformations. It amasses and then disperses, it accumulates and then sows, it devours and then creates. It receives all the waste and refuse waters of the earth, and converts them into treasure. It is solid in the iceberg, liquid in the wave, fluid in suspension. Regarded as matter, it is a mass ; regarded as a force, it is an abstraction. It equalizes and unites all phenomena. It may be called the infinite in combination. By force and disturbance, it arrives at transparency. It dissolves all differences, and absorbs them into its own unity. One of its drops is complete, and represents the whole. From the abundance of its tempests, it attains equilibrium. Plato beheld the mazy dances of the spheres. Strange as the assertion may seem, it is nevertheless true that the ocean, in its vast terrestrial journey round the sun, becomes, with its flux and reflux, the balance of the globe.

Any marine phenomenon is only a repetition of some other natural phenomenon. The sea is expelled from a waterspout as from a syphon; the storm carries out the principle of the pump; lightning issues from the sea as well as from the air. Aboard ships faint shocks are sometimes felt, and an odour of sulphur issues from the receptacles of chain cables. The ocean seethes and boils. "The devil has put the sea in his caldron," said De Ruyter. In the tempests which characterize the equinoxes and the restoration of equilibrium to the prolific power of Nature, vessels breasting the foam seem to emit a kind of fire; phosphoric lights chase each other along the rigging, so close sometimes to the sailors at their work that the latter stretch forth their hands and try to catch these birds of flame as they fly past. After the great earthquake of Lisbon, a blast of hot air, as from a furnace, drove before it towards the city a wave sixty feet high. The convulsions of the ocean are closely related to the convulsions of the earth.

These immeasurable forces sometimes produce extraordinary inundations. At the end of the year 1864, one of the Maldive Islands, a hundred leagues from the Malabar coast, actually foundered in the sea. It sunk to the bottom like a ship-wrecked vessel. The fishermen who sailed from it in the morning found nothing when they returned at night. They could scarcely distinguish their villages under the sea. On this occasion, boats were spectators of the wreck of houses.

In Europe, where Nature seems restrained by the presence of civilization, such events are rare and are supposed to be impossible. Nevertheless, Jersey and Guernsey originally formed a part of Gaul; and even now, as we write these lines, an equinoctial gale has just demolished the cliff on the frontier of England and Scotland, called the "First of the Fourth" (*Première des Quatre*).

Nowhere do these terrific forces appear more formidably conjoined than in the surprising strait known as the Lyse-Fiord. The Lyse-Fiord is the most dangerous of all the

2

Gut reefs of the ocean. Their terrors are there complete.
It is in the Norwegian sea, near the inhospitable Gulf of
Stavanger, and in the 59th degree of latitude. The water
is black and heavy, and subject to intermitting storms. In
this sea, and in the midst of this solitude, there is a great
sombre passage-way,— a passage-way for no human foot.
None ever pass through it; no ship ever ventures in. It is
a corridor ten leagues in length, between two rocky walls three
thousand feet in height. The defile has its elbows and angles
like all such marine thoroughfares,— never straight, having
been formed by the irregular action of the water. In the
Lyse-Fiord, the sea is almost always tranquil; the sky above
is serene; but the place is terrible. Where is the wind? Not
on high. Where is the thunder? Not in the heavens. The
wind is under the sea; the lightnings within the rock. Now
and then there is a convulsion of the water. At certain
moments, when there is perhaps not a cloud in the sky, nearly
half way up the perpendicular rock, at a thousand or fifteen
hundred feet above the water, and usually on the southern
rather than on the northern side, the rock suddenly thunders,
lightnings dart forth, and then retire like those toys which
lengthen out and spring back again in the hands of children.
They contract and enlarge; strike the opposite cliff, re-enter
the rock, issue forth again, recommence their play, multiply
their heads and tips of flame, strike wherever they can, begin
again, and then begin again with startling abruptness.
Flocks of birds fly away in terror. Nothing could be more
mysterious than this artillery issuing out of the invisible. One
cliff attacks the other, raining lightning blows from side to
side. Their warfare is not waged against mankind. It is the
old enmity of two rocks in the impassable gulf.

In the Lyse-Fiord, the rock performs the function of the
clouds, and the thunder breaks forth like volcanic fire. This
strange defile is a voltaic pile, the plates of which are the
double line of cliffs.

CHAPTER VI

A STABLE FOR THE HORSE

GILLIATT was sufficiently familiar with marine rocks to grapple effectively with the Douvres. First of all, as we have just said, it was necessary to find a safe shelter for the sloop.

The double row of reefs, which stretched in a sinuous form behind the Douvres, was connected here and there with other rocks, and suggested the existence of blind passages opening out in a straggling way, and attached to the principal ridge like branches to the trunk of a tree.

The lower part of these rocks was covered with kelp, the upper part with lichens. The uniform level of the sea-weed indicated the high-water mark in calm weather. The parts which the water had not touched presented those silver and golden hues imparted to marine rocks by the white and yellow lichen.

A sort of leprosy of conoidal shells covered the rock at certain points,— the dry rot of the granite.

At other points in the retreating angles, where fine sand had accumulated, worn from the surface by the wind rather than by the action of the waves, appeared tufts of blue thistles.

In the indentations, sheltered from the winds, could be traced the little perforations made by the sea-urchin. This shelly mass of prickles, which moves about like a living ball, by rolling on its spines, and the armour of which is composed of ten thousand pieces, artistically adjusted and welded together,— the sea-urchin, which is popularly called, for some unknown reason, " Aristotle's lantern," gnaws away the granite with his five teeth, and then lodges himself in the hole. It is in such holes that the cockle gatherers find them. They cut them in halves and eat them raw, like an oyster. Some

steep their bread in the soft flesh.   Hence its other name,
" Sea egg."

The tops of the further reefs, left visible by the receding tide, extended close to the escarpment of " The Man "
and into a sort of creek, enclosed on nearly all sides by rocky
walls.   Here was evidently a possible harbourage.

It was shaped like a horseshoe, and was open only on
the side of the east wind, which was the least violent of
all winds in this marine labyrinth.   The water was consequently protected there, and almost motionless.

The shelter seemed comparatively safe.   Gilliatt, moreover, had not much choice.

If he wished to take advantage of the low water, it was
necessary to make haste.

The weather continued to be fine and calm.   The insolent
sea was for a while in a gentle mood.

Gilliatt descended, put on his shoes again, unmoored the
cable, re-embarked, and pushed out into the water.

He used his oars, and kept quite close to the side of the
rock.

Having reached " The Man " rock, he examined the entrance to the little creek.

A fixed, wavy line in the motionless sea, a sort of wrinkle,
imperceptible to any eye save that of a sailor, marked the
channel.

Gilliatt studied its curve for a moment, then he held off a
little in order to veer easily, and steer well into the channel;
and suddenly with a stroke of the oars he entered the little
bay.

He sounded.

The anchorage appeared to be excellent.

The sloop would be safe there against almost any of the
contingencies of the season.

The most formidable reefs have quiet nooks of this sort
The ports which are thus found among the breakers are
like the hospitality of the fierce Bedouin,— friendly and
sure.

Gilliatt got the sloop as near to " The Man," as he could, but still far enough off to escape grazing the rock; then he cast his two anchors.

This done, he folded his arms, and reflected on his position.

The sloop was protected. Here was one problem solved. But another remained. Where could he find shelter himself?

He had the choice of two places,— the sloop itself, with its bit of cabin, which was scarcely habitable, and the summit of " The Man " rock, which could be scaled without much difficulty.

From both of these refuges it was possible at low water, by jumping from rock to rock, to reach the passage between the Douvres where the Durande was fixed, almost without wetting one's feet.

But low water lasts only a little while, and all the rest of the time he would be cut off either from his shelter or from the wreck by more than two hundred fathoms. Swimming among breakers is difficult at all times; if there is the least commotion in the sea it is impossible.

He was obliged to give up the idea of a shelter in the sloop or upon " The Man."

No resting-place was possible among the neighbouring rocks.

The summits of the lower ones disappeared twice a day beneath the rising tide.

The summits of the higher ones were constantly swept by flakes of foam, and promised nothing but an inhospitable drenching.

No choice remained but the wreck itself

Was it possible to find a refuge there?

Gilliatt hoped it might be.

CHAPTER VII

A CHAMBER FOR THE VOYAGER

HALF AN HOUR afterwards, Gilliatt having returned to the wreck, climbed to the deck, and soon afterwards descended into the hold, thus completing the summary survey begun on his first visit.

By the help of the capstan he had raised to the deck of the Durande the bale into which he had made the cargo of the sloop. The capstan had worked well. Bars for turning it were not wanting. Gilliatt had only to select one from a pile of rubbish.

He found among the *débris* a cold chisel, dropped, no doubt, from the carpenter's box, and which he gladly added to his little stock of tools.

Besides this, for in such a dearth of appliances every little counts, he had his jack-knife in his pocket.

Gilliatt worked all day long on the wreck, clearing away, propping, and arranging.

By nightfall he had discovered the following facts:

The entire wreck shook in the wind, and trembled with every step he took. There was nothing stable or strong except that portion of the hull which was jammed between the rocks and which contained the engine. There, the beams were effectually supported by the granite walls.

Establishing his home in the Durande would be imprudent. It would increase the weight; and instead of adding to her burden, it was important to lighten it. To burden the wreck in any way was indeed the very contrary of what he wanted.

The dilapidated mass required, in fact, the most careful management. It was like a sick man on the verge of dissolution. A strong wind would suffice to put an end to it.

It was, moreover, bad enough to be compelled to work

there. The amount of disturbance which the wreck would have to withstand would necessarily strain it, perhaps beyond its strength.

Besides, if any accident should happen in the night while Gilliatt was sleeping, he would necessarily perish with the vessel. No assistance was possible; all would be over. In order to save the shattered vessel, it was absolutely necessary to remain outside of it.

How to be outside and yet near it,—this was the problem.

The difficulty became complicated.

Where could he find a shelter under such conditions?

Gilliatt reflected.

Nothing remained but the two Douvres. They seemed hopeless enough.

From below it was impossible to tell with certainty whether the upper surface of the Great Douvre was flat or conical.

High rocks with flattened summits like the Great Douvre and " The Man," are usually decapitated peaks. They abound among mountains and in the ocean. Certain rocks, particularly those which are met with in the open sea, bear marks like half-felled trees. They appeared to have received a terrific blow from an axe. They have been subjected, in fact, to the blows of the gale, that indefatigable wood-cutter of the sea.

There are other and still more powerful causes of marine convulsions. Hence the innumerable bruises upon these primeval masses of granite. Some of these sea giants have had their heads struck off; and sometimes these heads, from some inexplicable cause, do not fall, but remain shattered on the summit of the mutilated trunk. These cases are by no means rare. The Devil's Rock, at Guernsey, and the Table, in the Valley of Anweiler, illustrate some of the most surprising examples of this strange geological enigma.

Some such phenomenon had probably fashioned the summit of the Great Douvre.

If the protuberance which Gilliatt fancied he could discern on the plateau were not a natural irregularity in the stone, it must necessarily be some remaining fragment of the shattered summit.

Perhaps the fragment might contain some excavation,— some hole into which a man could creep for cover, Gilliatt asked for no more.

But how could he reach the plateau? How could he scale that perpendicular wall, hard and polished as a pebble, half covered with a growth of glutinous confervæ, and having the slippery look of a soapy surface?

The edge of the plateau was at least thirty feet above the deck of the Durande.

Gilliatt took from his box of tools the knotted rope, hooked it to his belt by the grapnel, and set to work to scale the Little Douvre. The ascent became more difficult as he climbed. He had forgotten to take off his shoes, — a fact which increased the difficulty. With great labour and straining, however, he reached the edge. Once there, he raised himself and stood erect. There was scarcely room for his two feet. To make it his lodging would be difficult. A Stylite might have contented himself there; Gilliatt, more luxurious in his requirements, wanted something more commodious.

The Little Douvre, leaning towards the great one, looked from a distance as if it was saluting it, and the space between the Douvres, which measured a score of feet below, was only eight or ten at the highest point.

From the spot to which he had climbed, Gilliatt could see more distinctly a rocky excrescence which partly covered the plateau of the Great Douvre.

This plateau was at least twenty feet above his head.

A precipice separated him from it. The curved escarpment of the Little Douvre sloped away out of sight beneath him.

He detached the knotted rope from his belt, took a rapid glance at the dimensions of the rock, and slung the grapnel up to the plateau.

The grapnel scratched the rock, and slipped. The knotted rope with the hooks at its end fell beneath his feet, swinging against the side of the Little Douvre.

He renewed the attempt; slung the rope farther, aiming at the granite protuberance, in which he could perceive crevices and scratches.

The cast was so neat and skilful this time, that the hooks caught.

He pulled on it with all his strength. A piece of the rock broke, fell, and the knotted rope with its heavy iron came down once more, striking the escarpment beneath his feet.

He slung the grapnel a third time.

It did not fall.

He put a hard strain upon the rope; it resisted. The grapnel was firmly anchored at last.

The hooks had caught in some fracture in the plateau which he could not see.

It was necessary to trust his life to that unknown support.

He did not hesitate.

The case was urgent. He was compelled to adopt the quickest course.

Moreover, to descend again to the deck of the Durande, in order to devise some other step, was impossible. A slip was probable, and a fall almost certain. It was easier to climb than to descend.

Gilliatt's movements were decisive, like those of all good sailors.

He never wasted force. He always proportioned his efforts to the work in hand. Hence the wonderful feats of strength he performed with ordinary muscles. His biceps were no more powerful than those of ordinary men, but his heart was firmer. He added, in fact, to physical strength, the energy which is one of the most potent of the mental faculties.

The feat to be accomplished was appalling.

It was to cross the space between the two Douvres, supported only by this slender line.

Oftentimes in the path of duty and devotion, the gaunt form of death rises before men to present this momentous question: —

"Wilt thou dare this?" asks the shadow.

Gilliatt tested the cord again; the grappling-iron held firm.

Wrapping his left hand in his handkerchief, he grasped the knotted rope with his right hand, which he covered with his left; then stretching out one foot, and striking the rock vigorously with the other in order that the impetus might prevent the rope twisting, he hurled himself from the top of the Little Douvre upon the side of the larger one.

The shock was severe.

In spite of his precautions, the rope twisted, and his shoulder struck the rock.

There was a rebound.

In their turn his clinched fists struck the rocks, and the handkerchief having become loosened, they were terribly scratched. They had, indeed, narrowly escaped being crushed.

Gilliatt remained hanging there a moment with his brain whirling wildly.

He was sufficiently master of himself not to let go his hold of the rope.

A few moments passed in unavailing jerks and oscillations before he could seize the rope with his feet; but he succeeded at last.

Recovering himself, and holding the rope at last between his feet as with two hands, he gazed into the depth below.

He had no anxiety about the length of the rope, which had many a time served him for great heights, and which, in fact, trailed upon the deck of the Durande.

Assured of being able to descend again, he began to climb.

In a few moments he had gained the summit.

Never before had any wingless creature found a footing there. The plateau was covered in parts with the dung of birds. It was an irregular trapezium, a mass broken from the colossal granitic prism of the Great Douvre. This block was hollowed in the centre like a basin,— the work of the rain.

Gilliatt, in fact, had guessed correctly.

At the southern angle of the block he found a mass of superimposed rocks,— probably fragments of the fallen summit. These rocks, which looked like a heap of gigantic paving-stones, would have afforded plenty of room for a wild beast to secrete himself between them, if one could have found its way there, for they were piled one upon the other, leaving interstices like a heap of ruins. They did not form grottoes or caves, but the pile was full of holes like a sponge. One of these holes was large enough to admit a man.

The floor of this recess was covered with moss and a few tufts of grass. Gilliatt could fit himself in it as in a kind of sheath. The entrance was about two feet high, but it became smaller near the bottom. Stone coffins are sometimes of this form. The mass of rocks behind lying towards the south-west, the recess, though protected from showers, was open to the cold north wind.

Gilliatt was satisfied with the place.

The two chief problems were solved,— the sloop had a harbour, and he himself had found a shelter.

The chief merit of his cave was its accessibility from the wreck.

The grappling-iron of the knotted cord having fallen between two blocks, had become firmly hooked, but Gilliatt prevented any possibility of its giving way by rolling a huge stone upon it.

He was now free to operate at leisure upon the Durande.

Henceforth he was at home.

The Great Douvre was his dwelling, the Durande his workshop.

It was a comparatively easy matter for him to go to and fro, ascending and descending.

He dropped down easily by means of the knotted rope on to the deck.

The day's work was a good one, the enterprise had begun well; he was satisfied, and began to feel hungry.

He untied his basket of provisions, opened his knife, cut a slice of smoked beef, took a bite from his brown loaf, took a draught from his can of fresh water, and thus supped admirably.

To do well and eat well are two great comforts. A full stomach resembles an easy conscience.

This supper ended, there was still a little more daylight at his disposal. He took advantage of it to begin the lightening of the wreck,— an urgent necessity.

He had passed part of the day in gathering up the fragments. He now put to one side, in the strong compartment which contained the engine, all articles that might prove of use to him, such as wood, iron, cordage, and canvas; all that was useless he cast into the sea.

The cargo of the sloop, hoisted on to the deck by the capstan, compact as he had made it, was an encumbrance. Gilliatt surveyed the sort of niche, at a height within his reach, in the side of the Little Douvre. These natural closets, not entirely shut in, it is true, are often seen in rocks. It struck him that it would be possible to intrust some stores to their keeping, and he accordingly placed in the back of the recess the two boxes containing his tools and his clothing, and his two bags of rye-meal and biscuit. In front — a little too near the edge perhaps, but he had no other place — he deposited his basket of provisions.

He had taken care to remove from the box of clothing his sheepskin, his big coat with a hood, and his water-proof overalls.

To lessen the action of the wind upon the knotted cord, he made the lower extremity fast to one of the riders of the Durande.

This rider being bent a good deal, held the end of the cord as firmly as a stalwart hand.

There was still some difficulty concerning the upper end of the cord. To control the lower part was all very well, but at the summit of the escarpment, at the spot where the knotted cord touched the ridge of the plateau, there was reason to fear that it would be fretted and worn away by the sharp edge of the rock.

Gilliatt searched in a pile of rubbish, and took from it some scraps of sail, and from a bunch of old cables pulled out some strands of rope-yarn with which he filled his pockets.

Any sailor would have suspected that he intended to bind with these pieces of canvas and ends of yarn that portion of the knotted rope which rubbed against the edge of the rock, so as to preserve it from friction,— an operation which is called " keckling."

Having provided himself with these things, he drew his overalls over his legs, put his waterproof coat over his jacket, drew its hood over his red cap, tied the sheep-skin around his neck by the two legs, and arrayed in this complete panoply, he grasped the rope, now firmly fastened to the side of the Great Douvre, and again began the assault of this grim citadel of the sea.

In spite of his scratched hands, Gilliatt easily regained the summit.

The last pale tints of sunset were fading from the sky. It was night upon the sea below.

A little light still lingered upon the top of the Douvre.

Gilliatt profited by this remnant of daylight to bind the knotted rope. He wound around it again and again at the part which passed over the edge of the rock, a bandage of several thicknesses of canvas strongly tied at every turn. The whole resembled somewhat the padding which actresses place upon their knees, to prepare them for the agonies and supplications of the fifth act.

This accomplished, Gilliatt rose from his stooping position.

While he had been busied in his task, he had had a vague sense of a strange fluttering in the air.

It resembled, in the silence of evening, the noise which an immense bat might make with the beating of its wings.

Gilliatt raised his eyes.

A big black circle was revolving above his head in the pale twilight sky.

Such circles are seen around the heads of saints in old pictures. These, however, are golden on a dark ground, while the circle around Gilliatt was dark upon a pale ground. The effect was strange. It spread round the Great Douvre like an aureole of night.

The circle came nearer, then retired; grew narrower and then spread wide again.

It was an immense flock of gulls, sea-mews, and cormorants; a vast multitude of affrighted sea-birds.

The Great Douvre was probably their lodging-place, and they were coming to rest for the night. Gilliatt had appropriated their home. It was evident that their unexpected fellow-lodger annoyed them.

A man there was an object they had never beheld before.

Their wild fluttering continued for some time.

They seemed to be waiting for the stranger to leave the place.

Gilliatt followed them dreamily with his eyes.

The flying multitude at last seemed to abandon their design. The circle suddenly assumed a spiral form, and the cloud of sea-birds settled down upon " The Man " rock at the extremity of the group, where they seemed to be conferring and deliberating.

Gilliatt, after settling down in his granite alcove, and

covering a stone for a pillow for his head, could hear the birds for a long time chattering to one another, or croaking, as if by turn.

Then they were silent, and finally they all fell asleep — the birds upon their rocks, Gilliatt upon his.

CHAPTER VIII

IMPORTUNÆ VOLUCRES

GILLIATT slept well; but he was cold, and this caused him to wake from time to time. He had naturally placed his feet at the end and his head at the mouth of his cave. Unfortunately, he had not taken the precaution to remove from his couch a number of angular stones, which did not by any means conduce to sleep.

Now and then he half opened his eyes.

At intervals he heard loud noises. It was the rising tide entering the caverns below with the sound like the report of a cannon.

All the circumstances of his position conspired to produce the effect of a vision. Hallucinations seemed to surround him. The darkness strengthened this impression; and Gilliatt felt himself plunged into a region of unrealities. He asked himself if it were not all a dream?

Then he dropped to sleep again, and this time in a veritable dream, fancied himself at the Bu de la Rue, at the Bravées, at St. Sampson. He heard Déruchette singing; everything seemed real now. While he slept he seemed to wake and live; it was when he awoke again that he appeared to be sleeping.

In fact, from this time on he lived in a dream.

Towards the middle of the night a confused murmur filled the air. Gilliatt had a vague consciousness of it even in his sleep. It was perhaps a breeze rising.

Once, awakened by a cold shiver, he opened his eyes a little wider than before. Clouds were moving in the zenith; the moon was flying through the sky, with one large star following closely in her wake.

Gilliatt's mind was full of the incidents of his dreams. The fantastic outlines of the objects around him as seen in the darkness mingled confusedly with the impressions of his sleeping hours.

By daybreak he was half frozen; but he slept on soundly. The sudden daylight aroused him from a slumber which might have proved dangerous. The alcove faced the rising sun.

Gilliatt yawned, stretched himself, and sprang out of his resting-place.

His slumber had been so deep that he could not at first recall the circumstances of the night before.

By degrees the sense of reality returned, and he began to think of breakfast.

The weather was calm; the sky cool and serene. The clouds were gone; the night wind had cleared the horizon, and the sun rose brightly. Another fine day was dawning. Gilliatt felt cheerful and hopeful.

He threw off his overcoat and his overalls, rolled them up in the sheepskin with the wool inside, fastened the roll with a bit of rope-yarn, and pushed it into the cave for protection in case of rain.

This done, he made his bed,— that is, he removed the stones.

His bed made, he slid down the rope to the deck of the Durande and approached the niche where he had placed his basket of provisions.

The basket was not there; as it was very near the edge, the wind in the night had blown it down, and rolled it into the sea.

This seemed to indicate that the rock was defending itself.

There was an evident spirit of mischief and malice in a wind which had sought out his basket in that position.

It was the beginning of hostilities. Gilliatt understood the token.

To those who live in a state of familiarity with the sea, it is natural to regard the wind as an individual, and the rocks as sentient beings.

Nothing remained for Gilliatt but the biscuit and the rye-meal, except the shell-fish, on which the shipwrecked sailor had supported a lingering existence upon " The Man " rock.

It was useless to think of fishing. Fish are naturally averse to the neighbourhood of rocks. The drag and bow net fishers would only waste their time among the reefs, the sharp tops of which would prove destructive only to their nets.

Gilliatt breakfasted on a few limpits which he plucked with difficulty from the rocks. He narrowly escaped breaking his knife in the attempt.

While he was making his frugal meal, he became aware of a strange disturbance on the sea. He looked around.

It was a swarm of gulls and sea-mews which had just alighted upon some low rocks, and were beating their wings and tumbling over each other, screaming and shrieking the while. All were swarming noisily around the same object. This horde with beaks and talons were evidently pillaging something.

It was Gilliatt's basket.

Blown down upon a sharp point by the wind, the basket had burst open, and the birds had gathered round it immediately. They were carrying off in their beaks all sorts of fragments of provisions. Gilliatt, even at that distance recognized his smoked beef and salt fish.

It was their turn now to be aggressive. The birds were retaliating. Gilliatt had robbed them of their lodging, they deprived him of his supper.

3

CHAPTER IX

THE ROCK, AND HOW GILLIATT USED IT

A WEEK passed.

Although this was the rainy season no rain fell, a fact for which Gilliatt felt very thankful.

But the work he had entered upon was apparently beyond the power of human strength or skill. Success appeared so improbable that the attempt seemed like madness.

It is not until a task is fairly grappled with that its difficulties and perils become fully manifest. There is nothing like a beginning for proving how difficult it will be to reach the end. Every beginning is a struggle against resistance. The first step is an exorable undeceiver. A difficulty that one touches pricks like a thorn.

Gilliatt found himself immediately confronted by obstacles.

In order to raise the engine of the Durande from the wreck in which it was three-fourths buried,— in order to accomplish a salvage in such a place and in such a season, it seemed necessary to be a legion of men. Gilliatt was alone; a complete complement of carpenters' and engineers' tools and implements were needed. Gilliatt had a saw, a hatchet, a chisel, and a hammer. He needed both a good workshop and a good shed; Gilliatt had not a roof to cover him. Provisions, too, were necessary, and Gilliatt had not even bread.

Any one who could have seen Gilliatt working on the rock during that first week might have been puzzled to determine the nature of his operations. He seemed to have no thought either of the Durande or the two Douvres. He was busy only among the breakers; he seemed absorbed in saving the smaller portions of the wreck. He took advantage of every high tide to strip the reefs of everything that the shipwreck had distributed among them. He went from rock to rock, picking up whatever the sea had scattered,— bits of sail, pieces of

iron, splintered panels, shattered planking, broken yards,—
here a beam, there a chain, there a pulley.

At the same time, he carefully examined all the recesses
in the rocks. To his great disappointment none were habitable. He suffered greatly from the cold in the night in his
present lodgings on the summit of the rock, and he would have
been glad to find some better shelter.

Two of those recesses were quite large. Although the
natural pavement of rock was for the most part oblique and
uneven, it was possible to stand upright, and even to walk
within them. The wind and the rain entered there at will,
but the highest tides did not reach them. They were near
the Little Douvre, and were approachable at any time. Gilliatt decided that one should serve him as a storehouse, the
other as a forge.

With all the lanyards, rope-bands, and reef-points he could
collect, he tied the wood and iron in bundles, and the canvas in
rolls, then lashed all these together carefully. As the rising
tide approached these packages, he began to drag them
across the reefs to his storehouse. In a hollow in the rocks
he had found a top-rope, by means of which he had been able
to haul even the large pieces of timber. In the same manner
he dragged from the sea the numerous pieces of chain which
he found scattered among the breakers.

Gilliatt worked at these tasks with astonishing activity and
tenacity. He accomplished whatever he attempted; nothing
could withstand his ant-like perseverance.

By the end of the week he had gathered into this granite
warehouse of marine stores, and arranged in order, this mis-
cellaneous mass of salvage. There was a corner for the tacks
of sails and a corner for sheets. Bow-lines were not mixed
with halliards; parrels were arranged according to their number of holes. The coverings of rope-yarn, unwound from the
broken anchorings, were tied in bunches; the dead-eyes without pulleys were separated from the tackle-blocks. Belay-
ing-pins, bulls-eyes, preventer-shrouds, down-hauls, snatch-
blocks, pendents, kevels, trusses, stoppers, and sailbooms, if

they were not too much damaged by the storm, were placed in different compartments. All the cross-beams, timber-work, up-rights, stanchions, mast-heads, binding-strakes, portlids, and clamps were heaped up apart. Whenever it was possible, he arranged the broken planks from the vessel's bottom in their proper order. There was no mixing up reef-points with nippers, or crow's-feet with tow lines, or pulleys for the small with pulleys for the large ropes, or fragments from the waist with fragments from the stern. A place had even been reserved for the cat-harpings, which had supported the shrouds of the top-mast and the futtock-shrouds. Every part had its appointed place. The entire wreck was there classed and ticketed.

A stay-sail, fixed by huge stones, served, though torn and damaged, to protect what the rain might have injured.

Shattered as the bows of the boat were, he had succeeded in saving the two cat-heads with their three pulley-blocks.

He had found the bowsprit too, and had had much trouble in unrolling its gammoning; it was very hard and tight, having been, according to custom, made by the help of the windlass, and in dry weather. Gilliatt, however, persevered until he had detached it; for this heavy rope was likely to be very useful to him.

He had been equally successful in discovering the little anchor which had become fast in the hollow of a reef, where the ebb tide had left it uncovered.

In what had once been Tangrouille's cabin he found a piece of chalk, which he preserved carefully. He reflected that he might have some marks to make.

A fire-bucket and several pails in pretty good condition completed this stock of working materials.

All that remained of the Durande's supply of coal he carried into the warehouse.

In a week this salvage of *débris* was finished; the rock was swept clean, and the Durande was lightened. Nothing was left to burden the hull now except the machinery.

The portion of the fore-side bulwarks which hung to it

did not distress the hull. The mass hung without dragging, being partly sustained by a ledge of rock. It was large and broad, however, and heavy to drag, and would have encumbered his warehouse too much. These bulwarks strongly resembled the stocks in a shipyard.

Gilliatt left the mass where it was.

He had been profoundly thoughtful during all this labour. He had sought in vain for the figurehead,— the " doll," as the Guernsey folks called it,— of the Durande. It was one of the things that the waves had swept away forever.

Gilliatt would have given his right hand to find it, if he had not been in such urgent need of both his hands just at that time.

At the entrance to the storehouse and outside it were two piles of rubbish,— a pile of iron that would do for forging, and a pile of wood for fuel.

Gilliatt was always at work by early dawn. He did not take a moment's rest except at night.

The wild sea-birds, flying hither and thither, watched him curiously at his work.

CHAPTER X

THE FORGE

THE warehouse completed, Gilliatt constructed his forge. The other recess which he had chosen had within it a sort of passage like a gallery in a mine. He at first conceived the idea of making this his lodging; but the draught was so continuous and so strong in this passage that he had been compelled to abandon the plan. This current of air so incessantly renewed first gave him the notion of the forge. As it would not answer for a chamber, he was determined that this recess should be his blacksmith's shop. To make obsta-

cles serve our purpose, it is a great step towards triumph.
The wind was Gilliatt's enemy. He set about making it his
servant.

The proverb applied to certain kinds of men —" fit for
everything, good for nothing "— may also be applied to the
hollows in rocks. They give no advantages gratuitously.
Here we find a hollow fashioned in the shape of a bath; but
it allows the water to run off through a fissure; there is a
rocky chamber, but without a roof; here a bed of moss, but
reeking with moisture; here an arm-chair, but one of hard
stone.

The forge which Gilliatt intended to establish had been
roughly outlined by nature; but it was a troublesome matter
to reduce this rough sketch to manageable shape; — to transform this cave into a laboratory and smith's shop. Out of
three or four large rocks, shaped like a funnel and ending
in a narrow fissure, chance had constructed a sort of ponderous, ill-shapen blower, of very different power from those
huge old forge bellows fourteen feet long, which poured out at
every breath ninety-eight thousand inches of air. This was
quite a different kind of machine. The proportions of the
hurricane cannot be definitely measured.

This excess of power was an embarrassment. The incessant draught was difficult to regulate.

The cavern had two inconveniences,— the wind traversed
it from end to end; so did the water.

This was not sea-water, but a continual little trickling
stream, more like a spring than a torrent.

The foam which the surf hurled upon the rocks and sometimes more than a hundred feet in the air, had filled with sea-
water a natural cave situated among the high rocks overlooking the excavation. The overflowings of this reservoir
formed, a little back of the escarpment, a tiny waterfall about
an inch in breadth, but twelve or fourteen feet high. An occasional contribution from the rains also helped to fill the
reservoir. From time to time a passing cloud dropped a
shower into this rocky basin which was always overflowing,

The water was brackish and unfit to drink, but clear, and fell in graceful drops from the ends of the long marine grasses, as from the ends of a length of hair.

He was struck with the idea of making this water serve to regulate the draught in the cave. By means of a funnel made of rough planks and hastily put together to form two or three pipes, one of which was furnished with a valve, and of a large tub arranged as a lower reservoir, without checks or counterweight, and completed solely by air-tight stuffing above and air-holes below, Gilliatt, who, as we have said before, was handy at the forge and at the mechanic's bench, succeeded in constructing, instead of the forge-bellows, which he did not possess, an apparatus less perfect than what is known nowadays by the name of a " *cagniardelle*," but less rude than that which the people of the Pyrenees formerly called a " *trompe*."

He had some rye-meal, and out of it he manufactured some paste. He had also some white rope, which he picked out into tow. With this paste and tow, and some scraps of wood, he stopped all the crevices of the rock, leaving only a tiny air-hole made of a powder-flask which he had found aboard the Durande, and which had served for loading the signal gun. This powder-flask was directed horizontally upon a large stone, which Gilliatt made the hearth of the forge. A stopper made of a piece of tow served to close it in case of need.

After this he heaped up the wood and coal upon the hearth, struck his steel against the bare rock, caught a spark upon a handful of loose tow, and having ignited it, soon lighted his forge fire.

He tried the blower: it worked well.

Gilliatt felt the pride of a Cyclops: he was now the master of air, water, and fire. Master of the air; for he had given lungs to the wind, and changed the rude draught into a useful blower. Master of water, for he had converted the little cascade into a " *trompe*." Master of fire, for out of this moist rock he had struck a flame.

The cave being almost everywhere open to the sky, the

smoke issued freely, blackening the curved escarpment. The rocks which seemed made only for foam became now familiar with soot.

Gilliatt selected for an anvil a large, smooth stone, of about the required shape and dimensions. It formed a substantial base for the blows of his hammer; but one that was very dangerous inasmuch as fragments were liable to fly off from it. One of the extremities of this block, rounded and ending in a point, might, for want of something better, serve instead of a conoid horn; but the other kind of horn of the pyramidal form was wanting. It was the ancient stone anvil of the Troglodytes. The surface, polished by the waves, had almost the firmness of steel.

He regretted not having brought his anvil. As he did not know that the Durande had been broken in two by the tempest, he had hoped to find the carpenter's chest and all the tools generally kept in the forehold. But it was the forepart of the vessel that had been carried away.

The two excavations which he had found in the rock were contiguous. The warehouse and the forge communicated with each other.

Every evening, when his work was ended, he supped on a small biscuit, moistened in water, a sea-urchin or a crab, or a few *châtaignes de mer*, the only food to be found among these rocks; and shaking like his knotted rope, mounted again to his cell on the Great Douvre.

The very drudgery of his daily occupation increased the sort of abstraction in which he lived. To be steeped too deeply in realities is in itself a cause of visionary moods. His bodily labour, with its infinite variety of details, did not lessen the feeling of stupor which arose from the strangeness of his position and his work. Ordinary physical fatigue is a thread which binds man to earth; but the very peculiarity of the enterprise he was engaged in kept him in a kind of ideal. There were times when he seemed to be striking at the clouds. At other times, his tools seemed to him like weapons. He had a singular feeling as if he were repressing or providing against some latent danger of attack. Untwisting ropes, unravelling threads of yarn in a sail, or propping up a couple of beams seemed to him at such times like fashioning engines of war. The infinite pains which he had taken in his salvage operations seemed at last so many precautions against probable aggressions. His instincts became less and less those of a worker, and more and more those of a keeper of wild beasts.

His business there was that of a tamer. He had a vague perception of the fact.

Around him, far as eye could reach, was the spectacle of infinite labour wasted and lost. Nothing is more disturbing to the mind than the contemplation of the diffusion of forces at work in the unfathomable and illimitable space of the ocean. The mind tends naturally to seek the object of these forces. The incessant movement in space, the ever restless sea, the clouds that seem continually hurrying somewhere, the vast mysterious prodigality of effort,— all this is a problem. Whither does all this perpetual movement tend? What are these winds constructing? What are all these giant blows building up? These howling, shriekings, and sobbings of the storm, what do they result in? and what is the object of this tumult? The ebb and flow of these questionings is eternal as the tide. Gilliatt could answer for himself; he knew his work, but the agitation which surrounded him on all sides and at all times perplexed him with its eternal questionings. Unknown to himself, mechanically, by the mere pressure of external things, and without any other effect than a strange, unconscious bewilderment, Gilliatt, in this dreamy mood, blended his own toil somehow with the prodigious, wasted labour of the sea. How under such circumstances could he hope to escape the influence of that mystery of this dread, laborious ocean? how do other than meditate, so far as meditation was possible, upon the vacillation of the waves, the perseverance of the foam, the imperceptible wearing away of the rocks, the furious beatings of the winds, and all this travail and weariness for no apparent object.

For no object? No! O Thou Unknown, Thou only knowest for what!

CHAPTER XI

DISCOVERY

A ROCK near the coast is sometimes visited by men; a rock in mid-ocean never. What object would any one have in visiting it? It is not an island. No supplies can be obtained there; there are no fruit-trees, no pasturage, no beasts, no springs of water fit for man's use. Nothing is to be found there but inevitable ship-wreck.

This kind of rocks, which in the old sea dialect were called *Isolés*, are, as we have said, strange places. The sea is their only visitor; she works her own will with them. There is no sign of terrestrial life to disturb her. Man is a terror to the sea; she is shy of his approach, and hides her deeds from him. But she among the lone sea rocks is bolder. The unceasing murmur of the waves is not interrupted here. She labours at the rock, repairs its damage, sharpens its peaks, makes them rugged or renews them. She pierces the granite, wears down the soft stone, and denudes the hard; she rummages, dismembers, bores, perforates, and grooves; she fills the rock with cells, and makes it sponge-like, hollows out the inside, or adorns the outside with sculptures. She makes caves, sanctuaries, and palaces for herself in this lonely spot. She has her exuberant and hideous vegetation, composed of floating plants which bite, and of monsters which take root; and she hides away all this terrible magnificence in her secret depths. No eye watches her on these isolated rocks; no spy embarrasses her movements. Here she freely develops her mysterious side, which is inaccessible to man. Here she deposits all her strange secretions. Here, all the unknown wonders of the sea are congregated.

Promontories, capes, headlands, breakers, and shoals are veritable works of art. The geological formations of the earth are nothing in comparison with the vast operations of the ocean. These breakers, these submarine habitations, these pyramids, and crests of foam are all productions of that mysterious art which the author of this book has somewhere called " the Art of Nature." Their style is recognizable by its vastness. The effects of chance seem to be design. Its works are multiform. They reproduce the mazy labyrinths of the coral groves, the sublimity of the cathedral, the extravagance of the pagoda, the amplitude of the mountain, the delicacy of the jeweller's work, the horrors of the sepulchre. They are filled with cells like wasps' nests, with dens like menageries, with subterranean passages like the haunts of moles, with dungeons like bastiles, with ambuscades like a hostile camp. They have their doors, but they are barricaded; their columns, but they are shattered; their towers, but they are tottering; their bridges, but they are broken. Their compartments are unaccommodating; these are fitted for the birds only, those only for fish. Their style of architecture is varied and inconsistent; it regards or disregards at will the laws of equilibrium,— breaks off, stops short, begins in the form of an archivolt, and ends in an architrave. Enceladus is the mason.

A wondrous science of dynamics here exhibits its problems ready solved. Fearful overhanging blocks threaten, but fall not; the human mind cannot guess what power supports the toppling masses. Blind entrances, gaps, and ponderous suspensions multiply and vary infinitely. The laws which regulate this Babel baffle human induction. The Unknown, that great architect, plans nothing, but succeeds in all. Rocks massed together in confusion form a monstrous monument, defy reason, yet maintain equilibrium. Here is something more than solidity: it is eternity. But order is wanting. The wild tumult of the waves seems to have passed into the wilderness of stone. It is like a tempest petrified forever. Nothing could be more impressive than this architecture; always standing, yet always seeming to fall; in which everything seems to give support, and yet to withdraw it. A struggle between opposing lines has resulted in the construction of an edifice, filled with traces of the efforts of those old antagonists,— the ocean and the storm.

This architecture has its hideous masterpieces, of which the Douvres was one.

The sea had fashioned and perfected it with grim solicitude. The snarling waters had licked it into shape. It was hideous, treacherous, dark, full of hollows.

It had a complete venous system of submarine caverns ramifying and losing themselves in unfathomable depths. Some of the orifices of this labyrinth of passages were left exposed by the low tides. A man might enter there, but only at the peril of his life.

Gilliatt was obliged to explore all these grottoes, for the purpose of his salvage labour. There was not one which was not repulsive in aspect. Each cave bore that strong resemblance to an abattoir which is a characteristic of such formations.

A person who has never seen these hideous natural frescoes upon walls of everlasting granite, in excavations of this kind, can form no idea of the strange effect they produce.

These pitiless caverns, too, were crafty and treacherous. Woe betide him who might loiter there! The rising tide filled them to their very roofs.

Rock limpets and edible mosses abounded among them.

They were obstructed by quantities of shingle, heaped together in their recesses. Some of the big smooth stones weighed more than a ton. They were of every size, and every hue; but the greater part were blood-coloured. Some, covered with a hairy and glutinous seaweed, looked like big green moles boring their way into the rock.

Several of the caverns terminated abruptly in the form of a half cupola. Others, main arteries of a mysterious circulation, lengthened out in the rock in dark and tortuous fissures. They were the streets of the submarine city; but they contracted more and more, and at length left no way for a man to pass. Peering in with the help of a lighted torch, he could see nothing but dark hollows dripping with moisture.

One day Gilliatt in his explorations, ventured into one of these fissures. The state of the tide favoured the attempt. It was a beautiful, calm, sunshiny day. There was no fear of any accident from the sea to increase the danger.

Two necessities, as we have said, compelled him to undertake these explorations. He had to gather fragments of wreck and other things to aid him in his labour, and also to search for crabs and crayfish for his food. The shell-fish on the rocks had begun to fail him.

The fissure was narrow, and the passage difficult. Gilliatt could see daylight beyond. He made an effort, contorted himself as much as he could, and penetrated into the cave as far as possible.

He had reached, without suspecting it, the middle of the rock, the very point upon which Clubin had steered the Durande. Though abrupt and almost inaccessible without, it was hollow within. It was full of galleries, pits, and chambers, like the tomb of an Egyptian king. This network of caverns was one of the most complicated of the labyrinths created by the restless sea.

The branches of this submarine tunnel probably communicated with the sea outside by more than one issue; some, opening on a level of the waves, others, deep and invisible.

It was near here, but Gilliatt knew it not, that Clubin had dived into the sea.

In this crocodile cave,— where crocodiles, it is true, were not among the dangers,— Gilliatt wound in and out striking his head occasionally, bent low and rose again, lost his footing and regained it many times, advancing laboriously the while. By degrees the gallery widened; a glimmer of daylight appeared, and he found himself suddenly at the entrance to a cavern of a singular kind.

CHAPTER XII

THE INTERIOR OF AN EDIFICE UNDER THE SEA

THIS gleam of daylight was most fortunate.

One step further, and Gilliatt must have fallen into a pool that was, perhaps, bottomless. The waters of these cavern pools are so cold and paralyzing as to prove fatal to the strongest swimmers.

There is, moreover, no means of remounting or of clinging to any part of their steep walls.

He stopped short. The passage from which he had just emerged ended in a narrow and slippery projection, a sort of corbel in the peaked wall. He leaned against the side and surveyed it.

He was in a large cave. Over his head was a roof not unlike the inside of a vast skull, which had just been dissected. The dripping ribs of the striated indentations of the roof seemed to imitate the branching fibres and jagged sutures of the bony cranium. A stony ceiling and a watery floor. The rippling waters between the four walls of the cave looked like wavy paving tiles. The grotto was shut in on all sides. Not a window, not even an air-hole visible. No breach in the wall, no crack in the roof. The light came from below and through the water, a strange sombre light.

Gilliatt, the pupils of whose eyes had contracted during his explorations of the dusky corridor, could distinguish everything around him in the pale glimmer.

He was familiar, from having often visited them, with the caves of Plémont in Jersey, the Creux-Maillé at Guernsey, the Botiques at Sark; but none of these marvellous caverns could compare with the subterranean and submarine chamber into which he had made his way.

Under the water at his feet he could discern a sort of arch. This arch, a natural ogive, fashioned by the waves, glittered brightly between its two dark and deep supports. It was through this kind of submerged porch that the daylight entered the cave from the open sea. A strange light shooting upward from the gulf.

The glimmer spread out beneath the waters like a large fan, and was reflected on the rocks. The direct rays, divided into long, broad shafts, shone out in strong relief against the darkness below; while the refracted rays being much duller looked as if they were seen through panes of glass. There was light in the cave it is true; but it was an unearthly light. The beholder might have dreamed that he had entered some other planet. The glimmer was an enigma, like the glaucous light from the eye of a Sphinx. The whole cave represented the interior of a death's head of enormous proportions, and of a strange splendour. The vault was the hollow of the brain, the arch the mouth; the sockets of the eyes were wanting. The cavern, swallowing and disgorging by turn the flux and reflux through its mouth opened to the full noonday without, seemed to drink in the light and vomit forth bitterness, like some intelligent but malevolent human beings. The light, traversing this inlet through the vitreous medium of the sea-water, became green, like a ray of starlight from Aldebaran; and the pool seen in this light looked like a liquid emerald. A tint of aquamarine of marvellous delicacy pervaded the entire cave. The roof, with its cerebral lobes and countless ramifications, like fibres of nerves, gave out a tender reflection of chrysoprase. The ripples reflected on the roof enlarged and contracted their glittering scales in a mysterious and mazy dance. They gave the beholder an impression of something weird and spectral; he wondered what prey secured, or what expectation about to be realized, moved with a joyous thrill this magnificent network of living fire. From the projections of the vault and the angles of the rock hung lengths of delicate fibrous plants, bathing their roots probably through the granite in some pool above, and distilling from their silky tips, one by one, a pearly drop. These drops fell in the water now and then with a gentle splash. The effect of the scene was singular. Nothing more beautiful or more mournful could be imagined.

It was a wondrous palace, in which death sat smiling and content.

CHAPTER XIII

WHAT WAS SEEN THERE; AND WHAT WAS HALF-SEEN

CONTRADICTORY as the terms appear, this strange cave was a place of dazzling gloom.

The palpitation of the sea made itself felt throughout the cavern. The oscillation without raised and depressed the level of the waters within, with the regularity of respiration. A mysterious spirit seemed to pervade this vast organism, as it swelled and subsided in silence.

The water had a magical transparency; and Gilliatt distinguished at various depths submerged recesses, and jutting rocks of a deeper and deeper green. Certain dark hollows, too, were there, probably too deep for soundings.

On each side of the submarine portico, elliptical arches indicated the position of small lateral cave, low alcoves of the central cavern, accessible, perhaps, at low tides.

These openings had roofs in the shape of inclined planes, and at more or less acute angles. Little sandy beaches of a few feet wide, laid bare by the action of the water, extended inward, until they were lost to view in these recesses.

Here and there sea-weeds more than a yard in length undulated beneath the water, like long tresses waving in the wind; and one caught glimpses of dense masses of aquatic plants.

Above and below the surface of the water, the walls of the cave were covered from top to bottom with that wonderful efflorescence of the sea, rarely seen by human eyes, which the old Spanish navigators called *praderias de mar*. A luxuriant moss of varied tints of olive concealed and adorned the rough granite. From every jutting point hung the thin fluted strips of tangle which sailors use as barometers. The light breath which stirred in the cavern waved their glossy lengths to and fro.

Under this mossy covering, one caught occasional glimpses of some of the rarest gems in the casket of the ocean,— ivory shells, whorls, mitres, casks, purple-fish, univalves, struthiolaires, and turriculated cerites. Many bell-shaped limpet shells adhered to the rocks, forming settlements like tiny huts between alleys in which prowled oscabrions, those beetles of the sea. As very few large pebbles found their way into the cavern, many shell-fish took refuge there. The crustacea are the grandees of the sea, who, in their lacework and embroidery, avoid the rude contact of the pebbly crowd. The glittering heaps of shells, in certain spots under the wave, gave out singular irradiations, among which the eye caught glimpses of confused azure and gold, and mother-of-pearl of every tint of the water.

Upon the side of the cave, a little above the water-line, a strange but magnificent plant, attaching itself like a fringe to the border of the sea-weed, continued and completed it. This plant, thick, fibrous, inextricably intertwined, and almost black, hung in big dusky festoons, dotted with thousands of tiny flowers of the colour of lapis-lazuli. In the water they seemed to glow like small blue flames. Out of the water they were flowers; beneath it they were sapphires. When the water rose and inundated the base of the wall clothed with these plants, the rock seemed to be covered with gems.

With every swelling of the wave these flowers increased in splendour, and at every subsidence grew dull again. So it is with the destiny of man; aspiration is life, expiration is death.

One of the greatest marvels of the cave was the rock itself. Forming here a wall, there an arch, and here again a pillar or pilaster, it was often rough and bare; while sometimes the rock close beside it was enriched with the most del-

4

icate natural carving. It was the wondrous art-work of the ocean. Here a sort of panel, cut square and covered with round embossments simulated a bas-relief. Seeing this sculpture, with its shadowy designs, a man might have fancied that Prometheus had sketched it for Michael Angelo. It seemed as if that great genius with a few blows of his mallet could have finished the labours of the giant. In other places the rock was damasked like a Saracen buckler, or engraved like a Florentine vase. There were portions which looked like Corinthian brass, others like arabesques, as on the door of a mosque; others like Runic stones with indistinct and mystical designs. Plants with twisted creepers and tendrils, crossing and re-crossing upon the groundwork of lichens, covered it with filigree. The grotto reminded one not a little of the Alhambra. It was a strange compound of barbarism and the goldsmith's art, with the imposing and rugged architecture of ocean.

The magnificent sea-mosses covered the angles of granite as with velvet. The escarpments were festooned with flowering bindweed, sustaining itself with graceful ease, and ornamenting the walls with a tasteful design. Wallpellitories showed their strange clusters here and there. All the beauty possible to a cavern was there. The wondrous light of Eden which came from beneath the water, at once a submarine twilight and a heavenly radiance, softened down and blended all harsh lineaments. Every wave was a prism. The outlines of things under these rainbow-tinted undulations produced the chromatic effect of a too convex glass. Solar spectra shot through the waters. Fragments of rainbows seemed floating in that auroral diaphany. In more secluded corners, there was a sort of moonlight effect discernible on the water. Every kind of splendour seemed to unite there, forming a strange twilight. Nothing could be more perplexing or enigmatical than the weird beauties of this cavern. It seemed to be an enchanted region. The fantastic vegetation and the rude masonry of the place seemed to harmonize.

The effect of all these strange contrasts was marvellously

lovely. The branches seemed to droop under their weight of bloom. The savage rock and the delicate flower closely embraced each other. Massive pillars had for capitals and bands frail quivering garlands; it was like the fingers of fairies tickling the feet of Behemoth, and the rock sustained the plant, and the plant enfolded the rock with wondrous grace.

The result of these mysteriously harmonized deformities was one of sovereign beauty. The works of Nature, no less supreme than those of genius, contain something of the Absolute, and have an imposing air. Their very unexpectedness makes a profound impression on the mind, and are never more ravishing than when they suddenly cause the Exquisite to spring forth from the Terrible.

This unknown grotto was, so to speak, siderealized. One felt overwhelmed with amazement there. This crypt was filled with an Apocalyptic light. You were not sure what this or that thing was. There was reality stamped with impossibility before one's eyes. It could be seen, it could be touched, it was there, but it was difficult to believe it.

Was it really daylight that entered through this submarine casement? Was it really water that trembled in this dusky pool? Were not these arched roofs and porches fashioned out of sunset clouds? What stone was that beneath one's feet? Was not this solid shaft about to melt away and vanish in thin air? What was this cunning jewelry of glittering shells, half-seen beneath the wave? How very remote life, and the green earth, and human faces were! What strange enchantment haunted this mystic twilight!

At the extremity of the cave, which was oblong in form, rose a Cyclopean archivolt, singularly perfect in form. It was a sort of cave within a cave, a tabernacle within a sanctuary. Here, behind a sheet of brilliant verdure, interposed like the veil of a temple, a square rock bearing some resemblance to an altar rose out of the water. The water surrounded it on all sides. It seemed as if a goddess had just descended from it. One might have fancied that some celestial creature dwelt there in pensive beauty, but became in-

visible on the approach of mortals. It was hard to conceive
of that superb chamber without a majestic vision within it.
The imagination of the intruder might evoke again the marvellous apparition. A flood of chaste light falling upon white
shoulders; a forehead bathed in the light of dawn; an oval-
shaped Olympian visage; a bust of marvellous beauty; arms
modestly drooping; floating tresses forming a sort of aureole;
a delicately modelled body of snowy whiteness, half-envel-
oped in a sacred cloud, the form of a nymph with a glance
of a virgin; a Venus rising from the sea, or an Eve emerging
from Chaos,— this was the vision that filled the mind.

There could be no doubt that a supernatural form inhabited
this sanctuary. Some woman in celestial nudity, with the soul
of a star, had probably been there just now. On that pedes-
tal, whence an ineffable ecstasy emanated, imagination beheld
a gleaming whiteness, living and erect. The mind pictured
for itself, in the midst of the silent wonders of this cave, an
Amphitrite, a Tethys, a Diana with the power to love. It
was she, who, departing, had left in the cave this wonderful
effulgence, this sort of perfumed light. The dazzling glory
of the vision was no longer there; this female, created to be
seen only by the unseen, was not visible, but was felt. The
goddess was absent; but the divine influence was present.

The beauty of the recess seemed specially adapted for this
celestial presence. It was for the sake of this deity, this fairy
of the pearl caverns, this queen of the Zephyrs, this goddess
born of the waves, it was for her — or so, at least, the mind
imagined — that this subterranean dwelling had been thus religiously walled in, so that nothing might ever trouble the
majestic silence in which she dwelt.

Gilliatt, who was a kind of seer amid the secrets of Nature,
stood there musing,— a prey to varied and bewildering emotions.

Suddenly he became aware of a strange object rapidly approaching through the wonderfully transparent water, a few
feet from him. A sort of long ragged band was moving
amidst the oscillation of the waves. It did not float, but swam.

It seemed to have an object in view; it was advancing somewhere rapidly. The object resembled a jester's bawble, in
shape, with points that hung flabby and undulating, and
seemed to be covered with a thick slime. It was worse than
horrible; it was foul. The beholder felt that it was something
monstrous. It was a living thing, unless indeed, it were only
an illusion. It seemed to be seeking the darker portions of the
cave, where it finally vanished. The deep waters grew darker
as its sinister form ˜lided into them and disappeared.

BOOK II

THE TASK

————

CHAPTER I

THE RESOURCES OF ONE WHO HAS NOTHING

THE cavern seemed loath to part with its visitor. The entrance had been difficult; the return proved more difficult still. Gilliatt finally succeeded in extricating himself, however; but he did not return to the spot. He had found nothing that he was in quest of, and he had no time to indulge his curiosity.

He put the forge in operation at once. Tools were wanting; he set to work and made them.

For fuel he had the wreck; for motive power, the water; for his bellows, the wind; for his anvil, a stone; for skill, his instinct.

He entered upon his herculean task with ardour.

The weather seemed to smile upon his work. It continued to be as dry and serene. The month of March had come, but it was tranquil. The days grew longer. The blue sky, the gentleness of the breeze, the serenity of the noontide,— all seemed to preclude any idea of mischief. The waves danced merrily in the sunlight. A kiss is the first step in treachery; the ocean is prodigal of such caresses. Her smile, like that of woman's sometimes, cannot be trusted.

There was very little wind, and the hydraulic bellows

worked all the better on that account. Much wind would have hindered rather than aided it.

Gilliatt had a saw; he manufactured for himself a file. With the saw he attacked the wood; with the file, the metal. Then he availed himself of the two iron hands of the smith, the pincers and the pliers. The pincers gripe, the pliers handle; one is like the closed hand, the other like the fingers. Tools are organs. By degrees he made for himself a number of auxiliaries, and constructed his armour. He made a screen for his forge-fire with a piece of barrel hoop.

One of his principal labours was the sorting and repairing of pulleys. He mended both the blocks and the sheaves of tackle. He cut down the irregularities of all broken joists, and re-shaped the extremities. He had, as we have said, a great many pieces of wood, stored away and arranged according to their shape and dimensions, as well as the nature of their grain; the oak on one side, the pine on the other; the short pieces like riders, separated from the straight pieces like binding strakes. This formed his reserve of supports and levers, which he might need at any moment.

A person who intends to construct hoisting tackle ought, of course, to provide himself with beams and blocks; but these are not sufficient. He must have cordage as well. Gilliatt restored the cables, large and small. He frayed out the tattered sails, and succeeded in converting them into an excellent yarn of which he made twine. With this he joined the ropes. The joins, however, were liable to rot. It was necessary, therefore, to make use of these cables as soon as possible. He had only been able to make white tow, for he was without tar.

The ropes mended, he proceeded to repair the chains.

Thanks to the lateral point of the stone anvil, which served the part of the conoid horn, he was able to forge rings, rude in shape, it is true, but strong. With these he fastened together the severed lengths of chains, and made long pieces.

To work at a forge without assistance is a difficult matter; nevertheless, he succeeded. It is true that he had only **to** forge and shape comparatively small articles, which he was able to hold by his pliers with one hand, while he hammered with the other.

He cut into small pieces the iron bars of the captain's bridge, by which Clubin used to pass to and fro from paddle-box to paddle-box giving his orders; fashioned one end of each piece into a point, and affixed a flat head to the other. In this way he manufactured huge nails nearly a foot in length. These nails, much used in pontoon making, are useful in fixing anything in rocks.

What was his object in all these labours? We shall see.

He was several times compelled to renew the blade of his hatchet and the teeth of his saw. For renotching the saw he had manufactured a three-sided file.

Occasionally he made use of the capstan of the Durande. The hook of the chain broke: he made another.

By the aid of his pliers and pincers, and by using his chisel as a screwdriver, he set to work to remove the two paddle-wheels of the vessel,— a task which he finally accomplished. This was rendered practicable by reason of a peculiarity in their construction. The paddle-boxes which covered them were of great service to him in stowing them away. With the planks from these paddle-boxes he made two cases, in which he deposited the two paddles, piece by piece, each part being carefully numbered.

His lump of chalk became precious for this purpose.

He kept the two cases on the strongest part of the wreck.

When these preliminaries were completed, he found himself face to face with the great difficulty. The problem of the engine of the Durande was now clearly before him.

Taking the paddle-wheels to pieces had proved practicable. It was very different with the machinery.

In the first place, he was almost entirely ignorant of the details of the mechanism. Working thus blindly he might do some irreparable damage. If he ventured to dismember it, very different tools would be required than those he could fabricate with a cavern for a forge, a draught of wind for a bellows, and a stone for an anvil. In attempting, therefore, to take the machinery to pieces, there was great danger of destroying it.

The attempt seemed, at first wholly impracticable.

The apparent impossibility of the project rose up before him like a stone wall, blocking further progress.

What was to be done?

CHAPTER II

HOW SHAKSPEARE MAY MEET ÆSCHYLUS

A PLAN at last occurred to Gilliatt.

Since the time of the carpenter-mason of Salbris, who, in the sixteenth century, in the dark ages of science,— long before Amontons had discovered the first law of friction, or Lahire the second, or Coulomb the third,— without any other helper than a child, his son, with ill-fashioned tools, in the chamber of the great clock of La Charité-sur-Loire, solved at one stroke five or six problems in statics and dynamics inextricably intervolved like the wheels in a block of carts and wagons,— since the time of that grand and marvellous achievement of the poor workman, who found means, without breaking a single piece of wire, without throwing one of the teeth of the wheels out of gear, to lower in one piece, by a marvellous simplification, from the second story of the clock-tower to the first, that massive monitor of the hours, made all of iron and brass, " large as the room in which the man watches at night, from the tower," with its movements, its cylinders, its barrels, its drums, its hooks and its weights, the barrel of its spring steelyard, its horizontal pendulum, the holdfasts of its escapement, its reels of large and small chains, its stone weights, one of which weighed five hundred pounds, its bells, its peals, its jacks that strike the hours,

— since the time, I say, of the man who accomplished this miracle, and of whom posterity knows not even the name, nothing that could be compared with the project which Gilliatt was meditating had ever been attempted. What Gilliatt dreamed of doing was still harder, that is, still grander.

The ponderousness, the delicacy, the manifold difficulties, were no less in the machinery of the Durande than in the clock of La Charité-sur-Loire.

The untaught mechanic had his helpmate, his son; Gilliatt was alone.

A crowd gathered from Meung-sur-Loire, from Nevers, and even from Orleans, able in time of need to assist the mason of Salbris, and to encourage him with their friendly voices. Gilliatt had no voices but those of the wind around him; no crowd but the assemblage of waves.

There is nothing more remarkable than the timidity of ignorance, unless it be its temerity. When ignorance becomes daring, she has sometimes a sort of compass within herself,— the intuition of the truth, clearer oftentimes in a simple mind than in a learned brain.

Ignorance impels to an attempt. It is a state of wonderment, which, with its concomitant curiosity, forms a power. Knowledge often disconcerts one and makes one over-cautious. Gama, had he known what lay before him, would have recoiled before the Cape of Storms. If Columbus had been a great geographer, he might have failed to discover America.

The second successful climber of Mont Blanc was the savant, Saussure; the first, the goatherd, Balmat.

These instances, I admit, are exceptions, which detract nothing from science, which remains the rule. The ignorant man may discover; it is the learned who invent.

The sloop was still at anchor in the creek of " The Man " rock, where the sea left it in peace. Gilliatt, it will be remembered, had arranged everything for maintaining constant communication with it. He visited the sloop and measured her beam carefully in several parts, but particularly her midship frame. Then he returned to the Durande and measured the diameter of the floor of the engine-room. This diameter, of course, without the paddles, was two feet less than the broadest part of the deck of his bark. The machinery, therefore, might be put aboard the sloop.

But how could it be got there?

CHAPTER III

GILLIATT'S MASTERPIECE COMES TO THE RESCUE OF LETHIERRY'S MASTERPIECE

ANY fisherman, who was insane enough to loiter at that season in the neighbourhood of Gilliatt's labours, would have been repaid for his hardihood by a singular sight between the two Douvres.

Before his eyes would have appeared four stout beams, at equal distances, stretching from one Douvre to the other, and apparently forced into the rock, which is the firmest of all holds. On the Little Douvre, their extremities were laid and buttressed upon the projections of rock. On the Great Douvre, they had been driven in by blows of a hammer, by the powerful hand of a workman standing upright upon the beam itself. These supports were a little longer than the distance between the rocks. Hence the firmness of their hold; and hence, also, their slanting position. They touched the Great Douvre at an acute, and the Little Douvre at an obtuse, angle. Their inclination was slight; but it was unequal, which was a defect. But for this defect, they might have been supposed to be prepared to receive the planking of a deck. To these four beams were attached four sets of hoisting apparatus, each having its pendent and its tackle-fall with the bold peculiarity of having the tackle-blocks with two sheaves at one extremity of the beam, and the simple pulleys at the opposite end. This distance, which was too great not to be perilous, was necessitated by the operation to be effected. The blocks were firm, and the pulleys strong. To this tackle-gear cables were attached, which looked like threads from a distance; while beneath this apparatus of pulleys and spars, the massive hull of the Durande seemed to be suspended in the air by threads.

It was not yet suspended, however. Under the cross beams, eight perpendicular holes had been made in the deck, four on the port, and four on the starboard, side of the engine; eight other holes had been made beneath them through the hull. The cables, descending vertically from the four tackle-blocks, through the deck, passed out at the starboard side under the keel and the machinery, re-entered the ship by the holes on the port side, and passing upward again through the deck, returned, and were wound around the beams. Here a sort of jigger-tackle held them in a bunch bound fast to a single cable, capable of being directed by one arm. The single cable passed over a hook, and through a deadeye, which completed the apparatus and kept it in check. This combination compelled the four tacklings to work together, and, acting as a complete restraint upon the suspending powers, became a sort of dynamical rudder in the hand of the pilot of the operation, maintaining the movements in equilibrium.

The ingenious adjustment of this system of tackling had some of the simplifying qualities of the Weston pulley of these days, with a mixture of the antique polyspaston of Vitruvius. Gilliatt had invented the arrangement, although he knew nothing of the dead Vitruvius or of the still unborn Weston. The length of the cables varied, according to the unequal inclination of the cross-beams. The ropes were dangerous, for the untarred hemp was liable to give way. Chains would have been better in this respect, but chains would not have passed through the tackle-blocks easily.

The apparatus was full of defects; but as the work of one man, it was surprising.

For the rest, it will be understood that many details are omitted which would render the construction perhaps intelligible to practical mechanics, but obscure to others.

The top of the funnel passed between the two beams in the middle.

Gilliatt, unconscious plagiarist, without suspecting it, had reconstructed, three centuries later, the mechanism of the Salbris carpenter,— a mechanism rude and incorrect, and fraught with no little danger to him who might venture to use it.

Here let us remark that defects do not prevent a piece of machinery from working after a fashion. It may limp, but it moves.

The obelisk in the square of St. Peter's at Rome is erected in a way which offends against all the principles of statics. The carriage of the Czar Peter was so constructed that it looked ready to overturn at every step; but it travelled onward for all that. What blunders characterize the machinery at Marly! Everything that is heterodox in hydraulics! Yet did it not supply Louis XIV. with water all the same?

Come what might, Gilliatt had faith. He even anticipated success so confidently as to fix in the bulwarks of the sloop, on the very day when he measured its proportions, two pair of corresponding iron rings on each side, exactly at the same distances as the four rings on board the Durande, to which the four chains of the funnel were attached.

He had a very complete and settled plan in his mind. All the chances being against him, he had evidently determined that all the precautions at least should be on his side.

He did some things which seemed useless; a sign of careful premeditation.

His manner of proceeding would, as we have said, have puzzled an observer, even though he was familiar with mechanical operations.

A witness of his labour who had seen him, for example, with enormous efforts and at the risk of breaking his neck, driving eight or ten huge nails which he had forged into the base of the two Douvres at the entrance to the passage between them, would have had some difficulty in understanding the object of these nails, and would probably have wondered what could be the use of all that trouble.

If he had then seen him measuring the portion of the fore bulwark which had remained hanging to the wreck, then attaching a strong cable to the upper edge of that portion, cutting away with strokes of his hatchet the fastenings which held it, then dragging it out of the defile with the aid of the receding tide, pushing the lower part while he dragged the upper part, and, finally, with great labour, fastening with the cable this heavy mass of planks and piles wider than the entrance of the defile itself, with the nails driven into the base of the Little Douvre, the observer would perhaps have found the operation still more difficult to comprehend, and might have wondered why Gilliatt, if he wanted, for the purpose of his operations, to disencumber the space between the two rocks of this mass, had not allowed it to fall into the sea, where the tide would have carried it away.

Gilliatt had his reasons, however.

In fixing the nails in the base of the rocks, he had taken advantage of all the cracks in the granite, enlarging them when needful, and inserting, first of all, wooden wedges in which he drove the nails. He made a rough beginning of similar preparations in the two rocks which stood at the other end of the narrow passage on the eastern side. He placed plugs of wood in all the crevices, as if he desired to have them, too, in readiness; but this appeared to be a mere precaution, for he made no use of them. He was compelled to economize, and to use his materials only when he had need of them. This was another great drawback.

As fast as one task was accomplished, another became necessary. Gilliatt passed unhesitatingly from one to another, making gigantic strides all the while.

CHAPTER IV

SUB RE

THE aspect of the man who accomplished all these labours became terrible.

Gilliatt expended all his strength at once in his multifarious tasks, and regained it with difficulty.

Privations on the one hand, and fatigue on the other, had greatly reduced him in flesh. His hair and beard had grown long. He had only one shirt that was not in rags. He went about barefooted, the wind having carried away one of his shoes, and the sea the other. Flying fragments of the rude and dangerous stone anvil which he used had left small wounds upon his hands and arms. These wounds, or rather scratches, were not deep; but the keen air and the salt water irritated them continually.

He was hungry, thirsty, and cold.

His store of fresh water was gone; his rye-meal was used up. He had nothing left but a little hard tack.

This he gnawed with his teeth, having no water in which to steep it.

Little by little, and day by day, his strength decreased.

These terrible rocks were consuming his life.

How to obtain food was a problem; how to get drink was a problem; how to find rest was a problem.

He ate when he was fortunate enough to find a crayfish or a crab; he drank when he chanced to see a sea-bird descend upon a point of rock; for on climbing up to the spot he generally found a hollow there, with a little fresh water. He drank from it after the bird, sometimes with the bird; for the gulls and sea-mews had become accustomed to him, and no longer flew away on his approach. Even in his greatest need of food he did not attempt to molest them. He had, as will be remembered, a superstition about birds. The birds on their part, now that his hair was rough and wild, and his beard long, had no fear of him. The change in his face gave them confidence; he had lost all resemblance to man and taken the form of the wild beast.

In fact, the birds and Gilliatt had become good friends. Companions in poverty, they helped each other. So long as he had had any meal, he had crumbled for them some bits of the cakes he made. In his deeper distress they showed him, in their turn, the places where he could find tiny pools of water.

He ate the shell-fish raw. Shell-fish help in a certain degree to quench thirst. The crabs he cooked. Having no kettle, he roasted them between two stones heated red-hot in his fire, after the manner of the Färöe island savages.

Meanwhile, signs of the equinoctial season had begun to appear. Then came rain,— an angry rain. No showers or steady torrents, but fine, sharp, icy points which penetrated to his skin through his clothing, and to his bones through his skin. It was a rain which yielded very little drinking water, but which drenched him none the less.

Chary of assistance, prodigal of misery, such was the character of these rains. For one entire week Gilliatt suffered from them day and night.

At night, in his rocky recess, nothing but the overpowering fatigue occasioned by his daily toil enabled him to sleep. The big sea-gnats stung him, and he generally awoke covered with blisters.

He had a kind of slow fever, which sustained him; but this fever is a succour which destroys. By instinct he chewed the mosses, or sucked the leaves of wild cochlearia, scanty tufts of which grew in the dry crevices of the rocks. Of his suffering, however, he took little heed. He had no time to devote to the consideration of his own privations. The rescue of the machinery of the Durande was progressing well. That sufficed for him.

Every now and then, as the necessities of his work demanded, he jumped into the water, swam to some point, and gained a footing there. He plunged into the sea and left it, as a man passes from one room to another in his dwelling.

His clothing was never dry. It was saturated with rain water, which had no time to evaporate, and with sea water, which never dries.

Living in wet clothing is a habit which may be acquired. The poor groups of Irish people,— old men, mothers, half naked girls and infants,— who spend the winter in the open air, in the snow and rain, huddled together at the corners of the London streets, live and die in this condition.

To be soaked through, and yet be thirsty: Gilliatt became accustomed to this strange torture. There were times when he was glad to suck the sleeve of his big coat.

The fire that he made scarcely warmed him. A fire in the open air yields very little comfort. It burns a person on one side, while he freezes on the other.

Gilliatt often shivered while sweating over his forge.

Everywhere about him resistance loomed amid a terrible silence. He felt himself to be the enemy of an unseen combination.

There is a dismal *non possumus* in Nature.

The inertia of matter is like a grim threat.

A mysterious persecution environed him. He suffered equally from sudden flushes and sudden chills. The fire ate into his flesh; the water froze him; feverish thirst tormented him; the wind tore his clothing; hunger undermined the organs of the body. The mental depression all this caused was terribly exhausting. Obstacles silent, immense, seemed to converge from all points towards him with the blind irresponsibility of fate, yet full of a savage unanimity. He felt them pressing inexorably upon him. There was no way of escaping them. His sufferings produced the impression of some living persecutor. He had

5

a constant sense of something working against him, of a hostile form ever present, ever labouring to circumvent and to subdue him.

He could flee from the struggle; but so long as he remained, he had no choice but to war against this secret hostility. He asked himself what it was. It took hold of him, grasped him tightly, overpowered him, deprived him of breath. The invisible persecutor was destroying him by slow degrees. Every day the feeling of depression became greater, as if the mysterious screw had received another turn.

His situation in this dreary spot resembled a duel, in which a suspicion of treachery haunts the mind of one of the combatants.

It seemed to be a coalition of obscure forces which surrounded him. He felt that there was an invincible determination to be rid of his presence. It is thus that the glacier drives away the loitering ice-block.

Almost without seeming to touch him, this latent coalition had reduced him to rags; had left him bleeding, distressed, and, as it were, *hors de combat*, even before the real battle began. He toiled no less assiduously and unremittingly but as the work progressed the workman himself seemed to lose ground. One might have fancied that Nature — that wild beast in dread of the soul — had resolved to undermine the man. Gilliatt toiled on and left the rest to the future. The sea had begun by consuming him; what would come next?

The double Douvres,— that granite dragon lying in ambush in mid-ocean,— had sheltered him. It had allowed him to enter, and to do his will but its hospitality resembled the welcome of devouring jaws.

The unfathomable space around and above him, so full of opposition to man's will; the mute, inexorable determination of phenomena, following their appointed course; the great general law of things, implacable and passive; the ebbs and flows; the rock itself, a dark Pleiad, whose points were each a star amid vortices, the centre of radiating currents; the strange, indefinable conspiracy to crush with indifference the temerity of a living being; the wintry winds, the clouds, and the beleaguering waves which enveloped him,— closed in around him slowly, and shut him out from all companionship, like a dungeon built up stone by stone around a living man. Everything against him; nothing for him; he felt himself isolated, abandoned, enfeebled, sapped, forgotten. His storehouse empty, his tools broken or defective, he was tormented with hunger and thirst by day, with cold by night, with wounds and tatters, rags covering sores, torn hands, bleeding feet, wasted limbs, pallid cheeks. But there was unquenchable fire in his eye.

Superb fire, will-power made visible! Such is the eye of man. The eyeball tells how much of the man there is in us. We reveal ourselves by the light under our eyebrows. Petty consciences wink; grand consciences flash. If there is no spark in the eyeball, there is no thought in the brain, no love in the heart. He who loves, wills, and he who wills, lightens and flashes. Resolution gives fire to the look,— a fire composed of the combustion of timid thoughts.

The headstrong are really the sublime. The man who is only brave owes it to impulse; the man who is only valiant merely possesses that temperament; the man who is courageous has only one virtue; the man who is headstrong in the truth is sublime. All the secrets of great souls lie in the one word, *Perseverando*. Perseverance is to courage what the winch is to the lever, a perpetual renewal of the point of support. Let the goal be on earth or in heaven, to reach the goal is everything; in the first case one is Columbus, in the second case, Jesus. Never to disobey the dictates of your conscience, never to allow your will to be disarmed, results in suffering, but in triumph as well. The propensity of morals to fall does not preclude the possibility of soaring. From the fall comes the ascension. Weak souls are disconcerted by specious obstacles; strong souls, never. Perish, they possibly may; conquer, they certainly will. You might give Stephen all sorts of good reasons why he should not let himself be stoned. This contempt for sensible objections gives birth to that sublime victory which is called martyrdom.

All his efforts seemed to tend to the impossible. His success was meagre and slow. He was compelled to expend much labour to accomplish very trivial results. It was this that gave to his struggle such a noble and pathetic character.

That it should have required so many preparations, so much toil, so many cautious experiments, such nights of hardship, and such days of danger merely to set up four beams over a shipwrecked vessel, to divide and isolate the portion that could be saved, and to adjust to that wreck within a wreck four tackle-blocks with their cables was merely due to his solitary position.

But Gilliatt had merely accepted this solitary position. He had deliberately chosen it. Dreading a competitor because a competitor might have proved a rival, he had asked no assistance. The gigantic undertaking, the risk, the danger, the arduous toil, the possible destruction of the salvor in his work, famine, fever, nakedness, distress,— he had chosen all these for himself! Such was his selfishness.

He was like a man placed in the bell of an air-pump, which is being slowly exhausted of air. His vitality was failing him little by little. He scarcely perceived the fact.

The decline of physical strength does not necessarily impair the will. Faith is only a secondary power; the will is the first. The mountains, which faith is proverbially said to move, are nothing in comparison with what the will can accomplish. All that Gilliatt lost in vigour, he gained in tenacity. The deterioration of the physical man under the depressing influence of the surrounding sea and rock and sky only seemed to reinvigorate his moral nature.

Gilliatt felt no fatigue, or, rather, he would not yield to any. The refusal of the mind to recognize the failings of the body is in itself an immense power.

He saw nothing, except the steps attending the progress of his labours. His object — now seeming so near attainment — wrapped him in perpetual illusions. He endured all this suffering without any other thought than that contained in the word " Forward." His work flew to his head; the strength of the will is intoxicating. This intoxication is called heroism.

He had become a kind of Job, with the ocean as the scene of his sufferings.

But he was a Job wrestling with difficulties, a Job combating and making way against afflictions; a conquering Job; and if such names are not too great to be applied to a poor sailor and fisher of crabs and crayfish, a combination of Job and Prometheus.

CHAPTER V

SUB UMBRA

SOMETIMES in the night Gilliatt woke and peered into the darkness.

He felt a strange emotion.

As his eyes opened upon the blackness of the night, the situation seemed unspeakably dismal and full of disquietude.

There is such a thing as the pressure of darkness.

A strange roof of shadow; a deep obscurity, which no diver can explore; a light of a strange, subdued, and sombre kind, mingled with that obscurity; floating atoms of rays, like the dust of seeds or of ashes; millions of lamps, but no illumination; a vast sprinkling of fire, of which no man knows the secret; a diffusion of shining points, like a drift of sparks arrested in their course; the disorder of the whirlwind, with the fixedness of death; a mysterious

and abysmal depth; an enigma, at once showing and concealing its face; the Infinite in its mask of darkness,— these
are the synonyms of night. Its weight lies heavily on the
soul of man.

This combination of all mysteries,— the mystery of the
Cosmos and the mystery of Fate,— overpowers the human
brain.

The pressure of darkness acts in inverse proportion upon
different natures. In the presence of night man feels his
own incompleteness. He perceives the dark void, and realizes
his frailty. The sky is black, the man blind. Face to face
with night, man bends, kneels, prostrates himself, crouches
on the earth, crawls towards a cave, or seeks for wings. Almost always he shrinks from that vague presence of the
Unknown. He asks himself what it is; he trembles and
bows the head. Sometimes he desires to go to it.

To go whither?

He can only answer, " There! "

There! But what is it like? and what will be found
there?

This curiosity is evidently forbidden to the spirit of man;
for all around him the roads which bridge that gulf are
demolished or gone. There is no arch to enable him to span
the Infinite. But there is a fascination about forbidden
knowledge, as in the edge of the abyss. Where the foot
cannot tread, the eye may reach; where the eye can penetrate
no further, the imagination may soar. There is no man,
however feeble or insufficient his resources, who does not make
the attempt. According to his nature he questions or recoils
before this great mystery. With some it has the effect of
repressing, with others it enlarges, the soul. The spectacle
is sombre, indefinite.

Is the night calm and cloudless? It is then a mass of
shadow. Is it stormy? It is then a sea of cloud. Its
limitless depths reveal themselves to us, and yet baffle our
gaze; close themselves against research, but remain open
to conjecture. Its innumerable dots of light only make the

obscurity beyond deeper. Jewels, scintillations, stars; proofs of the existence of unknown universes which bid defiance to man's approach; landmarks of the infinite creation; boundaries there, where there are no bounds; landmarks impossible, and yet real, revealing the immensity of those infinite deeps. One microscopic glittering point; then another; then another; imperceptible, yet enormous. Yonder light is a focus; that focus is a star; that star is a sun; that sun is a universe; that universe is nothing. For all numbers are as zero in the presence of the Infinite.

These worlds, which yet are nothing, exist. Through this fact we feel the difference which separates the *being nothing* from the *not to be*.

The inaccessible added to the inexplicable, such are the heavens.

A sublime phenomenon is evolved from this thought,— the development of the soul by awe.

Awe is peculiar to man; the beast knows it not. Intelligence finds in this sublime terror its eclipse and the proof of its existence.

Darkness is unity, hence horror; at the same time it is complex, hence terror. Its unity crushes the spirit, and destroys all inclination to resist. Its complexity makes us look anxiously around on all sides; it seems as if some accident were about to happen. We surrender, yet are on our guard. One is in the presence of Omnipotence, hence submission; and in the presence of the many, hence distrust. The unity of darkness contains a multiple, visible in matter and realizable in thought. Its very silence is only another reason for one to be on the watch.

Night — as the writer has said elsewhere — is the proper, normal state of the special creation to which we belong. Day, brief in duration as in space, is merely proximity to a star.

The wonderful mystery of night is not accomplished without friction, and the friction of such a machine is the contusions of life. This friction of the machine we call Evil.

In the darkness we are conscious of this Evil, this covert lie against divine order, this open blasphemy of fact rebelling against the ideal. Evil disturbs the vast Whole of the Cosmos with a strange hundred-headed teratology. Evil is always present to oppose. It is the hurricane that stops the ship; it is chaos and checks the budding of a world. Good is characterized by unity, Evil by ubiquity; Evil disarranges life; it makes the bird destroy the fly, and the comet destroy the planet. Evil is an erasion in the book of Nature.

The darkness of night makes the brain whirl. One who attempts to sound its depths is submerged, and struggles in vain. No task is so hard as an examination of the land of shadows. It is the study of an effacement.

There is no definite spot where the spirit can rest. There are points of departure, no points of arrival. The decussation of contradictory solutions; all the different diversities of doubt simultaneously presented; the ramifications of phenomena perpetually exfoliating under an indefinite power of growth; an inexplicable promiscuity which makes minerals vegetate, vegetation live, thought ponder, love radiate, and gravitation attract; a simultaneous attack upon all questions deploying in a limitless obscurity; the half-seen sketching the unknown; cosmic simultaneousness in full view, not to the eye but to the mind, in the vast indistinct of space; the invisible become a vision,— such are the night and the shades of darkness.

He knows no details; he bears, to an extent proportionate to his spirit, the monstrous load of the Whole. It was this that drove the Chaldean shepherds to astronomy. Involuntary revelations come from the pores of Nature; an exudation of science is in some way self-produced, and wins the ignorant. Every person who leads a lonely life under this mysterious impregnation, becomes, often unconsciously, a natural philosopher.

The Darkness is indivisible; it is inhabited,— sometimes inhabited without change of place by the Absolute, sometimes inhabited but subject to change of place. To move therein is alarming. A holy creative power accomplishes its phases therein. Premeditations, powers, self-chosen destinies work out their measureless task there. A terrible and horrible life is in it. There are vast evolutions of stars, the stellar family, the planetary family, the zodiacal star-dust; the *quid divinum* of currents, of influences, of polarization and attraction. There are affinities and antagonisms in it; a stupendous ebb and flow of the universal antithesis; the imponderable at liberty in the midst of centres; the wandering atom, the scattered germ; circles of fecundation, osculations, and repugnancies; unheard-of profusion, distances like dreams; giddy revolutions; worlds plunging into the incalculable; prodigies pursuing each other in the gloom; the pantings of flying spheres and whirling wheels. The learned conjecture, the simple assent and tremble; it is, and it vanishes; it is impregnable, beyond reach, beyond approach. Conviction becomes oppression; some — we know not what — black evidence lies heavy on us; we can grasp nothing; we are crushed by the impalpable.

Everywhere around us we see the incomprehensible, nowhere the intelligible!

And then add the momentous question, Is this Immanence endowed with a soul?

We are in doubt. We look and listen.

Still the sad earth moves and rolls; the flowers are conscious of the mighty movement; the silenia opens at eleven o'clock in the evening, the hemerocallis at five in the morning. Striking regularity.

Each drop of water is a miniature world; the infusoria come to life. Think of the marvellous fecundity of an animalcule! The imperceptible displays its grandeur; the antistrophe of immensity is revealed; a diatome in a single hour produces thirteen hundred millions of diatomes.

Surely every enigma is summed up in this.

The irreducible equation is here. We are constrained to have faith. But to have faith does not suffice to give one tranquillity. Faith has a strange need of forms. Hence religions.   Nothing is so unsatisfying as a belief without outlines.

Whatever we think, whatever we wish, whatever may be our repugnance, to look into the darkness is not to look, but to contemplate.

What can be done with these phenomena? How move in the spot where they converge? To dispel this pressure is impossible. Darkness is a silence, but an eloquent silence. One conclusion stands out majestically,— the existence of a God. This belief in God is inherent in man. Syllogisms, quarrels, negations, systems, religions, pass over it without diminishing it. This thought is confirmed by darkness. The marvellous harmony of forces of Nature is manifested by their power to maintain all this obscurity in equilibrium. The universe is suspended in mid-air, yet nothing falls. Incessant, immeasurable change takes place without accident or fracture. Man participates in this transition movement; and the wonderful oscillations to which he is subjected, he calls destiny. Where does destiny begin? Where does Nature end? What is the difference between an event and a season, between a sorrow and a rain-storm, between a virtue and a star? Is not an hour a wave? The machinery in motion continues its passionless revolutions, without any regard to man. The starry heaven is a system of wheels, beams, and counterweights. It is supreme contemplation coupled with supreme meditation, all reality *plus* all abstraction. Nothing beyond; here we are stopped. The darkness reveals not the secret. We are in the train of a complicated mechanism, an integral part of an unknown Whole, and feel the Unknown within us fraternize mysteriously with an Unknown without us.

It is this which tells us that death is inevitable. What anguish, and at the same time what rapture! To be absorbed in the Infinite, and thereby brought to attribute to one's self a necessary immortality, or — who knows? — a possible eternity! to feel in the immense flood of the deluge of universal life the insubmersible will of the I! To look on the

stars and say, " I am a soul like you ; " to look into the darkness and say, " I am an abyss like you ! "

Such are the thoughts and visions awakened by the night!

All these vague fancies, multiplied and intensified by solitude, weighed upon Gilliatt.

He comprehended them not, but he felt them. His was
a powerful though uncultivated intellect, a noble though
unsophisticated heart.

CHAPTER VI

GILLIATT PLACES THE SLOOP IN READINESS

THIS rescue of the machinery of the wreck as meditated
by Gilliatt was, as we have already said, like the
escape of a criminal from a prison and necessitated all the
patience and industry recorded of such achievements,— industry carried to the point of a miracle, patience only to be
compared with a long agony. A certain prisoner named
Thomas, at the Mont St. Michel, found means of secreting
the greater part of a wall in his paillasse. Another at Tulle,
in 1820, cut away a quantity of lead from the terrace where
the prisoners walked for exercise. With what kind of a
knife? No one could guess. With what fire he melted this
lead no one has ever discovered; but it is known that he cast
it in a mould made by a bit of bread. With this lead and
this mould he made a key, and with this key he succeeded in
opening a lock of which he had never seen anything but the
keyhole. Gilliatt possessed some of this marvellous ingenuity. He had once climbed and descended from the cliff at
Boisrosé. He was the Baron Trenck of the wreck, and the
Latude of her machinery.

The sea, like a jailer, kept watch over him.

For the rest, mischievous and inclement as the rain had

been, he had contrived to derive some benefit from it. He had partially replenished his stock of fresh water; but his thirst was inextinguishable, and he emptied his can as fast as he filled it.

One day — it was on the last day of April or the first of May — everything was in readiness.

The engine-room was as it were enclosed between the eight cables hanging from the tackle-blocks, four on one side, four on the other. The sixteen holes on the deck and under the keel, through which the cables passed, had been hooped around. The planking had been sawed, the timber cut with the hatchet, the iron-work with a file, the sheathing with a chisel. The part of the keel immediately under the machinery was cut so as to descend with it while still supporting it. The whole ponderous mass was held by only a single chain, which was itself only kept in position by a filed notch. At this stage of proceedings, in such a task and so near its completion, haste is prudence.

The water was low, the moment favourable.

Gilliatt had succeeded in removing the axle of the paddle-wheels, the extremities of which might have proved an obstacle and checked the descent. He had contrived to make this heavy portion fast in a vertical position within the engine-room itself.

It was time to bring his work to an end. The workman, as we have said, was not worn out, for his will was strong; but his tools were. The forge was fast becoming useless. The blower had begun to work badly. The little hydraulic fall being of sea-water, saline deposits had incrusted the joints of the apparatus, and now prevented its free action.

Gilliatt visited the creek of "The Man" rock, examined the sloop, and assured himself that everything was in good condition, particularly the four iron rings fixed to starboard and to larboard; then he weighed anchor, and worked the heavy barge-shaped craft with the oars till he brought it alongside the two Douvres.

The defile between the two rocks was wide enough to admit it. There was also depth enough. On the day of his arrival he had satisfied himself that it was possible to push the sloop under the Durande.

The feat, however, was difficult; it required the minute precision of a watchmaker. The operation was all the more delicate from the fact that, in order to accomplish his object, he was compelled to force it in by the stern, rudder first. It was necessary that the mast and the rigging of the sloop should project beyond the wreck in the direction of the sea.

All this made Gilliatt's task very difficult. It was not like entering the creek of " The Man," where it was a mere affair of the tiller. It was necessary to push, drag, row, and take soundings all at once. Gilliatt spent but a quarter of an hour in these manœuvres; but he was successful.

In fifteen or twenty minutes the sloop was fastened under the wreck. It was almost wedged in there. By means of his two anchors he moored the boat at bow and stern. The stronger of the two was placed so as to hold against the strongest wind that blew, which was that from the south-west. Then by the aid of a lever and the·capstan, he lowered into the sloop the two cases containing the pieces of the paddle-wheels. These two cases were to serve as ballast.

Relieved of these encumbrances, he fastened the gearing that was to regulate the action of the pulleys to the hook of the chain of the capstan.

In the work that now devolved upon her, the defects of the old sloop became useful qualities. It had no deck; so the cargo could go all the deeper down into the hold. Her mast was far forward,— too far forward indeed for general purposes,— but that only gave more room; and the mast standing thus beyond the bulk of the wreck, there would be nothing to hinder its disembarkation.

While engaged in these operations, Gilliatt suddenly perceived that the sea was rising. He looked around to see from what quarter the wind was coming.

CHAPTER VII

SUDDEN DANGER

THE breeze was scarcely perceptible; but what there was came from the west,— a disagreeable habit of the winds during the equinoxes.

The effect of the sea upon the Douvres rocks depended greatly upon the quarter from which the wind came. The waves entered the rocky corridor either from the east or from the west, according to the gale which drove them along before it. Entering from the east, the sea was comparatively gentle; coming from the west, it was always violent. The reason for this was, that the wind from the east blowing from the land had not had time to gather much force; while the westerly winds, coming from the Atlantic, blew unchecked from a vast ocean. Even a very slight breeze, if it came from the west was serious. It rolled up huge billows in the illimitable expanse and dashed the waves against the narrow defile in greater bulk than could find entrance there.

A sea which rolls into a gulf is always terrible. It is the same with a crowd of people. When the quantity that can enter is less than the quantity that is endeavouring to force its way in, there is a fatal crush in the crowd, a fierce convulsion on the water. As long as the west wind blows, however slight the breeze, the Douvres are subjected to that rude assault twice a day. The sea rises, the tide breasts up, the narrow gorge gives little entrance; the waves, driven violently against it, rebound and roar, and a tremendous surf beats upon both sides of the passage. Thus the Douvres, during the slightest wind from the west, present the singular spectacle of a comparatively calm sea without, while a storm is raging within. This tumult of waters is much too circumscribed in character to be called a tempest. It is merely a local outbreak among the waves, but a terrible one. As regards the winds from the north and south, they strike the rocks crosswise, and create little surf in the passage. The entrance on the east, it must be remembered, was close to " The Man " rock. The dangerous opening on the west was at the opposite end of the passage, exactly between the two Douvres.

It was at this western entrance that Gilliatt found himself with the wrecked Durande, and the sloop made fast beneath it.

A catastrophe seemed inevitable. There was not much wind, but it was sufficient to make mischief.

Before many hours, the swell which was rising would be rushing with full force into the gorge between the Douvres. The first waves were already breaking. This swell, and eddy of the entire Atlantic, would have the boundless sea behind it. There would be no squall; no tempest, but a huge overwhelming wave, which beginning on the coast of America rolls towards the shores of Europe with an impetus gathered in a journey over two thousand leagues. This wave, a gigantic ocean barrier, meeting the gap of the rocks, must be caught between the two Douvres, standing like watch-towers at the entrance of the causeway. Thus swelled by the tide, augmented by resistance, and urged on by the wind, it would hurl itself against the cliffs and rush between the rocky walls, where it would reach the sloop and the Durande, and in all probability destroy them.

A protection against this danger was needed. Gilliatt had one.

The problem was to prevent the sea reaching it at one bound; to prevent it from striking, while allowing it to rise; to bar the passage without refusing it admission; to prevent the compression of the water in the gorge, which was the whole danger; to turn an eruption into a flood; to deprive the waves of their violence, and compel the furies to be gentle; it was, in fact, to substitute an obstacle which would appease for an obstacle which would irritate.

Gilliatt with that agility which is so much more potent

than mere strength, sprang upon the rock like a chamois among the mountains, or a monkey in the forest; using the smallest projection for his tottering and dizzy strides, leaping into the water, and emerging from it again; swimming among the shoals and clambering upon the rocks, with a rope between his teeth and a mallet in his hand. He detached the cable which held the forward end of the Durande to the base of the Little Douvre; fashioned out of some ends of hawsers some rough hinges, with which he affixed this bulwark to the huge nails fixed in the granite like the gates of a dock, turning their sides, as he would turn a rudder, outward to the waves, which pushed one end towards the Great Douvre, while the rope hinges held the other end to the Little Douvre; next, he contrived, by means of the huge nails placed beforehand for the purpose, to fix the same kind of fastenings on the Great Douvre as on the little one, made the huge mass of wood-work fast to the two pillars of the gorge, slung a chain across this barrier like a baldric upon a cuirass, and in less than an hour this barricade against the sea was complete, and the gorge was closed as by a folding-door.

This powerful apparatus, a heavy mass of beams and planks, had with the aid of the water been handled by Gilliatt with all the adroitness of a juggler. It might almost have been said that the obstruction was completed before the rising sea had time to discover it.

It was one of those occasions on which Jean Bart would have used the famous expression which he applied to the sea every time he narrowly escaped shipwreck. "We have cheated the Englishman;" for it is well known that when that famous admiral meant to speak contemptuously of the ocean he called it "the Englishman."

The entrance to the defile being thus protected, Gilliatt thought of the sloop. He loosened sufficient cable for the two anchors to allow her to rise with the tide,— an operation similar to what the mariners of old called "mouiller avec des embossures." In all this Gilliatt was not taken the least by surprise; this possibility had been foreseen. A seaman would have perceived it by the two pulleys of the top ropes cut in the form of snatch-blocks, and fixed behind the sloop, through which passed two ropes, the ends of which were slung through the rings of the anchors.

Meanwhile the tide was rising fast; the half flood had arrived,— a moment when the shock of the waves, even in comparatively moderate weather, may become considerable. Exactly what Gilliatt expected came to pass. The waves rolled violently against the barrier, struck it, broke heavily, and passed beneath it. Outside there was a heavy swell; within, the waters were quiet. He had invented a sort of marine Caudine Fork. The sea was conquered.

CHAPTER VIII

MOVEMENT RATHER THAN PROGRESS

THE long dreaded moment had come.

The problem now was to get the machinery into the sloop.

Gilliatt remained thoughtful for some moments, supporting the elbow of his left arm in his right hand, and pressing his left hand to his forehead.

Then he climbed upon the wreck. The part of it which contained the engine was to be separated from it, and the other part left.

He severed the four straps which held the four chains that extended from the funnel to the larboard and the starboard sides. The straps being only of rope, his knife served him well enough for this purpose.

The four chains, set free, hung down the sides of the funnel.

From the wreck he climbed up to the apparatus which he had constructed, stamped upon the beams, inspected the

6

tackle-blocks, looked to the pulleys, handled the cables, examined the eking-pieces, assured himself that the untarred hemp was not saturated, found that nothing was wanting and that nothing had given way; then springing from the height of the suspending props on to the deck, he took up his position near the capstan, in that portion of the Durande which he intended to leave edged between the two Douvres. This was to be his post during his labours.

Gravely, but calmly, he gave a final glance at the hoisting-tackle, then seized a file and began to sever the chain which held the whole suspended. The rasping of the file was audible amid the roaring of the sea. The chain from the capstan, attached to the regulating gear, was within Gilliatt's reach, quite near his hand.

Suddenly there was a crash. The link which he was filing snapped when only half cut through; the whole apparatus lunged violently. He had barely time to seize the regulating gear.

The severed chain struck against the rock; the eight cables creaked; the huge mass, sawed and cut through, detached itself from the wreck; the bottom of the hull opened, and the iron flooring of the engine-room became visible below the keel.

If he had not seized the regulating-tackle at that instant, it would have fallen. But his powerful hand was there, and the mass descended steadily.

When the brother of Jean Bart, Peter Bart, that powerful and sagacious toper, that poor Dunkirk fisherman, who thee'd and thou'd the Grand Admiral of France, went to the rescue of the galley " Langeron," in distress in the Bay of Ambleteuse, in the hope of saving the heavy floating mass in the breakers of that dangerous bay, he rolled up the mainsail, tied it with sea-reeds, and trusted to the ties to break away of themselves, and give the sail to the wind at the right moment. In like manner Gilliatt had trusted to the breaking of the chain; and the same eccentric feat of daring was crowned with the same success.

The tackle, taken in hand by Gilliatt, held out and worked well. Its function, it will be remembered, was to regulate the powers of the apparatus, thus reduced from many to one, by bringing them into united action. This gearing somewhat resembled the bridle of a bowline, except that instead of trimming a sail it served to balance a complicated mechanism.

Erect, and with his hand upon the capstan, Gilliatt was able to feel the pulse of the apparatus, so to speak.

It was here that his inventive genius manifested itself.

A remarkable coincidence of forces was the result.

While the machinery of the Durand, detached in a mass, was being lowered into the sloop, the sloop slowly rose to receive it. The wreck and the salvage vessel thus assisting each other as it were, saved half the labour of the operation.

The tide swelling between the two Douvres raised the sloop and brought it nearer to the Durande. The sea was more than conquered,— it was tamed and broken in. It became, in fact, part and parcel of the mechanism.

The rising waters lifted the vessel without any shock, but as gently, and almost as cautiously, as one would handle porcelain.

Gilliatt combined and proportioned the two labours, that of the water and that of the apparatus; and standing steadfast at the capstan, like some grim statue, watched every movement that went on around him, and regulated the slowness of the descent by the slow rise of the sea.

There was no jerk given by the waters, no slip among the tackle. It was a strange combination of all the natural forces. On one side, gravitation lowering the large bulk, on the other the sea raising the bark. The attraction of heavenly bodies which causes the tide, and the attractive force of the earth, which men call weight, seemed to conspire together to aid Gilliatt in his plans. There was no hesitation, no stoppage in their service; under the dominion of intellect these passive forces become active auxiliaries. From minute to minute the work advanced; and the distance between the

wreck and the sloop slowly diminished. The approach continued in silence, and as if in a sort of terror of the man who
stood there. The elements received his orders and obeyed
them.

Almost at the precise moment when the tide ceased to
rise; the cable ceased to slide. Suddenly, but without any
commotion, the pulleys stopped. The huge machine had
taken its place in the sloop, as if placed there by a powerful
hand. It stood straight, upright, motionless, firm. The
iron floor of the engine-room rested its four corners evenly
upon the hold.

The work was accomplished.

Gilliatt contemplated it, lost in thought.

He was not the spoiled child of success. He staggered
under the weight of his great joy. He felt his limbs give
way under him; and as he contemplated his triumph, this
man, who had never been dismayed by danger, began to
tremble.

He gazed upon the sloop under the wreck, and at the machinery in the sloop. He could hardly believe his own eyes.
It might have been supposed that he had never looked forward to that which he had accomplished. A miracle had
been wrought by his hands, and he contemplated it in bewilderment.

His reverie lasted but a short time.

Starting like one suddenly awakened from a deep sleep,
he seized his saw, cut the eight cables now separated from
the sloop, thanks to the rising of the tide, by only about ten
feet; sprang aboard, took a coil of rope, made four slings,
passed them through the rings prepared beforehand and
fastened to both sides of the sloop the four funnel chains
which had been still fastened to their places aboard the Durande only an hour before.

The funnel being secured, he disengaged the upper part
of the machinery. A portion of the planking of the Durande was adhering to it; he struck off the nails and relieved
the sloop of this encumbrance of planks and beams, which

fell over on to the rocks,— a great assistance in lightening it.

The sloop, however, as has been foreseen, behaved well under the burden of the machinery. It had sunk in the water, but only to a good water-line. Although massive, the engine of the Durande was less heavy than the pile of stones and the cannon which he had once brought back from Herm in the sloop.

His task was now ended; he had only to depart.

* * *

CHAPTER IX

A SLIP BETWEEN CUP AND LIP

BUT all was not yet ended.

To re-open the gorge closed by a portion of the Durande's bulwarks, and push out into the open sea, seemed a very easy and simple matter. But on the ocean every minute tells. There was little wind; scarcely a ripple on the open sea. The afternoon was beautiful, and promised a fine night. The sea, indeed, was calm, but the ebb had begun. The moment was favourable for starting. There would be the ebb tide for leaving the Douvres; and the flood would carry him into Guernsey. He could be at St. Sampson's by daybreak.

But an unexpected obstacle presented itself. There was a flaw in his arrangements which had baffled all his foresight.

The machinery was freed, but the chimney was not.

The tide, by raising the sloop towards the wreck suspended in the air, had diminished the dangers of the descent, and abridged the labour. But this diminution of distance had left the top of the funnel entangled in the gaping frame formed by the open hull of the Durande. The funnel was held fast there as between four walls.

The services rendered by the sea had been accompanied by this unfortunate drawback. It seemed as if the waves, constrained to obey, had avenged themselves by a malicious trick.

It is true that what the flood tide had done, the ebb would undo.

About eight feet of the funnel was entangled in the wreck. The water level would fall about twelve feet. Thus the funnel descending with the falling tide would have four feet of room to spare, and could easily clear itself.

But how much time would elapse before that release would be completed? Six hours.

In six hours it would be nearly midnight. How could he attempt to start at such an hour? How could he find his way among all these reefs, so full of danger even by day? How could he risk his vessel in the dead of night in that inextricable labyrinth, that ambuscade of shoals.

There was no help for it. He must wait for the morrow. The six hours lost entailed a loss of at least twelve hours.

He could not even hasten matters by opening the mouth of the gorge. His breakwater would be needed against the next tide.

He was compelled to wait. Folding his arms was almost the only thing which he had not done since his arrival on the rocks.

This forced inaction irritated him almost as much as if it had been his own fault. He thought, " What would Déruchette say of me if she saw me here doing nothing? "

And yet this interval for regaining his strength was not unnecessary.

The sloop was now at his service; he determined to spend the night in it.

He mounted once more to fetch his sheepskin from the great Douvre; descended again; supped off a few limpets and *châtaignes de mer;* drank, being very thirsty, a few draughts of water from his can, which was nearly empty; wrapped himself in the skin, the wool of which felt very comfortable to him; stretched himself out like a big watch-dog beside the engine, drew his red cap over his eyes, and slept.

His sleep was profound. It was such sleep as men enjoy after the completion of a herculean task.

CHAPTER X

SEA-WARNINGS

IN the middle of the night he suddenly awoke with a jerk like the recoil of a spring.

He opened his eyes.

The Douvres, towering high above his head, were illumined as if by a reflection from dying embers.

Over all the dark escarpment of the rock there was a light like the reflection of a fire.

Where did this fire come from?

It was from the water.

The appearance of the sea was extraordinary.

The water seemed on fire. As far as the eye could reach, among the reefs and beyond them, the sea was covered with flame. The flame was not red; it had nothing in common with the grand living fires of volcanic craters or of great furnaces. There was no sparkling, no glare, no purple edges, no noise. Long trails of pale light simulated upon the water the folds of a winding-sheet. It was the ghost of a great fire, rather than the fire itself.

It was in some degree like the livid glow of unearthly flames lighting the inside of a sepulchre.

A gleaming darkness.

The night itself, dim, vast, and widely diffused, was the fuel of that cold flame. It was a strange illumination issuing out of gloom. Even the shadows formed a part of that phantom fire.

The sailors of the Channel are familiar with these wonderful phosphorescent displays, so full of warning for the navigator. Nowhere are they more startling than in the " Great V," near Isigny.

In this light, surrounding objects lose their reality. A spectral glimmer renders them, as it were, transparent. Rocks become no more than outlines. Cables of anchors look like iron bars heated to a white heat. The nets of the fishermen seem webs of fire beneath the water. The half of the oar above the waves is dark as ebony, the part in the sea like silver. The drops from the blades uplifted from the water fall in starry showers upon the sea. Every boat leaves a furrow behind it like a comet's tail. The sailors seem to be on fire. If you plunge your hand into the water, you withdraw it clothed in flame. The flame is dead, and is not felt. Your arm becomes a firebrand. The foam twinkles. The fish are tongues of flame or fragments of forked lightning, moving in the palid depths.

The reflection of this brightness had passed through the closed eyelids of Gilliatt aboard the sloop. It was this that had awakened him.

His waking was most opportune.

The ebb tide had run out, and the waters were beginning to rise again. The funnel, which had become disengaged during his sleep, was about to re-enter the yawning gap above it.

It was rising slowly but surely.

A rise of another foot would have entangled it in the wreck again. A rise of one foot is equivalent to half-an-hour's tide. If he intended, therefore, to take advantage of the temporary deliverance once more within his reach, he had just half-an-hour before him.

He leaped to his feet.

Urgent as the situation was, he stood for a few moments meditating as he contemplated the phosphorescence on the waves.

Gilliatt was familiar with the sea in all its phases. Not-

withstanding all her tricks, and often as he had suffered from
her terrors, he had long been her companion. That mysterious entity which we call the ocean had nothing in its secret
thoughts which he could not divine. Observation, meditation, and solitude, had given him a quick perception of coming changes, of wind or cloud or wave, and had made him
weatherwise.

Gilliatt hastened to the top ropes and payed out some
cable; then being no longer held fast by the anchors, he
seized the boat hook of the sloop, and pushed her towards
the entrance to the gorge some fathoms from the Durande,
and quite near to the breakwater. Here, as the Guernsey
sailors say, it had *du rang*. In less than ten minutes the
sloop was withdrawn from beneath the remains of the wreck.
There was no further danger of the funnel being caught in a
trap. The tide might rise now.

And yet Gilliatt's manner was not that of one about to
take his departure.

He stood gazing at the light upon the sea again; but he
had no intention of starting. He was thinking how he could
fasten the sloop again, and fasten it more securely than ever,
though much nearer the mouth of the gorge.

Up to this time he had used the two anchors of the sloop,
but had not yet employed the little anchor of the Durande,
which he had found, as the reader will remember, among the
rocks. This anchor had been deposited in readiness for any
emergency, in a corner of the sloop, with a quantity of hawsers, and coils of top-ropes, and his cable, all furnished beforehand, with large knots, which prevented its dragging. He
now dropped this third anchor, taking care to fasten the
cable to a rope, one end of which was slung through the anchor ring, while the other was attached to the windlass of
the sloop.

In this manner he made a kind of fore-and-aft mooring,
much stronger than the moorings with two anchors. All this
indicated keen anxiety, and a redoubling of precautions. A
sailor would have seen in this operation something similiar to

an anchorage in bad weather, when there is fear of a current which might carry the vessel to leeward.

The phosphorescence which he had been observing, and upon which his eye was again fixed, was ominous, but at the same time useful. But for it he would have been held fast locked in sleep, and betrayed by the night. The strange appearance upon the sea had awakened him, and made things about him visible.

The light which it shed upon the rocks was, indeed, threatening; but alarming as it appeared to Gilliatt, it had served to show him the dangers of his position, and had rendered it possible for him to extricate the sloop. Now, whenever he was able to set sail, the vessel, with its freight of machinery, would be free.

And yet the idea of departing was further than ever from his mind. The sloop being securely fixed in its new position, he went in quest of the strongest chain which he had in his store-house, and attaching it to the nails driven into the two Douvres, he strengthened on the inside with this chain the rampart of planks and beams, already protected from without by the cross chain. Instead of opening the entrance to the defile, he made the barrier more complete.

The phosphorescence still lighted him, but it was diminishing. Day, however, was beginning to break.

Suddenly he paused to listen.

CHAPTER XI

MURMURS IN THE AIR

A FEEBLE, indistinct sound seemed to reach his ear from somewhere in the dim distance.

At certain times the depths of ocean give out a murmuring sound.

He listened a second time. The distant noise recommenced. Gilliatt shook his head like one who recognizes at last something familiar to him.

A few minutes later he was at the other end of the opening between the rocks, at the entrance facing the east, which had remained open until then, and with heavy blows of his hammer was driving large nails into the sides of the gully near " The Man " rock, as he had done in the gully at the Douvres.

The crevices of these rocks were prepared and well furnished with timber, almost all of which was heart of oak. The rock on this side being much broken up, there were abundant cracks, and he was able to fix even more nails there than in the base of the two Douvres.

Suddenly, and as if some great breath had passed over it, the luminous appearance on the waters vanished. The light of dawn which was becoming brighter every moment, took its place.

The nails being driven, Gilliatt dragged beams and ropes and chains to the spot, and, without taking his eyes off his work, or permitting his mind to be diverted for a moment, began to construct across the gorge at " The Man " rock with horizontal beams, made fast by cables, one of those open barriers which science has now adopted under the name of breakwaters.

Those who have witnessed, for example, at La Rocquaine in Guernsey, or at Bourg-d'Eau in France, the effect produced by a few posts fixed in the rock, will understand the efficacy of these simple preparations. This sort of breakwater is a combination of what is known in France as an *épi* with what is known in England as " a dam." Breakwaters are the *chevaux-de-frise* of fortifications against tempests. Man can struggle successfully with the sea only by taking advantage of this principle of dividing its forces.

Meanwhile, the sun had risen, and was shining brightly. The sky was clear, the sea calm.

Gilliatt hastened on with his work. He, too, was calm;

but there was anxiety in his haste. He passed with long strides from rock to rock, and returned dragging sometimes a rider, sometimes a binding strake. The utility of this preparation soon became manifest. It was evident that he was about to confront a danger which he had foreseen.

A strong iron bar served him as a lever for moving the beams.

The work was executed so fast that it was a rapid growth rather than a construction. One who has never seen a military pontooner at his work can scarcely form an idea of the rapidity with which this work progressed.

The eastern opening was even narrower than the western. The rocks were only five or six feet apart. The smallness of this opening was a great help. The space to be fortified and closed up being very small, the apparatus would be stronger and more simple. Horizontal beams, therefore, sufficed, the upright ones being useless.

The first cross-pieces of the breakwater being fixed, Gilliatt climbed upon them and listened once more.

The murmurs had become significant.

He continued the construction of his breakwater. He supported it with the two cat-heads of the Durande, bound to the frame of beams by cords passed through the three pulley-sheaves, and made the whole fast with chains.

The apparatus was nothing more or less than a collossal hurdle, having beams for rods, and chains in place of wattles.

It seemed woven together, quite as much as built.

He multiplied the fastenings, and added nails where they were needed.

Having obtained a great quantity of bar iron from the wreck, he had been able to make a large number of these heavy nails.

While he worked, he ate a biscuit or two. He was thirsty, but he could not drink, having no more fresh water. He had emptied the can at his meal of the evening before.

He added afterwards four or five more pieces of timber, then climbed again upon the barrier and listened.

The noises from the horizon had ceased; all was still.

The sea was smooth and quiet, deserving all those complimentary phrases which worthy people bestow upon it when well satisfied with a trip. " A mirror," " a pond," " like oil," and so forth. The deep blue of the sky responded to the deep green tint of the ocean. The sapphire and the emerald hues vied with each other. Each was perfect. Not a cloud on high, not a line of foam below. In the midst of all this splendour, the April sun rose magnificently. It was impossible to imagine a lovelier day.

On the edge of the horizon a flock of birds of passage formed a long dark line against the sky. They were flying towards land as if alarmed.

Gilliatt set to work again to raise the breakwater.

He raised it as high as he could,— as high, indeed, as the curvature of the rocks would permit.

Towards noon the sun seemed to emit more than its usual warmth. Noon is the critical time of the day. Standing upon the powerful frame which he had built up, he paused again to survey the wide expanse.

The sea was more than tranquil. A dull, dead calm reigned. No sail was visible. The sky was everywhere clear; but it had changed from blue to white in colour. The whiteness was peculiar. To the west, and upon the horizon, was a small spot of a sickly hue. The spot remained in the same place, but grew larger by degrees. Near the breakers the waves shuddered, but very gently.

Gilliatt had done well to build his breakwater.

A tempest was at hand.

The elements had determined to give him battle.

BOOK III

THE STRUGGLE

———

CHAPTER I

EXTREMES MEET

NOTHING is more dangerous than a late equinox.
The appearance of the sea presents a strange phenomenon, resulting from what may be called the arrival of
the ocean winds.

In all seasons, but particularly at the epoch of the Syzy-
gies, when least expected, the sea sometimes becomes singularly tranquil. That vast perpetual movement ceases ; a
sort of drowsiness and languor overspreads it, and it seems
weary and about to rest. Every rag of bunting, from the
tiny streamer of the fishing-boat to the great flag of ships
of war, droops against the mast. The admiral's flag and
Royal and Imperial ensigns sleep alike.

Suddenly all these streamers began to flutter gently.

If there happen to be clouds, the moment has come for
noting the formation of the *cirri;* if the sun is setting, for
observing the red tints of the horizon ; or if it be night and
there is a moon, for looking for the halo.

It is then that the captain or commander of a squadron,
if he happen to possess one of those storm glasses, the inven-
tor of which is unknown, watches his instrument carefully,
and takes his precautions against the south wind if the clouds

94

look like dissolved sugar, or against the north wind if they exfoliate in crystallizations like brakes or brambles, or like fir-trees. Then, too, the poor Irish or Breton fisherman, after having consulted some mysterious gnomon engraved by the Romans or by demons upon one of those straight enigmatical stones, which are called in Brittany " Menhir," and in Ireland " Cruach," hauls his boat up on the shore.

Meanwhile, the serenity of sky and ocean continues. The day dawns radiant, and Aurora smiles. It was this which filled the old poets and seers with religious horror, terrified at the thought that men dared to fancy the falsity of the sun. " Solem quis dicere falsum audeat? "

The power to discern latent possibilities in the world of Nature is prevented in man by the fatal opacity of surrounding things. The most terrible and perfidious of her aspects is that which masks the convulsions of the deep.

Hours and sometimes even days, pass thus. Pilots direct their telescopes here and there. The faces of old seamen always have an expression of severity left upon them by the annoyance of perpetually looking for changes.

Suddenly a great confused murmur is heard. A sort of mysterious dialogue takes place in the air.

Nothing unusual is seen.

The wide expanse is tranquil.

Yet the noises increase. The dialogue becomes more audible.

There is something moving beyond the horizon.

Something terrible. It is the wind.

The wind, or rather that nation of Titans we call the gale, — the unseen mob.

India knew them as the Maruts, Judea as the Keroubim, Greece as the Aquilones. They are the invisible winged creatures of the infinite. Their blasts sweep over the earth.

CHAPTER II

THE OCEAN WINDS

THEY come from the immeasurable deep. Their wide wings need the breadth of the ocean gulf, the spaciousness of desert solitudes. The Atlantic, the Pacific — those vast blue expanses — are their delight. They hasten thither in flocks. Commander Page witnessed, far out at sea, seven waterspouts at once. They roam there, wild and terrible! The eternal flux and reflux is their work. The extent of their power, the limits of their will, no one knows. They are the Sphinxes of the deep: Gama was their Œdipus. In that dark, ever-moving expanse, they appear with faces of cloud. He who perceives their pale lineaments in that wide arena, the horizon of the sea, feels himself in presence of an unsubduable power. It might be imagined that the proximity of human intelligence disquieted them, and that they revolted against it. The mind of man is invincible, but the elements baffle him. He can do nothing against these ubiquitous powers which no one can bind. The gentle breeze becomes a gale, smites with the force of a war-club, and then become gentle again. The winds attack with a terrible crash, and defend themselves by relapsing into nothingness. He who would contend with them must use artifice. Their varying tactics, their swift redoubled blows, confuse one. They fly as often as they attack. They are tenacious and impalpable. Who can circumvent them? The prow of the Argo, cut from an oak of Dodona's grove, that mysterious pilot of the bark, spoke to them, and they insulted that pilot-goddess. Columbus, beholding their approach towards the " Pinta," mounted upon the poop, and addressed them with the first verses of St. John's Gospel. Surcouf defied them: " Here come the gang," he used to say. Napier greeted them with cannon balls. They assume the dictatorship of chaos.

Chaos is theirs, in which to wreak their mysterious vengeance; the cave of the winds is more appalling than that of lions. How many corpses lie in its deep recesses, where the howling gusts sweep relentlessly over that obscure and ghastly mass! The winds are heard wheresoever they go, but they give ear to none. Their acts resemble crimes. No one knows upon whom they may hurl their hoary surf; with what ferocity they hang over shipwrecks, looking at times as if they flung their impious foam-flakes in the face of heaven. They are the tyrants of unknown regions. " Luoghi spaventosi," murmured the Venetian mariners.

The fields of space are subjected to their fierce assaults. Strange things happen in those lonely regions. Sometimes a horseman rides through the gloom; sometimes the air is full of a faint rustling as in a forest; again nothing is visible, but the tramp of a cavalcade is heard. The noonday is overcast with sudden night: a tornado passes. Or midnight suddenly becomes bright as day: the polar lights are in the heavens. Whirlwinds pass in opposite directions, and in a sort of hideous dance, a stamping of the storm fiends upon the waters. An over-burdened cloud opens and falls to earth. Other clouds filled with lurid light, flash and roar, then frown again ominously. Emptied of their lightnings, they are but as spent brands. Pent-up rains dissolve in mists. Yonder sea looks like a fiery furnace, into which the rains are falling; flames seem to issue from the waves. The white gleam of the ocean under the shower is reflected to marvellous distances. The different masses transform themselves into uncouth shapes. Monstrous whirlpools make strange hollows in the sky. The vapours revolve, the waves spin, the giddy Naiads roll. The sea, solid and yielding, moves, but does not change place; all is livid; shrieks as of despair resound through the air.

Great sheaves of shadow and darkness are gathered up in the distant sky. Now and then comes a convulsion. The murmur becomes uproar as the wave becomes surge. The horizon, a confused mass of strata oscillating ceaselessly, mut-

7

ters in a continual undertone. Strange and abrupt outbursts break the monotony. Cold blasts burst forth, followed by hot blasts. The restlessness of the sea betokens anxious expectation, agony, profound terror. Suddenly the hurricane sweeps down, like a wild beast, to drink of the ocean: a monstrous draught! The sea rises to the invisible mouth; a mound of water is formed; the swell increases, and the waterspout appears: the Prester of the ancients, stalactite above, stalagmite below, a whirling double-inverted cone, the kiss of two mountains,— a mountain of foam ascending, a mountain of vapour descending,— terrible coition of the cloud and the wave. Like the column in Holy Writ, the waterspout is dark by day and luminous by night. In its presence the thunder itself is silent and seems cowed.

The vast commotion of these solitudes has its gamut, a terrible crescendo. There are the gust, the squall, the storm, the gale, the tempest, the whirlwind, and the waterspout,— the seven chords of the wind's lyre, the seven notes of the great deep. The heavens are a huge arena; the sea a vast round; but a breath passes, they have vanished, and all is fury and wild confusion.

Such are these inhospitable realms.

The winds rush, fly, swoop down, die away, commence again, hover about, whistle, roar, and smile; they are frenzied, wanton, unbridled, or sink to ease upon the raging waves. Their howlings have a harmony of their own. They make the entire heavens resound. They blow in the cloud as in a trumpet; they sing through infinite space with the mingled tones of clarions, horns, bugles, and trumpets,— a sort of Promethean fanfare.

Such was the music of ancient Pan. Their harmonies are terrible. They revel in darkness. They drive and disperse great ships. Night and day, in all seasons, from the tropics to the pole, there is no truce; sounding their fatal trumpet through the tangled thickets of clouds and waves, they pursue their grim chase of vessels in distress. They have their packs of bloodhounds, and amuse themselves by setting them to barking at the rocks and billows. They drive the clouds together, and then roughly disperse them. They mould and knead the supple waters as with a million hands.

The water is supple because it is incompressible. It slips away without effort. Borne down on one side, it escapes on the other. It is thus that water becomes waves, and the billows are a token of its liberty.

CHAPTER III

THE MYSTERIOUS SOUNDS EXPLAINED

THE fiercest descent of the winds upon the earth takes place at the equinoxes. At this period the balance of tropic and pole librates, and the vast atmospheric tides pour their flood upon one hemisphere and their ebb upon another. The signs of Libra and Aquarius have reference to these phenomena.

It is the time of tempests.

The sea awaits their coming in silence.

Sometimes the sky looks sickly. Its face is wan. A thick dark veil obscures it. The mariners observe with uneasiness the threatening aspect of the clouds.

But it is its air of calm contentment which they dread most. A smiling sky in the equinoxes is a tempest in disguise. It was under skies like these that " The Tower of Weeping Women," in Amsterdam, was filled with wives and mothers scanning the far horizon.

When the vernal or autumnal storms loiter by the way, they are only gathering strength, hoarding up their fury for greater destruction. Beware of the gale that has been long delayed. It was Ango who said that " the sea pays old debts handsomely."

When the delay is unusually long, the sea reveals her impatience only by a deeper calm; but the magnetic intensity manifests itself in what might be called a fiery humour in the sea. Fire issues from the waves; electric air, phosphoric water. The sailors feel a strange lassitude. This time is particularly dangerous for iron vessels; their hulls are then liable to produce variations of the compass, leading them to destruction. The transatlantic steam-vessel " Iowa " perished from this cause.

To those who are familiar with the sea, its aspect at these moments is peculiar. It might be imagined to be both desiring and fearing the approach of the cyclone. Certain unions, though strongly urged by Nature, are attended by this strange compound of terror and desire. The lioness in her tenderest moods flies from the lion. Thus the sea, in the fire of her passion, trembles at the near approach of her union with the tempest. The nuptials are prepared. Like the marriages of the ancient emperors, they are celebrated with immolations. The *fête* is seasoned with disasters.

Meanwhile, from yonder deep, from the great open sea, from the unapproachable latitudes, from the lurid horizon of the watery waste, from the furthermost limits of ocean, the winds rush in.

Beware! for this is the famous equinox.

The storm plots all sorts of mischief. In ancient mythology there personalities were recognized taking part in this grand drama of Nature. Eolus plotted with Boreas. The alliance of element with element is necessary; they divide their task. One has to give impetus to the wave, the cloud, the stream: night too is an auxiliary, and must be employed. There are compasses to be falsified, beacons to be extinguished, lanterns of lighthouses to be masked, stars to be hidden. The sea must lend her aid. Every storm is preceded by a murmur. Beyond the horizon there is a premonitory whispering among the hurricanes.

This is the noise which is heard afar off in the darkness amid the terrible silence of the sea.

It was this significant whispering that Gilliatt had noticed. The phosphorescence on the water had been the first warning; this murmur the second.

If the demon Legion really exists, he is assuredly no other than the wind.

The entire heavens take part in a tempest: the entire ocean also. All their forces are marshalled for the strife. A contest with a storm is a contest with all the powers of sea and sky.

It was Messier, that great authority among naval men, the thoughtful astronomer of the little lodge at Cluny, who said, " The wind from everywhere is everywhere." He had no faith in the idea of winds imprisoned even in inland seas. With him there were no Mediterranean winds; he declared that he recognized them as they wandered about the earth. He declared that on a certain day and at a certain hour, the Föhn of the Lake of Constance, the ancient Favonius of Lucretius, had traversed the sky of Paris; on another day, the Bora of the Adriatic; on another day, the whirling Notus, which is supposed to be confined in the round of the Cyclades. He indicated their currents. He did not think it impossible that even the Autan, which circulates between Malta and Tunis, and the Autan, which circulates between Corsica and the Balearic Isles, could escape their bounds. He did not admit the theory of winds imprisoned like bears in their dens. It was he, too, who said that, " every rain comes from the tropics, and every flash of lightning from the pole." The wind in fact, becomes saturated with electricity at the intersection of the colures which marks the extremity of the axis, and with water at the equator, thus bringing moisture from the equatorial line and the electric fluid from the poles.

The wind is ubiquitous.

We certainly do not mean by this that wind zones do not exist. Nothing is better established than the existence of those continuous air currents; and aërial navigation by means of wind boats, to which the passion for Greek terminology has given the name of " aëroscaphes," may one day succeed in utilizing these rivers of air. The regular course of air

streams is an incontestable fact.   There are rivers of wind
and streams of wind and brooks of wind, although their
branches are exactly the opposite of water currents; for in the
air the brooks flow out of the streams, and the streams flow
out of the rivers instead of flowing into them.   Hence, instead of concentration we have dispersion.

The united action of the winds and the unity of the atmosphere is the natural result of this dispersion.   The displacement of one molecule produces the displacement of another.
The vast body of air becomes subject to one agitation.

To these profound causes of coalition we must add the irregular surface of the earth, whose mountains furrow the atmosphere, contorting and diverting the winds from their
course, and determining the directions of counter currents in
infinite radiations.

The phenomenon of the wind is the oscillation of two oceans
one against the other; the ocean of air, superimposed upon
the ocean of water, rests upon these currents, and is convulsed
with this vast agitation.

The indivisible cannot produce separate action.   No parti-
tion divides wave from wave.   The islands of the Channel feel
the influence of the Cape of Good Hope.   Navigation is
everywhere obliged to contend with the same monster; the sea
is one and the same hydra.   The waves cover it as with a fish-
skin.   The ocean is Ceto.

Upon that unity reposes an infinite variety.

CHAPTER IV

TURBA, TURMA

ACCORDING to the compass there are thirty-two winds.
But these may be subdivided indefinitely.   Classed
by its direction, the wind is uncalculable; classed by its kind,
it is infinite.   Homer himself would have shrunk from the task
of enumerating them.

The polar current encounters the tropical current. Heat and cold are thus combined; the equilibrium is disturbed by a shock; a wave of wind issues forth and is distended, scattered, and broken up in every direction in fierce streams. The dispension of the gusts shakes the streaming locks of the wind upon the four corners of the horizon.

All the winds that blow are there. The wind of the Gulf Stream, which disgorges the great fogs on Newfoundland; the wind of Peru, in the region of silent heavens, where no man ever head the thunder roar; the wind of Nova Scotia, where flies the great auk (*Alca impennis*) with his furrowed beak; the whirlwinds of Ferro in the China seas; the wind of Mozambique, which destroys the canoes and junks; the electric wind of Japan, foretold by the gong; the African wind, which blows between Table Mountain and the Devil's Peak, where it gains its liberty; the currents of the equator, which pass over the trade winds, describing a parabola, the summit of which is always to the west; the Plutonian wind, which issues from craters and is the terrible breath of flames; the singular wind peculiar to the volcano Awa, which forms an olive-hued cloud to the northward; the Java monsoon, against which the people construct those casemates known as hurricane houses; the branching north winds called by the English " Bush winds; " the curved squalls of the Straits of Malacca; observed by Horsburgh; the powerful south-west wind, called " pampero " in Chili, and " rebojo " in Buenos Ayres, which carries the great condor out to sea, and saves him from the pit where the Indian, concealed under a newly stripped bullock-hide, watches for him, lying on his back and bending his great bow with his feet; the chemical wind, which, according to Lemery, produces thunderbolts from the clouds; the Harmattan of the Caffres; the Polar snow-driver, which harnesses itself to the everlasting icebergs; the wind of the Gulf of Bengal, which sweeps over a continent to pillage the triangular town of wooden booths at Nijni-Novgorod, in which the great fair of Asia is held; the wind of the Cordilleras, agitator of great waves and forests; the wind of the Australian Archipelago, where the bee-hunters take the wild hives hidden under the forked branches of the giant eucalyptus; the sirocco, the mistral, the hurricane, the dry winds, the inundating and diluvian winds, the torrid winds, which scatter dust from the plains of Brazil upon the streets of Genoa; those which obey the diurnal rotation, those which revolt against it, and of which Herrara said, " Malo viento torna contra el sol; " those winds which hunt in couples, conspiring mischief, the one undoing the work of the other; and those old winds which assailed Columbus on the coast of Veragua, and which for forty days,— from the 21st of October to the 28th of November, 1520,— delayed and nearly frustrated Magellan's approach to the Pacific; and those which dismasted the Armada and confounded Philip II.   Others, too, there are, of whose names there is no end.   The winds, for instance, which carry showers of frogs and locusts, and drive before them clouds of living things across the ocean; those which blow in what are called " wind-leaps," and whose function is to destroy ships at sea; those which at a single blast throw the cargo out of trim, and compel the vessel to continue her course half broadside over; the winds which construct the circum-cumuli; the winds which mass together the circum-strata; the dark heavy winds bloated with rain; the winds of hailstorms; the fever winds. whose approach sets the salt springs and sulphur springs of Calabria boiling; those which impart a glittering appearance to the fur of the African panthers, prowling among the bushes of Cape Ferro; those which come quivering from the cloud, like the tongue of a trigonocephal, the terrible forked lightning; and those which bring whirlwinds of black snow. Such is the legion of winds.

The Douvres rock heard their distant tramp at the very moment that Gilliatt was constructing his breakwater.

As we have said, the wind means a combination of all winds.   The entire horde was advancing,— on one side, a legion of demons; on the other, Gilliatt.

CHAPTER V

GILLIATT'S ALTERNATIVES

THE mysterious forces had chosen their time well. Chance, if chance exists, is sometimes far-seeing. So long as the sloop was anchored in the little creek of " The Man " rock, and so long as the machinery was imprisoned in the wreck, Gilliatt's position was impregnable. The sloop was safe, the machinery sheltered. The Douvres, which held the hull of the Durande fast, condemned it to slow destruction, but protected it against unexpected accidents. At all events, one resource had remained to him. If the engine had been destroyed, Gilliatt would have been safe, for he would still have had the sloop with which to make his escape.

But to wait till the sloop was removed from the anchorage where she was so well protected; to allow it to be placed in the defile of the Douvres; to watch until the sloop, too, was entangled in the rocks; to permit him to complete the salvage, the moving, and the final embarkation of the machinery; to inflict no injury upon the wonderful apparatus by which one man was enabled to put the whole aboard his bark; to further, in fact, the success of his exploits so far,— this was only the trap which the elements had laid for him. Now, for the first time, he began to perceive in all its sinister characteristics the trick which the sea had been meditating so long.

The machinery, the sloop, and their master were all within the gorge now. One blow, and the sloop might be dashed to pieces on the rock, the machinery destroyed, and Gilliatt drowned.

The situation could not have been more critical.

The Sphinx, which men have pictured as concealing herself in the cloud, seemed to mock him with a dilemma.

" Should he go or stay? "

To go would have been madness; to remain was terrible.

CHAPTER VI

THE COMBAT

GILLIATT climbed to the summit of the great Douvre.

From there he could command a view of the entire horizon.

The western side was appalling. A wall of cloud spread across it, barring the wide expanse from side to side, and was now ascending slowly from the horizon towards the zenith. This wall, straight, perpendicular, without a single crack or crevice throughout its whole extent, seemed to have been built by the quare and measured by the plumb-line. It was cloud in the likeness of granite. Its escarpment, perfectly perpendicular at the southern end, curved a little towards the north, like a bent sheet of iron, presenting the steep slippery face of an inclined plane. The dark wall enlarged and grew; but its entablature remained parallel with the horizon line, which was almost indistinguishable in the gathering darkness. Silently, and in one solid mass, the battlements ascended. No undulation, no wrinkle, no projection changed its shape or relative position in the heavens. The appearance of this slowly ascending immobile mass of cloud was impressive. The sun, overhung by a strange sickly transparent haze, lighted up this outline of the Apocalypse. Already the cloudy bank had blotted out one half the sky. It was like a huge mountain uprising between earth and heaven.

It was night suddenly blotting out midday.

A heat like that from an oven door proceeded from that mysterious mass. The sky, which had changed from blue to white, was now turning from white to a slaty grey. The sea beneath was leaden-hued and dull. There was not a breath, not a wave, not a sound. As far as eye could reach, the ocean was deserted. Not a sail was visible in any direction. The birds had disappeared. Some deed of frightful treachery seemed impending.

The wall of cloud grew visibly larger.

This moving mountain of vapour, which was approaching the Douvres, was one of those clouds which might be justly called war clouds. Grim and sinister of aspect, it seemed to threaten with destruction anything and everything that stood in its way.

Its approach was terrible.

Gilliatt observed it closely, muttering to himself, " I am thirsty enough, but you will give me plenty to drink."

He stood there motionless a few moments, with his eye fixed upon the cloud bank, as if mentally taking a sounding of the tempest.

His cap was in his jacket pocket; he took it out and placed it on his head. Then he fetched from the cave, which he had so long served him as a sleeping-room, a few articles which he had kept there in reserve; he put on his overalls, and attired himself in his waterproof overcoat, like a knight who puts on his armour at the moment of battle. He had no shoes; but his naked feet had become hardened to the rocks.

This preparation for the storm being completed, he looked down upon his breakwater, grasped the knotted cord hurriedly, descended from the plateau of the Douvre, stepped on to the rocks below, and hastened to his storehouse. A few moments later he was again at work. The vast silent cloud might have heard the strokes of his hammer. With the nails, ropes, and beams which still remained, he constructed a second frame for the eastern gully, which he succeeded in fastening ten or twelve feet from the other.

The silence was still unbroken. The blades of grass between the crevices in the rocks did not move.

The sun suddenly disappeared. Gilliatt looked up.

The rising cloud had just reached it. It was like the blotting out of day, succeeded by a pale hazy reflection.

The immense wall of cloud had changed in appearance. It no longer retained its unity. It curved on reaching the zenith,

where it spread out horizontally over the rest of the
heavens.

The tempest formation was now distinctly visible, like the
strata in the side of a deep trench. It was possible to distinguish the layers of the rain from the beds of hail. There
was no lightning, but a horrible, diffused glare,— for the idea
of horror may be attached to light. The breathing of the
storm was audible; the silence was broken by an obscure
palpitation. Gilliatt silently watched the gigantic masses of
vapour grouping themselves overhead. On the horizon
brooded a band of mist of ashen hue; in the zenith, another
band of lead colour. Pale, ragged fragments of cloud
drooped from the great mass above upon the mist below. The
pile of cloud which formed the background was wan, dull,
gloomy, indescribable. A thin, whitish transverse cloud, coming no one could tell whither, cut the high dark well obliquely
from north to south. One of the extremities of this cloud
trailed along the surface of the sea. At the point where it
touched the water, a dense red vapour was visible in the midst
of the darkness. Below it, smaller clouds, quite black and
very low, were flying as if bewildered, or as if moved by opposite currents of air. The immense cloud beyond increased
from all points at once, heightened the eclipse, and continued
to spread its sombre pall over the firmament. In the east,
behind Gilliatt, there was only one clear bit of sky, and that
was rapidly becoming overcast. Without a breath of wind
in the air, a strange flock of grey downy particles seemed to
pass; they were fine and scattered, as if some gigantic bird
had been plucked of its plumage behind the bank of
cloud.

A dark compact roof had gradually formed, which touched
the sea on the verge of the horizon, and became merged into
it. The beholder had a vague sense of something advancing
steadily towards him. It was vast, heavy, ominous. Suddenly an immense peal of thunder shook the air.

Gilliatt himself felt the shock. Thunder belongs to dream-
land, and the rude reality in the midst of that visionary region

has something terrific in it. The listener might fancy that he hears something falling in the chamber of giants.

No electric flash accompanied the report. It was a blind peal. The silence was profound again. There was an interval, as when combatants take their places. Then appeared slowly, one after the other, great shapeless flashes; these flashes were silent. The wall of cloud was now a vast cavern, with fantastic roofs and arches. Outlines of giant forms were traceable among them; monstrous heads were vaguely shadowed forth; necks seemed to stretch out; elephants bearing turrets, seen for a moment, vanished. A column of vapour, straight, round, and dark, and surmounted by a white mist, simulated the form of a colossal steam-vessel ingulfed, hissing, and smoking beneath the waves. Trailing clouds undulated like folds of immense flags. In the centre, under a thick purple pall, a nucleus of dense fog hung motionless, inert, unpenetrated by the electric fires,— a sort of hideous fœtus in the bosom of the tempest.

Suddenly Gilliatt felt a breath move his hair. Two or three large spots of rain fell heavily around him on the rock. Then there was a second thunder-clap. The wind was rising.

The darkness was at its height. The first peal of thunder had shaken the sea; the second rent the wall of cloud from top to bottom; a breach was visible; the pent-up deluge rushed towards it; the rent became like a gulf filled with rain. The outpouring of the tempest had begun.

The moment was terrible.

Rain, wind, lightnings, thunder, waves swirling upwards to the clouds, foam, hoarse noises, and whistling sounds mingled together like monsters suddenly unloosed.

For a solitary man, imprisoned with an overloaded vessel, between two dangerous rocks in mid-ocean, no crisis could have been more menacing. The danger of the tide, over which he had triumphed, was nothing compared with the danger of the tempest.

Surrounded on all sides by perils, Gilliatt, at the last

moment, and before the crowning peril, resorted to an ingenious stratagem. He had secured his base of operations in the enemies' territory; had pressed the rock into his service. The Douvres, originally his enemy, had become his second in the impending duel. Out of that sepulchre he had constructed a fortress. He had intrenched himself among these formidable sea ruins. He was blockaded, but well defended. He had, so to speak, placed his back to the wall, and now stood face to face with the hurricane. He had barricaded the narrow strait, that highway of the waves. This, indeed, was the only possible course. It seemed as if the ocean, like other despots, might be brought to reason by the aid of barricades. The sloop might be considered secure on three sides. Closely wedged between the two inner walls of the rock, and made fast by three anchors, she was also sheltered on the north by the Little Douvre, and on the south by the Great Douvre,— terrible escarpments, more accustomed to wreck vessels than to save them. On the western side she was protected by the frame of timbers made fast and nailed to the rocks,— a tried barrier which had withstood the rude flood tide of the sea; a veritable citadel-gate, having for its sides two huge columns of rock,— the two Douvres themselves. Nothing was to be feared from that side. It was on the eastern side only that there was danger.

On that side there was no protection but the breakwater. A breakwater is an apparatus for dividing and distributing the waves. It requires at least two frames. Gilliatt had only had time to construct one. He was compelled to build the second in the very face of the tempest.

Fortunately the wind came from the north-west. The wind is not always adroit in its attacks. The north-west wind, which is the ancient " galerno," had very little effect upon the Douvres. It assailed the rocks on their flank, and drove the waves against neither of the two gorges; so that instead of rushing into the defile, they merely dashed themselves against a wall.

It was more than probable that there would be a sudden

change, however. It it should veer to the eastward before the second frame could be constructed, the peril would be great. The irruption of the sea into the gorge would be complete, and all would probably be lost.

All the while the storm was increasing in fury. In a tempest, blow hastily follows blow. That is its strength; but it is also its weakness. Its very fury gives human intelligence an opportunity to discover its weak points. Man defends himself, but under what overwhelming difficulties! No respite, no interruption, no truce, no pause for taking breath. There seems to be unspeakable cowardice in that prodigality of inexhaustible resources.

All the tumult of the wide expanse rushed towards the Douvres. Voices were heard in the darkness. What could they be? At times shouts were heard, as if some one was uttering words of command. There were wild clamours, strange trepidation, and then that majestic roar which mariners call the " cry of ocean." The flying eddies of wind whistled, while curling the waves and flinging them like giant quoits, cast by invisible hands against the rocks. The surf dashed over the rocks. There were torrents above, dashing foam below. Then the roar redoubled. No uproar of men or beasts could give one any idea of the wild din which mingled with the incessant breaking of the surf. The clouds cannonaded, the hailstones poured down in volleys, the surf mounted to the assault. As far as the eye could reach, the sea was white; ten leagues of yeasty water filled the horizon. Doors of fire were opened, clouds seemed burned by clouds, and something like smoke rose above a nebulous red mass, resembling burning embers. Floating conflagrations rushed together and amalgamated, each changing the shape of the other. A huge arsenal seemed to be emptied from the middle of the dark roof, hurling downward pell-mell, waterspouts, hail, torrents, purple fire, phosphoric gleams, darkness, and lightnings.

Meanwhile Gilliatt seemed to pay no attention to the storm. His head was bent over his work. The second framework was rapidly nearing completion. To every clap of thunder he replied with a blow of his hammer, making a cadence which was audible even amidst that tumult. He was bareheaded, for a gust of wind had carried away his cap.

He suffered from a burning thirst. Little pools of rain had formed in the rocks around him. From time to time he took some water in the hollow of his hand and drank. Then, without even looking upward to observe the storm, he applied himself anew to his task.

Everything might depend upon a single moment. He knew the fate that awaited him if his breakwater was not completed in time. What was the use of wasting a moment in watching for the approach of death?

The turmoil around him was like that of a vast bubbling caldron. Crashing and uproar resounded everywhere. Sometimes the lightning seemed to descend a sort of ladder. The electric flame played incessantly on projections of the rock, where there were probably metallic veins. Hailstones of enormous size fell. Gilliatt was compelled to shake the folds of his overcoat, for even the pockets of it became filled with hail.

The storm had now rotated to the west, and was expending its fury upon the barricades of the two Douvres. But Gilliatt had faith in his breakwaters, and with reason. These barricades, made of a large portion of the fore-part of the Durande, stood the shock of the waves easily. Elasticity is a powerful resistant. The experiments of Stephenson establish the fact that a raft of timber, joined and chained together in a certain fashion, will form a more powerful obstacle against the waves, which are themselves elastic, than a breakwater of solid masonry. The barriers of the Douvres fulfilled these conditions. They were, moreover, so ingeniously hung that the action of the waves only fastened them more securely to the rocks. To demolish them it would have been necessary to overthrow the Douvres themselves. The surf, in fact, was only able to hurl a few flakes of foam on the sloop. On that side, thanks to the barricade, the tempest had to content itself with harmless insult. Gilliatt turned his back upon the scene. He heard it vent its futile rage upon the rocks behind him, with the utmost tranquillity of mind.

The angry ocean deluged the rocks, dashed over them, penetrated the net-work of internal fissures, and emerged again from the granitic masses through the narrow chinks, forming a kind of inexhaustible fountain playing peacefully in the midst of the deluge. Here and there a silvery water-fall fell gracefully from these openings into the sea.

The second frame for the eastern barrier was completed. A few more knots of rope and ends of chains and this new rampart would be ready to play its part in barring out the storm.

Suddenly there was a strange brightness; the rain ceased; the clouds rolled asunder; the wind had just shifted; a sort of high, dark window opened in the zenith, and the lightning died out. The end seemed to have come, but it was only the beginning.

The change of wind was from the north-west to the north-east.

The storm was preparing to burst forth again with a new legion of hurricanes. The north was about to mount to the assault. Sailors call this dreaded moment of transition the " return storm." The southern wind brings most rain, the north wind most lightning.

The attack, coming now from the east, was directed against the weak point of the position.

This time Gilliatt paused in his work and looked around him.

He stood erect, upon a projection of rock behind the second barrier, which was now nearly finished. If the first frame was carried away, it would necessarily demolish the second, which was not yet completed, and crush him. Gilliatt, in the place that he had chosen, must in that case be destroyed before seeing the sloop, the machinery, and all his work shattered and swallowed up in the gulf,— such was the possibility which awaited him. He accepted it unflinchingly.

8

In the event of the wreck of all his hopes, it would certainly be his desire to die at once,— to die first as he would have expressed it; for he had come to regard the machinery as a living being. He pushed aside his hair, which had been blown into his eyes by the wind, grasped his trusty mallet, drew himself up in a defiant attitude, and awaited the shock.

He was not kept long in suspense.

A flash of lightning gave the signal; the livid opening in the zenith closed; a fierce torrent of rain fell; then all became dark, save where the lightnings burst forth once more. The attack had recommenced in earnest.

A heavy swell, visible from time to time in the glare of the lightning, was rolling in the east beyond " The Man " rock. It resembled a huge wall of glass. It was green, without a fleck of foam, and stretched across the whole wide expanse. It was fast advancing towards the breakwater, increasing in volume as it approached. It was a strange sort of gigantic cylinder rolling along the ocean. The thunder kept up a continuous rumbling.

The huge wave struck " The Man " rock, broke in twain, and passed on. The broken wave, rejoined, formed a mountain of water, and instead of advancing in a parallel line as before, came down perpendicularly upon the breakwater. It was a wave assuming the form of a beam.

This battering-ram hurled itself upon the breakwater.

The shock was terrific: the whole wave became a roaring avalanche.

It was impossible for those who have not witnessed them to imagine these foaming avalanches which the sea precipitates, and under which it ingulfs for the moment rocks more than a hundred feet in height,— such, for example, as the Great Anderlo at Guernsey, and the Pinnacle at Jersey. At St. Mary of Madagascar it sometimes passes completely over Tintingue Point.

For several minutes the water covered everything. Nothing was visible except the furious sea,— one vast expanse of foam, white winding-sheet blowing in the draught of a

"He pushed aside his hair, which had been blown into his eyes,—
grasped his trusty mallet, drew himself up in a defiant atttiude, and awaited
the shock."

Toilers of the Sea.   Vol. II, Page 114.

sepulchre; nothing was heard but the roaring storm working devastation around.

When the foam subsided, Gilliatt was still standing at his post.

The barrier had stood firm. Not a chain was broken, not a nail displaced. It had exhibited under the ordeal the two best qualities of a breakwater; it had proved flexible as a wicker hurdle and firm as a wall. The surf falling upon it had dissolved into a shower of spray.

A river of foam rushing along the zig-zags of the defile subsided as it approached the sloop.

The man who had put this curb upon the fury of the ocean took no rest.

The storm fortunately vented its fury elsewhere for a moment. The fierce attack of the waves was renewed upon the wall of rock. There was a respite, and Gilliatt took advantage of it to complete the inner barrier.

The day went down upon his labours. The hurricane continued its assault upon the flank of the rocks with a mournful solemnity. The stores of fire and water in the sky poured forth incessantly without any apparent diminution. The undulations of the wind above and below were like the movements of a dragon.

Nightfall brought no deeper darkness. The change was hardly noticeable, for the darkness was never complete. Tempests, alternately darkening and illumining by their lightnings, are merely intervals of the visible and invisible. One moment all is pale glare, then all is darkness. Spectral shapes suddenly issue forth, and return as suddenly into the gloom.

A phosphoric zone, tinged with the hue of the aurora borealis, rose like ghastly flames from behind the dense clouds, giving everything a wan aspect, and making the rain-drifts luminous.

This uncertain light aided Gilliatt, and directed him in his operations. Once he even turned to the lightning and cried, " Give me a light!" By its glare he was able to raise the forward barrier. The breakwater was now almost com-

plete. As he was engaged in making a powerful cable fast
to the last beam, the wind struck him full in the face. This
fact caused him to raise his head. The wind had shifted
abruptly to the north-east. The assault upon the eastern
end of the gorge had begun again. Gilliatt cast his eyes
over the horizon. Another great wall of water was approaching.

The wave broke with a great shock; a second followed;
then another and still another; then five or six almost together;
then a last shock of tremendous force.

This last wave, which was an accumulation of many waves,
bore a singular resemblance to a living thing. It would not
have been difficult to imagine in the midst of that swelling
mass the shapes of fins and gills. It fell heavily and broke
upon the barriers. Its almost animal form was shattered in
the recoil. It looked as if some immense sea-monster were
being crushed to death upon that block of rocks and timbers.
The swell rushed through, subsiding but devastating as it
went. The huge wave seemed to bite and cling to its victim
as it died. The rock shook to its base. A savage howling
mingled with the roar; the foam flew high in the air like the
spouting of a leviathan.

The subsidence showed the extent of the surf's ravages.
This last assault had not been altogether ineffectual. The
breakwater had suffered considerably this time. A long and
heavy beam, torn from the first barrier, had been swept over
the second, and hurled violently upon the projecting rock on
which Gilliatt had been standing only a moment before.
Fortunately he had not returned there. Had he done so, his
death would have been inevitable.

There was a remarkable circumstances connected with the
fall of this beam, which by preventing the timber from re-
bounding, saved Gilliatt from even greater dangers. It even
proved useful to him, as will be seen, in another way.

Between the projecting rock and the inner wall of the
gorge there was an opening something like the notch made
by an axe, or wedge. One of the ends of the timber hurled

into the air by the waves had stuck fast in this notch in falling. The gap had become enlarged.

Gilliatt was struck with an idea. It was that of bearing heavily on the other extremity.

The beam caught by one end in the nook, which it had widened, projected from it as straight as an outstretched arm. This arm was parallel with the anterior wall of the defile, and the disengaged end extended about eighteen or twenty inches beyond the point of support.

Gilliatt raised himself by means of his hands, feet, and knees to the escarpment, and then turning his back upon it pressed both his shoulders against the enormous lever. The beam was long, which increased its power. The rock was already loosened; but he was compelled to renew his efforts again and again. Great drops of sweat streamed from his forehead. The fourth attempt exhausted all his strength. There was a cracking noise; the gap spreading in the shape of a fissure, opened its vast jaws, and the heavy mass fell into the narrow space below with a sound like the reverberation of the distant thunder.

The mass fell straight, and without breaking, resting in its bed like a menhir precipitated intact.

The beam which had served as a lever went down with the rock, and Gilliatt, staggering forward as it gave way, narrowly escaped falling.

The bed of the pass at this part was full of huge round stones, and there was very little water. The monolith lying in the boiling foam, the flakes of which reached Gilliatt where he stood, stretched from side to side of the great parallel rocks of the defile, and formed a transversal wall, a sort of bridge between the two escarpments. Its two ends touched the rocks. It had been a little too long to lie flat, but its summit of soft rock was shattered by the fall. The result of this fall was a singular sort of *cul-de-sac*, which may still be seen. The water behind this stony barrier is almost always tranquil.

This was an even more invincible rampart than the forward timbers of the Durande fastened between the two Douvres.

The addition of this new barrier proved most opportune.

The assaults of the sea continued. The obstinacy of the waves is always increased by an obstacle. The first frame began to show signs of breaking up. One breach, however small, in a breakwater, is always serious. It inevitably enlarges; and there is no way of repairing it, for the sea would sweep away the workmen.

A flash which lighted up the rocks revealed to Gilliatt the nature of the mischief,— the beams broken down, the ends of rope and fragments of chain swinging in the winds, and a rent in the centre of the apparatus. The second frame was intact.

Though the block of stone overturned by Gilliatt in the gorge behind the breakwater was the strongest possible barrier, it had one defect. It was too low. The surge could not destroy, but might sweep over it.

It was useless to think of building it higher. Nothing but masses of rock would be of any service upon a stone barrier; but how could such masses be detached; or, if detached, how could they be moved, or raised, or piled, or fixed? Timbers may be added, but rocks cannot.

Gilliatt was not Enceladus.

The extremely limited height of this rocky isthmus rendered him anxious.

The effects of this fault were not long in showing themselves. The assaults upon the breakwater were incessant; the heavy seas seemed not merely to rage, but to attack with a firm determination to destroy it. A sort of trampling noise was heard upon the jolted frame-work.

Suddenly the end of a binding strake, detached from the dislocated frame, was swept over the second barrier and across the transversal rock, falling in the gorge, where the water seized and carried it into the sinuosities of the pass. Gilliatt lost sight of it. It seemed probable that it would do some injury to the sloop. Fortunately the water in the passage, being shut in on all sides, was very little affected by the commotion without. The waves there were comparatively small, and the shock was not likely to be very severe. Besides, he had very little time to spare for reflection upon this mishap. Every variety of danger was threatening him at once; the tempest was concentrated upon the most vulnerable point; destruction was imminent.

The darkness was profound for a moment: the lightning ceased,— a bit of sinister connivance. The cloud and the sea became one; there was a dull peal of thunder.

This was followed by a terrible outburst.

The frame which formed the front of the barriers was swept away. The fragments of beams were visible in the rolling waters. The sea was using the first breakwater as an engine for making a breach in the second.

Gilliatt experienced the feeling of a general who sees his advance guard driven in.

The second construction of beams resisted the shock. The apparatus was powerfully secured and buttressed. But the broken frame was heavy, and was completely at the mercy of the waves, which were incessantly hurling it forward and withdrawing it. The ropes and chains which remained unsevered prevented it from breaking up entirely, and the substantial qualities with which Gilliatt had endowed it made it all the more effective as a weapon of destruction. Instead of a buckler, it had become a mace. Besides this, it was now full of irregularities, bits of timbers projected on every side; and it was, as it were, covered with teeth and spikes. No sort of weapon could have been more effective, or better fitted for the handling of the tempest.

It was the projectile, while the sea played the part of the catapult.

The blows succeeded each other with dismal regularity. Gilliatt, standing thoughtful and anxious behind that barricaded portal, listened to death knocking loudly for admittance.

He reflected with bitterness that, but for the fatal entanglement of the funnel of the Durande in the wreck, he would have been at that very moment safe in port in Guernsey, with the sloop out of danger and the machinery saved.

The dreaded moment arrived. The destruction was complete. There was a sound like a death-rattle. The entire frame of the breakwater, both barriers, crushed and mingled inextricably, came rushing like chaos upon a mountain upon the stone barricade, where it stopped. Here the fragments lay together,— a mass of beams penetrable by the waves, but still breaking their force. The conquered barrier struggled nobly against destruction. The waves had shattered it, and in their turn were shattered against it. Though overthrown, it still remained tolerably effective. The rock which barred its passage, an immovable obstacle, held it fast. The passage, as we have said before, was very narrow at the point where the victorious whirlwind had driven and piled up the shattered breakwater. The very violence of the assault, by heaping up the mass and driving the broken ends one within the other, had helped to make the pile firm. It was destroyed, but immovable. Only a few pieces of timber had been swept away and dispersed by the waves. One passed through the air very near to Gilliatt. He felt the counter current upon his forehead.

Some of the immense waves which rise in great tempests with imperturbable regularity, swept over the ruins of the breakwater. They rushed into the gorge, and in spite of the many angles in the passage, set the waters in commotion. The waves began to roll ominously through the gorge.

Was there any means of preventing this agitation from extending as far as the sloop? It would not require long for the blasts of wind to create a tempest through all the windings of the pass. A few heavy seas would be sufficient to stave in the sloop and scatter her burden.

Gilliatt shuddered at the thought.

But he was not disconcerted. No peril could daunt his soul.

The hurricane had now discovered the best plan of attack, and was rushing fiercely between the two walls of the strait.

Suddenly a crash was heard, resounding and prolonging itself through the defile some distance behind him,— a crash more terrible than any he had yet heard.

It came from the direction of the sloop.

Something disastrous was happening there.

Gilliatt hastened towards it.

He could not see the sloop from where he was standing on account of the sharp turns in the pass.   At the last turn he stopped and waited for the lightning.

The first flash revealed the state of affairs.

The rush of the sea through the eastern entrance had encountered a blast of wind from the other end.   A disaster was imminent.

The sloop had received no apparent damage; anchored as she was, the storm had little power over her, but the remains of the Durande were in jeopardy.

The wreck presented considerable surface to the storm, while the breach which Gilliatt had made, and through which the machinery had been removed, rendered the hull still weaker.   The keelson was cut the vertebral column of the skeleton was broken.

The hurricane came down upon it.

This was all that was needed to complete its destruction. The planking of the deck bent like an open book.   The dismemberment had begun.   It was this noise which had reached Gilliatt's ears in the midst of the tempest.

The disaster which presented itself as he approached seemed almost irremediable.

The square opening which he had cut in the keel had become a gaping wound.   The wind had converted the smooth-cut hole into a ragged fracture.   This transverse breach separated the wreck in two parts.   The after-part nearest to the sloop, remained firmly wedged in its bed of rocks.   The forward portion, which faced him, was hanging. A fracture, while it holds, is a sort of hinge. The whole mass oscillated with a doleful sound, as the wind moved it. Fortunately the sloop was no longer under it.

But this swinging movement shook the other portion of the hull, still wedged and immovable as it was between the two Douvres. From shaking to loosening completely is but a step. Under the fierce assaults of the gale, the dislocated part might suddenly carry away the other portion, which almost touched the sloop. In that case, the whole wreck, together with the sloop and the engine, would be swept into the sea and swallowed up.

This catastrophe seemed almost inevitable.

Could it be prevented, and how?

Gilliatt was one of those who are accustomed to snatch the means of safety out of danger itself. He set his wits to work for a moment.

Then he hastened to his arsenal and brought his axe.

The mallet had served him well. It was now the axe's turn.

He climbed upon the wreck, got a footing on that part of the flooring which had not given way, and leaning over the gorge between the Douvres, he began to cut away the broken joists and planking which supported the hanging portion of the hull.

His object was to effect the separation of the two parts of the wreck, to disencumber the half which remained firm, to throw overboard what the waves had seized, and thus divide the prey with the storm. The hanging portion of the wreck, borne down by the wind and by its own weight, adhered at only one or two points. The entire wreck resembled a folding-screen, one leaf of which, half hanging, beat against the other. Only five or six pieces of flooring, bent and cracked, but not broken, still held. Their fractures creaked and enlarged at every gust, and the axe, so to speak, had merely to assist the gale in its work. This more than half-severed condition, while it increased the facility of

the work, also rendered it much more dangerous. The whole
might give way under him at any moment.

The tempest had reached its height. The convulsions
of the sea extended to the heavens. Hitherto the storm had
been supreme; it had seemed to work its own imperious will,
to give the impulse, to drive the waves to frenzy, while still
preserving a sort of grim composure. Below was fury;
above, anger. The heavens are the breath, the ocean only
the foam, hence the supremacy of the wind. But the intoxication of its own power had confused it. It had become
a mere whirlwind; it was a blindness bordering on madness.
There are times when tempests become frenzied, when the
heavens are seized with a sort of delirium, when the firmament
raves and hurls its lightnings blindly. Nothing could be
more appalling. It is a frightful moment. The trembling
of the rock was at its height. Every storm has its mysterious course; but at such times it loses its way. It is the most
dangerous moment of the tempest. " At such times," says
Thomas Fuller, " the wind becomes a furious maniac." It
is at this period that that continuous discharge of electricity
takes place which Piddington calls " the cascade of lightning."
It is at this time, too, that in the blackest spot in the clouds,
no one knows why, unless it be to observe the universal terror,
a circle of blue light appears, which the Spanish sailors of
ancient times called the eye of the tempest,—" el ojo de la
tempestad." That terrible eye now looked down on Gilliatt.

Gilliatt was surveying the heavens in his turn. He raised
his head defiantly now. After every stroke of his axe he
stood erect and gazed upwards, almost haughtily. He was,
or seemed to be, too near destruction not to feel self-sustained.
Would he yield to despair? No! In the presence of the
wildest fury of ocean he was watchful as well as bold. He
planted his feet only where the wreck was firm. He ventured his life, and yet was careful; for his determination, too,
had reached its highest point. His strength had grown ten-
fold greater. He had become excited by his own intrepidity.
The strokes of his axe were like blows of defiance. He seemed

to have gained in directness what the tempest had lost. A
pathetic struggle! On the one hand an indefatigable will;
on the other, inexhaustible power. It was a contest with the
elements for the prize at his feet. The clouds took the shape
of Gorgon masks in the immensity of the heavens; every possible form of terror appeared; the rain came from the sea,
the surf from the cloud; phantoms of the wind bent down;
meteoric faces revealed themselves and were again eclipsed,
leaving the darkness still more intense; then nothing was visible but the torrents raging on all sides,— a boiling sea;
cumuli heavy with hail, ashen-hued, ragged-edged, seemed
seized with a sort of whirling frenzy; strange rattlings filled
the air; the inverse currents of electricity observed by Volta
darted their sudden flashes from cloud to cloud. The prolongation of the lightning was terrible; the flashes passed
close to Gilliatt. The very ocean seemed appalled. Gilliatt
moved to and fro on the tottering wreck, though the deck
trembled under his feet, striking, cutting, hacking with the
axe in his hand, his features pallid in the gleam of the lightning, his long hair streaming, his feet naked, his face covered with the foam of the sea, but still grand amid the wild
tumult of the storm.

Against the fury of the elements man has no weapon but
his own powers of invention. Gilliatt owed his eventual triumph to his ingenuity. His object was to make all the dislocated portions of the wreck fall together. For this reason
he cut away the broken portions without entirely separating
them, leaving some parts on which they still swung. Suddenly he stopped, holding his axe in the air. The operation was complete. The entire dislocated portion fell with a
crash.

The mass rolled down between the two Douvres, just below
Gilliatt, who stood upon the wreck, leaning over and watching the fall. It fell perpendicularly into the water, struck
the rocks, and stopped in the defile before it touched the bottom. Enough remained out of the water to project more
than twelve feet above the waves. The vertical mass

formed a wall between the two Douvres. Like the rock overturned crosswise higher up the defile, it allowed only a slight stream of foam to pass through at its two extremities, and thus a fifth barricade against the tempest was improvised by Gilliatt.

The hurricane itself, in its blind fury, had assisted in the construction of this last barrier.

It was fortunate that the close proximity of the two walls had prevented the mass of wreck from falling to the bottom. This circumstance gave the barricade greater height; the water, besides, could flow under the obstacle, which diminished the power of the waves. That which passes below does not leap over. This is in part the secret of the floating breakwater.

Henceforth, let the storm rage as it would, there was nothing to fear for the sloop or the machinery. The water around them could not become much agitated again. Between the barrier of the Douvres, which covered them on the west, and the barricade which protected them from the east, no heavy sea or wind could reach them.

Gilliatt had wrested success out of the very catastrophe itself. The storm had been his co-labourer in the work.

This done, he took a little water in the palm of his hand from one of the rain-pools, and drank; and then, looking upward at the storm, said with a smile, " Bungler! "

Human intelligence combating with brute force experiences an ironical joy in demonstrating the stupidity of its antagonist, and in compelling it to aid the very victims of its fury, and Gilliatt felt something of that memorable desire to insult his invisible enemy which is as old as the heroes of the Iliad.

He descended to the sloop and examined it by the glare of the lightning. The relief which he had been able to afford his distressed bark was well-timed. She had been much shaken during the last hour, and had begun to give way. A hasty glance revealed no serious injury. Nevertheless, he was certain that the vessel had been subjected to a violent strain. As soon as the waves subsided, the hull had righted itself; the anchors had held fast; as for the machinery, the four chains had supported it admirably.

While Gilliatt was completing this survey, something white passed before his eyes and vanished in the gloom. It was a sea-mew.

No sight is more welcome in tempestuous weather. When the birds reappear, the storm is departing.

The thunder re-doubled,— another good sign.

The violent efforts of the storm had broken its force. All mariners knew that the last ordeal is severe, but short. A marked increase of violence in a thunder-storm is a forerunner of the end.

The rain stopped suddenly. Then there was only a surly rumbling in the heavens. The storm ceased with the suddenness of a plank falling to the ground. The immense mass of clouds became disorganized.

A strip of clear sky appeared between them. Gilliatt was astonished; it was broad daylight.

The tempest had lasted nearly twenty hours.

The wind which had brought the storm carried it away; the broken clouds were soon flying in confusion across the sky. From one end of the line to the other, there was a retreating movement; a dull muttering was heard. This gradually became fainter and fainter; a few last drops of rain fell, then all those dark masses of cloud charged with thunder departed like a multitude of chariots.

Suddenly the wide expanse of sky became blue.

Then, for the first time, Gilliatt discovered that he was terribly weary. Sleep swoops down upon the exhausted frame like a bird upon its prey. Sinking down on the deck of the sloop, he fell into a heavy slumber.

Stretched out at full length, he remained there perfectly motionless for several hours, scarcely distinguishable from the joists and beams among which he lay.

BOOK IV

PIT-FALLS IN THE WAY

CHAPTER I

HE WHO IS HUNGRY IS NOT ALONE

WHEN he awoke he was very hungry.

The sea was growing calmer. But there was still a heavy swell, which made his departure impossible,— at least, for the present. The day, too, was far advanced. For the sloop with its burden to reach Guernsey before midnight, it would be necessary to start in the morning.

Although sorely pressed by hunger, Gilliatt began by stripping himself,— the only means of getting warm. His clothes were saturated, but the rain had washed out the sea-water, which made it possible to dry them.

He kept on nothing but his trousers, which he rolled up nearly to his knees.

His overcoat, jacket, overalls, and sheepskin he spread out and fastened down with large round stones here and there.

Then he thought of eating.

He had recourse to his knife, which he was careful to keep always in a good condition, and detached from the rocks a few limpets, similar in kind to the *clonisses* of the Mediterranean. It is a well-known fact that these can be eaten raw: but after such arduous and prolonged toil, the ration was but a meagre one. His biscuit was gone; but he now had an abundance of water.

He took advantage of the receding tide to wander over the rocks in search of crayfish. There was enough rock exposed now for him to feel tolerably sure of success.

But he had forgotten that he could do nothing with these without fire to cook them. If he had taken the trouble to go to his storehouse, he would have found it inundated. His wood and coal were drenched, and of his store of tow, which served him for tinder, there was not a fibre which was not saturated. No means of lighting a fire remained.

His blower, too, was completely ruined. The screen of the hearth of his forge was broken down; the storm had sacked and devastated his workshop. With the tools and apparatus which had escaped the general wreck, he might still have done a little carpentry work; but he could not have accomplished any of the labours of the smith. Gilliatt, however, never thought of his workshop for a moment.

Drawn in another direction by the pangs of hunger, he pursued his search for food without much reflection. He wandered, not in the gorge, but outside among the smaller rocks where the Durande, ten weeks before, had first struck upon the sunken reef.

For the search that Gilliatt was prosecuting, this part was more favourable than the interior. At low water the crabs are accustomed to crawl out into the air. They seem to like to warm themselves in the sun, where they swarm sometimes to the disgust of loiterers, who see in these creatures, with their awkward sidelong gait, climbing clumsily from crack to crack upon the rocks, a species of sea vermin.

For two months Gilliatt had lived almost entirely upon these creatures.

This time, however, the crayfish and crabs were both wanting. The tempest had driven them into their solitary retreats, and they had not yet mustered up courage to venture abroad.

Gilliatt held his open knife in his hand, and from time to time scraped a cockle from under the bunches of seaweed, which he ate as he walked on.

He could not have been far from the very spot where Sieur Clubin had perished.

As Gilliatt was trying to make up his mind to be content with the sea-urchins and the *châtaignes de mer,* a little clattering noise at his feet aroused his attention. A large crab, startled by his approach, had just dropped into a pool. The water was shallow, and he did not lose sight of it.

He chased the crab along the base of the rock; but the crab moved fast, and at last it suddenly disappeared.

It had buried itself in some crevice under the rock.

Gilliatt clutched the projections of the rock, and leaned over to look where it shelved away under the water.

As he suspected, there was an opening in which the creature had evidently taken refuge. It was more than a crevice; it was a kind of porch.

The water beneath it was not deep, and the bottom, covered with large pebbles, was plainly visible. The stones were green and clothed with *confervæ,* indicating that they were never dry. They looked like the tops of a number of infants' heads, covered with a kind of green hair.

Holding his knife between his teeth, Gilliatt descended, by the aid of his feet and hands, from the upper part of the escarpment, and leaped into the water. It reached almost to his shoulders.

He made his way through the porch, and found himself in a blind passage, with a roof shaped like a rude arch over his head. The walls were polished and slippery. The crab was nowhere visible.

As Gilliatt advanced the light grew fainter, so that he began to lose the power to distinguish objects.

When he had gone about fifteen yards the vaulted roof overhead ended. He had penetrated beyond the low passage. There was more space here, and consequently more daylight. The pupils of his eyes, moreover, had dilated, and he could see pretty clearly. The discovery he made amazed him.

He had found his way again into the singular cavern which he had visited the month before.

9

The only difference was that he had entered by way of the sea.

It was through the submarine arch, that he had remarked before, that he had just entered. At certain low tides it was accessible.

His eyes became more accustomed to the place. His vision became clearer and clearer. He was astonished. He found himself again in that extraordinary palace of shadows; saw again before his eyes the vaulted roof, those fantastic columns, those purple, blood-like stains, the vegetation rich with gems, and at the farther end, the crypt or sanctuary, and that huge stone which so resembled an altar.

He took little notice of these details, but they were so strongly impressed upon his mind that he saw that the place was unchanged.

He observed before him, at a considerable height in the wall, the crevice through which he had penetrated the first time, and which, from the point where he now stood, seemed inaccessible.

Nearer the moulded arch, he noticed those low, dark grottoes, those caves within caves, which he had already observed from a distance. He was now much nearer to them. The entrance to the nearest was out of the water, and easily approached.

Nearer still than this recess he noticed, above the level of the water, and within reach of his hand, a horizontal fissure.

It seemed to him probable that the crab had taken refuge there, and he plunged his hand in as far as he was able, and grouped in that dusky aperture.

Suddenly he felt himself seized by the arm. A strange, indescribable horror thrilled him.

Some living thing, thin, rough, flat, cold, and slimy had twisted itself round his naked arm, in the dark depth below. It crept upward towards his chest. Its pressure was like a tightening cord, its steady persistence like that of a screw. In another instant the same mysterious spiral form had wound

around his wrist and elbow, and had reached his shoulder.   A
sharp point penetrated beneath the armpit.

Gilliatt recoiled, but he had scarcely power to move! He
was, as it were, nailed to the place.   With his left hand, which
was disengaged, he seized his knife, which he still held between his teeth, and with that hand gripping the knife, he
supported himself against the rocks, while he made a desperate effort to withdraw his arm; but he only succeeded in disturbing his persecutor, which wound itself still tighter.   It
was supple as leather, strong as steel, cold as night.

A second form, sharp, elongated, and narrow issued from
the crevice like a tongue out of monstrous jaws.

It seemed to lick his naked body; then suddenly stretching
out, it became longer and thinner, as it crept over his skin,
and wound itself around him.   At the same time a terrible
sensation of pain, utterly unlike any he had ever known, made
all his muscles contract.   It seemed as if innumerable suckers had fastened themselves in his flesh and were about to
drink his blood.

A third long undulating shape issued from the hole in the
rock, seemed to feel its way around his body to lash itself
around his ribs like a cord, and fix itself there.

Intense agony is dumb.   Gilliatt uttered no cry.   There
was sufficient light for him to see the repulsive forms which
had wound themselves about him.

A fourth ligature,— but this one swift as an arrow,—
darted towards his stomach, and wound around him there.

It was impossible to sever or tear away the slimy bands
which were twisted tightly around his body, and which were
adhering to it at a number of points.   Each of these points
was the focus of frightful and singular pangs.   It seemed
as if innumerable small mouths were devouring him at the
same time.

A fifth long, slimy, ribbon-shaped strip issued from the
hole.   It passed over the others, and wound itself tightly
around his chest.   The compression increased his sufferings.
He could scarcely breathe.

These living thongs were pointed at their extremities, but broadened like the blade of a sword towards its hilt.   All five evidently belonged to the same centre.   They crept and glided about him; he felt the strange points of pressure, which seemed to him like so many mouths, change their position from time to time.

Suddenly a large, round, flattened, glutinous mass issued from beneath the crevice.   It was the centre; the five thongs were attached to it like spokes to the hub of a wheel.   On the opposite side of this disgusting monster appeared the beginning of three other similar tentacles, the ends of which remained under the rock.   In the middle of this slimy mass were two eyes.

These eyes were fixed on Gilliatt.

He recognized the Devil Fish.

CHAPTER II

THE MONSTER

IT is difficult for those who have not seen it to believe in the existence of the devil-fish.

Compared with this creature, the ancient hydras are insignificant.

At times we are tempted to imagine that the shadowy forms which haunt our dreams may encounter in the realm of the Possible attractive forces which have the power to create living beings out of these visions of our slumbers.   The Unknown is cognizant of these strange visions, and concocts monsters out of them.

Orpheus, Homer, and Hesiod created only fabulous monsters.   Providence created the devil-fish.

When God chooses, he excels in creating what is execrable.   The wherefore of this perplexes and affrights the devout thinker.

If terror were the object of its creation, nothing more perfect than the devil-fish could be imagined.

The whale is enormous in bulk, the devil-fish is comparatively small; the jararaca makes a hissing noise, the devil-fish is mute; the rhinoceros has a horn, the devil-fish has none; the scorpion has a dart, the devil-fish has no dart; the shark has sharp fins, the devil-fish has no fins; the vespertilio-bat has wings with claws, the devil-fish has no wings; the porcupine has his spines, the devil-fish has no spines; the swordfish has his sword, the devil-fish has none; the torpedo has its electric spark, the devil-fish has none; the toad has its poison, the devil-fish has none; the viper has its venom, the devil-fish has no venom; the lion has its claws, the devil-fish has no claws; the griffon has its beak, the devil-fish has no beak; the crocodile has its jaws, the devil-fish has no jaws.

The devil-fish has no muscular organization, no menacing cry, no breastplate, no horn, no dart, no claw, no tail with which to hold or bruise; no cutting fins, or wings with nails, no prickles, no sword, no electric discharge, no poison, no claws, no beak, no jaws. Yet he is of all creatures the most formidably armed.

What, then, is the devil-fish? It is a huge cupping-glass.

The swimmer who, attracted by the beauty of the spot, ventures among reefs far out at sea, where still waters hide the wonders of the deep, or in the hollows of unfrequented rocks, or in unknown caverns abounding in marine plants, testacea, and crustacea, under the deep portals of the ocean, runs the risk of meeting it. If that fate should be yours, be not curious, but fly. The intruder enters there dazzled, but quits the spot in terror.

This frightful monster which is so often encountered amid the rocks in the open sea, is of a greyish colour, about five feet long, and about the thickness of a man's arm. It is ragged in outline, and in shape strongly resembles a closed umbrella, without a handle. This irregular mass advances slowly towards you. Suddenly it opens, and eight radii issue abruptly from around a face with two eyes. These radii are alive; their undulation is like lambent flames; they resemble, when opened, the spokes of a wheel measuring four or five feet in diameter.

This monster winds itself around its victim, covering and entangling him in its long folds. Underneath it is yellow; above, it is of a dull greyish hue. It is spider-like in form, but its tints are those of the chameleon. When irritated it becomes violent. Its most horrible characteristic is its softness.

Its folds strangle; its contact paralyzes.

It has the aspect of gangrened or scabrous flesh. It is a monstrous embodiment of disease.

It clings closely to its prey, and cannot be torn away,— a fact which is due to its power of exhausting air. The eight antennæ, large at their roots, diminish gradually, and end in needle-like points. Underneath each of these feelers are two rows of suckers, decreasing in size, the largest ones near the head, the smallest at the extremities. Each row contains twenty-five of these. There are, therefore, fifty suckers to each feeler, and the creature possesses four hundred in all. These suckers act like cupping-glasses.

They are cartilaginous substances, cylindrical, horny, and livid. Upon the large species they diminish gradually from the diameter of a five-franc piece to the size of a split pea. These small tubes can be thrust out and withdrawn by the animal at will. They are capable of piercing to a depth of more than an inch.

This sucking apparatus has all the regularity and delicacy of a key-board. It projects one moment and disappears the next. The most perfect sensitiveness cannot equal the contractibility of these suckers; always proportioned to the internal movement of the animal, and its exterior circumstances. The monster is endowed with the qualities of the sensitive plant.

This animal is the same as those which mariners call poulps; which science designates cephalopods, and which ancient legends call krakens. It is the English sailors who call them " devil-fish," and sometimes bloodsuckers. In the Channel Islands they are called *pieuvres*.

They are rare in Guernsey, and very small in Jersey; but near the island of Sark they are numerous as well as very large.

An engraving in Sonnini's edition of Buffon represents a cephalopod crushing a frigate. Denis Montfort, in fact, considers the polypus, or octopod, of high latitudes, strong enough to destroy a ship. Bory Saint Vincent doubts this; but he shows that in our latitude they will attack men. Near Brecq-Hou, in Sark, they show a cave where a devil-fish seized and drowned a lobster-man a few years ago. Péron and Lamarck are mistaken in their belief that the polypus having no fins cannot swim. The writer of these lines once saw with his own eyes a *pieuvre* pursuing a bather among the rocks called the Boutiques, in Sark. When captured and killed, this specimen was found to be four English feet broad, and it possessed four hundred suckers. The monster thrust them out convulsively in the agony of death.

According to Denis Montfort, one of those observers whose marvellous intuition degrades or elevates them to the level of magicians, the polypus is almost endowed with the passions of man: it has its hatreds. In fact, in the animal world to be hideous is to hate.

Hideousness has to contend against the natural law of elimination, which necessarily renders it hostile.

While swimming, the devil-fish remains, so to speak, in its sheath. It swims with all its parts drawn close together. It might be likened to a sleeve sewed up with a closed fist within. This protuberance, which is the head, pushes the water aside and advances with an undulatory movement. The two eyes, though large, are indistinct, being the colour of the water.

When it is lying in ambush, or seeking its prey, it retires into itself as it were, becomes smaller and condenses itself. It is then scarcely distinguishable in the dim, submarine light. It looks like a mere ripple in the water. It resembles anything except a living creature.

The devil-fish is crafty. When one is least expecting it, it suddenly opens.

A glutinous mass, endowed with a malevolent will, what could be more horrible.

It is in the most beautiful azure depths of limpid water that this hideous, voracious sea-monster delights.

It always conceals itself,— a fact which increases its terrible associations. When they are seen, it is almost invariably after they have captured their victim.

At night, however, and particularly in the breeding season, it becomes phosphorescent. These horrible creatures have their passions, their submarine nuptials. Then it adorns itself, glows, and illumines; and from some rock it can sometimes be discerned in the deep obscurity of the waves below, expanding with a pale irradiation,— a spectral sun.

The devil-fish not only swims, but crawls. It is part fish, part reptile. It crawls upon the bed of the sea. At such times, it makes use of its eight feelers, and creeps along after the fashion of a swiftly moving caterpillar.

It has no blood, no bones, no flesh. It is soft and flabby; a skin with nothing inside. Its eight tentacles may be turned inside out like the fingers of a glove.

It has a single orifice in the centre of its radii, which appears at first to be neither the vent nor the mouth. It is in fact both. The orifice performs a double function.

The entire creature is cold.

The jelly-fish of the Mediterranean is repulsive. Contact with that animated gelatinous substance, in which the hands sink, and at which the nails tear ineffectually; which can be rent in twain without killing it, and which can be plucked off without entirely removing it, that soft and yet tenacious creature which slips through the fingers,— is disgusting; but no horror can equal the sudden apparition of the devil-fish, that Medusa with its eight serpents.

No grasp is like the sudden strain of the cephalopod.

It is with the sucking apparatus that it attacks. The victim is oppressed by a vacuum drawing at numberless points; it is not a clawing or a biting, but an indescribable scarification. A tearing of the flesh is terrible, but less terrible than a sucking of the blood. Claws are harmless in comparison with the terrible action of these natural cupping-glasses. The claws of the wild beast enter your flesh; but with the cephalopod, it is you who enter the creature that attacks you.

The muscles swell, the fibres of the body are contorted, the skin cracks under the loathsome oppression, the blood spurts out and mingles horribly with the lymph of the monster, which clings to its victim by innumerable hideous mouths. The hydra incorporates itself with the man; the man becomes one with the hydra. The spectre lies upon you; the tiger can only devour you; the horrible devil-fish sucks your life-blood away. He draws you to and into himself; while bound down, glued fast, powerless, you feel yourself gradually emptied into this horrible pouch, which is the monster itself.

To be eaten alive is terrible; to be absorbed alive is horrible beyond expression.

Science, in accordance with its usual excessive caution, even in the face of facts at first rejects these strange animals as fabulous; then she decides to observe them; then she dissects, classifies, catalogues, and labels them; then procures specimens, and exhibits them in glass cases in museums. They enter then into her nomenclature; are designated mollusks, invertebrata, radiata: she determines their position in the animal world a little above the calamaries, a little below the cuttle-fish; she finds an analogous creature for these hydras of the sea in fresh water called the argyronectes: she divides them into large, medium, and small kinds; she more readily admits the existence of the small than of the large species, which is, however, the tendency of science in all countries, for she is rather microscopic than telescopic by nature. Classifying them according to their formation, she calls them cephalopods; then counts their antennæ, and calls then octopods. This done, she leaves them. Where science drops them, philosophy takes them up.

Philosophy, in her turn, studies these creatures. She goes farther and yet not so far. She does not dissect, she meditates. Where the scalpel has laboured, she plunges the hypothesis. She seeks the final cause. Eternal perplexity of the thinker. These creatures disturb his ideas of the Creator. They are hideous surprises. They are the death's-head at the feast of contemplation. The philosopher determines their characteristics in dread. They are the concrete forms of evil. What attitude can he assume in regard to this treachery of creation against herself? To whom can he look for the solution of this enigma?

The Possible is a terrible matrix. Monsters are mysteries in a concrete form. Portions of shade issue from the mass, and something within detaches itself, rolls, floats, condenses, borrows elements from the ambient darkness; becomes subject to unknown polarizations, assumes a kind of life, furnishes itself with some unimagined form from the obscurity, and with some terrible spirit from the miasma, and wanders ghost-like among living things. It is as if night itself assumed the forms of animals. But for what good? with what object? Thus we come again to the eternal question.

These animals are as much phantoms as monsters. Their existence is proved and yet improbable. It is their fate to exist in spite of *a priori* reasonings. They are the amphibia of the shore which separates life from death. Their unreality makes their existence puzzling. They touch the frontier of man's domain and people the region of chimeras.

We deny the possibility of the vampire, and the devil-fish appears to disconcert us. Their swarming is a certainty which disconcerts our confidence. Optimism, which is nevertheless in the right, becomes silenced in their presence. They form the visible extremity of the dark circles. They mark the transition of our reality into another. They seem to belong to that commencement of terrible life, which the dreamer sees confusedly through the loop-hole of the night.

This multiplication of monsters, first in the Invisible, then in the Possible, has been suspected, perhaps perceived by magi and philosophers in their austere ecstasies and profound contemplations. Hence the conjecture of the material hell. The demon is simply the invisible tiger. The wild beast which devours souls has been presented to the eyes of human beings by Saint John, and by Dante in his vision of hell.

If, in truth, the invisible circles of creation continue indefinitely, if after one there is yet another, and so on and on in illimitable progression; if that chain, which we for our part are resolved to doubt, really exists, the devil-fish at one end proves Satan at the other.

It is certain that the wrong-doer at one end proves wrong-doing at the other.

Every malignant creature, like every perverted intelligence, is a sphinx.

A terrible sphinx propounding a terrible riddle,— the riddle of the existence of Evil.

It is this perfection of evil which has sometimes sufficed to incline powerful intellects to a belief in the duality of the Deity, towards that terrible bifrons of the Manichæans.

A piece of silk stolen during the last war from the palace of the Emperor of China represents a shark eating a crocodile, who is eating a serpent, who is devouring an eagle, who is preying on a swallow, who in his turn is eating a caterpillar.

All Nature, which is under our observation, is thus alternately devouring and devoured. The prey prey upon each other.

Learned men, however, who are also philosophers, and therefore optimists in their view of creation, find or think they find, an explanation. Among others, Bonnet of Geneva, that mysterious, exact thinker, who was opposed to Buffon, as in later times Geoffroy St. Hillaire has been to Cuvier, was struck with the idea of the final object. His notions may be summed up thus: universal death necessitates universal sepulture; the devourers are the sextons of the system of Nature.

Every created thing eventually enters into and forms a part of some other created thing. To decay is to nourish. Such is the terrible law from which not even man is exempt.

In our world of twilight this fatal order of things produces monsters. You ask for what purpose. We find the solution here.

But *is* this the solution? Is this the answer to our questionings? And if so, why not some different order of things? Thus the question returns.

We live: so be it. But let us try to believe that death means progress. Let us aspire to an existence in which these mysteries shall be made clear.

Let us obey the conscience which guides us thither.

For let us never forget that the best is only attained through the better.

CHAPTER III

ANOTHER KIND OF SEA-COMBAT

SUCH was the creature in whose power Gilliatt had fallen.

The monster was the mysterious inmate of the grotto; the terrible genius of the place; a kind of marine demon.

The splendours of the cavern existed for it alone.

The shadowy creature, dimly discerned by Gilliatt beneath the rippling surface of the dark water on the occasion of his first visit, was the monster. This grotto was its home. When he entered the cave a second time in pursuit of the crab, and saw a crevice in which he supposed the crab had taken refuge, the *pieuvre* was there lying in wait for prey.

No bird would brood, no egg would burst to life, no flower would dare to open, no breast to give milk, no heart to love, no spirit to soar, under the influence of that impersonation of evil watching with sinister patience in the dim light.

Gilliatt had thrust his arm deep into the opening; the monster had snapped at it.

It held him fast, as the spider holds the fly.

He was in the water up to his belt; his naked feet clutching the slippery roundness of the huge stones at the bottom; his right arm bound and rendered powerless by the flat coils of the long tentacles of the creature, and his body almost hidden under the folds and cross folds of this horrible bandage.

Of the eight arms of the devil-fish, three adhered to the rock, while five encircled Gilliatt. In this way, clinging to the granite on one side, and to its human prey on the other, it chained him to the rock. Two hundred and fifty suckers were upon him, tormenting him with agony and loathing. He was grasped by gigantic hands, each finger of which was nearly a yard long, and furnished inside with living blisters eating into the flesh.

As we have said, it is impossible to tear one's self from the clutches of the devil-fish. The attempt only results in a firmer grasp. The monster clings with more determined force. Its efforts increase with those of his victim; every struggle produces a tightening of its ligatures.

Gilliatt had but one resource,— his knife.

His left hand only was free; but the reader knows with what power he could use it. It might have been said that he had two right hands.

His open knife was in his hand.

The antennæ of the devil-fish cannot be cut; it is a leathery substance upon which a knife makes no impression; it slips under the blade; its position in attack too is such that to sever it would be to wound the victim's own flesh.

The creature is formidable, but there is a way of resisting it. The fishermen of Sark know it, and so does any one who has seen them execute certain abrupt movements in the sea. Porpoises know it, too; they have a way of biting the cuttle-fish which decapitates it.   Hence the frequent sight on the sea of headless pen-fish, polypuses, and cuttle-fish.

In fact, its only vulnerable part is its head.

Gilliatt was not ignorant of this fact.

He had never seen a devil-fish of this size.   His first encounter was with one of the largest species.   Any other man would have been overwhelmed with terror.

With the devil-fish, as with a furious bull, there is a certain instant in the conflict which must be seized.   It is the instant when the bull lowers his neck; it is the instant when the devil-fish advances its head.   The movement is rapid.   One who loses that moment is irrevocably doomed.

The events we have described occupied only a few seconds. Gilliatt, however, felt the increasing power of the monster's innumerable suckers.

The monster is cunning; it tries first to stupefy its prey. It seizes and then pauses awhile.

Gilliatt grasped his knife; the sucking increased.

He looked at the monster, which seemed to return the look.

Suddenly it loosened from the rock its sixth antenna, and darting it at him, seized him by the left arm.

At the same moment, it advanced its head with a quick movement.   In one second more its mouth would have fastened on his breast.   Bleeding in the sides, and with his two arms entangled, he would have been a dead man.

But Gilliatt was watchful.

He avoided the antenna, and at the very instant the monster darted forward to fasten on his breast, he struck it with the knife clinched in his left hand.

There were two convulsive movements in opposite directions,— that of the devil-fish, and that of its prey.

The movements were as rapid as a double flash of lightning.

Gilliatt had plunged the blade of his knife into the flat, slimy substance, and with a rapid movement, like the flourish of a whiplash in the air, had described a circle round the two eyes, and wrenched off the head as a man would draw a tooth.

"At the very instant the monster darted forward to fasten on his breast, he struck it with the knife clinched in his left hand.

Toilers of the Sea. Vol. II, Page 142.

The struggle was ended. The slimy bands relaxed. The air-pump being broken, the vacuum was destroyed. The four hundred suckers, deprived of their sustaining power, dropped at once from the man and the rock. The mass sank to the bottom of the water.

Breathless with the struggle, Gilliatt could dimly discern on the stones at his feet two shapeless, slimy heaps, the head on one side, the rest of the monster on the other.

Nevertheless, fearing a convulsive return of the death agony, he recoiled to be out of the reach of the dreaded tentacles.

But the monster was quite dead.

Gilliatt closed his knife.

CHAPTER IV

NOTHING IS HIDDEN, NOTHING LOST

IT was time that he killed the devil-fish. He was almost suffocated. His right arm and his chest were purple. Hundreds of small swellings were visible upon them; the blood flowed from them here and there. The remedy for these wounds is sea-water. Gilliatt plunged into it, rubbing himself vigorously at the same time with the palms of his hands. The swellings disappeared under the friction.

By stepping further into the waters he had, without perceiving it, approached to the sort of recess already noticed by him near the crevice where he had been attacked by the devil-fish.

This recess stretched obliquely under the great walls of the cavern, and was dry. The large pebbles which had become heaped up there had raised the bottom above the level of ordinary tides. The entrance was a rather large elliptical arch; a man could enter it by stooping. The green light of the submarine grotto penetrated and faintly illumined it.

While hastily rubbing his skin, Gilliatt raised his eyes mechanically.

He was able to see far into the tiny grotto.

He shuddered, for he fancied he perceived, at the farther depth of the dusky recess, a face wreathed with a ghastly smile.

Gilliatt had never heard the word " hallucination," but he was familiar with the idea. Those mysterious encounters with the invisible, which we call hallucinations in order to spare ourselves the trouble of explaining them, are a part of Nature. Whether they be illusions or realities, visions are an unquestionable fact. One who has the gift is sure to see them.

Gilliatt, as we have said, was a dreamer. He had at times the power of a seer. It was not in vain that he had spent his life musing among solitary places.

He imagined himself the dupe of one of those mirages which he had more than once beheld in his dreamy moods.

The opening was shaped something like a lime-burner's kiln. It was a low niche with projections like basket-handles. The sharp groins contracted gradually as far as the extremity of the crypt, where the heaps of round stones and the rocky roof joined.

Gilliatt entered, and lowering his head, advanced towards the object in the distance.

There was indeed something smiling at him.

It was a death's-head. There was not only the head, but the entire skeleton.

A complete human skeleton was lying in the cave.

Under such circumstances a bold man will continue his researches.

Gilliatt glanced around him. He was surrounded by a multitude of crabs. The multitude did not stir. They were but empty shells.

These groups were scattered here and there among the

masses of pebbles, forming all sorts of odd figures on the floor of the cave.

Gilliatt, having his eyes fixed elsewhere, had walked over them without perceiving them.

At the farther end of the crypt, where he had now penetrated, there was a still larger pile of remains. It was a confused mass of legs, antennæ, and mandibles. Claws stood wide open; bony shells lay quiet under their bristling horns; some reversed showed their livid hollows. The heap was like a *mêlée* of besiegers who had fallen, and lay massed together entangled like so much brush-wood.

The skeleton was partly buried in this heap.

Under this confused mass of scales and tentacles, the eye could distinguish the cranium, the vertebræ, the thigh bones, the tibias, and the long-jointed finger bones with their nails. The frame formed by the ribs was filled with crabs. A heart had once beat there. The green mould of the sea had settled round the sockets of the eyes. Limpets had left their slime upon the bony nostrils. Within this rocky cave there was neither sea-gull, nor weed, nor a breath of air. All was still. The teeth grinned hideously.

The gloomy side of laughter is that strange mockery of its expression which is peculiar to a human skull.

This marvellous palace of the deep, inlaid and incrusted with all the gems of the sea, had at last revealed its secret. It was a savage haunt; the devil-fish inhabited it; it was also a tomb, in which the body of a man reposed.

The skeleton and the creatures around it seemed to oscillate slightly by reason of the reflections from the water which trembled upon the roof and wall. The multitude of crabs looked as if they were finishing their repast. These crustacea seemed to be devouring the carcass.

Gilliatt had the storehouse of the devil-fish before his eyes.

It was a dismal sight. The crabs had devoured the man; the devil-fish had devoured the crabs.

There were no remains of clothing visible anywhere. The man must have been seized naked.

10

Gilliatt began to remove the shells from the skeleton. Who was this man? The body looked as if it had been prepared for an anatomical study. All the flesh was stripped off; not a muscle remained; but not a bone was missing. If Gilliatt had been skilled in physiology he could have demonstrated the fact. The periostea, denuded of their covering, were as white and smooth as if they had been polished. But for some green mould from sea-mosses here and there, they would have been like ivory. The cartilaginous divisions were delicately inlaid and arranged. The tomb sometimes produces this dismal mosaic work.

The body was, as it were, buried under a heap of dead crabs. Gilliatt disinterred it.

Suddenly he stooped and examined it more closely.

He had perceived around the vertebral column a sort of belt.

It was the leathern girdle, which had evidently been worn buckled around the waist of the man when alive.

The leather was moist; the buckle rusty.

Gilliatt pulled the girdle; the vertebræ of the skeleton resisted, and he was compelled to break through them in order to remove it. A crust of small shells had begun to form upon it.

He felt it, and discovered a hard substance inside. It was useless to endeavour to unfasten the buckle, so he cut the leather with his knife.

The girdle contained a small iron box and several pieces of gold. Gilliatt counted twenty guineas.

The iron box was a sailor's tobacco-box, that opened and shut with a spring. It was very tight and rusty. The spring being completely oxidized would not work.

Once more the knife served Gilliatt in a difficulty. A pressure with the point of the blade caused the lid to fly up.

The box was open.

There was nothing inside but some pieces of paper.

These were damp, but uninjured. The box, hermetically sealed, had preserved them. Gilliatt unfolded them.

They were three bank-notes of one thousand pounds sterling each, making in all seventy-five thousand francs.

Gilliatt folded them up again, replaced them in the box, taking advantage of the space which remained to add the twenty guineas; and then re-closed the box as well as he could.

Next he examined the belt.

The leather, which had originally been smooth outside, was rough within. Upon this tawny ground some letters had been traced in thick, black ink. Gilliatt deciphered them, and read the words " Sieur Clubin."

CHAPTER V

THE FATAL DIFFERENCE BETWEEN SIX INCHES AND TWO FEET

GILLIATT replaced the box in the girdle, and crammed the girdle in his trousers' pocket.

He left the skeleton among the crabs, with the remains of the devil-fish beside it.

While he had been occupied with the devil-fish and the skeleton, the rising tide had submerged the entrance to the cave. He was only able to leave it by diving under the arched entrance. He got through without any difficulty; for he knew the ground well, and was a proficient in such manœuvres.

It is easy to understand the drama that had taken place there the ten weeks before. One monster had seized another monster, the devil-fish had captured Clubin.

These two embodiments of treachery had met in the inexorable darkness. There had been an encounter at the bottom of the sea between these two compounds of cruelty and watchfulness; the monster had destroyed the man: a terrible fulfilment of justice.

The crab feeds on carrion, the devil-fish on crabs. The devil-fish seizes anything within its reach,— be it otter, dog, or man,— sucks the blood, and leaves the body at the bottom of the sea. The crabs are the scavengers of the deep. Putrefying flesh attracts them; they crowd round it, devour the body, and are in their turn consumed by the devil-fish. Dead creatures disappear in the crab, the crab disappears in the *pieuvre*. This is the law which we have already pointed out.

The devil-fish had laid hold of Clubin and drowned him. Some wave had carried his body into the recess at the farther end of this cave, where Gilliatt had discovered it.

He returned searching among the rocks for sea-urchins, and limpets, as he went. He had no desire for crabs; to have eaten them now would have seemed to him like feeding upon human flesh.

There was nothing now to prevent his departure. Heavy tempests are always followed by a calm, which sometimes lasts several days. There was, therefore, no danger to be apprehended from the sea. Gilliatt had resolved to leave the rocks on the following day. It was important, on account of the tide, to keep the barrier between the two Douvres during the night, but he intended to remove it at daybreak, to push the sloop out to sea, and set sail for St. Sampson. The light breeze which was blowing came from the south-west, which was precisely the wind he needed.

It was in the first quarter of the moon, in the month of May; and the days were long.

When Gilliatt, having finished his wanderings among the rocks, and appeased his appetite to some extent, returned to the passage between the two Douvres, where he had left the sloop, the sun had set, the twilight was increased by the pale light which comes from a crescent moon; the tide had attained its highest point and was beginning to ebb. The funnel standing upright above the sloop had been covered by the foam during the tempest with a coating of salt which glittered in the light of the moon.

This circumstance reminded Gilliatt that the storm had in-

undated the sloop, both with surf and with rain, and that if
he meant to start in the morning, it would be necessary to bale
it out.

Before leaving to go in quest of crabs, he had ascertained
that there was about six inches of water in the hold. The
scoop which he used for the purpose would, he thought, be
sufficient for throwing the water overboard.

On arriving at the barrier, Gilliatt was horrified to perceive that there were nearly two feet of water in the sloop.
A terrible discovery! The vessel had sprung a leak.

The water had been gaining gradually during his absence.
Heavily loaded as the sloop was, two feet of water was a
perilous addition. A little more, and she must inevitably
founder. If he had returned but an hour later, he would
probably have found nothing above water but the funnel and
the mast.

There was not a minute to lose. It was absolutely necessary to find the leak, stop it, and then empty the vessel, or at
all events, lighten it. The pumps of the Durande had been
lost in the break-up of the wreck.

To find the leak was the most urgent.

Gilliatt set to work immediately, and without even giving
himself time to dress. He shivered; but he was no longer
conscious of either hunger or cold.

The water continued to gain in his vessel. Fortunately
there was no wind. The slightest swell would have been
fatal.

The moon went down.

Bent low, and covered with water higher than his waist,
he groped about for a long time.

At last he discovered the leak.

At the critical moment when the sloop swerved, during the
gale, the strong bark had bumped violently upon the rocks.
One of the projections of the Little Douvre had made a fracture in the starboard side of the hull.

The leak, unfortunately, was near the joint of the two
riders, a fact which in the confusion caused by the hurricane

had prevented him perceiving it during his hasty survey in
the height of the storm.

The fracture was alarming on account of its size; but fortunately, although the vessel was sunk lower than usual by
the weight of the water, it was still above the ordinary water-
line.

At the time when the accident occurred, the waves had
rolled heavily into the defile, and had flooded the vessel
through the breach, so she had sunk a few inches under the
additional weight. Even after the subsidence of the water,
the weight had kept the hole still below the surface. Hence
the imminence of the danger.

The depth of water had increased from two to twenty
inches. But if he could succeed in stopping the leak, he
could bail out the sloop; the hole once stanched, the vessel
would rise to its usual water-line, the fracture would be above
water, and in this position the repair would be easy, or at
least possible. His carpenter's tools, as we have already said,
were still in fair condition.

But meanwhile what uncertainty must he not endure!
What perils, what chances of accidents! He heard the water
rising inexorably. One shock, and all would be lost! Perhaps his endeavours would prove futile even now!

He reproached himself bitterly. He said to himself that
he ought to have discovered the damage immediately. The
six inches of water in the hold ought to have suggested it
to him. He had been stupid enough to attribute these six
inches of water to the rain and surf. He was angry with
himself for having slept and eaten; he blamed himself even
for his weariness, and almost for the storm and the intense
darkness of the night. It all seemed to have been his
fault.

These bitter self-reproaches filled his mind while engaged
in his labour, but they did not prevent him from giving close
attention to his work.

The leak had been discovered; that was the first step; to
stanch it was the second. That was all it was possible to do

for the present. Carpentering cannot be carried on under water.

It was a favourable circumstance that the breach in the hull was in the place between the two chains which held the funnel fast on the starboard side. The material used in stopping the leak could be secured by these chains.

Meanwhile the water was gaining. It was now between two and three feet deep.

It reached above Gilliatt's knees.

CHAPTER VI

DE PROFUNDIS AD ALTUM

GILLIATT had among his store of surplus rigging for the sloop a large tarpaulin, provided with long lanyards at the four corners.

He took this tarpaulin, made fast two corners of it by the lanyards to the two rings of the funnel chains on the same side as the leak, and threw it over the gunwale. The tarpaulin hung like a sheet between the Little Douvre and the bark, and sunk in the water. The pressure of the water as it endeavoured to enter the hold, kept the tarpaulin close to the hull. The heavier the pressure the closer the sail adhered. The water kept it directly over the fracture. The wound in the bark was stanched.

The tarred canvas formed a barrier between the interior of the hold and the waves outside. Not a drop of water entered.

The leak was covered, but it was not stopped. It was a respite only.

Gilliatt took the scoop and began to bale out the sloop. It was time that she were lightened. The labour warmed him a little, but his weariness was extreme. He was forced to acknowledge to himself that he could not complete the work of emptying the hold.   He had scarcely eaten anything, and he had the humiliation of feeling himself exhausted.

He measured the progress of his work by the sinking of the level of water below his knees.   The fall was slow.

Moreover, the leakage was only interrupted; the evil was moderated, not repaired.   The tarpaulin pushed into the gap began to bulge inside, looking as if a fist were under the canvas, endeavouring to force it through.   The canvas, strong and pitchy, resisted; but the swelling and the tension increased.   It was by no means certain that it would not give way.   The swelling might become a rent at any moment. The entrance of the water would then begin again.

In such a case, as the crews of vessels in distress know very well, there is no other remedy than stuffing.   The sailors take everything in the shape of rags they can lay hands upon,— everything, in fact, which they can make of " service; " and with they push the bulging sail-cloth as far as they can into the hole.

But unfortunately all the rags and tow which Gilliatt had stored up had been used in his operations, or carried away by the storm.

If necessary, he might possibly have been able to find some remains by searching among the rocks.   The sloop was sufficiently lightened for him to leave it with safety for a quarter of an hour; but how could he make this search without a light?   The darkness was complete.   There was no longer any moon,— nothing but the starry sky.   He had no dry tow to serve as a match, no tallow to make a candle, no fire to light one, no lantern to shelter it from the wind.   In the sloop and among the rocks everything was blurred and indistinct.   He could hear the water lapping against the injured hull, but he could not even see the crack.   It was with his hands that he had ascertained the bulging of the tarpaulin. In the darkness it was impossible to make any effectual search for rags of canvas or pieces of tow scattered over the rocks. Who could find these waifs and strays without being able to see his path? Gilliatt looked sorrowfully at the sky: "All those stars," he thought, "and yet no light!"

The water in the hold having diminished, the pressure from without increased. The bulging of the canvas became greater and was constantly increasing, like a frightful abscess about to burst. The situation, which had been improved for a short time, began to be threatening.

Some means of stopping it effectually was absolutely necessary. He had nothing left but his clothes, which he had spread out to dry upon the projecting rocks of the Little Douvre.

He hastened to fetch them and hung them on the gunwale of the sloop.

Then he took his tarpaulin overcoat, and kneeling in the water thrust it into the hole, and swelling the sail outward, emptied it of water. To the tarpaulin coat he added the sheepskin, then his Guernsey shirt, and then his jacket. The hole held them all and more. He had nothing left but his sailor's trousers, which he took off, and pushed in with the other articles. This increased and strengthened the stuffing.

The stopper was made, and it seemed to be sufficient.

These clothes passed partly through the gap, the sail-cloth outside enveloping them. The sea in its efforts to enter, pressed against the obstacle, spread it over the gap, and blocked it. It was a sort of exterior compression.

Inside, only the centre of the bulge having been driven out, there remained all around the gap and the stuffing just thrust through, a sort of circular pad formed by the tarpaulin, which was rendered still firmer by the irregularities of the break in which it had become entangled.

The leak was stanched, but nothing could be more precarious. Those sharp splinters which held the tarpaulin might pierce it, thus making other holes by which the water would enter; while he would not even perceive it in the darkness.

There was little probability that the stuffing would last until daylight. Gilliatt's anxiety changed in form; but he felt it increase all the more rapidly in proportion as he found his strength failing him.

He had again set to work to bale out the hold, but his arms, in spite of all his efforts, could scarcely lift a scoopful of water. He was naked and shivering.

He felt as if the end was at hand.

One possible chance flashed across his mind. There might be a sail in sight. Some fishing-boat might come to his assistance. The moment had arrived when a help-mate was absolutely necessary. With a man and a lantern, all might yet be saved. If there were two persons, they might easily bale the vessel. As the leak was stanched temporarily, as soon as the vessel could be relieved of her burden, she would rise to her usual level. The leak would then be above the surface of the water, so repairs would be practicable, and he would be able to replace the rags with a piece of plank. If not, it would be necessary to wait till daylight,— to wait the whole night long; a delay which might prove ruinous. Gilliatt was in a fever of haste.

If by chance some ship's lantern should be in sight, Gilliatt would be able to signal it from the top of the Great Douvre. The weather was calm; there was no wind or rolling sea; there was a possibility of the figure of a man being observed moving against the background of the starry sky. A captain of a ship, or even the master of a fishing-boat, would not be in the vicinity of the Douvres at night without directing his glass upon the rock, by way of precaution.

Gilliatt hoped that some one might notice him.

He climbed upon the wreck, grasped the knotted rope, and climbed to the top of the Great Douvre.

Not a sail was visible in the horizon, nor a single ship's lantern. The wide expanse, as far as eye could reach, was deserted.

No assistance was possible, and no resistance was possible.

Gilliatt felt himself without resources,— a feeling which he had not experienced until then.

A grim fatality was now his master. In spite of all his

labour, all his success, all his courage, he and his bark, with its precious burden, were about to become the plaything of the waves. He had no other means of continuing the struggle. How could he prevent the tide from returning, the water from rising, the darkness from continuing? The stuffing he had made was his sole dependence. He had exhausted and stripped himself in constructing and completing it; he could neither strengthen nor add to it. The stop-gap was such that it must remain as it was, and any further efforts would be useless. How would this inert obstacle work? It was this obstacle, not Gilliatt, that would have to sustain the combat now. The mere pressure of a wave would suffice to re-open the fracture. It was simply a question of a little more or less pressure.

Henceforth Gilliatt could neither aid his auxiliary, nor hinder his adversary. He was now a mere spectator of this struggle, though it was one of life or death for him. He, who had maintained the struggle with such rare skill and intelligence, was at the last moment compelled to resign all to a mere blind resistance.

No trial, no terror that he had yet undergone, could be compared with this.

From the time he had first taken up his abode upon the Douvres, he had found himself environed, and as it were possessed by solitude. This solitude more than surrounded, it enveloped him. A thousand dangers had menaced him. The wind was always there, ready to buffet him; the sea, ready to roar. There was no stopping that terrible mouth, the wind; no imprisoning that dread monster, the sea.

And yet he had striven undaunted. He, a solitary man, had fought hand to hand with the ocean, had wrestled even with the tempest.

There was no form of misery with which he had not become familiar. He had been compelled to work without tools, to move vast burdens without aid, to solve problems without science, to eat and drink without provisions of any kind; to find shelter and sleep.

Upon that solitary rock, a dreary couch, he had been subjected by turns to all the varied and cruel tortures of Nature, who is oftentimes a kind mother, but quite as often a pitiless destroyer.

He had conquered his isolation, conquered hunger, conquered thirst, conquered cold, conquered fever, conquered labour, conquered sleep. He had encountered a mighty coalition of obstacles formed to bar his progress. After his privations, there were the elements to contend with; after the sea, the tempest; after the tempest, the devil-fish; after the monster, the spectre.

Ah, the dismal irony of the *dénouement*. Upon this rock, whence he had thought to depart triumphant, the spectre of Clubin had arisen to mock him with a hideous smile.

The spectre had cause to sneer, for Gilliatt, too, was ruined. He, too, like Clubin, was in the clutches of death.

Winter, famine, fatigue, the dismemberment of the wreck, the removal of the machinery, the equinoctial gale, the thunder, the sea-monster, were all as nothing compared with this small fracture in a vessel's side.

One could fight against cold, with fire; against hunger, with the shell-fish on the rocks; against thirst, with the rain; against the difficulties of his great task, with industry and energy; against the sea and the storm, with the breakwater; against the devil-fish, with a trusty knife; but against the terrible leak he had no weapon.

The hurricane had left him this grim farewell, this last retort, this traitorous thrust, this treacherous side blow of a vanquished foe. In its flight the tempest had turned and shot this parting arrow behind it.

It was possible to contend with the tempest, but how could he hope to wrestle with the insidious enemy who now attacked him?

If the leak re-opened, nothing could prevent the sloop from foundering. It would be like the bursting of the ligature of the artery; and once under the water with its heavy burden, no power could raise it. Was his noble struggle, and two months of herculean labour, to end in naught? To begin again would be impossible. He had neither forge nor materials. By dawn, in all probability, he would see his work swallowed up completely and irrevocably in the gulf.

How terrible, to feel that sombre power beneath him! to see the ocean snatching his prize from his hands.

His bark ingulfed, there was nothing left for him but to perish of cold and hunger, like the poor shipwrecked sailor on " The Man " rock.

For two long months this desperate struggle had been going on between the wide expanse of ocean, the waves, the winds, and the lightnings, on one hand, and a man on the other. On one hand the sea, on the other a human mind; on one hand the infinite, on the other a mere atom.

The battle had been fierce, and behold the abortive issue of those prodigies of valour.

Must this unparalleled heroism end in utter powerlessness, this formidable struggle end in impotent despair?

Gilliatt gazed wildly about him.

He had no clothing. He stood naked in the midst of that immensity.

Then, overwhelmed by a consciousness of an unknown but infinite power, bewildered by this relentless persecution, confronted by the shadows of night and impenetrable darkness, in the midst of the murmuring waves, the tossing foam, the roaring surf, beneath the mighty firmament studded with glittering constellations, and with the great unfathomable deep around him, he sank down, gave up the struggle, and throwing himself upon the rock with his face turned upward to the stars, completely humbled, he lifted his clasped hands to heaven, and cried aloud: " Have mercy ! "

Crushed to earth by that immensity, he prayed.

He was there alone, in the darkness, upon the rock, in the open sea, stricken down with exhaustion like one smitten by lightning, naked like the gladiator in the arena, save that for an arena he had the vast horizon, instead of wild beasts, the shadows of darkness, instead of the faces of the crowd, the eyes of the great Unknown, instead of the Vestals, the stars, instead of Cæsar, God!

His whole being seemed to dissolve in cold, fatigue, powerlessness, prayer, and darkness, and his eyes closed.

CHAPTER VII

THE APPEAL IS HEARD

SEVERAL hours passed.

The sun rose in a cloudless sky.

Its first ray shone upon a motionless form on the Great Douvre. It was Gilliatt.

He was still lying stretched out upon the rock.

He was naked, cold, and stiff; but he did not shiver. His closed eyelids were wan. It would have been difficult for a beholder to determine whether the form before him was not a corpse.

The sun seemed to be gazing down upon him.

If he were not dead, he was so near death that a single cold blast would have sufficed to extinguish life.

The wind began to blow, warm and animating,— the revivifying breath of spring.

Meanwhile the sun mounted higher in the clear, blue sky; its light became warmth. It enveloped the slumbering form.

But Gilliatt did not move. If he breathed at all, it was only with that feeble respiration which would scarcely sully the surface of a mirror.

The sun continued its ascent; its rays striking less and less obliquely upon the naked man. The gentle breeze which had been merely tepid, became hot.

The rigid and naked body still remained perfectly motionless, but the skin was less livid in hue.

The sun, approaching the zenith, shone almost perpendicularly upon the plateau of the Douvres. A flood of light descended from the heavens; the reflection from the glassy sea increased its splendour; the rock itself imbibed the hot rays and warmed the sleeper.

A sigh heaved his breast.

He lived.

The sun continued its kindly offices. The wind, which was already the breath of summer and of noon, approached him like loving lips that breathed softly upon him.

Gilliatt moved.

The sea was perfectly calm. Its murmur was like the droning of a nurse beside a sleeping infant. The rock seemed cradled in the waves.

The sea-birds, who knew that recumbent form, fluttered around it,— not with their former wild astonishment, but with a sort of fraternal tenderness. They uttered plaintive cries: they seemed to be calling to him.

A sea-mew, who no doubt knew him, was tame enough to approach him. It began to caw gently, as if talking to him.

The sleeper seemed not to hear. The bird hopped upon his shoulder, and pecked his lips softly.

Gilliatt opened his eyes.

The birds, content and shy, dispersed, chattering wildly.

Gilliatt arose, stretched himself like a roused lion, ran to the edge of the platform, and looked down into the gulf between the two Douvres.

The sloop was there, intact; the stopper had not failed him; the sea had probably disturbed it but little.

All was well.

His weariness was forgotten. His strength had returned. His swoon had ended in a refreshing sleep.

He descended and baled out the sloop, thus raising the leak above the water-line, dressed himself, ate, drank some water, and gave thanks.

The gap in the side of the vessel, examined in broad daylight, was found to require more labour than he had thought.

It was a serious fracture. The entire day would be consumed in repairing it.

At daybreak the next morning, after removing the barrier and re-opening the entrance to the gorge, dressed in the tattered clothing which had served to stop the leak, with Clubin's belt containing the seventy-five thousand francs, around his waist, standing erect in the sloop, now thoroughly repaired, beside the machinery he had rescued, with a favourable breeze and a calm sea, Gilliatt pushed off from the Douvres.

He headed the sloop straight for Guernsey.

Had any one chanced to be on the Douvres at the moment of the sloop's departure, he would have heard Gilliatt singing, in an undertone, the air of " Bonnie Dundee."

PART III

DERUCHETTE

BOOK I

NIGHT AND THE MOON

CHAPTER I

THE HARBOR BELL

THE St. Sampson of the present day is almost a city; the St. Sampson of forty years ago was little more than a village.

When the winter was ended and spring had come, the inhabitants were not long out of bed after sundown. St. Sampson was an ancient parish which had long been accustomed to the sound of the curfew-bell, and which had a traditional habit of blowing out the candle at an early hour. The people there went to bed and got up with the sun. These old Norman villages are wonderfully successful with poultry.

The people of St. Sampson, except a few rich families among the townsfolk, are also a population of quarrymen and carpenters. The port is a great port for repairs. The quarrying of stone and the fashioning of timber go on all day long; here stands a labourer with his pickaxe, there a workman with his mallet. At night they are ready to drop with fatigue, and sleep like lead. Heavy labour brings heavy slumbers.

One evening, in the early part of the month of May, after watching the crescent moon for some instants through the trees, and listening to the step of Déruchette walking along in the cool air in the garden of the Bravées, Mess Lethierry had returned to his room overlooking the harbour, and had retired to rest. Douce and Grace were already in bed. The entire household was asleep with the exception of Déruchette. The doors and shutters were everywhere closed. The streets were silent and deserted. Some few lights, like winking eyes about to close in rest, showed here and there in windows in the roofs, indicating that the domestics were going to bed. Nine had already struck in the old Romanesque belfry, wreathed in ivy, which shares with the church of St. Brelade at Jersey the peculiarity of having for its date four ones (IIII), used to signify the year eleven hundred and eleven.

The popularity of Mess Lethierry at St. Sampson had been founded on his success. His success at an end, his popularity departed. One might almost imagine that ill-fortune is contagious, and that the unsuccessful have a plague, so rapidly are they put in quarantine. The young men of well-to-do families avoided Déruchette. The isolation around the Bravées was so complete that its inmates had not even heard the news of the great local event which had that day set all St. Sampson in a ferment. The rector of the parish, the Rev. Ebenezer Caudray, had become rich. His uncle, the noted Dean of St. Asaph, had just died in London. The news had been brought by the mail sloop, the " Cashmere," arrived from England that very morning, and the mast of which could be seen in the harbour of St. Peter's Port. The " Cashmere " was to sail for Southampton at noon on the morrow, and would, so rumour said, convey the reverend gentleman, who had been suddenly summoned to England, to be present at the official opening of the will, not to speak of other urgent matters connected with an important inheritance. All day long St. Sampson had been conversing excitedly upon this subject. The " Cashmere," the Rev. Ebenezer, his deceased uncle, his wealth, his speedy departure, his possible preferment in the future, had formed the foundation of this perpetual buzzing. One solitary house, still uninformed on these matters, had remained unperturbed. This was the Bravées.

Mess Lethierry had thrown himself in his hammock all dressed as he was.

Since the accident to the Durande, his hammock had been his only consolation. Every prisoner has the privilege of stretching himself out on his pallet, and Mess Lethierry was the prisoner of grief. To go to bed was a truce, a gain in breathing time, a suspension of thought. He neither slept nor watched. Strictly speaking, for two months and a half, or ever since his misfortune had befallen him, Mess Lethierry had been in a sort of a dream. He had not yet regained possession of his faculties. He was in that cloudy and confused condition of mind with which those who have undergone overwhelming afflictions are familiar. His reflections were not thought, his sleep was not repose. He was not awake by day or asleep by night. He was up, and then went to rest,— that was all. When he was in his hammock forgetfulness came to him. He called that sleeping. Chimeras floated about him, and within him. A nocturnal cloud, full of confused faces, flitted through his brain. Sometimes it was the Emperor Napoleon dictating to him the story of his life; sometimes there were several Déruchettes; strange birds peopled the trees; the streets of Lons-le-Saulnier turned into serpents. Such nightmares as these were brief respites in his despair. He spent his nights in dreaming, and his days in reverie.

Sometimes he remained all the afternoon at the window of his room, which overlooked the harbour, with his head drooping, his elbows on the sill, his ears resting on his fists, his back turned to the whole world, his eyes fixed on the old massive iron ring fastened in the wall of the house, only a few feet from his window, where he used to moor the Durande. He was looking at the rust which gathered on the ring.

He was reduced to the mere mechanical habit of living.

The bravest men, when deprived of their most cherished hope, often come to this. His life had become a void. Life is a voyage; the idea is the itinerary. The plan of their course gone, they stop. The object is lost, the strength of purpose gone. Fate has a secret discretionary power. It is able to touch even our mental being with its rod. Despair is destitution of the soul. Only the greatest minds can resist it.

Mess Lethierry was always meditating,— if absorption can be called meditation,— in the depths of a sort of cloudy abyss. Broken words like these sometimes escaped him. "There is nothing left for me now, but to ask for leave to go."

There was a certain contradiction in that nature, complex as the sea, of which Mess Lethierry was, so to speak, the product. Mess Lethierry's grief did not seek relief in prayer.

To be powerless is almost a comfort under some circumstances. In the presence of those two relentless powers — destiny and Nature — it is by his very powerlessness that man has been led to seek support in prayer.

Man seeks relief from his terror; his anxiety bids him kneel.

Prayer, that wondrous power peculiar to the soul, is addressed to the magnanimity of the Invisible; it gazes into mystery with the very eyes of the grave, and before this potent fixity of regard and supplication, we feel a possible disarmament of the Unknown.

The mere possibility of such a thing is a consolation.

But Mess Lethierry prayed not.

In the days when he was happy, God had been a palpable presence to him. Lethierry addressed him almost familiarly, pledged his word to him, seemed at times to hold close intercourse with him. But in the hour of his misfortune, the idea of God had become eclipsed in his mind,— a phenomenon which is not infrequent. This almost invariably happens when the mind has created for itself a deity invested with human attributes.

In his present frame of mind there was but one thing of

which Lethierry was clearly cognizant,— the smile of Déruchette. Everything else was dim and shadowy.

For some time, apparently on account of the loss of the Durande, and of the blow which it had been to them, this pleasant smile had been rare. She seemed always thoughtful. Her bird-like playfulness, her child-like ways, were gone. She was never seen now in the morning, at the sound of the cannon which announced daybreak, saluting the rising sun with "Boom! Daylight! Come in, please!" At times her expression was very serious,— an unusual thing for that sweet nature. She sometimes made an effort, however, to laugh before Mess Lethierry, and to divert him; but her cheerfulness diminished from day to day,— grew dim like the wing of an empaled butterfly. Either through sorrow for her uncle's sorrow,— for there are griefs which are the reflections of other griefs,— or for some other reason, she about this time became very religiously inclined. In the time of the old rector, M. Jaqueim Hérode, she scarcely went to church, as we have already said, four times a year; now, on the contrary, she was assiduous in her attendance at church. She missed no service, either Sunday or Thursday. Pious souls in the parish noted this fact with great satisfaction. It is a great blessing when a girl who runs so many risks in the world turns her thoughts towards God.

It at least enables the poor parents to feel easy on the subject of love-making.

In the evening, whenever the weather permitted, she walked for an hour or two in the garden of the Bravées. She was almost as quiet there as Mess Lethierry, and almost always alone. Déruchette went to bed last. This, however, did not prevent Douce and Grace from watching her a little, with that instinct for spying which is common to servants. Spying is such a relaxation after household work.

As for Mess Lethierry, in the abstracted state of his mind, these little changes in Déruchette's habits escaped him. Moreover, his nature had little in common with the duenna. He had not even remarked her regular attendance at church. Tenacious of his prejudices against the clergy and their sermons, he would scarcely have approved such close attendances at the parish church.

Not that his own moral condition was not undergoing change however. Sorrow often undergoes a marked change in its form.

Robust natures, as we have said, are sometimes almost overwhelmed by sudden great misfortunes; but not quite. Manly characters, such as Lethierry's, experience a reaction in a given time. Sorrow has many different stages. From utter despair we rise to dejection; from dejection to grief; from grief to melancholy. Melancholy is a twilight state; suffering melts into it and becomes a gloomy joy.

Melancholy is the pleasure of being sad.

Such moods were not for Lethierry. Neither the nature of his temperament nor the character of his misfortune suited those delicate shades. But at the time of which we speak his apathy had begun to wear off a little, leaving him no less sad, however. He was just as inactive, and quite as dull; but he was no longer overwhelmed. A certain perception of events and circumstances was returning to him, and he began to experience something that might be called a return to reality.

Thus by day in the great lower room, though he did not listen to the words of those about him, he heard them. Grace came one morning, quite exultant, to tell Déruchette that he had undone the cover of a newspaper.

This half acceptance of realities is in itself a good symptom, — a token of convalescence. Great afflictions produce a stupor; it is by such little acts that men return to their former selves. This improvement, however, is at first only an aggravation of the evil. The dreamy condition of mind in which the sufferer has lived, served, while it lasted, to blunt his grief. His sight before was dim. He felt little. Now his view is clear, nothing escapes him; and his wounds re-open. Every detail that he notices serves to remind him of his sorrow. He lives over everything again in memory; every recollection is a pang. All kinds of bitter aftertastes lurk in that return to life. He is better, and yet worse. Such was the condition of Lethierry. In returning to consciousness, his sufferings had become more keen.

It was a sudden shock that first recalled him to a sense of reality.

One afternoon, between the 15th and 20th of April, a double-knock at the door of the great lower room of the Bravées had signalled the arrival of the postman. Douce had opened the door; there was a letter.

The letter came from beyond the sea; it was addressed to Mess Lethierry, and bore the postmark " Lisbon."

Douce had taken the letter to Mess Lethierry, who was in his room. He took it, placed it mechanically on the table, and did not look at it.

The letter remained an entire week upon the table without being opened.

It happened, however, one morning that Douce said to Mess Lethierry: —

" Shall I brush the dust off your letter, sir? "

Lethierry seemed to arouse from his lethargy.

" Ay, ay! You are right," he said; and he opened the letter, and read as follows: —

AT SEA, 10th March.

To Mess Lethierry of St. Sampson: —

You will be gratified to receive news of me. I am aboard the " Tamaulipas," bound for the port of " No-return." Among the crew is a sailor named Ahier-Tostevin, from Guernsey, who will return, and will have some facts to communicate to you. I take the opportunity of our speaking a vessel, the " Hernan Cortes," bound for Lisbon, to forward you this letter.

You will be astonished to learn that I am an honest man.

As honest as Sieur Clubin.

I am almost sure that you know of certain recent events ere this; nevertheless, it is, perhaps, not altogether superfluous to send you a full account of them.

To proceed:

I have returned your money.

Some years ago, I borrowed from you, under rather unfortunate circumstances, the sum of fifty thousand francs. Before leaving St. Malo lately, I paid into the hands of your confidential man of business, Sieur Clubin, on your account, three bank-notes of one thousand pounds each;

making together seventy-five thousand francs. You will no doubt find this reimbursement sufficient.

Sieur Clubin acted for you, and received your money, in a remarkably energetic manner; indeed, he seemed to me singularly zealous. This is, indeed, my reason for apprising you of the facts.

Your other confidential man of business,

RANTAINE.

Postscript.— Sieur Clubin was in possession of a revolver, which may explain to your satisfaction the fact of my having no receipt.

One who has touched a torpedo, or a Leyden-jar fully charged, may form some idea of the effect the reading of this letter produced on Mess Lethierry.

This common-place looking missive to which he had at first paid so little attention, contained a veritable thunderbolt.

He recognized the writing and the signature. As for the facts to which the letter referred, he did not understand them in the least. But the excitement of the event soon set his mind to working again.

The most potent part of the shock he had received lay in the mystery of the seventy-five thousand francs intrusted by Rantaine to Clubin. This was an enigma which taxed Lethierry's brain to the uttermost. Conjecture is a healthy occupation for the mind. Reason is awakened; logic is called into play.

For some time past public opinion in Guernsey had been undergoing a reaction on the subject of Clubin,— the man who had enjoyed such a high reputation for honour for so many years, the man so unanimously regarded with esteem. People had begun to question and to doubt; there were wagers for and against. Some new light had been thrown on the question in singular ways. The character of Clubin began to become clearer,— that is to say, he began to appear blacker in the eyes of the world.

A judicial inquiry had taken place at St. Malo, for the purpose of ascertaining what had become of coast-guardsman No. 619. Legal perspicacity had got upon a false scent,— a thing which frequently happens. It had started with the hypothesis that the man had been enticed away by Zuela, and had shipped aboard the " Tamaulipas " for Chili. This ingenious supposition led to a considerable amount of wasted conjecture. The short-sighted authorities had failed to take any note of Rantaine; but as the inquiry progressed, other clews were developed and the affair became complicated. Clubin, too, became mixed up with the enigma. A coincidence, perhaps a direct connection, had been found between the departure of the " Tamaulipas " and the loss of the Durande. At the wine-shop near the Dinan Gate, where Clubin thought himself entirely unknown, he had been recognized. The keeper of the wine-shop said that Clubin had bought a bottle of brandy that night. For whom? The gunsmith of St. Vincent street, too, had talked; Clubin had purchased a revolver of him. For what purpose? The landlord of the Auberge Jean had talked: Clubin had absented himself in an inexplicable manner. Captain Gertrais-Gaboureau had talked: Clubin had determined to start, although he had been warned, and knew that he might expect a great fog. The crew of the Durande had talked. In fact, the collection of freight had been strangely neglected, and the cargo badly stowed,— a neglect easy to comprehend, if the captain had determined to wreck the ship. The Guernsey passenger, too, had talked: Clubin had evidently believed that he had run upon the Hanways. The Torteval people had talked: Clubin had visited that neighbourhood a few days before the loss of the Durande, and had been seen walking in the direction of Pleinmont, near the Hanways. He had a travelling-bag with him. " He had set out with it, and come back without it." The birds'-nesters had talked; their story might be connected with Clubin's disappearance,— that is, if the lads' supposed ghosts were in reality smugglers. Finally, the haunted house of Pleinmont itself had spoken. Persons who were determined to get information had climbed up and entered the windows, and had found inside, what? The very travelling-bag which had been seen in Sieur Clubin's possession. The authorities of the *Douzaine* of Torteval had taken possession of the bag and had opened it. It was found to contain provisions, a telescope, a chronometer, a man's clothing, and linen marked with Clubin's initials. All this, according to the gossips of St. Malo and Guernsey, began to look more and more like a case of fraud. Obscure hints were brought together; there seemed to have been a singular disregard of advice on Clubin's part; a willingness to encounter the dangers of the fog; a suspected negligence in the stowage of the cargo. Then there was the mysterious bottle of brandy; a drunken helmsman; a substitution of the captain for the helmsman; a management of the rudder, that was, to say the least, very unskilful. The heroism of remaining behind upon the wreck began to look like knavery. Besides, Clubin had evidently been deceived as to the rock he was on. If he had really intended to wreck the vessel, it was easy to understand the choice of the Hanways, as the shore could easily be reached by swimming, and he could conceal himself in the haunted house while awaiting an opportunity for flight. The travelling-bag, that suspicious preparation, completed the proof. By what link this affair became connected with the affair of the disappearance of the coast-guardsman nobody knew. People imagined some connection, and that was all. They had a glimpse in their minds of look-out-man, No. 619, alongside of the mysterious Clubin,— quite a tragic drama. Perhaps Clubin was not an actor in it, but his presence was visible in the side scenes.

The supposition of a wilful destruction of the Durande did not explain everything however. There was a revolver in the story, with no part as yet assigned to it. The revolver was probably connected with the other affair.

The scent of the public is keen and true. Its instinct excels in these piecemeal discoveries of truth. Still, amid these facts, which seemed to point pretty clearly to a case of barratry, there were many uncertainties.

Everything was consistent, everything coherent; but a reason was lacking.

People do not wreck vessels merely for the pleasure of wrecking them. Men do not run all these risks of fog, rocks, swimming, concealment, and flight without an object. What could have been Clubin's object?

The act seemed evident, but the motive was puzzling.

Hence a doubt in many minds. Where there is no motive, it is natural to infer that there was no act.

The missing link was important. The letter from Rantaine seemed to supply it.

This letter furnished a motive for Clubin's supposed crime: seventy-five thousand francs to be appropriated.

Rantaine was the *Dues ex machina*. He had descended from the clouds with a lantern in his hand. His letter threw a light upon the affair. It explained everything, and even promised a witness in the person of Ahier-Tostevin.

The part the revolver had played in the affair was now apparent.

Rantaine's letter explained the mystery.

There could be no possible palliation of Clubin's crime. He had premeditated the shipwreck; the preparations discovered in the haunted house were conclusive proofs of that.

Even supposing him innocent, and admitting the wreck to have been accidental, would he not, at the last moment, when he determined to sacrifice himself with the vessel, have intrusted the seventy-five thousand francs to the men who escaped in the long-boat? The evidence was remarkably complete. But what had become of Clubin? He had doubtless become a victim of his blunder. He had probably perished upon the Douvres.

These numerous surmises, which really were not far from the truth, had been engrossing Mess Lethierry's mind for several days. The letter from Rantaine had done him the service of setting him to thinking. At first he was overwhelmed with surprise; then he made an effort to reflect. He made another effort more difficult still,— that of inquiry. He was induced to listen, and even engage in conversation. At the end of a week, he had become, to a certain degree, himself again; his thoughts had regained their coherence, and he was almost restored. He had emerged from his confused and troubled state.

Even if Mess Lethierry had ever entertained any hope of recovering his money, Rantaine's letter destroyed all chance of that.

It added to the catastrophe of the Durande this new loss of seventy-five thousand francs. It put him in possession of that amount just so far as to make him sensible of its loss. The letter revealed the full extent of his ruin.

After this, he experienced a new and poignant misery. When he began to take an interest in his household, to try and determine what it was to be in the future, and how he was to set things in order,— matters of which he had taken no heed for two months past,— these trifling cares wounded him like a thousand tiny pin-points, worse in the aggregate than the old despair. A sorrow is doubly burdensome which has to be endured in each particular, and while one is disputing inch by inch with fate for ground already lost. Ruin is endurable in the mass, but not in the dust and fragments of the fallen edifice. The great fact may overwhelm, but the details torture.

Humiliation tends to aggravate the blow. A second catastrophe follows the first, with even more repulsive features. You descend one degree nearer to annihilation. The winding-sheet becomes changed to sordid rags.

No thought is more bitter than that of one's gradual fall from a social position.

To be ruined does not seem to be such a terrible thing. A violent shock, a cruel turn of fortune's wheel, an overwhelming catastrophe,— be it so. We submit, and all is over. You are ruined; you are dead. No; you are still living. On the morrow you know it only to well. How? By a thousand pin-pricks? Yonder passer-by omits to bow to you; the tradesmen's bills rain down upon you; and yonder stands one of your enemies, smiling malevolently. Perhaps he is really thinking of Arnal's last pun; but it is all the same to you. The pun would not have seemed so inimitable to him but for your ruin. You read your own sudden insignificance even in looks of indifference. Friends who used to dine at your table become of the opinion that three courses were an extravagance. Your faults are patent to the eyes of everybody; ingratitude having nothing more to expect, proclaims itself openly; every idiot predicted your misfortunes. The malicious tear you to pieces; those who are even more malicious profess to pity you. And then come a hundred paltry details. Nausea succeeds to grief. You have been wont to indulge in wine; you must now drink cider. Two servants,— two! Why, one will be too many. It will be necessary to discharge this one, and get rid of that one. Flowers in your garden are superfluous; you should plant it with potatoes. You used to make presents of your fruits to friends; you must send them to market hereafter. As to the poor, it will be absurd to think of giving anything to them. Are you not poor yourself? And then there is the painful question of dress. To have to deny your wife a ribbon, what torture! To have to refuse a dress to one who has made you a gift of her beauty; to haggle over such matters, like a miser! Perhaps she will say to you, " What! rob my garden of its flowers, and now refuse me one for my bonnet!" Ah me! to have to condemn her to shabby dresses. The family table is silent. You fancy that those seated around it think harshly of you. Beloved faces have become clouded. This is what is meant by falling fortunes. It is to die daily. To be struck down is like a blast from a furnace; to decay like this is like being burned by inches.

An overwhelming blow is a sort of Waterloo, a slow decay, a St. Helena. Destiny, in the guise of Wellington, still has some dignity; but how sordid it appears in the shape of Hudson Lowe. Fate then becomes a paltry huckster. We find the man of Campo Formio quarrelling about a pair of stockings; we see that dwarfing of Napoleon which degrades England even more.

Waterloo and St. Helena! Reduced to humbler proportions, every ruined man has passed through those two phases.

On the evening which we have mentioned, and which was

one of the first evenings in May, Lethierry, leaving Déruchette
to walk alone by moonlight in the garden, had gone to bed
more depressed than ever.

All these sordid and repulsive details connected with
pecuniary misfortunes; all these petty cares, which are at
first merely tiresome, but subsequently harassing, were revolving in his mind. A dull load of misery! Mess Lethierry
felt that his fall was irremediable. What could he do?
What would become of them? What privations would he be
compelled to impose on Déruchette? Whom should he discharge,— Douce or Grace? Would they have to sell the
Bravées? Would they not be compelled to leave the island?
To be nothing where he had been everything,— it was a terrible fall indeed!

And to know that the good old times had gone forever!
To recall those journeys to and fro, uniting France with these
numerous islands; the Tuesday's departure, the Friday's return, the crowd on the quay, the large cargoes, the industry,
the prosperity, that proud direct navigation, that machinery
embodying the will of man, that all-powerful boiler! The
steamboat is really only the compass perfected, inasmuch as
the needle indicates the direct course, and the steam-vessel
follows it. One suggests, the other executes. Where was she
now, his Durande, that mistress of the seas, that queen who
had made him a king? To have been so long the leading man
on the island, a successful man too, a man who had revolu-
tionized navigation; and then to have to give up everything,
— to abdicate! To cease to exist, to become a by-word, a
laughing stock! To become a thing of the past, after having
so long represented the future. To be degraded to an object
of pity to fools, to witness the triumph of routine, obstinacy,
conservatism, selfishness, ignorance! To see the old barbarous
sailing cutters crawling to and fro upon the sea; to see old
prejudices revive again; to have wasted a whole lifetime; to
have been a shining light, and then suffer this eclipse. Ah,
what a fine sight it was upon the waves, that noble funnel,
that huge cylinder, that pillar with its column of smoke,— a

column grander than that on the Place Vendôme; for on that
there was only a figure of a man, while on this stood Progress.
The ocean was subdued; it was certainty upon the open sea.
And had all this been witnessed in that little island, in that
little harbour, in that little town of St. Sampson? Yes; it
had been witnessed. And could it be, that having seen it, it
had all vanished to be seen no more?

This series of regrets tortured Lethierry. There is such
a thing as a mental sobbing. Never, perhaps, had he felt
his misfortunes more acutely. A sort of numbness follows
this acute suffering. Under this burden of sorow, he gradually sank into a doze.

For about two hours he remained in this state, feverish,
sleeping a little, dreaming a good deal. Such torpor is accompanied with a feverish action of the brain, which is in-
expressibly wearisome. Towards the middle of the night, a
little before or a little after midnight, he shook off his lethargy, aroused himself, and opened his eyes. His window
was directly in front of his hammock. He saw something
extraordinary.

A form stood in front of his window,— a marvellous
form. It was the funnel of a steam-vessel.

Mess Lethierry started, and sat upright in bed. The
hammock oscillated like a bough in a tempest. Lethierry
stared.

A vision filled the window-frame. There was the harbour
flooded with moonlight, and in the glitter, close to his
house, stood out, tall and round and black, a magnificent
object.

The funnel of a steamboat!

Lethierry sprang out of his hammock, ran to the window,
lifted the sash, leaned out, and recognized it.

It was the smoke-pipe of the Durande he saw. It stood in
the old place.

Four chains supported it, made fast to the bulwarks of a
vessel, the irregular outlines of which he could dimly distinguish beneath the funnel.

Lethierry recoiled, turned his back to the window, and dropped in a sitting posture into his hammock again.

Then he returned, and once again beheld the vision.

An instant afterwards, or in about the time occupied by a flash of lightning, he was out on the quay, with a lantern in his hand.

A large sloop laden with some big unwieldy object, out of which rose the smoke-stack he had seen from the window of the Bravées, was made fast to the mooring-ring of the Durande. The bows of the sloop extended beyond the corner of the house, and were level with the quay.

There was no one aboard.

The vessel was of peculiar shape. Any Guernsey man would have recognized it. It was the old Dutch sloop.

Lethierry jumped aboard, and ran forward to the mass which he saw beyond the mast.

The boiler was there, entire, complete, intact, standing square and firm upon its cast-iron flooring. Not a rivet was missing; the axle of the paddle-wheels had been lifted and made fast near the boiler; the pump was in place; nothing was lacking.

Lethierry examined the machinery.

The lantern and the moon helped him in his scrutiny.

He went over every part of the machinery.

He noted the two cases on the sides of the vessel. He examined the axle of the wheels.

He went into the little cabin; it was empty.

He returned to the engine, and felt it, looked into the boiler, and knelt down to examine it inside.

He placed his lantern inside the furnace, where the light, illuminating all the machinery, produced almost the illusion of an engine-room with its fire.

Then he burst into a wild laugh, sprang to his feet, and with his eyes fixed on the engine, and his arms outstretched towards the funnel, he cried aloud, " Help, help! "

The harbour bell was on the quay, a few yards away. He ran to it, seized the rope, and began to pull it. violently.

CHAPTER II

THE HARBOUR BELL AGAIN

GILLIATT, after a passage that was uneventful but rather slow on account of the heavy cargo he had aboard, reached St. Sampson after dark, and at nearer ten than nine o'clock.

He had calculated the time. The half-flood had arrived. There was plenty of water, and the moon was shining; so he was able to enter the port without difficulty.

The little harbour was silent. A few vessels were moored there, with their sails brailed up to the yards, the yards on the caps, and without lanterns. At the far end a few others were visible, high and dry in the careenage, where they were undergoing repairs,— large hulls dismasted and stripped, with their planking open at various parts and looking like huge dead beetles lying on their backs with their legs in the air.

As soon as he had passed the mouth of the harbour, Gilliatt examined the port and the quay. There was no light to be seen either at the Bravées or elsewhere. The place was deserted, save, perhaps, by some one going or returning from the parsonage; nor was it possible to be sure of this even; for the night blurred every outline, and the moonlight always gives to objects a vague appearance. The distance added to the indistinctness. The parsonage at that time was situated on the other side of the harbour, where a shipyard now stands.

Gilliatt approached the Bravées quietly, and made the sloop fast to the ring of the Durande, under Mess Lethierry's window. Then he leaped over the bulwarks to the shore.

Leaving the sloop behind him at the quay, he turned the corner of the house, passed up a little narrow street, then along another, did not even notice the pathway which branched

12

off leading to the Bu de la Rue, and in a few minutes found himself at that corner of the wall where in June there were wild mallows with pink flowers, as well as holly, ivy, and nettles. Many a time seated on a stone, behind the bushes, on summer days, he had watched here for hours, even for whole months through a gap in the wall the garden of the Bravées and the two windows of a little room seen through the branches of the trees. The stone was there still, and the bushes, the low place in the wall, and the garden, as quiet and dark as ever. Like an animal returning to its lair, gliding rather than walking, he made his way in. Once seated there, he made no sound, but looked around, and beheld again the garden, the pathways, the flower-beds, the house, the two windows of the chamber. The moon flooded the scene with her silvery light. Gilliatt scarcely dared to breathe, and did all he could to prevent it.

He seemed to be gazing on a vision of paradise, and was afraid that it would vanish. It seemed almost impossible that these things could be really before his eyes; and if they were, it could only be with that imminent danger of melting into air which belongs to things divine. A breath, and the vision would fade away. He shuddered at the thought.

Before him, not far off, on the side of one of the paths in the garden, was a wooden bench painted green. The reader will remember this seat.

Gilliatt looked up at the two windows. He thought of the slumber of one who was possibly in that room. Behind that wall she was no doubt sleeping. He wished himself elsewhere, yet would sooner have died than go away. He pictured her lying there, her bosom rising softly with her gentle breathing. It was she,— that beauteous vision, that creature of spotless purity whose image haunted him day and night. She was there! He thought of her so far removed, and yet so near as to be almost within reach of his ecstasy. He thought of that fair being so long and ardently desired, so distant, so impalpable, with closed eyelids, and face resting on her hand; of the mystery of sleep in its relations with

that pure spirit, of what dreams might come to one who was
herself a dream.   He dared not think beyond, and yet he did.
He ventured on those familiarities which a lover's fancy
prompts; the thought of how much of the woman there
might be in this angelic being disturbed his thoughts.   The
darkness of night emboldens timid imaginations to take these
furtive glances.   He was vexed with himself, feeling on reflection as if it were profanity to think of her so boldly; yet
still constrained, in spite of himself, he tremblingly gazed into
the invisible.   He shuddered almost with a sense of pain as
he pictured her room, a skirt hanging on a chair, a mantle
fallen on the carpet, a belt unbuckled, a handkerchief.   He
imagined her corset with its lacing trailing on the ground,
her stockings, her little shoes.   His soul was among the stars.

The stars are made for the human heart of a poor man
like Gilliatt no less than for that of the rich and great.
There is a certain degree of passion by which every man becomes enveloped in a celestial light.   With a rough and
primitive nature, this truth is even more applicable.   An
uncultivated mind is especially susceptible to such fancies.

Delight is a fulness which overflows like any other.   To see
those windows was almost too much happiness for Gilliatt.

Suddenly, he beheld the object of this thoughts before
him.

From the branches of a clump of bushes, already densely
covered with foliage, issued with spectral slowness a celestial
figure, a divine face.

Gilliatt felt his strength failing him.   It was Déruchette.

Déruchette approached, then paused, walked back a few
yards, stopped again, then returned and seated herself upon
the wooden bench.   The moon shone brightly through the
branches, a few clouds floated among the pale stars; the sea
murmured to the shadows in an undertone, the town was
sleeping, a thin haze was rising from the horizon, the melancholy was profound.   Déruchette inclined her head, with those
thoughtful eyes which gaze intently yet see nothing.   She
had nothing on her head but a little cap which showed the

beginning of her hair upon her delicate neck. As she sat
twisting one of her ribbon strings of her cap mechanically
around her finger the hall light made her hands seem like
those of a statue; her dress was of one of those shades that
look white at night: the trees stirred as if they felt the enchantment which she shed around her. The tip of one foot
was visible. Her lowered eyelids had that vague contraction
which suggests a tear checked in its course, or a thought
suppressed. There was a charming indecision in the movements of her arms, which had no support to lean on; a sort
of floating grace mingled with every posture; the folds of her
dress were exquisite; her face, which might inspire adoration,
was meditative, like portraits of the Virgin. It was terrible to
think how near she was: Gilliatt could hear her breathe.

A nightingale was singing in the distance. The soft whispering of the breezes among the branches only seemed to in-
tensify the silence of the night. Déruchette, beautiful, divine,
looked in the dim light like a creation from those rays and
from the perfumes in the air. That wide-spread enchantment
seemed to concentrate and embody itself mysteriously in her;
she became its living manifestation. She seemed the out-
blossoming of all that shadow and silence.

But the shadow and silence which floated so lightly about
her weighed heavily on Gilliatt. He was bewildered; what
he experienced is not to be told in words. Emotion is always
new, and the word is always enough. Hence the impossibility
of expressing it. Joy is sometimes overwhelming. To see
Déruchette, to see her herself, to see her dress, her cap, her
ribbon, which she twined around her finger,— was it possible
to imagine it? Was it possible to be thus near her; to hear
her breathe? She breathed! then the stars might breathe also.
Gilliatt felt a thrill through him. He was the most miserable
and yet the happiest of men. He knew not what to do. His
delirious joy at seeing her annihilated him. Was it indeed
Déruchette there, and he so near? His thoughts, bewildered
and yet intent, were fascinated by that figure as by a dazzling
jewel. He gazed upon her neck — her hair. He did not

even say to himself that all this would soon belong to him, that before long,— to-morrow, perhaps,— he would have the right to take off that cap, to unknot that ribbon.   He was not guilty of the audacity of even thinking of such a thing. Touching in fancy is almost like touching with the hand. Love was to Gilliatt like honey to the bear,— an exquisite dream.   He thought confusedly; he knew not what possessed him.   The nightingale sang on.   He felt as if he were breathing his very life out.

The idea of rising, of jumping over the wall, of speaking to Déruchette, never once occurred to him.   If it had, he would have turned and fled.   If anything resembling a thought had begun to dawn in his mind, it was this: that Déruchette was there, that he asked nothing more, and that eternity had begun.

A noise aroused them both, her from her reverie, him from his ecstasy.

Some one was walking in the garden though it was impossible to see who was approaching on account of the trees. It was certainly the footstep of a man they heard.

Déruchette raised her eyes.

The sound came nearer, then ceased.   The person walking had stopped.   He must have been quite near.   The path beside which the bench stood, wound between two clumps of trees.   The stranger was there in the alley between the trees, a few yards from the seat.

Accident had so placed the branches that Déruchette could see the new-comer, but Gilliatt could not.

The moon cast on the ground beyond the trees a shadow which reached to the garden seat.

Gilliatt could see this shadow.

He looked at Déruchette.

She was quite pale; her mouth was partly open, as with a suppressed cry of surprise.   She half arose from the bench, and sank back on it again.   There was in her attitude a sort of fascination mingled with a desire to fly.   Her surprise was enchantment mingled with timidity.   She had a smile on her lips, with a fulness like tears in her eyes. She seemed trans-figured by that presence, as if the being whom she saw before her did not belong to earth. The reflection of an angel was in her look.

The stranger, who was to Gilliatt only a shadow, spoke. A voice issued from the trees, softer than the voice of a woman, though it was the voice of a man. Gilliatt heard these words :—

"I see you, mademoiselle, every Sunday and every Thursday. They tell me that you were not in the habit of coming so often formerly. I beg your pardon for repeating the remark. I have never spoken to you; it was my duty. I speak to you to-day, for it is still my duty. It is right that I speak to you first. The "Cashmere," sails to-morrow. This is why I have come. You walk every evening in your garden. It would be wrong of me to know your habits so well, if I had not the thought that I have. Mademoiselle, you are poor; since this morning I have become rich. Will you have me for your husband?

Déruchette clasped her two hands imploringly, and gazed at the speaker, silent, with fixed eyes, and trembling from head to foot.

The voice continued,—

"I love you. God does not wish man to silence the voice of his heart. He has promised him eternity with the intention that he should not be alone. There is but one woman on earth for me. It is you. I think of you as of a prayer. My faith is in God, and my hope is in you. You are my life, and already my supreme happiness."

"Sir," said Déruchette, "there is no one in the house to answer!"

The voice rose again : —

"Yes, I have encouraged this dream. Heaven has not forbidden us to dream. You are like an angel in my eyes. I love you deeply, mademoiselle. To me you are holy innocence personified. I know it is an hour when your household have retired to rest, but I could not choose my time.

Do you remember that passage of the Bible which some one read before us; it was the twenty-fifth chapter of Genesis. I have thought of it often since. M. Hérode said to me, ' You must have a rich wife.' I replied, ' No, I want a poor wife.' I say this to you, mademoiselle, without venturing to approach you; I will step even farther back if it be your wish that my shadow should not touch your feet. Your will is my law. You will come to me if such is your will. I love and wait. You are the living form of a benediction."

" I did not know, sir, that any one noticed me on Sundays and Thursdays," stammered Déruchette.

The voice continued,—

" We are powerless against it. The whole Law is love. Marriage is Canaan; you are to me the promised land of beauty."

Déruchette replied, " I do not mean to do wrong any more than persons who are much more strict."

The voice continued,—

" God manifests his will in the flowers, in the light of dawn, and in the gentle springtime; love, too, is of his ordaining. You are beautiful in this holy shadow of night. This garden has been tended by you; in its perfumes there is something of your breath. The affinities of our souls do not depend on us. They cannot be counted with our sins. You were there, that was all. I was there, that was all. I did nothing but feel that I loved you. Sometimes my eyes rested upon you. I was wrong, but what could I do? It was through looking at you that it all happened. I could not restrain my gaze. There are mysterious impulses which are beyond our control. The heart is the noblest of all temples. To have your presence in my home,— that is the terrestrial paradise for which I long. Say, will you be mine? As long as I was poor, I spoke not. I know your age. You are twenty-one; I am twenty-six. I go to-morrow; if you refuse me, I return no more. Oh, be my betrothed; will you not? More than once have my eyes, in spite of myself, addressed that question to you. I love you; answer me. I will speak to your uncle as soon as he is able to receive me; but I turn first to you. To Rebecca I plead for Rebecca,— unless you love me not."

Déruchette hung her head, and murmured,—

" Oh, I adore him! "

The words were spoken in a voice so low that only Gilliatt heard them.

She remained with her head lowered, as if by shading her face she hoped to conceal her thoughts.

There was a pause. Not a leaf stirred. It was one of those solemn and peaceful moments when inanimate objects appear to share the slumber of living creatures, and night seems to be listening to the beating of Nature's heart. In the midst of that retirement, like a harmony making the silence more complete, rose the wild murmur of the sea.

The voice was heard again.

" Mademoiselle! "

Déruchette started.

Again the voice spoke.

" You are silent."

" What would you have me say? "

" I wait for your reply."

" God has heard it," said Déruchette.

Then the voice became almost sonorous, and at the same time softer than before, and these words issued from the leaves as from a burning bush :—

" You are my betrothed. Then come to me. Let the blue sky, with all its stars, witness this taking of my soul to thine; and let our first embrace be mingled with that firmament."

Déruchette arose and remained an instant motionless, looking straight before her, doubtless into another's eyes; then, with slow steps, with head erect, her arms drooping, but with the fingers of her hands wide apart, like one who leans on some unseen support, she moved towards the trees, and out of sight.

A moment afterwards, instead of one shadow upon the

gravelled walk, there were two; then they intermingled. Gilliatt saw at his feet the embrace of those two shadows.

There are moments when we are entirely unconscious of the flight of time. These two enraptured lovers, who were ignorant of the presence of a witness, and saw him not; this witness of their joy who could not see them, but who knew of their presence,— how long did they remain in this sort of trance? It would be impossible to say. Suddenly a noise burst forth at a distance. A voice was heard crying " Help ! " and the harbour bell began to ring. It is probable that in their celestial transports of delight they heard no echo of the tumult.

The bell continued to ring. Any one who sought Gilliatt then at the corner of the wall would have failed to find him.

BOOK II

GRATITUDE AND DESPOTISM

————

CHAPTER I

JOY MINGLED WITH ANGUISH

MESS LETHIERRY pulled the bell furiously, then stopped abruptly. A man had just turned the corner of the quay. It was Gilliatt.

Lethierry ran towards him, or rather flung himself upon him, seized his hand, and looked him in the face for a moment without uttering a word. It was the silence of an explosion struggling to find a vent.

Then pulling and shaking and hugging him with all his might, he compelled him to enter the lower room of the Bravées, pushed back with his heel the door which had remained half opened, sat down, or sank into a chair beside a great table lighted by the moon, the reflection of which seemed to impart a strange pallor to Gilliatt's face, and with a voice of mingled laughter and tears, cried : —

" Ah, my son! my player of the bagpipe! I knew that it was you. The sloop, *parbleu!* Tell me the story. You went there, then. Why, they would have burned you a hundred years ago! It is magic! There isn't a screw missing. I have looked at everything already, examined everything, and handled everything. I guessed that the paddles were in the two cases. And here you are once more! I looked in the little cabin for you. I rang the bell. I wanted to see you.

186

I said to myself, 'Where is he?' I could wait no longer.
You must admit that wonderful things do come to pass. You
have brought me back to life again. *Tonnerre!* you are an
angel! Yes, yes; it is my engine! Nobody will believe it;
people will see it, and say, 'It can't be true.' Not a tap,
not a pin is missing. The feed-pipe has not budged an inch.
It is incredible that there should have been no more damage.
We have only to put on a little oil. But how did you accomplish it? To think that the Durande will be moving
again. The axle of the wheels must have been taken to pieces
by some watchmaker. Give me your word of honour that I
am not crazy."

He sprang to his feet, breathed a moment, and continued: —

" Swear it, I say! What a change. I had to pinch myself to be certain I was not dreaming. You are my child,
you are my son, you are my Providence! Brave lad! to go
and fetch my good old engine! And in the open sea among
those awful rocks! I have seen some strange things in my
life, but nothing to equal this. I have known Parisians who
were positive demons, but I'd defy them to have done this.
It beats the Bastille. I have seen *gauchos* ploughing in the
Pampas, with a crooked branch of a tree for a plow and a
bundle of thorn-bushes for a harrow, dragged by a leathern
strap; they get harvests of wheat that way, with grains as big
as hazel-nuts. But that is a trifle compared with your feats.
You have performed a miracle,— a real one. Ah, *gredin!*
let me hug you. How they will gossip in St. Sampson. I
shall set to work at once to rebuild the boat. It is astonishing
that the crank is all right. Gentlemen, he has been to the
Douvres: I say, to the Douvres! He went alone to the
Douvres! I defy you to find a worse spot. Do you know,
have they told you, that it's proved that Clubin sent the
Durande to the bottom to swindle me out of money which had
been intrusted to him for me. He made Tangrouille drunk.
It's a long story. I'll tell you all about his piratical tricks,
some day. I, stupid idiot, had confidence in Clubin. But he

trapped himself, the villain, for he couldn't have got away. There is a God above, my boy! We'll begin to re-build the Durande at once, Gilliatt. We'll have her twenty feet longer. They build them longer now than they did. I'll buy the wood from Dantzic and Bremen. Now I have got the machinery, they will give me credit again. They'll have confidence now."

Mess Lethierry stopped, turned his eyes devoutly heavenward, and muttered, "Yes, there is a power on high!"

Then he placed the middle finger of his right hand between his two eyebrows, and tapped with his nail there,— an action which indicates an important project passing through the mind, and continued: —

"Nevertheless, to begin again, on a grand scale, a little ready money would have been useful. Ah, if I only had my three bank-notes,— the seventy-five thousand francs that scoundrel Rantaine returned, and that villain Clubin stole."

Gilliatt silently felt in his pocket, and drew out something which he placed before Mess Lethierry. It was the leather belt that he had brought back. He opened it, and spread it out on the table; on the inside the word " Clubin " could be deciphered even in the light of the moon. He then took out of the pocket of the belt a box, and out of the box three pieces of paper, which he unfolded and handed to Lethierry.

Lethierry examined them. It was light enough to see the figure " 1000," and the word " *thousand* " was also perfectly visible. Mess Lethierry took the three notes, laid them on the table one after the other, looked at them, looked at Gilliatt, stood for a moment dumb; and then began again, like an eruption after an explosion: —

"These too! You are a marvel. My bank-notes! all three — of a thousand pounds each. My seventy-five thousand francs. Why, you must have gone down to the infernal regions. It is Clubin's belt. *Pardieu!* I can read his vile name. Gilliatt has brought back engine and money too. There will be something to put in the papers now. I will buy some timber of the finest quality. I guess how it was; you found his miserable carcass mouldering away in some corner.

We'll have some Dantzic pine and Bremen oak; we'll have a
first-rate planking,— oak within and pine without. In old
times they didn't build so well, but their work lasted longer;
the wood was better seasoned, because they did not build so
much. We'll build the hull of elm perhaps. Elm is good
for the parts in the water. To be sometimes dry, and sometimes wet, rots the timbers; elm needs to be always wet; it's a
wood that feeds upon water. What a splendid Durande we'll
build. The lawyers will not trouble me again. I shall want
no more credit. I have some money of my own. Did any-
body ever see a man like Gilliatt? I was struck all of a heap,
— I was a dead man! He comes and sets me up again as
firm as ever! And all the while I never once thought about
him,— he had gone clean out of my mind; but I recollect
everything now. Poor lad! Ah, by the way, you know you
are to marry Déruchette."

Gilliatt leaned back against the wall, like on who staggers,
and said in a tone that was very low but distinct: —

" No."

Mess Lethierry started.

" How, no! "

" I do not love her," Gilliatt replied.

Mess Lethierry went to the window, opened and reclosed
it, picked up the three bank-notes, folded them, placed them
the iron box on top of them, scratched his head, seized Clubin's
belt, flung it violently against the wall, and exclaimed: —

" You must be mad! "

He thrust his fists into his pocket, and exclaimed:

" You don't love Déruchette? What! was it at me, then,
that you used to play the bagpipe? "

Gilliatt, still supporting himself by the wall, turned as
pale as death. As he became paler. Lethierry became
redder.

" Here 's an idiot for you! He does n't love Déruchette.
Very good; make up your mind to love her, for she shall
never marry any one but you. A devilish pretty story that;
and you think that I believe you! If there is anything really

the matter with you, send for a doctor; but don't talk nonsense. You can't have had time to quarrel, or get out of
temper with her. It is true that lovers are great fools sometimes. Come now, what are your reasons? If you have any,
tell me. People don't make such geese of themselves without
some reason. But I have a piece of cotton in my ears; perhaps I didn't understand. Repeat what you said."

Gilliatt replied,—

"I said, No!"

"You said, No. He sticks to it, the lunatic. You must be
crazy. You said, No. Here's a stupidity beyond anything
ever heard of. Why, people have had their heads shaved for
much less than that. What! you don't like Déruchette? Oh,
then, it was out of affection for the old man that you did all
these things? It was for the sake of papa that you went to
the Douvres, that you endured cold and heat, and almost died
of hunger and thirst, and ate limpets off the rocks, and had
the fog, the rain, and the wind for your bedroom, and brought
me back my machinery, just as you might bring a pretty
woman her little canary that had escaped from its cage. And
that tempest we had three days ago. Do you think I don't
remember that? You must have had a fine time of it! It was
in the midst of all this misery, alongside of my old craft, that
you shaped, and cut, and turned, and twisted, and dragged
about, and filed, and sawed, and carpentered, and schemed,
and performed more miracles there by yourself than all the
saints in paradise. Ah, you annoyed me enough once with
your bagpipe. They call it a *biniou* in Brittany. Always
the same tune, too, silly fellow. And yet you don't love
Déruchette? I don't know what is the matter with you. I
recollect it all now. I was there in the corner; Déruchette
said, 'He shall be my husband;' and so you shall. You
don't love her! Either you must be mad, or else I am mad.
And you stand there, and won't say a word. I tell you you
are not at liberty to do all the things you have done, and then
say, 'I don't love Déruchette.' People don't do other people
services in order to put them in a passion. Well; if you

don't marry her, she shall remain single all her life. In the
first place, I need you. You must be the captain of the Durande. Do you imagine I mean to part with you like this?
No, no, my brave boy; I won't let you off! I have got you
now; I'm not even going to listen to you. Where can I find
a sailor like you? You are the man I want. But why don't
you speak?"

Meanwhile the harbour bell had aroused the household and
the neighbourhood. Douce and Grace had risen, and now entered the lower room, silent and astonished. Grace had a candle in her hand. A group of neighbours, townspeople, sailors, and labourers, who had rushed out of their houses, were
outside on the quay, gazing in wonder at the funnel of the
Durande and the sloop. Some, hearing Lethierry's voice in
the lower room, began to slip in through the half-open door.
Between the faces of two worthy old women appeared that of
Sieur Landoys, who seemed to have a happy faculty of always being where he wanted to be.

Men feel a satisfaction in having witnesses of their joy.
The sort of scattered support which a crowd gives, pleases
them at such times; they seem to draw new life from it. Mess
Lethierry suddenly perceived that there were people around
him; and he welcomed the audience at once.

" So you are here, my friends! I am very glad to see you.
You know the news? That man has been there, and brought
it back. How d' ye do, Sieur Landoys? When I woke up
just now, the first thing I spied was the smoke-stack. It
was under my window. There's not a nail missing. They
rave about Napoleon's exploits; but I think more of this than
of the battle of Austerlitz. You have just left your beds,
my good friends. The Durande caught you napping.
While you are putting on your night-caps and blowing out
your candles there are others working like heroes. We are a
set of cowards and do-nothings; we sit at home rubbing our
rheumatic limbs; but happily that does not prevent there being some men of another stamp. The man of the Bu de la
Rue has arrived from the Douvres. He has fished up the Du-

rande from the bottom of the sea; and fished up my money out of Clubin's pocket, from a still greater depth. But how did you contrive to do it? All the powers of darkness were against you, the wind and the sea, the sea and the wind. It must be true that you are a magician. Those who say so are not so stupid after all. The Durande is back again. The tempests may rage now; this cuts the ground from under their feet. My friends, I can inform you that there was no shipwreck after all. I have examined all the machinery. It is as good as new,— perfect. The valves move as easily as rollers. You would think they were made yesterday. You know that the waste water is carried away by a pipe inside another pipe, through which the water passes to the boilers; this is to economize heat. Well; the two pipes are there just as good as new. So is the entire engine, in fact. She is all there, paddle-wheels and all. Ah, he shall marry her!"

"Marry the engine?" asked Sieur Landoys.

"No, the girl; yes, the engine,— both of them. He shall be my double son-in-law. He shall be her captain. Goodday, Captain Gilliatt; for there will soon be a captain of the Durande. We are going to do a thundering business again. There will be trade and passengers and big cargoes of oxen and sheep. I wouldn't exchange St. Sampson for London now. And there stands the author of all this good fortune. It is a strange adventure, I can tell you. You will read about it on Saturday in old Mauger's 'Gazette.' What's the meaning of these louis-d'ors here?"

For Mess Lethierry had just noticed that there was some gold in the box that lay on the notes. He seized it, opened and emptied it into the palm of his hand, and put the handful of guineas on the table.

"For the poor, Sieur Landoys. Give those sovereigns to the constable of St. Sampson from me. You recollect Rantaine's letter. I showed it to you. Very well; I've got the bank-notes. Now we can buy some oak and fir, and go to carpentering. Look you! Do you remember the gale three days ago,— that hurricane of wind and rain? Gilliatt endured all that out on the Douvres. That didn't prevent his taking the wreck to pieces, as I might take my watch. Thanks to him, I am on my legs again. Old 'Lethierry's galley' is going to run again, ladies and gentlemen. A nut-shell with a couple of wheels and a funnel. I always had that idea. I used to say to myself, I will certainly do it some day. That was a long time ago. The idea came in my head one day in Paris, at the coffee-house on the corner of the Rue Christine and the Rue Dauphine, while I was reading a paper that contained an account of the new invention. Do you know that Gilliatt would think nothing of putting that engine at Marly in his pocket and walking off with it? He is wrought-iron, that man; tempered steel; a sailor that can't be beat, an excellent smith, an extraordinary fellow, much cleverer than the Prince of Hohenlohe. He is what I call a man of brain. We are children in comparison with him. We may think ourselves sea-wolves, but there is the sea-lion! Hurrah for Gilliatt! I do not know how he managed it. He certainly must be the very devil! And how can I do otherwise than give him Déruchette? "

Déruchette had been in the room several minutes. She had not spoken or moved since she entered. She had glided in like a shadow and sat down almost unperceived just back of where Mess Lethierry was standing, loquacious, excited, joyful, gesticulating wildly, and talking in a loud voice. A little while afterwards another silent apparition entered. A man attired in black, with a white cravat, holding his hat in his hand, appeared in the doorway. There were now several candles in the group, which had gradually increased in number. These lights were near the man attired in black. His profile and youthful and pleasing complexion showed itself against the dark background with the clearness of an engraving on a medal. He leaned his shoulder against the frame of the door, and held his left hand to his forehead,— an attitude of unstudied grace, which made his brow look even broader than it really was by reason of the smallness of his hand. There was an expression of anguish in his contracted

13

lips, as he looked on and listened with profound attention. The by-standers recognizing M. Caudray, the rector of the parish, had stepped back to allow him to pass; but he remained upon the threshold. There was hesitation in his posture, but decision in his eyes, which now and then met those of Déruchette. With regard to Gilliatt, whether by chance or design, he was in shadow, and could not be seen distinctly.

At first Mess Lethierry did not observe Caudray, but he saw Déruchette. He went to her and kissed her affectionately on the forehead, pointing at the same time towards the dark corner where Gilliatt was standing.

"Déruchette," he said, "we are rich again; and there is your future husband."

Déruchette raised her head, and looked towards the dusky corner, in evident bewilderment.

"The marriage will take place immediately, to-morrow, if possible," Mess Lethierry continued. "We will have a special license; the formalities here are not very troublesome; the dean can do what he pleases; people are married before they have time to turn round. It is not as it is in France, where you must have bans, and publications, and delays, and all that fuss. You will be able to boast of being the wife of a brave man. No one can say he is not. I thought so from the day when I saw him come back from Herm with the little cannon. But now he comes back from the Douvres with his fortune and mine, and the fortune of this country. A man of whom the world will have plenty to say some day. You said you would marry him, and you shall marry him; and you will have little children, and I will be a grandfather, and you will have the good fortune to be the wife of a noble fellow, who can work and who can be of use to his fellow-men,— a surprising fellow, worth a hundred others; a man who can rescue other people's inventions, a providence! At all events, you will not have married, like so many other silly girls about here, a soldier or a priest,— that is, a man who kills or a man who lies. But what are you doing there, Gilliatt? Nobody can see you. Douce, Grace, everybody, bring a light, I say.

Show up my son-in-law for me. I betroth you to each other, my children; here stands your husband, and here is my son,— Gilliatt of the Bu de la Rue, this noble fellow, this splendid sailor. I will have no other son-in-law, and you no other husband; I pledge my word to that once more in God's name. Ah, you are here, Monsieur the Curé. You must marry these young people for me."

Lethierry's eye had just lighted on Caudray.

Douce and Grace had done as they were directed. Two candles placed on a neighbouring table illumined Gilliatt from head to foot.

"There's a fine fellow for you," said Mess Lethierry.

Gilliatt's appearance was appalling.

He was in the same condition in which he had that morning set sail from the rocks,— in rags, his bare elbows showing through his sleeves, his beard long, his hair rough and wild, his eyes bloodshot, his skin peeling, his hands covered with wounds, his feet naked. Some of the blisters left by the devilfish were still visible upon his arms.

Lethierry gazed at him admiringly, nevertheless.

"This is my son-in-law," he said. "See how he has struggled with the sea. He's in rags, but what shoulders and hands! There's a fine fellow for you!"

Grace ran to Déruchette and supported her head. She had fainted.

CHAPTER II

THE LEATHER TRUNK

BY daybreak all St. Sampson was up and out and the people of St. Peter's Port began to flock there. The resurrection of the Durande caused a commotion in the island equal to that caused by the miracle of Salette in the south of France. There was a crowd on the quay staring at the funnel standing erect in the sloop. They were anxious to see and handle the machinery; but Lethierry, after making a new and triumphant survey of the whole by daylight, had placed two sailors aboard with instructions to prevent any one from approaching it. The smoke-stack, however, furnished sufficient food for contemplation. The crowd gaped with astonishment. They talked of nothing but Gilliatt. They remarked on his nickname of " Wicked Gilliatt; " and their admiring comments generally ended with the remark, " It is not pleasant to have people on the island who can do things like that."

Mess Lethierry was seen from outside the house, seated at a table before the window, writing, with one eye on the paper and another on the sloop. He was so completely absorbed that he had only stopped once to call Douce and ask after Déruchette. " Mademoiselle has risen, and has gone out," Douce replied. " She is wise to go out for a little air," answered Lethierry. " She was a little faint last night, owing to the heat. There was a crowd in the room. This, and her surprise and joy, and the windows being all closed, overcame her. She will have a husband to be proud of." Then he resumed his writing. He had already finished and sealed two letters, addressed to the most important ship-builders at Bremen. He soon finished a third.

A sound upon the quay caused him to look up. He leaned out of the window, and saw coming up the path which led from the Bu de la Rue, a boy pushing a wheel-barrow. The lad was going towards St. Peter's Port. In the barrow was a portmanteau of brown leather, studded with brass nails.

" Where are you going, my lad? " shouted Mess Lethierry.

The boy stopped, and replied,—

" To the ' Cashmere.' "

" What for? "

" To take this trunk aboard."

" Very good; you can take these three letters too."

Mess Lethierry opened his table drawer, took out a piece of string, tied the three letters which he had just written together, and threw the packet to the boy, who caught it between his hands.

"Tell the captain of the 'Cashmere' they are my letters, and to take good care of them. They are for Germany,— Bremen *via* London."

"I can't speak to the captain, Mess Lethierry."

"Why not?"

"The 'Cashmere' is not at the quay."

"Ah!"

"She is in the roads."

"Ay, true; on account of the tide."

"I can only speak to the man who takes the things aboard."

"You will tell him, then, to attend to the letters."

"Very well, Mess Lethierry."

"At what time does the 'Cashmere' sail?"

"At twelve."

"The tide will be coming in then."

"But the wind is favourable," answered the lad.

"Boy," said Mess Lethierry, pointing with his forefinger to the engine in the sloop, "do you see that? There is something that laughs at winds and tides."

The boy put the letters in his pocket, picked up his barrow again, and went on towards the town. Mess Lethierry called "Douce! Grace!"

Grace opened the door a little way.

"What is it, Mess?"

"Come in and wait a moment."

Mess Lethierry took a sheet of paper, and began to write. If Grace, standing behind him, had been curious, and had leaned forward to see what he was writing, she might have read as follows: —

"I have written to Bremen for the lumber. I have appointments all the morning with carpenters for the estimate. The rebuilding will go on fast. You must go to the Deanery for a licence yourself. It is my wish that the marriage should take place as soon as possible,— immediately would be better. I am busy about the Durande. Do you busy yourself about Déruchette"

He dated it, and signed " Lethierry." He did not take the trouble to seal it, but merely folded it, and handed it to Grace, saying,—

" Take that to Gilliatt."

" To the Bu de la Rue? "

" To the Bu de la Rue."

BOOK III

THE DEPARTURE OF THE CASHMERE

CHAPTER I

THE HAVELET NEAR THE CHURCH

WHEN there is a crowd at St. Sampson, St. Peter's Port is deserted. An object of curiosity at any given place is like an air-pump. News travels fast in small places. Going to see the funnel of the Durande under Mess Lethierry's window had been, since sunrise, the business of the Guernsey folks. Every other event was eclipsed by this. The death of the dean of St. Asaph was forgotten, together with the interest in the Rev. Mr. Caudray, his suddenly acquired wealth, and his intended departure on the "Cashmere." The machinery of the Durande brought back from the Douvres rocks was the topic of the day. People were incredulous. The shipwreck had appeared extraordinary, the salvage seemed impossible. Everybody hastened to assure himself of the truth by the help of his own eyes. Business of every kind was suspended. Long processions of towns-folk with their families, from the "Vesin" up to the "Mess," men and women, gentlemen, mothers with children, infants with dolls, were coming by every road or pathway to see "the thing to be seen" at the Bravées, and turning their backs upon St. Peter's Port. Many shops at St. Peter's Port were closed. In the Commercial Arcade there was an absolute stagnation in buying and selling. The Durande engrossed everybody's at-

tention. Not a single shopkeeper had made a sale that morning, except a jeweller, who marvelled much at having sold a
wedding-ring to " a man who seemed to be in a great hurry,
and who asked where the dean's house was." The shops that
remained open were centres of gossip, where loungers discussed the miraculous salvage. There was not a promenader
on the Hyvreuse, which is known in these days, nobody knows
why, as Cambridge Park; no one was visible on High Street,
then called the Grande Rue; nor in Smith Street, then known
as the Rue des Forges, nor in Hauteville. Even the Esplanade was deserted. One might suppose it was Sunday.
A visit from a royal personage to review the militia at the
Ancresse could not have drained the town more completely.
All this hubbub about a " nobody " like Gilliatt, caused a
good deal of shrugging of the shoulders among persons of
grave and correct habits.

The church of St. Peter's Port, with its three gable ends, its
transept and steeple, stands near the water's edge at the end
of the harbour, and nearly on the landing-place itself, where
it welcomes those who arrive, and bids the departing " God-
speed." This edifice is the most prominent feature in the
long line of buildings on the sea-front of the town.

It is both the parish church of St. Peter's Port and the
Deanery of the whole island. Its officiating minister is the
surrogate of the bishop, a clergyman invested with full
powers.

The harbour of St. Peter's Port, a very fine and large
port at the present day was at that epoch, and even up
to ten years ago, much smaller than the harbour of St.
Sampson. It was enclosed both on the right and left side
by massive walls which curved until they almost met again
at the mouth of the harbour, where a little white lighthouse
stood. Under this lighthouse a narrow opening, still furnished with two rings for the chain with which it was
customary to close the passage in ancient times, formed the
only entrance for vessels. The harbour of St. Peter's Port
might be compared to the claws of a huge lobster opened a

little way. These odd pincers tore a scrap of sea from old
ocean and tried to compel it to remain calm. But during
easterly winds the waves rolled heavily against the narrow entrance, the harbour was rough, and it was advisable not to
enter it. This having been the case on the " Cashmere's "
arrival, the vessel had anchored in the roads.

The vessels, during easterly winds, preferred this course,
which also saved them the port dues. At such times the
boatmen of the town, a hardy race of mariners whom the
new harbour had thrown out of employment, came in their
boats to fetch passengers from the landing-place or at sta-
tions on the shore, and carried them with their luggage, often
in heavy seas, but always without accident, to the vessels about
to sail. The east wind blows off the shore, and is very
favourable for the passage to England; the vessel at such
times rolls, but does not pitch.

When a vessel happened to be in the port, everybody
embarked from the quay. When it was in the roads they
took their choice, and embarked from any point on the coast.
In every creek or inlet there was a boat for hire. The
Havelet was one of these creeks. The little harbour (for
that is the signification of the word) was near the town, but
was such a lonely place that it seemed a long way off. This
seclusion was due to the shelter afforded by the high cliffs of
Fort St. George, which overlooked this retired inlet. The
Havelet was accessible by several paths. The most direct
was along the water's edge. This path had the advantage
of taking one from the town to the church in five minutes,
and the disadvantage of being covered by the sea twice a
day. The other paths were more or less abrupt, and led
into the creek through gaps in the steep rocks. Even in
broad daylight it was dusk in the Havelet. Huge walls of
granite hemmed it in on three sides, and thick bushes and
brambles cast a sort of soft twilight upon the rocks and
waves below. No spot could be more peaceful than this in
calm weather, nor more tumultuous during heavy seas. The
ends of some of the branches there were always wet with the

foam. In the springtime, the place was full of flowers, of birds' nests, of perfumes, of butterflies, and bees. Thanks to recent improvements, this romantic nook no longer exists. Fine straight lines have taken the place of these wild features; masonry, quays, and little gardens have made their appearance; terraces have become the rage, and modern taste has finally subdued the eccentricities of the cliff and the irregularities of the rocks below.

CHAPTER II

DESPAIR CONFRONTS DESPAIR

IT was a little before ten o'clock in the morning. The crowd at St. Sampson was apparently increasing. The multitude, feverish with curiosity, was moving towards the north; and the Havelet, which lies to the southward was more deserted than ever.

Notwithstanding this, there was a boat there and a boatman. In the boat was a travelling-bag. The boatman seemed to be waiting for some one.

The "Cashmere" was visible at anchor outside the harbour, and as she did not start till midday there was as yet no movement aboard.

Any one passing along the cliffs overhead might have heard the murmur of conversation in the Havelet, and if he had leaned over the overhanging cliff might have seen, some distance from the boat, in a nook among the rocks and bushes, where the eye of the boatman could not reach them, a man and a woman. It was Caudray and Déruchette.

These quiet nooks on the sea-shore, the favourite haunts of lady bathers, are not always so solitary as is believed. One is sometimes observed and watched there. Those who seek shelter and solitude in them may easily be followed through the thick bushes; and, thanks to the multiplicity and entanglement of the paths, the granite and the shrubs which favour the stolen interview, may also favour the witness.

Caudray and Déruchette stood face to face, looking into each other's eyes, and holding each other by the hand. Déruchette was speaking. Caudray was silent. A tear that had gathered upon his eye-lash hung there and did not fall.

Grief and profound emotion were imprinted on his strong, intellectual countenance. A painful resignation was there too,— a resignation hostile to faith, though springing from it. Upon this face which had seemed so angelic until now, there was a stern almost bitter expression. He who had hitherto meditated only on doctrine, had begun to meditate on Fate,— an unhealthy occupation for a priest. Faith dissolves under its action. Nothing disturbs the religious mind more than that bending under the weight of the unknown. Life seems a perpetual succession of misfortunes to which man is forced to submit. We never know from what side the sudden blow will come. Misery and happiness enter or make their exit like unexpected guests. Their laws, their orbit, their principle of gravitation, are beyond man's ken. Virtue does not lead to happiness, nor crime to retribution: conscience has one logic, fate another; and neither coincide. Nothing is foreseen. We live as we can,— from hand to mouth, as it were. Conscience is the straight line, life is the whirlwind which creates above man's head black chaos or blue sky as the case may be. Fate does not practise the art of gradations. Her wheel turns so fast sometimes that we can scarcely distinguish the interval between one revolution and another, or the link between yesterday and to-day. Caudray was a believer whose faith did not exclude reason, and whose priestly training did not shut him out from passion. The religions which impose celibacy on the priesthood know what they are about. Nothing is more destructive to the individuality of a priest than love. All sorts of clouds seemed to darken Caudray's soul.

He had looked too long into Déruchette's eyes.

These two beings evidently worshipped each other.

There was in Caudray's eye the mute adoration of despair.

Déruchette spoke : —

" You must not leave me. I cannot bear it. I thought I could bid you farewell. I cannot. Why did you come yesterday? You should not have come if you were going so soon. I never spoke to you. I loved you, but knew it not. That day, when M. Hérode read the story of Rebecca to us, and when your eyes met mine, my cheeks were like fire, and I thought, ' Oh, how Rebecca must have blushed!' And yet, if any one had told me yesterday that I loved you, I should have laughed at them. It is this that makes our love seem so terrible. It appears almost like an act of treachery. I was not on my guard. I went to church, I saw you, I thought everybody there was like myself. I am not reproaching you; you did nothing to make me love you; you did nothing but look at me; it is not your fault if you look at people; and yet it made me adore you. I did not even suspect it. When you took up the book it was a flood of light; when others took it, it was only a book. You raised your eyes sometimes; you spoke of archangels. Ah, you were my archangel! What you said penetrated my mind at once. Before you came I do not know whether I even believed in God. Since I have known you, I have learned to pray. I used to say to Douce, dress me quickly, lest I should be late at service; and I hastened to the church. I did not know the cause. I said to myself, ' How devout I am becoming!' It is from you that I have learned that I do not go to church for God's service. It is true; I went for your sake. You spoke so well, and when you raised your hands to heaven, you seemed to hold my heart within your two white hands. I was foolish, but I did not know it. Shall I tell you where you did wrong? It was in coming to me in the garden; it was in speaking to me. If you had said nothing, I should have known nothing. If you had gone away I should, perhaps, only have been sad, but now I should die.   Now I know that I love you, you cannot leave me. Of what are you thinking? You do not seem to listen to me."

" You heard what was said last night," Caudray responded.

"Ah me!"

" What can I do against that? "

They were silent for a moment.   Caudray continued:

" There is but one thing left for me to do,— depart."

" And me to die.   Oh, how I wish there was no sea, but only sky. It seems to me as if that would settle all, and that our departure would be the same.   It was wrong to speak to me; oh, why did you speak to me? Do not go! What will become of me?   I tell you I shall die. You will be far away when I am in my grave. Oh, my heart will break!   I am very wretched; yet my uncle is not unkind."

It was the first time in her life that Déruchette had ever said " my uncle."   Until then she had always said " my father."

Caudray stepped back, and made a sign to the boatman. Déruchette heard the sound of the boat-hook on the shingle, and the step of the man on the gunwhale of the boat.

" No! no! " cried Déruchette.

" It must be, Déruchette," replied Caudray.

" No! never! For the sake of an engine, impossible! Did you see that horrible man last night? You cannot leave me thus. You are wise; surely, you can find a way out of this trouble. It is impossible that you bade me come here this morning with the idea of leaving me. I have never done anything to deserve this; you can have no cause to reproach me. Is it by that vessel you intend to sail? I will not let you go. You shall not leave me! Heaven does not open thus to close so soon. I know you will remain. Besides, it is not yet time. Oh, how I love you! "

And pressing close to him, she interlaced the fingers of both her hands behind his neck, as if partly to make a bond of her two arms for detaining him, and partly, with clasped hands, to pray.

But he put her gently from him in spite of her determined resistance.

Déruchette sank down upon a projecting rock covered with ivy. As she did so, she unconsciously pushed the sleeve of her dress up to the elbow, showing her beautiful bare arm. There was a strangely haggard look in her eyes. The boat was approaching.

Caudray took her head between his hands. The maiden had the air of a widow, and the youth that of a grandfather.

He touched her hair with a sort of reverent care, fixed his eyes upon her for some moments, then kissed her tenderly but solemnly on the forehead, and in accents trembling with anguish, and which plainly revealed the struggle in his soul, he uttered the word which has so often resounded in the depths of the human heart, " Farewell! "

Déruchette burst into loud sobs.

At this moment they heard a voice near them, which said solemnly and deliberately : —

" Why do you not marry? "

Caudray raised his head. Déruchette looked up.

Gilliatt stood before them.

He had approached by a side path.

He did not look like the same man they had seen the night before. He had arranged his hair, shaved off his beard, put on his shoes and stockings, and a white shirt, with a broad collar turned over sailor fashion. He wore a sailor's costume, but every article was new. He had a gold ring on his little finger. He seemed perfectly calm.

His sunburnt skin had become pale.

They gazed at him astonished. Though so changed, Déruchette recognized him. But the words he had spoken were so foreign to what was passing in their minds at that moment, that they left no distinct impression.

Gilliatt spoke again.

"Why should you say farewell? Become man and wife, and go together."

Déruchette started. A nervous trembling shook her from head to foot.

"Miss Lethierry is of age," Gilliatt continued. "It depends entirely upon herself. Her uncle is only her uncle. You love each other —"

"How came you here?" Déruchette interrupted in a gentle voice.

"Make yourselves one," repeated Gilliatt.

Déruchette began to have some idea of the meaning of his words.

"My poor uncle!" she stammered out.

"If the marriage was still to take place he would refuse," said Gilliatt. "When it is over he will consent. Besides, you are going to leave Guernsey. When you return he will forgive you."

"Besides, he is thinking of nothing just now but the rebuilding of his boat," Gilliatt added, with a slight touch of bitterness. "This will occupy his mind during your absence. The Durande will console him."

"I cannot," said Déruchette, in a state of stupor which was not without its gleam of joy. "I cannot leave him unhappy."

"It will be only for a short time," answered Gilliatt.

Caudray and Déruchette had been, as it were, bewildered. They began partially to recover themselves now. The meaning of Gilliatt's words grew plainer as their surprise diminished. There was still a slight doubt in their minds, but they were not inclined to resist. We yield easily to those who come to save us. Objections to a return into paradise are weak. There was something in the attitude of Déruchette, as she leaned imperceptibly upon her lover, which seemed to make common cause with Gilliatt's words. The strangeness of this man's presence, and of his utterances, which, in the mind of Déruchette in particular, created intense astonishment, was a thing quite apart. He said to them, "Become

man and wife!" This was clear; if there was any responsibility, he assumed it. Déruchette had a vague feeling that
he, for many reasons, had a right to decide her fate. Caudray murmured thoughtfully,—

"True, an uncle is not a father."

His resolution was weakened by this sudden and fortunate
turn in affairs. The scruples of the clergyman melted in
the flame, in his love for Déruchette.

Gilliatt's tone became abrupt and harsh, and one could
detect a feverish pulsation in it.

"There must be no delay," he said curtly. "The 'Cashmere' sails in two hours. You have just time, but that is
all. Come."

Caudray surveyed him attentively, then suddenly exclaimed,—

"I recognize you. It was you who saved my life."

"I think not," Gilliatt replied.

"Yonder," said Caudray, "at the extremity of the
Banques."

"I do not know the place," said Gilliatt.

"It was on the very day I arrived here."

"Let us lose no time," interrupted Gilliatt.

"And if I am not mistaken you are the man we saw last
night."

"Possibly."

"What is your name?"

Gilliatt raised his voice:—

"Boatman! wait here for us. We shall return soon. You
asked me, Miss Lethierry, how I came to be here. The answer
is very simple. I followed you. You are twenty-one. In
this country, when persons are of age, and depend only on
themselves, they can be married when they please. Let us
take the path along the beach. It is passable; the tide will
not rise till noon. But we must lose no time. Come with me."

Déruchette and Caudray seemed to consult each other by
a glance. They were standing close together, motionless.
They were intoxicated with joy, but there is a strange hesi-

tation sometimes on the very threshold of happiness. They understood, as it were, without understanding.

" His name is Gilliatt," whispered Déruchette.

Gilliatt interrupted them with a tone of authority.

" What do you linger for? " he asked. " I tell you to follow me."

" Whither? " asked Caudray.

" There! "

And Gilliatt pointed toward the spire of the church.

Gilliatt walked on ahead, and they followed him. His step was firm, but they walked unsteadily.

As they approached the church, a dawning smile became visible on the pure and beautiful countenances of the two lovers. In the hollow eyes of Gilliatt there was the darkness of despair.

The beholder might have imagined that he saw a spectre leading two souls to paradise.

Caudray and Déruchette scarcely realized what had happened.

The interposition of this man was like the branch clutched at by the drowning. They followed their guide with the docility of despair, leaning on the first comer. Those who feel themselves near death easily accept the accident which seems to save. Déruchette, being most ignorant of life, was more confident. Caudray was thoughtful. Déruchette was of age, it is true. The English formalities of marriage are simple, especially in primitive regions, where the clergyman has almost a discretionary power; but would the dean consent to celebrate the marriage without even inquiring whether the uncle consented? This was the question. Nevertheless, they would soon learn. At all events, the attempt would afford them a respite.

But who was this man? And if it was really he whom Lethierry had declared should be his son-in-law the night before, what could be the meaning of his actions? The very obstacle itself seemed to have become a kind providence. Caudray yielded; but his yielding was only the hasty and

14

tacit assent of a man who feels himself saved from despair.

The pathway was uneven and sometimes wet and difficult to pass. Caudray, absorbed in thought, did not observe the occasional pools of water or the heaps of gravel. But from time to time Gilliatt turned and said to him, " Take heed of those stones. Give her your hand."

CHAPTER III

THE FORETHOUGHT OF SELF-SACRIFICE

THE clock struck ten as they entered the church. By reason of the early hour, and also on account of the deserted condition of the town that day, the church was empty.

At the farther end, however, near the table which in the reformed church fills the place of an altar, there were three persons,— the dean, his curate, and the registrar. The dean, who was the Reverend Jaquemin Hérode, was seated: the curate and the registrar stood beside him.

An open Bible lay on the table.

Beside the dean, upon a credence-table, was another book. It was the parish register. That, too, was open, and an observant eye might have detected a freshly written page on which the ink was not yet dry. A pen and writing materials lay beside the register.

The Reverend Jaquemin Hérode rose on perceiving Caudray.

" I have been expecting you," he said. " All is ready."

The dean, in fact, was attired in his clerical robes.

Caudray glanced at Gilliatt.

The Reverend Doctor added, " I am at your service, brother ; " and bowed.

It was a bow which turned neither to right nor left. It

was evident from the direction of the dean's glance that he did not recognize the existence of any one but Caudray, for Caudray was a clergyman and a gentleman. Neither Déruchette, who stood a little to one side, nor Gilliatt, who was in the rear, were included in the salutation. In his look was a sort of tacit understanding in which Caudray alone was included. The observance of these little niceties constitutes an important feature in the maintenance of order and the preservation of society.

The dean, with a graceful and dignified urbanity, continued: —

"I congratulate you, my colleague, from a double point of view. You have lost your uncle, and are about to take a wife; you are blessed with riches on the one hand, and happiness on the other. Moreover, thanks to the boat which they are about to rebuild, Mess Lethierry, too, will be rich, — which is as it should be. Miss Lethierry was born in this parish; I have verified the date of her birth in the register. She is of age, and her own mistress. Her uncle, too, who is her only relative, consents. You are anxious to be united immediately on account of your approaching departure.

"This I can understand; but it being the marriage of the rector of the parish, I should have been gratified to have seen it attended with a little more solemnity. I will consult your wishes by not detaining you longer than necessary. The essentials will be soon complied with. The form is already drawn up in the register, and only the names remain to be filled in. By the provisions of the law and custom, the marriage can be celebrated immediately after the issue of the license. The declaration necessary for the license has been duly made. I will hold myself responsible for a slight irregularity, inasmuch as the application for a license ought to have been registered seven days in advance; but I yield to necessity and the urgency of your departure. Be it so, then. I will proceed with the ceremony. My curate will be the witness for the bridegroom; as regards the witness for the bride —"

The dean turned towards Gilliatt. Gilliatt made a movement of his head.

" That is sufficient," said the dean.

Caudray remained motionless ; Déruchette was happy, but equally powerless to move.

" Nevertheless," continued the dean, " there is still one obstacle."

Déruchette started.

The dean continued : —

" The representative here present of Mess Lethierry applied for the license for you and signed the declaration on the register." And with the thumb of his left hand the dean pointed to Gilliatt, which prevented the necessity of pronouncing his name. " The messenger from Mess Lethierry," he added, " informed me this morning that being too much occupied to come in person, Mess Lethierry desired that the marriage should take place immediately. This desire expressed verbally, is not sufficient. In consequence of the slight irregularity attending the issue of the license, which I take upon myself, I cannot proceed so hastily without making a personal inquiry of Mess Lethierry, unless some one can produce his signature. However great my desire to serve you, I cannot be satisfied with a mere verbal message. I must have some written authority."

" That need not delay us," said Gilliatt, handing a paper to the dean. The dean took it, scanned it hastily, seemed to pass over some lines as unimportant, and read aloud : " Go to the dean for the license. I wish the marriage to take place as soon as possible. Immediately would be better."

He placed the paper on the table, and proceeded : —

" It bears Lethierry's signature. It would have been more respectful to have addressed it to me. But as it is a question of serving a colleague, I ask no more."

Caudray glanced again at Gilliatt. There are moments when mind and mind comprehend each other. Caudray felt that there was some deception but he had not the strength, perhaps he had not even the desire, to reveal it. Whether from obedience to a latent heroism which he but imperfectly divined, or whether from a deadening of the conscience, arising from the suddenness with which happiness had been placed within his reach, he uttered not a word.

The dean took the pen, and aided by the clerk, filled up the blanks on the page of the register; then rose, and by a gesture invited Caudray and Déruchette to approach the table.

The ceremony was begun.

It was a strange moment. Caudray and Déruchette stood side by side before the minister.

One who has ever dreamed of a marriage in which he himself was chief actor, may conceive of the feeling which they experienced.

Gilliatt stood at a little distance in the shadow of the pillars.

Déruchette, on rising that morning, unspeakably wretched and despairing, and thinking only of death and the winding-sheet, had dressed herself in white. The attire, which had been associated in her mind with the grave, was well suited to her nuptials. A white dress is all that is necessary for a bride.

Her face was radiant with happiness. Never had she appeared more beautiful. Her features were remarkable for prettiness rather than beauty. Their only fault, if fault it be, lay in a certain excess of grace. Déruchette in repose,— that is, neither disturbed by passion nor grief,— was graceful above all.

A face like this transfigured is our ideal of the Virgin. Déruchette, touched by sorrow and love, seemed to have caught that nobler and more holy expression. It makes the difference between the field daisy and the lily.

The tears had scarcely dried upon her cheeks; one perhaps still lingered in the midst of her smiles. Traces of tears indistinctly visible form a pleasing but touching accompaniment of joy.

The dean, standing near the table, placed his hand upon

the open book, and asked in a distinct voice whether they knew of any impediment to their union.

There was no reply.

Caudray and Déruchette advanced a step or two towards the table.

" Joseph Ebenezer, wilt thou have this woman to be thy wedded wife? " asked the dean.

Caudray replied, " I will."

" Durande Déruchette, wilt thou have this man to be thy wedded husband? " the dean continued.

Déruchette, in an agony of soul, springing from her very excess of happiness, murmured rather than uttered:

" I will."

Then followed the beautiful form of the Anglican marriage service.

The dean looked around, and in the dim light of the church, uttered the solemn words:

" Who giveth this woman to be married to this man? "

Gilliatt answered, " I do! "

There was an interval of silence.   Caudray and Déruchette felt a vague sense of oppression in spite of their joy.

The dean placed Déruchette's right hand in Caudray's; and Caudray repeated after him: —

" I take thee, Durande Déruchette, to be my wedded wife for better for worse, for richer for poorer, in sickness and in health, to love and to cherish till death do us part; and thereto I plight thee my troth."

The dean then placed Caudray's right hand in that of Déruchette, and Déruchette said after him: —

" I take thee to be my wedded husband for better for worse, for richer for poorer, in sickness or in health, to love, cherish, and obey, till death do us part; and thereto I plight thee my troth."

" Where is the ring? " asked the dean.

The question took them by surprise.   Caudray had no ring; but Gilliatt removed the gold ring which he wore upon his little finger.   It was doubtless the wedding-ring which had

been sold that morning by the jeweller in the Commercial
Arcade.

The dean laid the ring on the Bible; then handed it to
Caudray, who took Déruchette's little trembling hand, slipped
the ring on her fourth finger, and said:

"With this ring I thee wed!"

"In the name of the Father, and of the Son, and of the
Holy Ghost," continued the dean.

"Amen," said his curate.

Then the dean said, "Let us pray."

Caudray and Déruchette turned towards the table, and
knelt down.

Gilliatt, standing near, inclined his head.

They knelt before God; he was bending beneath the burden
of his fate.

CHAPTER IV

"FOR YOUR WIFE: WHEN YOU MARRY"

AS they left the church they could see the "Cashmere"
making preparations for departure.

"You are in time," said Gilliatt.

They again took the path leading to the Havelet.

Caudray and Déruchette went first; Gilliatt, this time,
walking behind them. They were like two somnambulists.
Their bewilderment had not passed away, but only changed
in form. They took no heed of where they were going, or of
what they did. They hurried on mechanically, scarcely conscious of the existence of anything,— feeling that they were
united forever, but scarcely able to connect two ideas in their
minds. In ecstasy like theirs it is as impossible to think as
it is to swim in a torrent. In the midst of their trouble and
despair they had been raised to the seventh heaven of delight.

They were in Elysium. They did not speak, but their souls were absorbed in sweet communion.

The footsteps of Gilliatt behind them reminded them of his presence now and then. They were deeply moved, but could find no words. Such excess of emotion results in stupor; theirs was delightful but overwhelming. They were man and wife: every other idea was secondary to that. Gilliatt had done them an inestimable kindness; that was all that they could grasp. In their secret hearts, they thanked him fervently, profoundly, Déruchette felt that there was some mystery to be explained later, but not now. Meanwhile they accepted their unexplained happiness. They submitted to the decision of this determined man who made them happy as if he had a right to do it. To question him, to talk with him, seemed impossible. Too many impressions were rushing upon them at once for that. Their mental absorption was pardonable.

Events sometimes succeed each other with the rapidity of hailstones. Their effect is overpowering; they deaden the senses and render incidents incomprehensible even to those whom they chiefly concern. We become scarcely conscious of our own adventures; we are overwhelmed without guessing the cause, or crowned with happiness without realizing it. For some hours Déruchette had been subjected to every kind of emotion: first, surprise and delight at meeting Caudray in the garden; then horror at the monster whom her uncle had presented to her as her husband; then anguish when the angel of her dreams spread his wings and seemed about to depart; and now joy, such joy as she had never known before, founded on an inexplicable enigma,— the restoration of her lover by the very monster who had so horrified her.

Gilliatt, her evil destiny of last night, to-day became her saviour! She could not explain it satisfactorily to her own mind. It was evident that Gilliatt had devoted the entire morning to preparing the way for their marriage. He had done everything; he had answered for Mess Lethierry, seen the dean, obtained the licence, signed the necessary declaration, and thus the marriage had been rendered possible. But Déruchette did not understand it. Even if she had, she would not have comprehended the reasons.

She could do nothing but close her eyes, and gratefully yield herself up to the guidance of this good spirit. There was no time for explanations, and expressions of gratitude seemed too insignificant.

The little power of thought which they retained was scarcely more than sufficient to guide them on their way, to enable them to distinguish the sea from the land, and the " Cashmere " from any other vessel.

In a few minutes they reached the little landing.

Caudray entered the boat first. As Déruchette was about to follow, she felt some one pluck her gently by the sleeve. It was Gilliatt who had placed a finger upon a fold of her dress.

" Madam," he said, " you are starting on a journey very unexpectedly. It has struck me that you will have need of dresses and linen. You will find a trunk aboard the ' Cashmere,' containing a lady's clothing. It came to me from my mother. It was intended for my wife if I should ever marry. Permit me to ask your acceptance of it."

Déruchette, partially aroused from her dream, turned towards him. In a voice that was scarcely audible, Gilliatt continued : —

" I do not wish to detain you, madam, but I feel that I ought to give you some explanation. On the day of the misfortune, you were sitting in the lower room ; you uttered certain words. It is not at all strange that you have forgotten them. We cannot be expected to remember every word we speak. Mess Lethierry was in great trouble. It was certainly a noble vessel, and one that did good service. The misfortune was recent ; there was a great excitement. There are things which one naturally forgets. It was only a vessel wrecked among the rocks ; one cannot be always thinking of an accident. But what I wished to tell you was that as it was said that no one would go, I went. They said it was impossible; but it was not. I thank you for listening to me a moment. You can understand, madam, that if I went there, it was not with the thought of displeasing you. This is a thing, besides, of old date. I know that you are in haste. If there was time, if we could talk about this, you might perhaps remember. But this is all useless now. The history of it goes back to a day when there was snow upon the ground. And then on one occasion, as I passed you, I thought you looked kindly on me. That is how it all happened. With regard to last night, I had not had time to go to my home. I came from my labour; I was all torn and ragged; I startled you, and you fainted. I was to blame; people do not go like that to strangers' houses; I ask your forgiveness. That is about all I wanted to say. You are about to sail. You will have fine weather; the wind is in the east. Farewell. You will not blame me for troubling you with these things. This is the last minute, you know."

"I am thinking of the trunk you spoke of," replied Déruchette. "Why do you not keep it for your wife, when you marry?"

"It is not likely that I shall ever marry, madam," replied Gilliatt.

"That would be a pity," said Déruchette; "you are so good. Thank you."

And Déruchette smiled. Gilliatt returned her smile. Then he assisted her into the boat.

In less than a quarter of an hour Caudray and Déruchette were aboard the " Cashmere."

CHAPTER V

THE GREAT TOMB

GILLIATT walked swiftly along the beach, passed hastily through St. Peter's Port, and then hurried towards St. Sampson by way of the shore. In his anxiety to avoid people he knew, he shunned the highways now crowded with pedestrians excited over his great achievement.

For a long time, as the reader knows, he had had a way of traversing the country in every direction without being seen by any one. He knew all the by-paths, and preferred lonely and circuitous routes; he had the shy habits of a wild beast who knows that he is disliked, and keeps at a distance. When quite a child, he had been quick to feel how little welcome men showed in their faces at his approach, and he had gradually contracted that habit of holding himself aloof which had since become an instinct.

He passed the Esplanade, then the Salerie. Now and then he turned and looked behind him at the " Cashmere " in the roads, which had just set sail. There was very little wind, and Gilliatt moved faster than the vessel as he walked with downcast eyes among the rocks on the water's edge. The tide was beginning to rise.

Suddenly he paused, and, turning his back upon the sea, contemplated for some minutes a clump of oaks beyond the rocks that hid the road to Vale. They were the oaks at the spot called the Basses Maisons. It was there that Déruchette once wrote the name of Gilliatt in the snow. Many a day had passed since that snow had melted away.

He continued on his way.

The day was beautiful,— more beautiful than any that had been seen that year. It was one of those spring days when May suddenly pours forth all its beauty, and when Nature seems to have no thought but to rejoice and be happy.

Amid the many murmurs from forest and village, from the sea
and the air, a sound of cooing could be distinguished. The
first butterflies of the year were resting on the early roses.
Everything in Nature seemed new,— the grass, the mosses, the
leaves, the perfumes, even the rays of light. The sun shone
as if it had never shone before. The pebbles seemed bathed
in coolness. Birds but lately fledged sang from the trees, or
fluttered among the boughs in their attempts to use their
new-found wings. There was a combined chattering of gold-
finches, pewits, tomtits, woodpeckers, bullfinches, and thrushes.
Lilacs, lilies of the valley, daphnes, and melilots mingled their
hues in the thickets. A beautiful aquatic plant peculiar to
Guernsey covered with an emerald green the pools where the
kingfishers and the water-wagtails, which make such graceful
little nests, came down to bathe. Through every opening in
the branches appeared the deep blue sky. A few wanton
clouds chased each other along the azure sky, with the undulating grace of nymphs. The ear seemed to catch the sound
of kisses wafted from invisible lips. Every old wall had its
bunch of gillyflowers like a bridegroom. The plum-trees and
laburnums were in bloom; their white and yellow blossoms
gleamed through the interlacing boughs. The spring had
showered all her gold and silver on the woods. The new
shoots and leaves were green and fresh. Calls of welcome were
in the air; the approaching summer opened her hospitable
doors for birds coming from afar. It was the time of the
arrival of the swallows. Clumps of furze-bushes bordered the
steep sides of the roads until it should be time for the haw-
thorn. The pretty and the beautiful reigned side by side;
the magnificent and the graceful, the great and the small.
No note in the grand concert of Nature was lost. Microscopic
beauties took their place in the vast universal plan in which
everything was as distinguishable as if seen in limpid water.
Everywhere a divine fulness, a mysterious sense of expansion,
suggested the unseen workings of the moving sap. Glittering
things glittered more than ever; loving natures seemed to
become more tender. There was a hymn in the flowers, and a

radiance in the sounds of the air. The widely diffused harmony of Nature burst forth on every side. All things that felt the dawn of life invited others to put forth shoots. A movement coming from below, and also from above, stirred vaguely every heart susceptible to the powerful though covert influence of germination. The flower gave promise of the fruit; young maidens dreamed of love. It was Nature's universal bridal. It was sunny and bright and warm; through the hedges in the meadows children could be seen laughing and playing games. The apple, peach, cherry, and pear trees filled the orchards with their masses of white and pink blossoms. In the fields were primroses, cowslips, milfoil, daffodils, daisies, speedwell, hyacinths, St. John's wort, violets, blue borage and yellow irises, together with those beautiful little pink star-shaped flowers which are always found in large patches, and which are consequently called " companions." Insects covered with golden scales glided between the stones. The flowering houseleek covered the thatched roofs with purple bloom; and the bees were abroad, mingling their humming with the murmurs from the sea.

When Gilliatt reached St. Sampson, the water had not yet risen at the farther end of the harbour, and he was able to cross it dry-shod and unobserved, behind the hulls of several vessels drawn up for repairs. A number of flat stones placed at regular distances were of great assistance to him in crossing. He was not noticed. The crowd was at the other end of the port near the narrow entrance, by the Bravées. There, his name was in everybody's mouth. They were, in fact, talking so much about him that no one paid attention to him. He passed, protected to some extent by the very commotion he had caused.

He saw the sloop lying where he had moored it, with the funnel standing between its four chains, the movements of carpenters at work, and confused outlines of figures passin to and fro; and he could distinguish the loud and cherry vo'c of Mess Lethierry giving orders.

He threaded the narrow alleys behind the Bravées. There

was no one else there. Public curiosity was concentrated on
the front of the house. He chose the footpath that skirted the
low wall of the garden, but stopped at the angle where the
wild mallow grew. He saw once more the big stone where he
used to spend his time,— the wooden bench where Déruchette
was wont to sit, and glanced again at the path where he had
seen the shadow of two forms which had vanished from his
gaze forever.

He soon went on his way, climbed the hill of Vale Castle,
descended it, and directed his steps towards the Bu de la Rue.

The Houmet-Paradis was a solitude.

His house was exactly as he had left it that morning after
dressing himself to go to St. Peter's Port.

A window was open, through which his bagpipe might
have been seen hanging to a nail upon the wall. Upon the
table was the little Bible given to him as a token of gratitude
by the stranger whom he now knew as Caudray.

The key was in the door. He approached, placed his hand
upon it, turned it twice in the lock, then put it in his pocket,
and departed.

He did not walk in the direction of the town, but towards
the sea.

He crossed the garden diagonally, taking the shortest cut
without regard to the beds, but taking care not to tread upon
the plants which he had placed there because he heard that
they were favourites with Déruchette.

He climbed the parapet, and let himself down upon the
rocks below. Going straight on, he began to follow the long
ridge which connected the Bu de la Rue with the huge granite
obelisk rising perpendicularly out of the sea, and known as
the Beast's Horn.

The famous Gild-Holm-'Ur seat was on this rock.

He strode from rock to rock like a giant striding over
mountain peaks. To make long strides over a ridge of
jagged rocks is like walking on the ridge of a roof.

A fisherwoman with dredge-nets, who had been wading bare-
footed among the pools of sea-water, and had just regained

the shore, called out to him, " Take care! The tide is coming in."

But he hastened on.

Having reached the big rock on the point,— the Horn, which rises like a pinnacle out of the sea,— he stopped. It was the extreme end of the promontory.

He looked around.

Out at sea were a few fishing-boats at anchor. From time to time, little rivulets of silver streamed from them in the sun,— it was the water running from the nets. The " Cashmere " was not yet off St. Sampson. She had set her maintopsail, and was between Herm and Jethou.

Gilliatt walked around to the other side of the rock, and came up under the Gild-Holm-'Ur seat, at the foot of the steep stairs where he had helped Caudray down less than three months before. He ascended.

Most of the steps were already under water. Only two or three were still dry. He mounted them.

The steps led up to the Gild-Holm-'Ur. He reached the niche, gazed at it for a moment, pressed his hand on his eyes, and let it glide gently from one eyelid to the other,— a gesture by which he seemed to obliterate the memory of the past, — then sat down in the hollow, with the perpendicular wall behind him and the ocean at his feet.

The " Cashmere " at that moment was passing the great round sea-washed tower, defended by one serjeant and a cannon, which marks half the distance between Herm and St. Peter's Port.

A few flowers waved among the crevices in the rock above Gilliatt's head. The sea was blue as far as eye could reach. The wind came from the east; there was a little surf in the direction of the island of Sark, of which only the western end is visible from Guernsey. In the distance one could dimly discern the coast of France like a line of mist, and the long strip of yellow sand at Carteret. Now and then a white butterfly fluttered by. Butterflies frequently fly out to sea.

The breeze was scarcely perceptible. The blue expanse

above as well as below was perfectly tranquil. Not a ripple agitated those serpent-like lines of more or less intense azure which indicate the contour of the reefs below.

The " Cashmere," making but slight progress, had set her topsail and studdingsails to catch the breeze. All her canvas was spread, but the wind being a side one, her studdingsails only compelled her to hug the Guernsey coast more closely.

She had passed the St. Sampson beacon, and was off the hill of Vale Castle. The moment was fast approaching when she would round Bu de la Rue Point.

Gilliatt watched her approach.

The air and sea were still. The tide rose not in waves, but by an imperceptible swell. The level of the water crept upwards, without any palpitation. The subdued murmur from the open sea was soft as the breathing of a child.

In the direction of the harbour of St. Sampson, the sound of carpenters' hammers could be faintly heard. The carpenters were probably at work constructing the tackle, gear, and apparatus for removing the engine from the sloop.

The sounds, however, scarcely reached Gilliatt by reason of the mass of granite at his back.

The " Cashmere " approached with the slowness of a phantom ship.

Gilliatt watched it intently.

Suddenly a touch and a sensation of cold caused him to look down. The sea had reached his feet.

He lowered his eyes, then raised them again.

The " Cashmere " was quite near now.

The side of the rock in which the rains had hollowed out the Gild-Holm-'Ur seat was so completely vertical, and there was so much water at its base, that in calm weather vessels were able to pass within a few cables' lengths of it without danger.

The " Cashmere " was abreast of the rock. It rose straight upwards as if it had grown out of the water; or like the lengthening out of a shadow.

The rigging stood out darkly against the sky and in the

magnificent expanse of the sea. The tall sails, passing for a
moment between the beholder and the sun, became illumined
with a singular glory and transparency. The water murmured softly, but no sound attended the majestic passing of
the vessel. The deck was as plainly visible to Gilliatt as if he
had been standing upon it.

The " Cashmere " almost grazed the rock.

The steersman was at the helm, a cabin-boy was climbing
the shrouds, a few passengers were leaning over the bulwarks
contemplating the beauty of the scene, the captain was smoking; but Gilliatt saw nothing of all this.

There was a nook on deck on which the broad sunlight fell.
It was on this corner that Gilliatt's eyes were fixed. In the
sunlight there, sat Déruchette and Caudray. They were sitting together side by side, like two birds, warming themselves
in the noonday sun, upon one of those covered seats with a
little awning which well-ordered packet-boats provided for
passengers, and which were marked " For ladies only," when
they happened to be on an English vessel. Déruchette's head
was resting on Caudray's shoulder; his arm was around her
waist; they held each other's hands with their fingers inter-
woven. A celestial light beamed on these two beautiful and
innocent faces, one so virginal, the other so heavenly in expression. Their chaste embrace was indicative at the same
time of their earthly union and their purity of soul. The
seat was a sort of alcove, almost a nest; at the same time it
formed a sort of halo around them,— the tender aureole of
love melting into a cloud.

The silence was like the silence of heaven.

Caudray's gaze was fixed in rapt contemplation. Déruchette's lips moved; and in that perfect silence, as the wind
carried the vessel near shore, and it glided within a few feet
of the Gild-Holm-'Ur, Gilliatt heard the soft and musical
voice of Déruchette exclaiming:

" Look yonder! It seems as if there were a man upon the
rock."

The vessel passed on.

15

Leaving the promontory of the Bu de la Rue behind her, the " Cashmere " glided out upon the broad expanse. In less than a quarter of an hour, her masts and sails formed upon the water merely a sort of white obelisk rapidly diminishing in size. Gilliatt felt that the water had reached his knees.

He watched the vessel speeding on her way.

The breeze freshened. He could see the " Cashmere " run out her lower studdingsails and her staysails in order to take advantage of the rising wind. She was already out of the waters of Guernsey. Gilliatt followed the vessel with his eyes. The waves had reached his waist.

The tide was rising. Time was passing.

The sea-mews and cormorants circled excitedly around him, as if trying to warn him of his danger. Perhaps some of his old companions of the Douvres were among them and had recognized him.

An hour passed.

The wind from the sea was scarcely felt in the roads; but the outlines of the " Cashmere " were rapidly fading in the distance. The sloop, according to all appearance, was sailing fast. It was already nearly off the Caskets.

But there was no foam around the Gild-Holm-'Ur; no wave beat against its granite sides. The water rose peacefully. It was nearly up to Gilliatt's shoulders.

Another hour passed.

The " Cashmere " was beyond the waters of Alderney. The Ortachs concealed it from view for a moment; it passed behind the rocks and emerged again as from an eclipse. The sloop was hastening northward. It was only a white speck now glittering in the sunlight.

The birds were still hovering over Gilliatt, uttering short, shrill cries.

Only his head was visible now. The tide was nearly at the flood.

Gilliatt was still watching the " Cashmere."

Evening was approaching. Behind him, in the roads, a few fishing-boats were returning home.

"Only his head was visible now. The tide was nearly at the flood."

Toilers of the Sea. Vol. II, Page 226.

Gilliatt's eyes remained fixed upon the vessel in the distant horizon.

Their expression resembled nothing earthly. A strange lustre shone in their calm yet tragic depths. There was in them the knowledge of hopes never to be realized; the calm but sorrowful acceptance of an end widely different from his dreams; the solemn acceptance of an accomplished fact. The flight of a star might be followed by such a gaze. By degrees the shadow of approaching death began to darken them, though they were still riveted upon that point in space. The wide water around the Gild-Holm-'Ur and the vast gathering twilight closed in upon them at the same instant.

The " Cashmere," now scarcely perceptible, had become a mere spot in the thin haze. Gradually, this spot grew paler. Then it dwindled still more. Then it disappeared altogether.

As the vessel vanished from sight in the horizon, the head of Gilliatt disappeared beneath the water. Nothing was visible now but the sea.

THE END

BUG-JARGAL

BUG-JARGAL

PROLOGUE

WHEN it came to the turn of Captain Leopold d'Auverney, he gazed around him with surprise, and hurriedly assured his comrades that he did not remember any incident in his life that was worthy of repetition.

"But, Captain d'Auverney," objected Lieutenant Henri, "you have — at least report says so — travelled much, and seen a good deal of the world; have you not been to the Antilles, to Africa, and to Italy? and above all, you have been in Spain. But see, here is your lame dog come back again!"

D'Auverney started, let fall the cigar that he was smoking, and turned quickly to the tent door, at which an enormous dog appeared, limping towards him.

In another instant the dog was licking his feet, wagging his tail, whining, and gambolling as well as he was able; and by every means testifying his delight at finding his master; and at last, as if he felt that he had done all that could be required of a dog, he curled himself up peaceably before his master's seat.

Captain d'Auverney was much moved, but he strove to conceal his feelings, and mechanically caressed the dog with one hand, while with the other he played with the chin-strap of his shako, murmuring from time to time, "So here you are once again, Rask, here you are!" Then, as if suddenly recollecting himself, he exclaimed aloud, "But who has brought him back?"

"By your leave, Captain —"

1

For the last few seconds Sergeant Thaddeus had been standing at the door of the tent, the curtain of which he was holding back with his left hand, while his right was thrust into the bosom of his great-coat. Tears were in his eyes as he contemplated the meeting of the dog and his master, and at last, unable to keep silence any longer, he risked the words, " By your leave, Captain."

D'Auverney raised his eyes.

" Why, it is you, Thaddeus? and how the deuce have you been able — eh? Poor dog, poor Rask! I thought that you were in the English camp. Where did you find him, Sergeant? "

" Thanks be to Heaven, Captain, you see me as happy as your little nephew used to be when you let him off his Latin lesson."

" But tell me, where *did* you find him? "

" I did not find him, Captain; I went to look for him."

Captain d'Auverney rose, and offered his hand to the sergeant, but the latter still kept his in the bosom of his coat.

" Well, you see, it was — at least, Captain, since poor Rask was lost, I noticed that you were like a man beside himself; so when I saw that he did not come to me in the evening, according to his custom, for his share of my ration bread,— which made old Thaddeus weep like a child; I, who before that had only wept twice in my life, the first time when — yes, the day when —" and the sergeant cast a sad look upon his captain. " Well, the second was when that scamp Balthazar, the corporal of the Seventh half brigade, persuaded me to peel a bunch of onions."

" It seems to me, Thaddeus," cried Henri, with a laugh, " that you avoid telling us what was the first occasion upon which you shed tears."

" It was doubtless, old comrade," said the captain kindly, as he patted Rask's head, " when you answered the roll-call as Tour d'Auvergne, the first grenadier of France."

" No, no, Captain; if Sergeant Thaddeus wept, it was

when he gave the order to fire on Bug-Jargal, otherwise called Pierrot."

A cloud gathered on the countenance of D'Auverney, then he again endeavoured to clasp the sergeant's hand; but in spite of the honour that was attempted to be conferred on him, the old man still kept his hand hidden under his coat.

" Yes, Captain," continued Thaddeus, drawing back a step or two, while D'Auverney fixed his eyes upon him with a strange and sorrowful expression,—" yes, I wept for him that day, and he well deserved it. He was black, it is true, but gunpowder is black also; and — and —"

The good sergeant would fain have followed out his strange comparison, for there was evidently something in the idea that pleased him; but he utterly failed to put his thoughts into words, and after having attacked his idea on every side, as a general would a fortified place, and failed, he raised the siege, and without noticing the smiles of his officers, he continued: —

" Tell me, Captain, do you recollect how that poor negro arrived all out of breath, at the moment when his ten comrades were waiting on the spot? We had had to tie them, though. It was I who commanded the party; and with his own hands he untied them, and took their place, although they did all that they could to dissuade him; but he was inflexible. Ah, what a man he was; you might as well have tried to move Gibraltar! And then, Captain, he drew himself up as if he were going to enter a ball-room, and this dog, who knew well enough what was coming, flew at my throat —"

" Generally, Thaddeus, at this point of your story you pat Rask," interrupted the captain; " see how he looks at you."

" You are right, sir," replied Thaddeus, with an air of embarrassment; " he *does* look at me, poor fellow; but the old woman Malajuda told me it was unlucky to pat a dog with the left hand, and —"

" And why not with your right, pray? " asked D'Auverney, for the first time noticing the sergeant's pallor, and the hand reposing in his bosom.

The sergeant's discomfort appeared to increase. " By your leave, Captain, it is because — well, you have got a lame dog, and now there is a chance of your having a one-handed sergeant."

" A one-handed sergeant! What do you mean? Let me see your arm. One hand! Great heavens! "

D'Auverney trembled, as the sergeant slowly withdrew his hand from his bosom, and showed it enveloped in a blood-stained handkerchief.

" This is terrible," exclaimed D'Auverney, carefully un-doing the bandage. " But tell me, old comrade, how this happened."

" As for that, the thing is simple enough. I told you how I had noticed your grief since those confounded English had taken away your dog,— poor Rask, Bug's dog. I made up my mind to-day to bring him back, even if it cost me my life, so that you might eat a good supper. After having told Mathelet, your *bât* man, to get out and brush your full-dress uniform, as we are to go into action to-morrow, I crept quietly out of camp, armed only with my sabre, and crouched under the hedges until I neared the English camp. I had not passed the first trench when I saw a whole crowd of red soldiers. I crept on quietly to see what they were doing, and in the midst of them I perceived Rask tied to a tree; while two of the *milords*, stripped to here, were knocking each other about with their fists, until their bones sounded like the big drum of the regiment. They were fighting for your dog. But when Rask caught sight of me, he gave such a bound that the rope broke, and in the twinkling of an eye the rogue was after me. I did not stop to explain, but off I ran, with all the English at my heels. A regular hail of balls whistled past my ears. Rask barked, but they could not hear him for their shouts of ' French dog! French dog! ' just as if Rask was not of the pure St. Domingo breed. In spite of all I crushed through the thicket, and had almost got clean away when two red coats confronted me. My sabre accounted for one, and would have rid me of the other had his pistol not unluckily had a bullet in it. My right arm suffered; but ' French dog ' leapt at his throat, as if he were an old acquaintance. Down fell the Englishman, for the embrace was so tight that he was strangled in a moment,— and here we both are. My only regret is that I did not get my wound in to-morrow's battle."

" Thaddeus, Thaddeus ! " exclaimed the captain in tones of reproach; " were you mad enough to expose your life thus for a dog? "

" It was not for a dog, it was for Rask."

D'Auverney's face softened as Thaddeus added: " For Rask, for Bug's dog."

" Enough, enough, old comrade ! " cried the captain, dashing his hand across his eyes; " come, lean on me, and I will lead you to the hospital."

Thaddeus essayed to decline the honour, but in vain; and as they left the tent the dog got up and followed them.

This little drama had excited the curiosity of the spectators to the highest degree. Captain Leopold d'Auverney was one of those men who, in whatever position the chances of nature and society may place them, always inspire a mingled feeling of interest and respect. At the first glimpse there was nothing striking in him,— his manner was reserved, and his look cold. The tropical sun, though it had browned his cheek, had not imparted to him that vivacity of speech and gesture which among the Creoles is united to an easy carelessness of demeanour, in itself full of charm.

D'Auverney spoke little, listened less, but showed himself ready to act at any moment. Always the first in the saddle, and the last to return to camp, he seemed to seek a refuge from his thoughts in bodily fatigue. These thoughts, which had marked his brow with many a premature wrinkle, were not of the kind that you can get rid of by confiding them to a friend; nor could they be discussed in idle conversation. Leopold d'Auverney, whose body the hardships of war could not subdue, seemed to experience a sense of insurmountable fatigue in what is termed the conflict of the feelings. He avoided argument as much as he sought warfare. If at any time he allowed himself to be drawn into a discussion, he would utter a few words full of common-sense and reason, and then at the moment of triumph over his antagonist he would stop short, and muttering " What good is it? " would saunter off to the commanding officer to glean what information he could regarding the enemy's movements. His comrades forgave his cold, reserved, and silent habits, because upon every occasion they had found him kind, gentle, and benevolent. He had saved many a life at the risk of his own, and they well knew that though his mouth was rarely opened, yet his purse was never closed when a comrade had need of his assistance.

D'Auverney was young; many would have guessed him at thirty years of age, but they would have been wrong, for he was some years under it. Although he had for a long period fought in the ranks of the Republican army, yet all were in ignorance of his former life. The only one to whom he seemed ever to open his heart was Sergeant Thaddeus, who had joined the regiment with him, and would at times speak vaguely of sad events in his early life. It was known that D'Auverney had undergone great misfortunes in America; that he had been married in St. Domingo, and that his wife and all his family had perished in those terrible massacres which had marked the Republican invasion of that magnificent colony. At the time of which we write, misfortunes of this kind were so general that any one could sympathize with, and feel pity for, such sufferers.

D'Auverney, therefore, was pitied less for his misfortunes than for the manner in which they had been brought about. Beneath his icy mask of indifference the traces of the incurably wounded spirit could be at times perceived. When he went into action his calmness returned, and in the fight he behaved as if he sought for the rank of general; while after victory he was as gentle and unassuming as if the position of a private soldier would have satisfied his ambition. His comrades, seeing him thus despise honour and promotion, could not understand what it was that lighted up his countenance with a ray of hope when the action commenced, and they did not for a moment divine that the prize D'Auverney was striving to gain was simply — *death*.

The Representatives of the People, in one of their missions to the army, had appointed him a Chief of Brigade on the field of battle; but he had declined the honour upon learning that it would remove him from his old comrade Sergeant Thaddeus. Some days afterwards, having returned from a dangerous expedition safe and sound, contrary to the general expectation and his own hopes, he was heard to regret the rank that he had refused. " For," said he, " since the enemy's guns always spare me, perhaps the guillotine, which ever strikes down those it has raised, would in time have claimed me."

Such was the character of the man upon whom the conversation turned as soon as he had left the tent.

" I would wager," cried Lieutenant Henri, wiping a splash of mud off his boot which the dog had left as he passed him, —" I would wager that the captain would not exchange the broken paw of his dog for the ten baskets of Madeira that we caught a glimpse of in the general's wagon."

" Bah! " cried Paschal the *aide-de-camp*, " that would be a bad bargain: the baskets are empty by now, and thirty empty bottles would be a poor price for a dog's paw; why, you might make a good bell-handle out of it."

They all laughed at the grave manner in which Paschal pronounced these words, with the exception of a young officer of Hussars named Alfred, who remarked,—

" I do not see any subject for chaff in this matter, gentlemen. This sergeant and dog, who are always at D'Auverney's heels ever since I have known him, seem to me more the objects of sympathy than raillery, and interest me greatly."

Paschal, annoyed that his wit had missed fire, interrupted

him: " It certainly is a most sentimental scene; a lost dog found, and a broken arm —"

" Captain Paschal," said Henri, throwing an empty bottle outside the tent, " you are wrong; this Bug, otherwise called Pierrot, excites my curiosity greatly."

At this moment D'Auverney returned, and sat down without uttering a word. His manner was still sad, but his face was more calm; he seemed not to have heard what was said. Rask, who had followed him, lay down at his feet, but kept a watchful eye on his master's comrades.

" Pass your glass, Captain D'Auverney, and taste this."

" Oh, thank you," replied the captain, evidently imagining that he was answering a question, " the wound is not dangerous; there is no bone broken."

The respect which all felt for D'Auverney prevented a burst of laughter at this reply.

" Since your mind is at rest regarding Thaddeus's wound," said Henri, " and, as you may remember, we entered into an agreement to pass away the hours of bivouac by relating to one another our adventures, will you carry out your promise by telling us the history of your lame dog, and of Bug,— otherwise called Pierrot, that regular Gibraltar of a man?"

To this request, which was put in a semi-jocular tone, D'Auverney at last yielded.

" I will do what you ask, gentlemen," said he; " but you must only expect a very simple tale, in which I play an extremely second-rate part. If the affection that exists between Thaddeus, Rask, and myself leads you to expect anything very wonderful, I fear that you will be greatly disappointed. However, I will begin."

For a moment D'Auverney relapsed into thought, as though he wished to recall past events which had long since been replaced in his memory by the acts of his later years; but at last, in a low voice and with frequent pauses, he began his tale.

CHAPTER I

I WAS born in France, but at an early age I was sent to St. Domingo, to the care of an uncle, to whose daughter it had been arranged between our parents that I was to be married. My uncle was one of the wealthiest colonists, and possessed a magnificent house and extensive plantations in the Plains of Acul, near Fort Galifet. The position of the estate, which no doubt you wonder at my describing so minutely, was one of the causes of all our disasters, and the eventual total ruin of our whole family.

Eight hundred negro slaves cultivated the enormous domains of my uncle. Sad as the position of a slave is, my uncle's hardness of heart added much to the unhappiness of those who had the misfortune to be his property. My uncle was one of the happily small number of planters from whom despotic power had taken away the gentler feelings of humanity. He was accustomed to see his most trifling command unhesitatingly obeyed, and the slightest delay on the part of his slaves in carrying it out was punished with the harshest severity; while the intercession either of my cousin or of myself too often merely led to an increase of the punishment, and we were only too often obliged to rest satisfied by secretly assuaging the injuries which we were powerless to prevent.

Among the multitude of his slaves, one only had found favour in my uncle's sight; this was a half-caste Spanish dwarf, who had been given him by Lord Effingham, the Governor of Jamaica. My uncle, who had for many years resided in Brazil, and had adopted the luxurious habits of the Portuguese, loved to surround himself with an establishment that was in keeping with his wealth. In order that nothing should be wanting, he had made the slave presented to him by Lord Effingham his fool, in imitation of the feudal lords

9

who had jesters attached to their households. I must say
that the slave amply fulfilled all the required conditions.

Habibrah, for that was the half-caste's name, was one of
those strangely formed, or rather deformed, beings who
would be looked upon as monsters if their very hideousness
did not cause a laugh. This ill-featured dwarf was short
and fat, and moved with wondrous activity upon a pair of
slender limbs, which, when he sat down, bent under him like
the legs of a spider. His enormous head, covered with a
mass of red curly wool, was stuck between his shoulders,
while his ears were so large that Habibrah's comrades were
in the habit of saying that he used them to wipe his eyes
when he wept. On his face there was always a grin, which
was continually changing its character, and which caused his
ugliness to be of an ever-varying description. My uncle was
fond of him, because of his extreme hideousness and his inextinguishable gayety. Habibrah was his only favourite, and
led a life of ease, while the other slaves were overwhelmed with
work. The sole duties of the jester were to carry a large fan,
made of the feathers of the bird of paradise, to keep away
the sandflies and the mosquitoes from his master. At meal-
times he sat upon a reed mat at his master's feet, who fed
him with tit-bits from his own plate. Habibrah appeared to
appreciate all these acts of kindness, and at the slightest sign
from my uncle he would run to him with the agility of a
monkey and the docility of a dog.

I had imbibed a prejudice against my uncle's favourite
slave. There was something crawling in his servility; for
though outdoor slavery does not dishonour, domestic service
too often debases. I felt a sentiment of pity for those slaves
who toiled in the scorching sun, with scarcely a vestige of
clothing to hide their chains; but I despised this idle serf,
with his garments ornamented with gold lace and adorned
with bells. Besides the dwarf never made use of his influence
with his master to ameliorate the condition of his fellow-suf-
ferers; on the contrary, I heard him once, when he thought
that he and his master were alone, urge him to increase his

severity towards his ill-fated comrades. The other slaves, however, did not appear to look upon him with any feelings of anger or rancour, but treated him with a timid kind of respect; and when, dressed in all the splendour of laced garments and a tall pointed cap ornamented with bells, and quaint symbols traced upon it in red ink, he walked past their huts, I have heard them murmur in accents of awe, " He is an *obi* " (sorcerer).

These details, to which I now draw your attention, occupied my mind but little then. I had given myself up entirely to the emotion of a pure love, in which nothing else could mingle,— a love which was returned me with passion by the girl to whom I was betrothed,— and I gave little heed to anything that was not Marie. Accustomed from youth to look upon her as the future companion of my life, there was a curious mixture of the love of a brother for a sister, mingled with the passionate adoration of a betrothed lover.

Few men have spent their earlier years more happily than I have done, or have felt their souls expand into life in the midst of a delicious climate and all the luxuries which wealth could procure, with perfect happiness in the present and the brightest hopes for the future. No man, as I said before, could have spent his earlier years more happily —

[D'Auverney paused for a moment, as if these thoughts of by-gone happiness had stifled his voice, and then added:]

And no one could have passed his later ones in more profound misery and affliction.

CHAPTER II

IN the midst of these blind illusions and hopes, my twentieth birthday approached. It was now the month of August, 1791, and my uncle had decided that this should be the date of my marriage with Marie. You can well understand that the thoughts of happiness, now so near, absorbed

all my faculties, and how little notice I took of the political
crisis which was then felt throughout the colony. I will not,
therefore, speak of the Count de Pernier, or of M. de
Blanchelande, nor of the tragical death of the unfortunate
Colonel de Marchiste; nor will I attempt to describe the jeal-
ousies of the Provincial House of Assembly of the North, and
the Colonial Assembly (which afterwards called itself the
General Assembly, declaring that the word " Colonial " had
a ring of slavery in it). For my own part, I sided with
neither; but if I did espouse any cause, it was in favour of
Cap, near which town my home was situate, in opposition to
Port au Prince.

Only once did I mix myself up in the question of the day.
It was on the occasion of the disastrous decree of the 15th of
May, 1791, by which the National Assembly of France ad-
mitted free men of colour to enjoy the same political privileges as the whites. At a ball given by the Governor of Cap,
many of the younger colonists spoke in impassioned terms of
this law, which levelled so cruel a blow at the instincts of
supremacy assumed by the whites, with perhaps too little
foundation. I had, as yet, taken no part in the conversation,
when I saw approaching the group a wealthy planter, whose
doubtful descent caused him to be received merely upon suf-
ferance by the white society. I stepped in front of him, and
in a haughty voice I exclaimed, " Pass on, sir! pass on! or
you may hear words which would certainly be disagreeable
to those with *mixed blood* in their veins." He was so enraged
at this insinuation that he challenged me. We fought, and
each was slightly wounded. I confess that I was in the
wrong to have thus provoked him, and it is probable that I
should not have done so on a mere *question of colour;* but I
had for some time past noticed that he had had the audacity
to pay certain attentions to my cousin, and had danced with
her the very night upon which I had insulted him.

However, as time went on, and the date so ardently desired
approached, I was a perfect stranger to the state of political
ferment in which those around me lived; and I never perceived

the frightful cloud which already almost obscured the horizon, and which promised a storm that would sweep all before it. No one at that time thought seriously of a revolt among the slaves,— a class too much despised to be feared; but between the whites and the free mulattoes there was sufficient hatred to cause an outbreak at any moment, which might entail the most disastrous consequences.

During the first days of August a strange incident occurred, which threw a slight shade of uneasiness over the sunshine of my happiness.

CHAPTER III

O N the banks of a little river which flowed through my uncle's estate was a small rustic pavilion in the midst of a clump of trees. Marie was in the habit of coming here every day to enjoy the sea breeze, which blows regularly in St. Domingo, even during the hottest months of the year, from sunrise until evening. Each morning it was my pleasant task to adorn this charming retreat with the sweetest flowers that I could gather.

One morning Marie came running to me in a great state of alarm. Upon entering her leafy retreat she had perceived, with surprise and terror, all the flowers which I had arranged in the morning thrown upon the ground and trampled under foot, and a bunch of wild marigolds, freshly gathered, placed upon her accustomed seat. She had hardly recovered from her terror, when, in the adjoining coppice, she heard the sound of a guitar, and a voice, which was not mine, commenced singing a Spanish song; but in her excitement she had been unable to catch the meaning of the words, though she could hear her own name frequently repeated. Then she had taken to flight, and had come to me full of this strange and surprising event.

This recital filled me with jealousy and indignation. My first suspicions pointed to the mulatto with whom I had fought; but even in the midst of my perplexity I resolved to do nothing rashly. I soothed Marie's fears as best I could, and promised to watch over her without ceasing, until the marriage tie would give me the right of never leaving her.

Believing that the intruder whose insolence had so alarmed Marie would not content himself with what he had already done, I concealed myself that very evening near the portion of the house in which my betrothed's chamber was situated.

Hidden among the tall stalks of the sugar-cane, and armed with a dagger, I waited; and I did not wait in vain. Towards the middle of the night my attention was suddenly attracted by the notes of a guitar under the very window of the room in which Marie reposed. Furious with rage, with my dagger clutched firmly in my hand, I rushed in the direction of the sound, crushing beneath my feet the brittle stalks of the sugar-canes. All of a sudden I felt myself seized and thrown upon my back with what appeared to be superhuman force; my dagger was wrenched from my grasp, and I saw its point shining above me; at the same moment I could perceive a pair of eyes and a double row of white teeth gleaming through the darkness, while a voice, in accents of concentrated rage, muttered, " Te tengo, te tengo!" (I have you, I have you).

More astonished than frightened, I struggled vainly with my formidable antagonist, and already the point of the dagger had pierced my clothes, when Marie, whom the sound of the guitar and the noise of the struggle had aroused, appeared suddenly at her window. She recognized my voice, saw the gleam of the knife, and uttered a cry of terror and affright. This cry seemed to paralyze the hand of my opponent. He stopped as if petrified; but still, as though undecided, he kept the point of the dagger pressed upon my chest. Then he suddenly exclaimed in French, " No, I cannot; she would weep too much," and, casting away the weapon, rose to his feet, and in an instant disappeared in the canes; and before

I could rise, bruised and shaken from the struggle, no sound and no sign remained of the presence or the flight of my adversary.

It was some time before I could recover my scattered faculties. I was more furious than ever with my unknown rival, and was overcome with a feeling of shame at being indebted to him for my life. "After all, however," I thought, "it is to Marie that I owe it; for it was the sound of *her* voice that caused him to drop his dagger."

And yet I could not hide from myself that there was something noble in the sentiment which had caused my unknown rival to spare me. But who could he be? One supposition after another rose in my mind, all to be discarded in turn. It could not be the mulatto planter to whom my suspicions had first been directed. He was not endowed with such muscular power; nor was it his voice. The man with whom I had struggled was naked to the waist; slaves alone went about half-clothed in this manner. But this could not be a slave; the feeling which had caused him to throw away the dagger would not have been found in the bosom of a slave,— and besides, my whole soul revolted at the idea of having a slave for a rival. What was to be done? I determined to wait and watch.

CHAPTER IV

MARIE had awakened her old nurse, whom she looked upon almost in the light of the mother who had died in giving her birth, and with them I remained for the rest of the night, and in the morning informed my uncle of the mysterious occurrence. His surprise was extreme, but, like me, his pride would not permit him to believe that a slave would venture to raise his eyes to his daughter. The nurse received the strictest orders from my uncle never to leave Marie alone for a moment; but as the sittings of the Provincial Assembly, the threatening aspect of the affairs of the colony, and the superintendence of the plantation allowed him but little leisure, he authorized me to accompany his daughter whenever she left the house, until the celebration of our nuptials; and at the same time, presuming that the daring lover must be lurking in the neighbourhood, he ordered the boundaries of the plantation to be more strictly guarded than ever.

After all these precautions had been taken, I determined to put the matter to further proof. I returned to the summer-house by the river, and repairing the destruction of the evening before, I placed a quantity of fresh flowers in their accustomed place.

When the time arrived at which Marie usually sought the sweet shades of this sequestered spot, I loaded my rifle and proposed to escort her thither. The old nurse followed a few steps behind.

Marie, to whom I had said nothing about my having set the place to rights, entered the summer-house the first. " See, Leopold," said she, " my nest is in the same condition in which I left it yesterday; here are your flowers thrown about in disorder and trampled to pieces, and there is that odious bouquet which does not appear at all faded since yesterday; indeed, it looks as if it had been freshly gathered."

I was speechless with rage and surprise. There was my morning's work utterly ruined, and the wild flowers, at whose freshness Marie was so much astonished, had insolently usurped the place of the roses that I had strewn all over the place.

" Calm yourself," said Marie, who noticed my agitation; " this insolent intruder will come here no more; let us put all thoughts of him on one side, as I do this nasty bunch of flowers."

I did not care to undeceive her, and to tell her that he *had* returned; yet I was pleased to see the air of innocent indignation with which she crushed the flowers under her foot. Hoping that the day would again come when I should meet my mysterious rival face to face, I made her sit down between her nurse and myself.

Scarcely had we done so when Marie put her finger on my lips: a sound, deadened by the breeze and the rippling of the stream, had struck upon her ear. I listened; it was the notes of a guitar, the same melody that had filled me with fury on the preceding evening. I made a movement to start from my seat, but a gesture of Marie's detained me.

" Leopold," whispered she, " restrain yourself; he is going to sing, and we shall learn who he is."

As she spoke, a few more notes were struck on the guitar, and then from the depths of the wood came the plaintive melody of a Spanish song, every word of which has remained deeply engraved on my memory: —

> Why dost thou fear me and fly me?
> Say, has my music no charms?
> Do you not know that I love you?
> Why, then, these causeless alarms?
> Maria!
>
> When I perceive your slight figure
> Glide through the cocoanut grove,
> Sometimes I think 't is a spirit
> Come to reply to my love.
> Maria!
>
> Sweeter your voice to mine ears
> Than the birds' song in the sky
> That, from the kingdom I've lost,
> Over the wide ocean fly.
> Maria!
>
> Far away, once I was king,
> Noble and powerful and free;
> All I would gladly give up
> For a word, for a gesture from thee,
> Maria!
>
> Tall and upright as a palm,
> Sweet in your young lover's eyes
> As the soft shade of the tree
> Mirrored in cool water lies.
> Maria!

2

But know you not that the storm
  Comes and uproots the fair tree?
Jealousy comes like that storm,
  Bringing destruction to thee,
                        Maria!

Tremble, Hispaniola's daughter,
  Lest all should fade and decay;
And vainly you look for the arm
  To bear you in safety away.
                        Maria!

Why, then, repulse my fond love?
  Black I am, while you are white;
Night and the day, when united,
  Bring forth the beautiful light.
                        Maria!

CHAPTER V

A PROLONGED quavering note upon the guitar, like a sob, concluded the song.

I was beside myself with rage. King! black! slave! A thousand incoherent ideas were awakened by this extraordinary and mysterious song. A maddening desire to finish for once and all with this unknown being, who dared to mingle the name of Marie with songs of love and menace, took possession of me. I grasped my rifle convulsively and rushed from the summer-house. Marie stretched out her arms to detain me, but I was already in the thicket from which the voice appeared to have come. I searched the little wood thoroughly, I beat the bushes with the barrel of my rifle, I crept behind the trunks of the large trees, and walked through the high grass.

Nothing, nothing, always nothing! This fruitless search added fuel to the fire of my anger. Was this insolent rival always to escape from me like a supernatural being? Was I never to be able to find out who he was, or to meet him? At this moment the tinkling of bells roused me from my revery.

I turned sharply round, the dwarf Habibrah was at my side.

"Good-day, master," said he, with a sidelong glance full of triumphant malice at the anxiety which was imprinted on my face.

"Tell me," exclaimed I, roughly, "have you seen any one about here?"

"No one except yourself, señor mio," answered he, calmly.

"Did you hear no voice?" continued I.

The slave remained silent as though seeking for an evasive reply.

My passion burst forth. "Quick, quick!" I exclaimed. "Answer me quickly, wretch! did you hear a voice?"

He fixed his eyes boldly upon mine; they were small and round, and gleamed like those of a wild cat.

"What do you mean by a voice, master? There are voices everywhere,— the voice of the birds, the voice of the stream, the voice of the wind in the trees —"

I shook him roughly. "Miserable buffoon!" I cried, "cease your quibbling, or you shall hear another voice from the barrel of my rifle. Answer at once; did you hear a man singing a Spanish song?"

"Yes, señor," answered he, calmly. "Listen, and I will tell you all about it. I was walking on the outskirts of the wood listening to what the silver bells of my *gorra* [cap] were telling me, when the wind brought to my ears some Spanish words,— the first language that I heard when my age could have been counted by months, and my mother carried me slung at her back in a hammock of red and yellow wool. I love the language; it recalls to me the time when I was little without being a dwarf,— a little child, and not a buffoon; and so I listened to the song."

"Is that all you have to say?" cried I, impatiently.

"Yes, handsome master; but if you like I can tell you who the man was who sang."

I felt inclined to clasp him in my arms. "Oh, speak!" I exclaimed; "speak! Here is my purse, and ten others fuller than that shall be yours if you will tell me his name."

He took the purse, opened it, and smiled. " Ten purses fuller than this," murmured he; " that will make a fine heap of good gold coins. But do not be impatient, young master, I am going to tell you all. Do you remember the last verse of his song,— something about ' I am black, and you are white, and the union of the two produces the beautiful light? ' Well, if this song is true, Habibrah, your humble slave, was born of a negress and a white, and must be more beautiful than you, master. I am the offspring of day and night, therefore I am more beautiful than a white man, and —"

He accompanied this rhapsody with bursts of laughter.

" Enough of buffoonery," cried I; " tell me who was singing in the wood! "

" Certainly, master; the man who sang such buffooneries, as you rightly term them, could only have been — a fool like me! Have I not gained my ten purses? "

I raised my hand to chastise his insolence, when a wild shriek rang through the wood from the direction of the summer-house. It was Marie's voice. Like an arrow I darted to the spot, wondering what fresh misfortune could be in store for us, and in a few moments arrived, out of breath, at the door of the pavilion. A terrible spectacle presented itself to my eyes.

An enormous alligator, whose body was half concealed by the reeds and water plants, had thrust his monstrous head through one of the leafy sides of the summer-house; his hideous, widely-opened mouth threatened a young negro of colossal height, who with one arm sustained Marie's fainting form, while with the other he had plunged the iron portion of a hoe between the sharp and pointed teeth of the monster. The reptile struggled fiercely against the bold and courageous hand that held him at bay.

As I appeared at the door, Marie uttered a cry of joy, and extricating herself from the support of the negro, threw herself into my arms with, " I am saved! I am saved! "

At the movement and exclamations of Marie the negro turned abruptly round, crossed his arms on his breast, and casting a look of infinite sorrow upon my betrothed, remained immovable, taking no heed of the alligator, which, having freed itself from the hoe, was advancing on him in a threatening manner. There would have been a speedy end of the courageous negro had I not rapidly placed Marie on the knees of her nurse (who, more dead than alive, was gazing upon the scene), and coming close to the monster, discharged my carbine into its yawning mouth. The huge reptile staggered back, its bleeding jaws opened and shut convulsively, its eyes closed; and after one or two unvailing efforts it rolled over upon its back, with its scaly feet stiffening in the air. It was dead.

The negro whose life I had so happily preserved turned his head, and saw the last convulsive struggles of the monster; then he fixed his eyes upon Marie, who had again cast herself into my arms, and in accents of the deepest despair, he exclaimed in Spanish, " Why did you kill him? " and without waiting for a reply leaped into the thicket and disappeared.

CHAPTER VI

THE terrible scene, its singular conclusion, the extraordinary mental emotions of every kind which had accompanied and followed my vain researches in the wood, had made my brain whirl. Marie was still stupefied with the danger that she had so narrowly escaped, and some time elapsed before we could frame coherent words, or express ourselves otherwise than by looks and clasping of the hands.

At last I broke the silence: " Come, Marie, let us leave this; some fatality seems attached to the place."

She rose eagerly, as if she had only been waiting for my permission to do so, and leaning upon my arm, we quitted the pavilion. I asked her how it had happened that succour had so opportunely arrived when the danger was so imminent,

and if she knew who the slave was who had come to her assistance; for that it *was* a slave, was shown by his coarse linen
trousers,— a dress only worn by that unhappy class.

" The man," replied Marie, " is no doubt one of my father's
negroes, who was at work in the vicinity when the appearance
of the alligator made me scream; and my cry must have
warned him of my danger. All I know is, that he rushed
out of the wood and came to my help."

" From which side did he come? " asked I.

" From the opposite side from which the song came, and
into which you had just gone."

This statement upset the conclusion that I had been drawing from the Spanish words that the negro had addressed to
me, and from the song in the same language by my unknown
rival. But yet there was a crowd of other similarities. This
negro of great height and powerful muscular development
might well have been the adversary with whom I had struggled on the preceding night. In that case his half-clothed
person would furnish a striking proof. The singer in the
wood had said, " I am black,"— a further proof. He had
declared himself to be a king, and this one was only a slave;
but I recollected that in my brief examination I had been
surprised at the noble appearance of his features, though of
course accompanied by the characteristic signs of the African
race.

The more that I thought of his appearance, the nobleness
of his deportment, and his magnificent proportions, I felt that
there might be some truth in his statement that he had been
a king. But then came the crushing blow to my pride: if
he had dared to gaze with an eye of affection upon Marie, if he
had made her the object of his serenades,— *he*, a *negro* and a
slave,— what punishment could be sufficiently severe for his
presumption? With these thoughts all my indecision returned again, and again my anger increased against the mysterious unknown. But at the moment that these ideas filled
my brain, Marie dissipated them entirely by exclaiming, in
her gentle voice,—

" My Leopold, we must seek out this brave negro, and pay him the debt of gratitude that we owe him; for without him I should have been lost, for you would have arrived too late."

These few words had a decisive effect. They did not alter my determination to seek out the slave, but they entirely altered the design with which I sought him; for it was to recompense and not to punish him that I was now eager.

My uncle learned from me that he owed his daughter's life to the courage of one of his slaves, and he promised me his liberty as soon as I could find him out.

CHAPTER VII

UP to that time my feelings had restrained me from going into those portions of the plantation where the slaves were at work; it had been too painful for me to see so much suffering which I was powerless to alleviate. But on the day after the events had taken place which I have just narrated, upon my uncle asking me to accompany him on his tour of inspection, I accepted his proposal with eagerness, hoping to meet among the labourers the preserver of my much-beloved Marie.

I had the opportunity in this visit of seeing how great a power the master exercises over his slaves, but at the same time I could perceive at what a cost this power was bought; for though at the presence of my uncle all redoubled their efforts, I could perceive that there was as much hatred as terror in the looks that they furtively cast upon him.

Irascible by temperament, my uncle seemed vexed at being unable to discover any object upon which to vent his wrath, until Habibrah the buffoon, who was ever at his heels, pointed out to him a young negro, who, overcome by heat and fatigue, had fallen asleep under a clump of date-trees. My uncle stepped quickly up to him, shook him violently, and in angry tones ordered him to resume his work.

The terrified slave rose to his feet, and in so doing disclosed a Bengal rose-tree upon which he had accidentally lain, and which my uncle prized highly. The shrub was entirely destroyed.

At this the master, already irritated at what he called the idleness of his slave, became furious. Foaming with rage, he unhooked from his belt the whip with wire-plated thongs, which he always carried with him on his rounds, and raised his arm to strike the negro who had fallen at his feet.

The whip did not fall. I shall, as long as I live, never forget that moment. A powerful grasp arrested the hand of the angry planter, and a negro (it was the very one that I was in search of) exclaimed, " Punish me, for I *have* offended you; but do not hurt my brother, who has but broken your rose-tree."

This unexpected interposition from the man to whom I owed Marie's safety, his manner, his look, and the haughty tone of his voice, struck me with surprise. But his generous intervention, far from causing my uncle to blush for his causeless anger, only increased the rage of the incensed master, and turned his anger upon the new comer.

Exasperated to the highest pitch, my uncle disengaged his arm from the grasp of the tall negro, and pouring out a volley of threats, again raised the whip to strike the first victim of his anger. This time, however, it was torn from his hand, and the negro, breaking the handle studded with iron nails as you would break a straw, cast it upon the ground and trampled upon the instrument of degrading punishment.

I was motionless with surprise; my uncle with rage, for it was an unheard-of thing for him to find his authority thus contemned. His eyes appeared ready to start from their sockets, and his lips quivered with passion.

The negro gazed upon him calmly, and then, with a dignified air, he offered him an axe that he held in his hand. " White man," said he, " if you wish to strike me, at least take this axe."

My uncle, beside himself with rage, would certainly have

complied with the request, for he stretched out his hand to grasp the dangerous weapon; but I in my turn interfered, and seizing the axe threw it into the well of a sugar-mill which was close at hand.

" What have you done? " asked my uncle, angrily.

" I have saved you," answered I, " from the unhappiness of striking the preserver of your daughter. It is to this slave that you owe Marie; it is the negro to whom you have promised liberty."

It was an unfortunate moment in which to remind my uncle of his promise. My words could not soothe the wounded dignity of the planter.

" His liberty! " replied he, savagely. " Yes, he has deserved that an end should be put to his slavery. His liberty indeed! we shall see what sort of liberty the members of a court-martial will accord him."

These menacing words chilled my blood. In vain did Marie later join her entreaties to mine. The negro whose negligence had been the cause of this scene was punished with a severe flogging, while his defender was thrown into the dungeons of Fort Galifet, under the terrible accusation of having assaulted a white man. For a slave who did this, the punishment was invariably death.

CHAPTER VIII

YOU may judge, gentlemen, how much all these circumstances excited my curiosity and interest. I made every inquiry regarding the prisoner, and some strange particulars came to my knowledge. I learned that all his comrades displayed the greatest respect for the young negro. Slave as he was, he had but to make a sign to be implicitly obeyed. He was not born upon the estate, nor did any one know his father or mother: all that was known of him was that some years ago a slave ship had brought him to St.

Domingo. This circumstance rendered the influence which he exercised over the slaves the more extraordinary, for as a rule the negroes born upon the island profess the greatest contempt for the *Congos*,— a term which they apply to all slaves brought direct from Africa.

Although he seemed a prey to deep dejection, his enormous strength, combined with his great skill, rendered him very valuable in the plantation. He could turn more quickly, and for a longer period, than a horse the wheels of the sugar-mills, and often in a single day performed the work of ten of his companions to save them from the punishment to which their negligence or incapacity had rendered them liable. For this reason he was adored by the slaves; but the respect that they paid him was of an entirely different character from the superstitious dread with which they looked upon Habibrah the Jester.

What was more strange than all was the modesty and gentleness with which he treated his equals, in contrast to the pride and haughtiness which he displayed to the negroes who acted as overseers. These privileged slaves, the intermediary links in the chain of servitude, too often exceed the little brief authority that is delegated to them, and find a cruel pleasure in overwhelming those beneath them with work. Not one of them, however, had ever dared to inflict any species of punishment on him, for had they done so, twenty negroes would have stepped forward to take his place, while he would have looked gravely on, as though he considered that they were merely performing a duty. The strange being was known throughout the negro quarter as Pierrot.

CHAPTER IX

THE whole of these circumstances took a firm hold upon my youthful imagination. Marie, inspired by compassion and gratitude, applauded my enthusiasm, and Pierrot excited our interest so much that I determined to visit him and offer him my services in extricating him from his perilous position. As the nephew of one of the richest colonists in the Cap, I was, in spite of my youth, a captain in the Acul Militia. This regiment, and a detachment of the Yellow Dragoons, had charge of Fort Galifet; the detachment was commanded by a non-commissioned officer, to whose brother I had once had the good fortune to render an important service, and who therefore was entirely devoted to me.

[Here the listeners at once pronounced the name of Thaddeus.]

You are right, gentlemen, and as you may well believe, I had not much trouble in penetrating to the cell in which the negro was confined. As a captain in the militia, I had of course the right to visit the fort; but to evade the suspicions of my uncle, whose rage was still unabated, I took care to go there at the time of his noon-day *siesta*. All the soldiers too, except those on guard, were asleep, and guided by Thaddeus I came to the door of the cell. He opened it for me, and then discreetly retired.

The negro was seated on the ground, for on account of his height he could not stand upright. He was not alone; an enormous dog was crouched at his feet, which rose with a growl, and moved toward me.

" Rask! " cried the negro.

The dog ceased growling and again lay down at his master's feet, and began eating some coarse food.

I was in uniform, and the daylight that came through the

loophole in the wall of the cell was so feeble that Pierrot could not recognize my features.

"I am ready," said he, in a clear voice.

"I thought," remarked I, surprised at the ease with which he moved, "that you were in irons."

He kicked something that jingled.

"Irons; oh, I broke them!"

There was something in the tone in which he uttered these words that seemed to say, "I was not born to wear fetters."

I continued: "I did not know that they had permitted you to have a dog with you."

"They did not allow it; I brought him in."

I was more and more astonished. Three bolts closed the door on the outside, the loop hole was scarcely six inches in width, and had two iron bars across it.

He seemed to divine my thoughts, and rising as nearly erect as the low roof would permit, he pulled out with ease a large stone placed under the loop-hole, removed the iron bars, and displayed an opening sufficiently large to permit two men to pass through. This opening looked upon a grove of bananas and cocoa-nut trees which covered the hill upon which the fort was built.

Surprise rendered me dumb; at that moment a ray of light fell on my face. The prisoner started as if he had accidentally trodden upon a snake, and his head struck against the ceiling of the cell. A strange mixture of opposing feelings passed over his face,— hatred, kindness, and astonishment being all mingled together; but recovering himself with an effort, his face once more became cold and calm, and he gazed upon me as if I was entirely unknown to him.

"I can live two days more without eating," said he.

I saw how thin he had become, and made a movement of horror.

He continued: "My dog will only eat from my hand, and had I not enlarged the loop-hole, poor Rask would have died of hunger. It is better that he should live, for I know that I am condemned to death."

" No," said I ; " no, you shall not die of hunger."

He misunderstood me. " Very well," answered he, with a bitter smile, " I could have lived two days yet without food, but I am ready : to-day is as good as to-morrow. Do not hurt Rask."

Then I understood what he meant when he said " I am ready." Accused of a crime the punishment for which was death, he believed that I had come to announce his immediate execution ; and yet this man endowed with herculean strength, with all the avenues of escape open to him, had in a calm and childlike manner repeated, " I am ready ! "

" Do not hurt Rask," said he, once more.

I could restrain myself no longer. " What ! " I exclaimed, " not only do you take me for your executioner, but you think so meanly of my humanity that you believe I would injure this poor dog, who has never done me any harm ! "

His manner softened, and there was a slight tremor in his voice as he offered me his hand, saying, " White man, pardon me ; but I love my dog, and your race have cruelly injured me."

I embraced him, I clasped his hand, I did my best to undeceive him. " Do you not know me ? " asked I.

" I know that you are white, and that a negro is nothing in the eyes of men of your colour ; besides, you have injured me."

" In what manner ? " exclaimed I, in surprise.

" Have you not twice saved my life ? "

This strange accusation made me smile ; he perceived it, and smiled bitterly : " Yes, I know it too well : once you saved my life from an alligator, and once from a planter ; and what is worse, I am denied the right to hate you. I am very unhappy."

The strangeness of his language and of his ideas surprised me no longer ; it was in harmony with himself. " I owe more to you than you can owe to me. I owe you the life of Marie, — of my betrothed."

He started as though he had received some terrible shock.

" Marie ! " repeated he in stifled tones, and his face fell in his hands, which trembled violently, while his bosom rose and fell with heavy sighs.

I must confess that once again my suspicions were aroused ; but this time there were no feelings of anger or jealousy. I was too near my happiness, and he was trembling upon the brink of death, so that I could not for a moment look upon him as a rival ; and even had I done so, his forlorn condition would have excited my compassion and sympathy.

At last he raised his head. " Go," said he ; " do not thank me." After a pause he added, " And yet my rank is as lofty as your own."

These last words roused my curiosity. I urged him to tell me of his position and his sufferings ; but he maintained an obstinate silence.

My proceedings, however, had touched his heart, and my entreaties appeared to have vanquished his distaste for life. He left his cell, and in a short time returned with some bananas and a large cocoa-nut ; then he reclosed the opening and began to eat. As we conversed, I remarked that he spoke French and Spanish with equal facility, and that his education had not been entirely neglected. He knew many Spanish songs, which he sang with great feeling. Altogether he was a mystery that I endeavoured in vain to solve, for he would give me no key to the riddle. At last, with regret, I was compelled to leave him, after having urged on my faithful Thaddeus to permit him every possible indulgence.

CHAPTER X

EVERY day at the same hour I visited him. His position rendered me very uneasy, for in spite of all our prayers, my uncle obstinately refused to withdraw his complaint. I did not conceal my fears from Pierrot, who however listened to them with indifference.

Often Rask would come in with a large palm-leaf tied round his neck. His master would take it off, read some lines traced upon it in an unknown language, and then tear it up. I had ceased to question him in any matters connected with himself.

One day as I entered he took no notice of me; he was seated with his back to the door of the cell, and was whistling in melancholy mood the Spanish air, " Yo que soy contrabandista " (" A smuggler am I "). When he had completed it, he turned sharply round to me, and exclaimed: " Brother, if you ever doubt me, promise that you will cast aside all suspicion on hearing me sing this air."

His look was earnest, and I promised what he asked, without noticing the words upon which he laid so much stress, " If you ever doubt me." He took the empty half of a cocoanut which he had brought in on the day of my first visit, and had preserved ever since, filled it with palm wine, begged me to put my lips to it, and then drank it off at a draught. From that day he always called me *brother*.

And now I began to cherish a hope of saving Pierrot's life. My uncle's anger had cooled down a little. The preparations for the festivities connected with his daughter's wedding had caused his feelings to flow in gentle channels. Marie joined her entreaties to mine. Each day I pointed out to him that Pierrot had had no desire to insult him but had merely interposed to prevent him from committing an act of perhaps too great severity; that the negro had at the risk of his life saved Marie from the alligator; and besides, Pierrot was the strongest of all his slaves (for now I sought to save his life, not to obtain his liberty); that he was able to do the work of ten men, and that his single arm was sufficient to put the rollers of a sugar-mill in motion. My uncle listened to me calmly, and once or twice hinted that he might not follow up his complaint.

I did not say a word to the negro of the change that had taken place, hoping that I should soon be the messenger to announce to him his restoration to liberty. What astonished me greatly was, that though he believed that he was under sentence of death, he made no effort to avail himself of the means of escape that lay in his power. I spoke to him of this.

"I am forced to remain," said he, simply, "or they would think that I was afraid."

CHAPTER XI

ONE morning Marie came to me radiant with happiness; upon her gentle face was a sweeter expression than even the joys of pure love could produce, for written upon it was the knowledge of a good deed.

"Listen," said she. "In three days we shall be married. We shall soon —"

I interrupted her.

"Do not say *soon*, Marie, when there is yet an interval of three days."

She blushed and smiled. "Do not be foolish, Leopold," replied she. "An idea has struck me which has made me very happy. You know that yesterday I went to town with my father to buy all sorts of things for our wedding. I only care for jewels because you say that they become me; I would give all my pearls for a single flower from the bouquet which that odious man with the marigolds destroyed. But that is not what I meant to say. My father wished to buy me every-thing that I admired; and among other things there was a *bas-quina* of Chinese satin embroidered with flowers, which I ad-mired. It was very expensive. My father noticed that the dress had attracted my attention. As we were returning home, I begged him to promise me a boon after the manner of the knights of old: you know how he delights to be com-pared with them. He vowed on his honour that he would grant me whatever I asked, thinking of course that it was the *basquina* of Chinese satin; but no, it is Pierrot's pardon that I will ask for as my nuptial present."

I could not refrain from embracing her tenderly. My uncle's word was sacred, and while Marie ran to him to claim its fulfilment, I hastened to Fort Galifet to convey the glad news to Pierrot.

"Brother," exclaimed I, as I entered, "rejoice! your life is safe; Marie has obtained it as a wedding present from her father."

The slave shuddered.

"Marie — wedding — my life! What reference have these things to one another?"

"It is very simple," answered I. "Marie, whose life you saved, is to be married —"

"To whom?" exclaimed the negro, a terrible change coming over his face.

"Did you not know that she was to be married to me?"

His features relaxed. "Ah, yes," he replied; "and when is the marriage to take place?"

"On August the 22d."

"On August the 22d! Are you mad?" cried he, with terror painted in his countenance.

He stopped abruptly; I looked at him with astonishment. After a short pause he clasped my hand: "Brother," said he, "I owe you so much that I must give you a warning. Trust to me; take up your residence in Cap, and get married before the 22d."

In vain I entreated him to explain his mysterious words.

"Farewell," said he, in solemn tones; "I have perhaps said too much, but I hate ingratitude even more than perjury."

I left the prison a prey to feelings of great uneasiness; but all these were soon effaced by the thoughts of my approaching happiness.

That very day my uncle withdrew his charge, and I returned to the fort to release Pierrot. Thaddeus, on hearing the noise accompanied me to the prisoner's cell; but he was

3

gone! Rask alone remained, and came up to me wagging his tail. To his neck was fastened a palm-leaf, upon which were written these words: "Thanks; for the third time you have saved my life. Do not forget your promise, friend;" while underneath, in lieu of signature were the words: "Yo que soy contrabandista."

Thaddeus was even more astonished than I was, for he was ignorant of the enlargement of the loop-hole, and firmly believed that the negro had changed himself into a dog. I allowed him to remain in this belief, contenting myself with making him promise to say nothing of what he had seen. I wished to take Rask home with me, but on leaving the fort he plunged into a thicket and disappeared.

CHAPTER XII

MY uncle was furiously enraged at the escape of the negro. He ordered a diligent search to be made for him, and wrote to the governor placing Pierrot entirely at his disposal should he be re-taken.

The 22d of August arrived. My union with Marie was celebrated with every species of rejoicing at the parish church of Acul. How happily did that day commence from which all our misfortunes were to date! I was intoxicated with my happiness, and Pierrot and his mysterious warning were entirely banished from my thoughts.

At last the day came to a close, and my wife had retired to her apartments, but for a time duty forbade me joining her there. My position as a captain of the militia required me that evening to make the round of the guards posted about Acul. This nightly precaution was absolutely necessary owing to the disturbed state of the colony, caused by occasional outbreaks among the negroes, which, however, had been promptly repressed. My uncle was the first to recall me to the recollection of my duty. I had no option but to yield, and, putting on my uniform, I went out. I visited the first few guards without discovering any cause of alarm; but towards midnight, as half buried in my own thoughts I was patrolling the shores of the bay, I perceived upon the horizon a ruddy light in the direction of Limonade and St. Louis du Morin. At first my escort attributed it to some accidental conflagration; but in a few moments the flames became so vivid, and the smoke rising before the wind grew so thick, that I ordered an immediate return to the fort to give the alarm, and to request that help might be sent in the direction of the fire.

In passing through the quarters of the negroes who belonged to our estate, I was surprised at the extreme disorder that reigned there. The majority of the slaves were afoot, and were talking together with great earnestness. One strange word was pronounced with the greatest respect: It was *Bug-Jargal*, which occurred continually in the almost unintelligible dialect that they used. From a word or two which I gathered here and there, I learned that the negroes of the northern districts were in open revolt, and had set fire to the dwelling-houses and the plantations on the other side of Cap. Passing through a marshy spot, I discovered a quantity of axes and other tools, which would serve as weapons, hidden among the reeds.

My suspicions were now thoroughly aroused and I ordered the whole of the Acul militia to get under arms, and gave the command to my lieutenant; and while my poor Marie was expecting me, I, obeying my uncle's orders (who, as I have mentioned, was a member of the Provincial Assembly) took the road to Cap, with such soldiers as I had been able to muster.

I shall never forget the appearance of the town as we approached. The flames from the plantations which were burning all around it threw a lurid light upon the scene, which was only partially obscured by the clouds of smoke which the wind drove into the narrow streets. Immense masses of sparks rose from the burning heaps of sugar-cane, and fell like fiery snow on the roofs of the houses, and on the rigging of the vessels at anchor in the roadsteads, at every moment threatening the town of Cap with as serious a conflagration as was already raging in its immediate neighbourhood. It was a terrible sight to witness the terror-stricken inhabitants exposing their lives to preserve from so destructive a visitant their habitations, which perhaps was the last portion of property left to them; while, on the other hand, the vessels, taking advantage of a fair wind, and fearing the same fate, had already set sail, and were gliding over an ocean reddened by the flames of the conflagration.

CHAPTER XIII

STUNNED by the noise of the minute-guns from the fort, by the cries of the fugitives and the distant crash of falling buildings, I did not know in what direction to lead my men; but meeting in the main square the captain of the Yellow Dragoons, he advised me to proceed direct to the governor.

Other hands have painted the disasters of Cap, and I must pass quickly over my recollections of them, written as they are in fire and blood. I will content myself with saying that the insurgent slaves were already masters of Dondon, of Terrier-Rouge, of the town of Ouanaminte, and of the plantation of Limbé. This last news filled me with uneasiness, owing to the proximity of Limbé to Acul. I made all speed to the Government House. All was in confusion there. I asked for orders, and begged that instant measures might be taken for the security of Acul, which I feared the insurgents were already threatening. With the governer (Monsieur de Blanchelande) were M. de Rouvray, the brigadier and one of the largest landholders in Cap; M. de Touzard, the lieutenant-colonel of the Regiment of Cap; a great many members of the Colonial and the Provincial Assemblies, and numbers of the leading colonists. As I entered, all were engaged in a confused argument.

"Your Excellency," said a member of the Provincial Assembly, "it is only too true,— it is the negroes, and not the free mulattoes. It has often been pointed out that there was danger in that direction."

"You make that statement without believing in its truth," answered a member of the Colonial Assembly, bitterly; "and you only say it to gain credit at our expense. So far from expecting a rising of the slaves, you got up a sham one in 1789,— a ridiculous farce, in which with a supposed insurgent force of three thousand slaves *one* national volunteer only was killed, and that most likely by his own comrades."

"I repeat," replied the Provincial, "that we can see farther than you. It is only natural. We remain upon the spot and study the minutest details of the colony, while you and your Assembly hurry off to France to make some absurd proposals, which are often met with a national reprimand *Ridiculus mus.*"

The member of the Colonial Assembly answered with a sneer: "Our fellow-citizens re-elected us all without hesitation."

"It was your Assembly," retorted the other, "that caused the execution of that poor devil who neglected to wear a tricoloured cockade in a *café*, and who commenced a petition for capital punishment to be inflicted on the mulatto Lacombe with that worn-out phrase, 'In the name of the Father, of the Son, and of the Holy Ghost.'"

"It is false!" exclaimed the other; "there has always been a struggle of principles against privileges between our Assemblies."

"Ha, monsieur! I see now you are an Independent."

"That is tantamount to allowing that you are in favour of the White Cockade: I leave you to get out of that confession as best you may."

More might have passed, but the governor interposed:

"Gentlemen, gentlemen, what has this to do with the present state of affairs, and the pressing danger that threatens us? Listen to the reports that I have received. The revolt began this night at ten o'clock among the slaves in the Turpin Plantation. The negroes, headed by an English slave named Bouckmann, were joined by the blacks from Clement, Trémés, Flaville, and Nöe. They set fire to all the plantations, and massacred the colonists with the most unheard-of barbarities. By one single detail I can make you comprehend all the horrors accompanying this insurrection. The standard of the insurgents is the body of a white child on the point of a pike."

A general cry of horror interrupted the governor's statement.

"So much," continued he, "for what has passed outside the town. Within its limits all is confusion. Fear has rendered many of the inhabitants forgetful of the duties of humanity, and they have murdered their slaves. Nearly all have confined their negroes behind bolts and bars. The white artisans accuse the free mulattoes of being participators in the revolt, and many have had great difficulty in escaping from the fury of the populace. I have had to grant them a place of refuge in a church, guarded by a regiment of soldiers; and now, to prove that they have nothing in common with the insurgents, they ask that they may be armed and led against the rebels."

"Do nothing of the kind, your Excellency!" cried a voice which I recognized as that of the planter with whom I had had a duel,—"do nothing of the kind! give no arms to the mulattoes!"

"What! do you not want to fight?" asked a planter with a sneer.

The other did not appear to hear him, and continued: "These men of mixed blood are our worst enemies, and we must take every precaution against them. It is from that quarter that the insurgents are recruited; the negroes have but little to do with the rising." The poor wretch hoped by his abuse of the mulattoes to prove that he had nothing in common with them, and to clear himself from the imputation of having black blood in his veins; but the attempt was too barefaced, and a murmur of disgust rose up on all sides.

"Yes," said M. de Rouvray, " the slaves *have* something to do with it, for they are forty to one; and we should be in a serious plight if we could only oppose the negroes and the mulattoes with whites like you."

The planter bit his lips.

" General," said the governor, " what answer shall be given to the petition? Shall the mulattoes have the arms? "

" Give them weapons, your Excellency; let us make use of every willing hand. And you, sir," he added, turning to the colonist of doubtful colour, " go arm yourself, and join your comrades."

The humiliated planter slunk away, filled with concentrated rage.

But the cries of distress which rang through the town reached even to the chamber in which the council was being held. M. de Blanchelande hastily pencilled a few words upon a slip of paper, and handed it to one of his *aides-de-camp*, who at once left the room.

" Gentlemen," he said, " the mulattoes will receive arms; but there are many more questions to be settled."

" The Provincial Assembly should at once be convoked," said the planter who had been speaking when first I entered.

" The Provincial Assembly!" retorted his antagonist; " what is the Provincial Assembly? "

" You do not know because you are a member of the Colonial Assembly," replied the favourer of the White Cockade.

The Independent interrupted him. " I know no more of the Colonial than the Provincial; I only recognize the General Assembly."

" Gentlemen," exclaimed a planter, " while we are losing time with this nonsense, tell me what is to become of my cotton and my cochineal."

"And my indigo at Lumbé?"

"And my negroes, for whom I paid twenty dollars a-head all round?" said the captain of a slave-ship.

"Each minute that you waste," continued another colonist, "costs me ten quintals of sugar, which at seventeen piastres the quintal makes one hundred and thirty livres, ten sous, in French money, by the —"

Here the rival upholders of the two Assemblies again sought to renew their argument.

"*Morbleu,*" said M. de Rouvray in a voice of thunder, striking the table violently, "what eternal talkers you are! What do we care about your two Assemblies? Summon both of them, your Excellency, and I will form them into two regiments; and when they march against the negroes we shall see whether their tongues or their muskets make the most noise."

Then turning towards me he whispered: "Between the two Assemblies and the governor nothing can be done. These fine talkers spoil all, as they do in Paris. If I was seated in his Excellency's chair, I would throw all these fellows out of the window, and with my soldiers and a dozen crosses of St. Louis to promise, I would sweep away all the rebels in the island. These fictitious ideas of liberty, which they have all run mad after in France, do not do out here. Negroes should be treated so as not to upset them entirely by sudden liberation; all the terrible events of to-day are merely the result of this utterly mistaken policy, and this rising of the slaves is the natural result of the taking of the Bastille."

While the old soldier thus explained to me his views,— a little narrow-minded perhaps, but full of the frankness of conviction,— the stormy argument was at its height. A certain planter, one among the few who were bitten with the rabid mania of the revolution, and who called himself Citizen General C——, because he had assisted at a few sanguinary executions, exclaimed:

"We must have punishments rather than battles. Every nation must exist by terrible examples: let us terrify the negroes. It was I who quieted the slaves during the risings of

June and July by lining the approach to my house with a double row of negro heads. Let each one join me in this, and let us defend the entrances to Cap with the slaves who are still in our hands."

"How?" "What do you mean?" "Folly!" "The height of imprudence!" was heard on all sides.

"You do not understand me, gentlemen. Let us make a ring of negro heads, from Fort Picolet to Point Caracole. The rebels, their comrades, will not then dare to approach us. I have five hundred slaves who have remained faithful: I offer them at once."

This abominable proposal was received with a cry of horror. "It is infamous! It is too disgusting!" was repeated by at least a dozen voices.

"Extreme steps of this sort have brought us to the verge of destruction," said a planter. "If the execution of the insurgents of June and July had not been so hurried on, we should have held in our hands the clew to the conspiracy, which the axe of the executioner divided forever."

Citizen C —— was silenced for a moment by this outburst; then in an injured tone he muttered: "I did not think that *I* above all others should have been suspected of cruelty. Why, all my life I have been mixed up with the lovers of the negro race. I am in correspondence with Briscot and Pruneau de Pomme Gouge, in France; with Hans Sloane, in England; with Magaw, in America; with Pezll, in Germany; with Olivarius, in Denmark; with Wadstiörn, in Sweden; with Peter Paulus, in Holland; with Avendaño, in Spain; and with the Abbé Pierre Tamburini, in Italy!"

His voice rose as he ran through the names of his correspondents among the lovers of the African race, and he terminated his speech with the contemptuous remark, "But after all, there are no true philosophers here."

For the third time M. de Blanchelande asked if anyone had anything further to propose.

"Your Excellency," cried one, "let us embark on board the 'Leopard,' which lies at anchor off the quay."

"Let us put a price on the head of Bouckmann," exclaimed another.

"Send a report of what has taken place to the Governor of Jamaica," suggested a third.

"A good idea, so that he may again send us the ironical help of five hundred muskets!" sneered a member of the Provincial Assembly. "Your Excellency, let us send the news to France, and wait for a reply."

"Wait! a likely thing indeed," exclaimed M. de Rouvray; "and do you think that the blacks will wait, eh? And the flames that encircle our town, do you think they will wait? Your Excellency, let the tocsin be sounded, and send dragoons and grenadiers in search of the main body of the rebels. Form a camp in the eastern division of the island; plant military posts at Trou and at Vallieres. I will take charge of the plain of Dauphin; but let us lose no more time, for the moment for action has arrived."

The bold and energetic speech of the veteran soldier hushed all differences of opinion. The general had acted wisely. That secret knowledge which every one possesses, most conducive to his own interests, caused all to support the proposal of General de Rouvray; and while the governor with a warm clasp of the hand showed his old friend that his counsels had been appreciated, though they had been given in rather a dictatorial manner, the colonists urged for the immediate carrying out of the proposals.

I seized the opportunity to obtain from M. de Blanchelande the permission that I so ardently desired, and leaving the room, mustered my company in order to return to Acul,—though, with the exception of myself, all were worn out with the fatigue of their late march.

CHAPTER XIV

D AY began to break as I entered the market-place of the town, and began to rouse up the soldiers, who were lying about in all directions wrapped in their cloaks, and mingled pell-mell with the Red and Yellow Dragoons, fugitives from the country, cattle bellowing, and property of every description sent in for security by the planters. In the midst of all this confusion I began to pick out my men, when I saw a private in the Yellow Dragoons, covered with dust and perspiration, ride up at full speed. I hastened to meet him; and in a few broken words he informed me that my fears were realized,— that the insurrection had spread to Acul, and that the negroes were besieging Fort Galifet, in which the planters and the militia had taken refuge. I must tell you that this fort was by no means a strong one, for in St. Domingo they dignify the slightest earthwork with the name of fort.

There was not a moment to be lost. I mounted as many of my soldiers as I could procure horses for, and taking the dragoon as a guide, I reached my uncle's plantation about ten o'clock. I scarcely cast a glance at the enormous estate, which was nothing but a sea of flame, over which hovered huge clouds of smoke, through which every now and then the wind bore trunks of trees covered with sparks. A terrible rustling and crackling sound seemed to reply to the distant yells of the negroes which we now began to hear, though we could not as yet see them. The destruction of all this wealth, which would eventually have become mine, did not cause me a moment's regret. All I thought of was the safety of Marie: what mattered anything else in the world to me? I knew that she had taken refuge in the fort, and I prayed to God that I might arrive in time to rescue her. This hope sustained me through all the anxiety I felt, and gave me the strength and courage of a lion.

At length a turn in the road permitted us to see the fort. The tricolour yet floated on its walls, and a well-sustained fire was kept up by the garrison. I uttered a shout of joy. " Gallop, spur on! " said I to my men, and redoubling our pace we dashed across the fields in the direction of the scene of action. Near the fort I could see my uncle's house; the doors and windows were dashed in, but the walls still stood, and shone red with the reflected glare of the flames, which owing to the wind being in a contrary direction, had not yet reached the building. A crowd of the insurgents had taken possession of the house, and showed themselves at the windows and on the roof. I could see the glare of torches and the gleam of pikes and axes, while a brisk fire of musketry was kept up on the fort. Another strong body of negroes had placed ladders against the walls of the fort and strove to take it by assault, though many fell under the well-directed fire of the defenders. These black men, always returning to the charge after each repulse, looked like a swarm of ants endeavouring to scale the shell of a tortoise, and shaken off by each movement of the sluggish reptile.

We reached the outworks of the fort, our eyes fixed upon the banner which still floated above it. I called upon my men to remember that their wives and children were shut up within those walls, and urged them to fly to their rescue. A general cheer was the reply, and forming column I was on the point of giving the order to charge, when a loud yell was heard; a cloud of smoke enveloped the fort and for a time concealed it from our sight; a roar was heard like that of a furnace in full blast, and as the smoke cleared away we saw a red flag floating proudly above the dismantled walls. All was over. Fort Galifet was in the hands of the insurgents.

"A tall black burst through a blazing fence, carrying in his arms a
young woman who shrieked and struggled."

Bug-Jargal. Page 45.

CHAPTER XV

I CANNOT tell you what my feelings were at this terrible spectacle. The fort was taken, its defenders slain, and twenty families massacred; but I confess, to my shame that I thought not of this. Marie was lost to me,— lost, after having been made mine, but a few brief hours before; lost, perhaps, through my fault, for had I not obeyed the orders of my uncle in going to Cap I should have been by her side to defend her, or at least to die with her. These thoughts raised my grief to madness, for my despair was born of remorse.

However, my men were maddened at the sight. With a shout of "Revenge!" with sabres between their teeth and pistols in either hand, they burst into the ranks of the victorious insurgents. Although far superior in numbers, the negroes fled at their approach; but we could see them on our right and left, before and behind us, slaughtering the colonists, and casting fuel on the flames. Our rage was increased by their cowardly conduct.

Thaddeus, covered with wounds, made his escape through a postern gate. "Captain," said he, "your Pierrot is a sorcerer,— an *obi* as these infernal negroes call him; a devil, I say. We were holding our position, you were coming up fast; all seemed saved,— when by some means, which I do not know, he penetrated into the fort, and there was an end of us. As for your uncle and Madame —"

"Marie!" interrupted I, "where is Marie?"

At this instant a tall black burst through a blazing fence, carrying in his arms a young woman who shrieked and struggled; it was Marie, and the negro was Pierrot!

"Traitor!" cried I, and fired my pistol at him; one of the rebels threw himself in the way, and fell dead.

Pierrot turned, and addressed a few words to me which I did not catch; and then grasping his prey tighter, he dashed into a mass of burning sugar-canes. A moment afterwards a huge dog passed me, carrying in his mouth a cradle in which lay my uncle's youngest child. Transported with rage, I fired my second pistol at him; but it missed fire.

Like a madman I followed on their tracks; but my night march, the hours that I had spent without taking rest or food, my fears for Marie, and the sudden fall from the height of happiness to the depth of misery, had worn me out. After a few steps I staggered, a cloud seemed to come over me, and I fell senseless.

CHAPTER XVI

WHEN I recovered my senses I found myself in my uncle's ruined house, supported in the arms of my faithful Thaddeus, who gazed upon me with an expression of the deepest anxiety. "Victory!" exclaimed he, as he felt my pulse begin to beat; "victory! the negroes are in full retreat and my captain has come to life again!"

I interrupted his exclamations of joy by putting the only question in which I had any interest: "Where is Marie?" I had not yet collected my scattered ideas: I felt my misfortune without the recollection of it.

At my question Thaddeus hung his head. Then my memory returned to me, and like a hideous dream I recalled once more the terrible nuptial day, and the tall negro bearing away Marie through the flames. The rebellion which had broken out in the colony caused the whites to look on the blacks as their mortal enemies, and made me see in Pierrot — the good, the generous, and the devoted, who owed his life three times to me — a monster of ingratitude and a rival. The carrying off my wife on the very night of our nuptials proved too plainly to me what I had at first only suspected; and I now knew that the singer of the wood was the wretch who had torn my wife from me. In a few hours how great a change had taken place!

Thaddeus told me that he had vainly pursued Pierrot and his dog when the negroes, in spite of their numbers retired; and that the destruction of my uncle's property still continued, without the possibility of its being arrested. I asked what had become of my uncle. He took my hand in silence and led me to a bed, the curtains of which he drew. My unhappy uncle was there, stretched upon his blood-stained couch, with a dagger driven deeply into his heart. By the tranquil expression of his face it was easy to see that the blow had been struck during his sleep.

The bed of the dwarf Habibrah, who always slept at the foot of his master's couch, was also profusely stained with gore, and the same crimson traces could be seen upon the laced coat of the poor fool, cast upon the floor a few paces from the bed. I did not hesitate for a moment in believing that the dwarf had died a victim to his affection for my uncle, and that he had been murdered by his comrades, perhaps in the effort to defend his master. I reproached myself bitterly for the prejudice which had caused me to form so erroneous an estimate of the characters of Pierrot and Habibrah; and of the tears I shed at the tragic fate of my uncle, some were dedicated to the end of the faithful fool. By my orders his body was carefully searched for, but all in vain; and I imagined that the negroes had cast the body into the flames. I gave instructions that in the funeral service over my uncle's remains prayers should be said for the repose of the soul of the devoted Habibrah.

CHAPTER XVII

FORT GALIFET had been destroyed, our house was in ruins; it was useless to linger there any longer, so that evening I returned to Cap. On my arrival there I was seized with a severe fever. The effort that I had made to overcome my despair had been too violent; the spring had been bent too far and had snapped. Delirium came on. My broken hopes, my profound love, my lost future, and, above all, the torments of jealousy made my brain reel. It seemed as if fire flowed in my veins; my head seemed ready to burst, and my bosom was filled with rage. I pictured to myself Marie in the arms of another lover, subject to the power of a master, of a slave, of Pierrot! They told me afterwards that I sprang from my bed, and that it took six men to prevent me from dashing out my brains against the wall. Why did I not die then?

The crisis, however, passed. The doctors, the care and attention of Thaddeus, and the latent powers of youth conquered the malady: would that it had not done so! At the end of ten days I was sufficiently recovered to lay aside grief, and to live for vengeance.

Hardly arrived at a state of convalescence, I went to M. de Blanchelande, and asked for employment. At first he wished to give me the command of some fortified post, but I begged him to attach me to one of the flying columns, which from time to time were sent out to sweep those districts in which the insurgents had congregated. Cap had been hastily put in a position of defense, for the revolt had made terrible progress, and the negroes of Port au Prince had begun to show symptoms of disaffection. Biassou was in command of the insurgents at Lumbé, Dondon and Acul; Jean François had proclaimed himself generalissimo of the rebels of Maribarou; Bouckmann, whose tragic fate afterwards gave him a certain celebrity, with his brigands ravaged the plains of Limonade; and lastly, the bands of Morne-Rouge had elected for their chief a negro called Bug-Jargal.

If report was to be believed, the disposition of this man contrasted very favourably with the ferocity of the other chiefs. While Bouckmann and Biassou invented a thousand different methods of death for such prisoners as fell into their hands, Bug-Jargal was always ready to supply them with the means of quitting the island. M. Colas de Marjue and eight other distinguished colonists were by his orders released from the terrible death of the wheel to which Bouckmann had condemned them; and many other instances of his humanity were cited, which I have not time to repeat.

My hoped-for vengeance, however, still appeared to be far removed. I could hear nothing of Pierrot. The insurgents commanded by Biassou continued to give us trouble at Cap; they had once even endeavoured to take position on a hill that commanded the town, and had only been dislodged by the battery from the citadel being directed upon them. The governor had therefore determined to drive them into the interior of the island. The militia of Acul, of Lumbé, of Ouanaminte, and of Maribarou, joined with the regiment of Cap and the Red and Yellow Dragoons, formed one army of attack; while the corps of volunteers under the command of the merchant Poncignon, with the militia of Dondon and Quartier-Dauphin, composed the garrison of the town.

The governor desired first to free himself from Bug-Jargal, whose incursions kept the garrison constantly on the alert; and he sent against him the militia of Ouanaminte and a battalion of the regiment of Cap. Two days afterwards the expedition returned, having sustained a severe defeat at the hands of Bug Jargal. The governor, however, determined to persevere, and a fresh column was sent out with fifty of the Yellow Dragoons and four hundred of the militia of Maribarou. This second expedition met with even less success than the first. Thaddeus, who had taken part in it, was in a violent fury, and upon his return vowed vengeance against the rebel chief Bug-Jargal.

[A tear glistened in the eyes of D'Auverney; he crossed his arms on his breast, and appeared to be for a few moments plunged in a melancholy reverie. At length he continued.]
4

CHAPTER XVIII

THE news had reached us that Bug-Jargal had left Morne-Rouge, and was moving through the mountains to effect a junction with the troops of Biassou. The governor could not conceal his delight. "We have them!" cried he, rubbing his hands. "They are in our power!"

By the next morning the colonial forces had marched some four miles to the front of Cap. At our approach the insurgents hastily retired from the positions which they had occupied at Port-Mayat and Fort Galifet, and in which they had planted siege guns that they had captured in one of the batteries on the coast. The governor was triumphant, and by his orders we continued our advance. As we passed through the arid plains and the ruined plantations, many a one cast an eager glance in search of the spot which was once his home; but in too many cases the foot of the destroyer had left no traces behind. Sometimes our march was interrupted, by the conflagration having spread from the lands under cultivation to the virgin forests.

In these regions, where the land is untilled and the vegetation abundant, the burning of a forest is accompanied with many strange phenomena. Far off, long before the eye can detect the cause, a sound is heard like the rush of a cataract over opposing rocks; the trunks of the trees flame out with a sudden crash, the branches crackle, and the roots beneath the soil all contribute to the extraordinary uproar. The lakes and the marshes in the interior of the forests boil with the heat. The hoarse roar of the coming flame stills the air, causing a dull sound, sometimes increasing and sometimes diminishing in intensity as the conflagration sweeps on or recedes. Occasionally a glimpse can be caught of a clump of trees surrounded by a belt of fire, but as yet untouched by the flames; then a narrow streak of fire curls round the stems, and in another instant the whole becomes one mass of gold-coloured fire. Then uprises a column of smoke, driven here and there by the breeze; it takes a thousand fantastic forms,— spreads itself out, diminishes in an instant; at one moment it is gone, in another it returns with greater density; then all becomes a thick black cloud, with a fringe of sparks; a terrible sound is heard, the sparks disappear, and the smoke ascends, disappearing at last in a mass of red ashes, which sink down slowly upon the blackened ground.

CHAPTER XIX

ON the evening of the third day of our march we entered the ravines of Grande-Riviere; we calculated that the negro army was some twenty leagues off in the mountains.

We pitched our camp on a low hill, which appeared to have been used for the same purpose before, as the grass had been trodden down and the brushwood cut away. It was not a judicious position in a strategical point of view, but we deemed ourselves perfectly secure from attack. The hill was commanded on all sides by steep mountains clothed with thick forests,— their precipitous sides having given these mountains the name of the Dompte-Mulâtre. The Grande-Riviere flowed behind our camp, which being confined within steep banks was just about here very deep and rapid. Both sides of the river were hidden with thickets, through which nothing could be seen. The waters of the stream itself were frequently concealed by masses of creeping plants, hanging from the branches of the flowering maples which had sprung up at intervals in the jungle, crossing and recrossing the stream, and forming a tangled net-work of living verdure. From the heights of the adjacent hills this mass of verdure appeared like a meadow still fresh with dew, while every now and then a dull splash could be heard as a teal plunged through the flower-decked curtain, and showed in which direction the river

lay. By degrees the sun ceased to gild the crested peaks of
the distant mountains of Dondon; little by little darkness
spread its mantle over the camp, and the silence was only
broken by the cry of the night-bird, or by the measured tread
of the sentinels.

Suddenly the dreaded war-songs of " Oua-Nassé " and of
" The Camp of the Great Meadow " were heard above our
heads; the palms, the acomas, and the cedars, which crowned
the summits of the rocks, burst into flames, and the lurid light
of the conflagration showed us numerous bands of negroes and
mulattoes, whose copper-hued skins glowed red in the firelight
upon the neighbouring hills. It was the army of Biassou.

The danger was imminent. The officers, aroused from
their sleep, endeavoured to rally their men. The drum beat
the " Assembly," while the bugles sounded the " Alarm." Our
men fell in hurriedly and in confusion; but the insurgents, instead of taking advantage of our disorder, remained motionless, gazing upon us, and continuing their song of " Oua-
Nassé."

A gigantic negro appeared alone on one of the peaks that
overhung the Grande-Riviere; a flame-coloured plume floated
on his head, and he held an axe in his right hand and a blood-
red banner in his left. I recognized Pierrot. Had a carbine
been within my reach I should have fired at him, cowardly
although the act might have been. The negro repeated the
chorus of " Oua-Nassé," planted his standard on the highest
portion of the rock, hurled his axe into the midst of our ranks,
and plunged into the stream. A feeling of regret seized me;
I had hoped to have slain him with my own hand.

Then the negroes began to hurl huge masses of rocks upon
us, while showers of bullets and flights of arrows were poured
upon our camp. Our soldiers, maddened at being unable to
reach their adversaries, fell on all sides, crushed by the rocks,
riddled with bullets, and transfixed by arrows. The army was
rapidly falling into disorder. Suddenly a terrible noise came
from the centre of the stream.

The Yellow Dragoons, who had suffered most from the

shower of rocks, had conceived the idea of taking refuge under the thick roof of creepers which grew over the river. It was Thaddeus who had at first discovered this —

Here the narrative was suddenly interrupted.

CHAPTER XX

MORE than a quarter of an hour had elapsed since Thaddeus, his arm in a sling, had glided into the tent without any of the listeners noticing his arrival, and taking up his position in a remote corner had by occasional gestures expressed the interest that he took in his captain's narrative; but at last, considering that this direct allusion to himself ought not to be permitted to pass without some acknowledgment on his part, he stammered out,—

" You are too good, Captain! "

A general burst of laughter followed this speech, and D'Auverney, turning towards him, exclaimed severely: " What, Thaddeus, you here?   And your arm? "

On being addressed in so unaccustomed a tone, the features of the old soldier grew dark; he quivered, and threw back his head, as though to restrain the tears which seemed to struggle to his eyes.   " I never thought," said he, in a low voice, " that you, Captain, could have omitted to say *thou* when speaking to your old sergeant."

" Pardon me, old friend," answered the captain, quickly; " I hardly knew what I said.   Thou wilt pardon me, wilt thou not? "

The tears sprang to the sergeant's eyes in spite of his efforts to repress them.   " It is the third time," remarked he, — " but these are tears of joy."

Peace was made, and a short silence ensued.

" But tell me, Thaddeus, why hast thou quitted the hospital to come here? " asked D'Auverney, gently.

"It was — with your permission, Captain — to ask if I should put the laced saddle-cloth on the charger for to-morrow."

Henri laughed. "You would have been wiser, Thaddeus, to have asked the surgeon-major if you should put two more pieces of lint on your arm," said he.

"Or to ask," continued Paschal, "if you might take a glass of wine to refresh yourself. At any rate, here is some brandy; taste it,— it will do you good, my brave sergeant."

Thaddeus advanced, saluted, and apologizing for taking the glass with his left hand, emptied it to the health of the assembled company: "You had got, Captain, to the moment when — yes, I remember, it was I who proposed to take shelter under the creepers, to prevent our men being smashed by the rocks. Our officer, who did not know how to swim, was afraid of being drowned, and, as was natural, was dead against it until he saw — with your permission, gentlemen — a great rock fall on the creepers without being able to get through them. 'It is better to die like Pharaoh than like Saint Stephen,' said he; 'for we are not saints, and Pharaoh was a soldier like ourselves.' The officer was a learned man, you see. And so he agreed to my proposal, on the condition that I should first try the experiment myself. Off I went; I slid down the bank and caught hold of the roof of the creepers, when all of a sudden some one took a pull at my legs. I struggled, I shouted for help, and in a minute I received half-a-dozen sabre-cuts. Down came the dragoons to help me, and there was a nice little skirmish under the creepers. The blacks of Morne-Rouge had hidden themselves there, never for a moment thinking that we should fall right on the top of them.

This was not the right time for fishing, I can tell you. We fought, we swore, we shouted. They had nothing particular on, and were able to move about in the water more easily than we were; but, on the other hand, our sabres had less to cut through. We swam with one hand and fought with the other.

Those who could not swim, like my captain, hung on to the creepers, while the negroes pulled them by the legs.

" In the midst of the hullabaloo I saw a big negro fighting like Beelzebub against five or six of ours. I swam up to him, and recognized Pierrot, otherwise called Bug — But I must n't tell that yet, must I, Captain? Since the capture of the fort I owed him a grudge, so I took him hard and fast by the throat; he was going to rid himself of me by a thrust of his dagger, when he recognized me, and gave himself up at once. That was very unfortunate, was it not, Captain? For if he had not surrendered, he would not — But you will know that later on, eh? When the blacks saw that he was taken they made a rush at me to get him off; when Pierrot, seeing no doubt that they would all lose their lives, said some gibberish or other, and in the twinkling of an eye they plunged into the water, and were out of sight in a moment. This fight in the water would have been pleasant enough if I had not lost a finger and wetted ten cartridges, and if the poor man — but it was to be, was it not, Captain? "

And the sergeant respectfully placed the back of his hand to his forage-cap, and then raised it to heaven with the air of an inspired prophet.

D'Auverney was violently agitated. " Yes," cried he, " thou art right, my old Thaddeus; that night was a fatal night for me ! "

He would have fallen into one of his usual reveries had they not urgently presed him to conclude his story. After a while he continued.

CHAPTER XXI

WHILE the scene which Thaddeus has just described was passing behind the camp, I had succeeded, by aid of the brushwood, with some of my men in climbing the opposite hills until we had reached a point called Peacock Peak, from the brilliant tints of the mica which coated the surface of the rock.

From this position, which was opposite a rock covered with negroes, we opened a withering fire. The insurgents, who were not so well armed as we were, could not reply warmly to our volleys, and in a short time began to grow discouraged. We redoubled our efforts, and our enemies soon evacuated the neighbouring rocks, first hurling the dead bodies of their comrades upon our army, the greater proportion of which was still drawn up on the hill. Then we cut down several trees, and binding the trunks together with fibres of the palm, we improvised a bridge, and by it crossed over to the deserted positions of the enemy, and thus managed to secure a good post of vantage. This operation completely quenched the courage of the rebels. Our fire continued. Shouts of grief arose from them, in which the name of Bug-Jargal was frequently repeated. Many negroes of the army of Morne-Rouge appeared on the rock upon which the blood-red banner still floated; they prostrated themselves before it, tore it from its resting-place, and then precipitated it and themselves into the depths of the Grande-Riviere. This seemed to signify that their chief was either killed or a prisoner.

Our confidence had now risen to such a pitch that I resolved to drive them from their last position at the point of the bayonet, and at the head of my men I dashed into the midst of the negroes.

The soldiers were about to follow me across the temporary bridge that I had caused to be thrown from peak to peak, when one of the rebels with a blow of his axe broke the bridge to atoms, and the ruins fell into the abyss with a terrible noise.

I turned my head: in a moment I was surrounded, and seized by six or seven negroes, who disarmed me in a moment. I struggled like a lion, but they bound me with cords made of bark, heedless of the hail of bullets that my soldiers poured upon them. My despair was somewhat soothed by the cries of victory which I heard from our men, and I soon saw the negroes and mulattoes ascending the steep sides of the rocks with all the precipitation of fear, uttering cries of terror.

My captors followed their example. The strongest among them placed me on their shoulders, and carried me in the direction of the forest, leaping from rock to rock with the agility of wild goats. The flames soon ceased to light the scene, and it was by the pale rays of the moon that we pursued our course.

CHAPTER XXII

AFTER passing through jungles and crossing many a torrent, we arrived in a valley situated in the higher part of the hills, of a singularly wild and savage appearance. The spot was absolutely unknown to me. The valley was situated in the heart of the hills, in what is called the "double mountains." It was a large green plain, imprisoned by walls of bare rock, and dotted with clumps of pines and palm-trees. The cold, which at this height is very severe, was increased by the morning air, the day having just commenced to break; but the valley was still plunged in darkness, and was only lighted by flashes from the negroes' fires. Evidently this spot was their headquarters; the shattered remains of their army had begun to reassemble and every now and then bands of negroes and mulattoes arrived, uttering groans of distress and cries of rage. New fires were speedily lighted, and the camp began to increase in size.

The negro whose prisoner I was had placed me at the foot of an oak, whence I surveyed this strange spectacle with entire carelessness. The black had bound me with his belt to the trunk of the tree, against which I was leaning, and carefully tightening the knots in the cords which impeded my movements, he placed on my head his own red woollen cap, as if to indicate that I was his property; and after making sure that I could not escape or be carried off by others, he was preparing to leave me, when I determined to address him; and

speaking in the creole dialect, I asked him if he belonged to
the band of Dondon, or of Morne-Rouge. He stopped at
once, and in a tone of pride replied, " Morne-Rouge." Then
an idea entered my head. I had often heard of the generosity of the chief Bug-Jargal; and though I had made up my
mind that death would soon end all my troubles, the thought
of the tortures that would inevitably precede it should I fall
into the hands of Biassou filled me with horror. All I wanted
was to be put to death without torment. It was perhaps a
weakness, but I believe that the mind of man ever revolts at
such a death. I thought then that if I could be taken from
Biassou, Bug-Jargal might give me what I desired,— a soldier's death. I therefore asked the negro of Morne-Rouge
to lead me to Bug-Jargal.

He started: " Bug-Jargal!" he repeated, striking on his
forehead in anguish; then, as if rage had suddenly overtaken
him, he shook his fist, and shouting, " Biassou, Biassou!" he
left me hastily.

The mingled rage and grief of the negro recalled to my
mind the events of the day, and the certainty we had acquired
of either the death or capture of the chief of the band of
Morne-Rouge. I felt that all hope was over, and resigned
myself to the threatened vengeance of Biassou.

CHAPTER XXIII

A GROUP of negresses came near the tree to which I was
fastened, and lit a fire. By the numerous bracelets of
blue, red and violet glass which ornamented their arms and
ankles; by the rings which weighed down their ears and
adorned their toes and fingers; by the amulets on their bosoms
and the collar charms suspended round their necks; by the
aprons of variegated feathers which were their sole coverings,
— I at once recognized them as *griotes*. You are perhaps
ignorant that among the African blacks there exists a certain

class with a rude talent for poetry and improvisation, which approaches closely to madness. These unhappy creatures, wandering from one African kingdom to another, are in these barbarian countries looked upon in the same light as the minstrels of England, the minne-singers of Germany, and the troubadours of France. They are called " griots," and their wives " griotes." The *griotes* accompany the barbaric songs of their husbands with lascivious dances, and form a grotesque parody on the *nautch* girls of India and the *almes* of Egypt.

It was a group of these women who came and sat down near me, and with their legs crossed under them according to their custom, and their hideous faces lighted up by the red light of a fire of withered branches. When they had formed a complete circle they all joined hands, and the eldest, who had a heron's plume stuck in her hair, began to exclaim, " Ouanga! " I at once understood that they were going through one of their performances of pretended witchcraft. Then the leader of the band, after a moment's silence, plucked a lock of hair from her head and threw it into the fire, crying out these words, " Malé o guiab," which in the jargon of the creoles means, " I shall go to the devil." All the *griotes* imitated their leader, and throwing locks of their hair in the fire, repeated gravely, " Malé o guiab." This strange invocation, and the extraordinary grimaces that accompanied it, caused me to burst into one of those hysterical fits of laughter which so often seize on one even at the most serious moments. It was in vain that I endeavoured to restrain it,— it would have vent; and this laugh, which escaped from so sad a heart, brought about a gloomy and terrifying scene.

Disturbed in their incantations, the negresses sprang to their feet. Until then they had not noticed me, but now they rushed close up to me, screaming " Blanco, Blanco! " I have never seen so hideous a collection of faces, contorted as they were with passion, their white teeth gleaming, and their eyes almost starting from their heads. They were, I believe, about to tear me in pieces, when the old woman with the heron's plume on her head stopped them with a sign of her hand, and exclaimed seven times, " Zoté cordé? " (" Do you agree? ") The wretched creatures stopped at once, and to my surprise tore off their feather aprons, which they flung upon the ground, and commenced the lascivious dance which the negroes call " La chica."

This dance, which should only consist of attitudes and movements expressive of gaiety and pleasure, assumed a very different complexion when performed by these naked sorceresses. In turn, each of them would place her face close to mine, and with a frightful expression of countenance would detail the horrible punishment that awaited the white man who had profaned the mysteries of their *Ouanga*. I recollected that savage nations had a custom of dancing round their victims that they were about to sacrifice, and I patiently awaited the conclusion of the performance which I knew would be sealed with my blood; and yet I could not repress a shudder as I perceived each *griote*, in strict unison with the time, thrust into the fire the point of a sabre, the blade of an axe, a long sail-maker's needle, a pair of pincers, and the teeth of a saw.

The dance was approaching its conclusion, and the instruments of torture were glowing red with heat. At a signal from the old woman, each negress in turn withdrew an implement from the fire, while those who had none furnished themselves with a blazing stick. Then I understood clearly what my punishment was to be, and that in each of the dancers I should find an executioner. Again the word of command was given, and the last figure of the dance was commenced. I closed my eyes that I might not see the frantic evolutions of these female demons, who in measured cadence clashed the red-hot weapons over their heads. A dull, clinking sound followed, while the sparks flew out in myriads. I waited, nerving myself for the moment when I should feel my flesh quiver in agony, my bones calcine, and my muscles writhe under the burning tortures of the nippers and the saws. It was an awful moment. Fortunately it did not last long.

In the distance I heard the voice of the negro whose prisoner

I was, shouting, " Que hacies, mujeres, ne demonio, que haceis alli, devais mi prisonero? " I opened my eyes again; it was already broad daylight. The negro hurried towards me, gesticulating angrily. The *griotes* paused, but they seemed less influenced by the threats of my captor than by the presence of a strange-looking person by whom the negro was accompanied.

It was a very stout and very short man,— a species of dwarf,— whose face was entirely concealed by a white veil, pierced with three holes for the eyes and mouth. The veil hung down to his shoulders, and displayed a hairy, copper-hued breast, upon which was hung by a golden chain the mutilated sun of a monstrance. The cross-hilt of a heavy dagger peeped from a scarlet belt, which also supported a kind of petticoat striped with green, yellow, and black, the hem of which hung down to his large and ill-shaped feet. His arms, like his breast, were bare; he carried a white staff, and a rosary of amber beads was suspended from his belt, in close proximity to the handle of his dagger. His head was surmounted with a pointed cap adorned with bells; and when he came close I was not surprised in recognizing in it the *gorra* of Habibrah, and among the hieroglyphics with which it was covered I could see many spots of gore: without doubt, it was the blood of the faithful fool. These blood-stains gave me fresh proofs of his death, and awakened in me once again a fresh feeling of regret for his loss.

Directly the *griotes* recognized the wearer of Habibrah's cap, they cried out all at once: " The Obi! " and prostrated themselves before him. I guessed at once that this was a sorcerer attached to Biassou's force.

" Basta, basta " (" enough "), said he, in a grave and solemn voice, as he came close up to them. " Devais el prisonero de Biassou." (" Let the prisoner be taken to Biassou.")

All the negresses leaped to their feet and cast their implements of torture on one side, put on their aprons, and at a gesture of the Obi fled like a cloud of grass-hoppers.

At this instant the glance of the Obi fell upon me. He started back a pace, and half waved his white staff in the direction of the retiring *griotes*, as if he wished to recall them; then muttering between his teeth the word " Maldicho " (" accursed "), he whispered a few words in the ear of the negro, and crossing his arms retired slowly, apparently buried in deep thought.

CHAPTER XXIV

MY captor informed me that Biassou had asked to see me, and that in an hour I should be brought before him.

This, I calculated, gave me another hour in which to live. Until that time had elapsed, I allowed my glances to wander over the rebel camp, the singular appearance of which the daylight permitted me to observe.

Had I been in any other position, I should have laughed heartily at the ostentatious vanity of the negroes, who were nearly all decked out in fragments of clerical and military dress, the spoils of their victims. The greater portion of these ornaments were not new, consisting of torn and blood-stained rags. A gorget could often be seen shining over a stole, while an epaulet looked strange when contrasted with a chasuble. To make amends for former years of toil, the negroes now maintained a state of utter inaction: some of them slept exposed to the rays of the sun, their heads close to a burning fire; others, with eyes that were sometimes full of listlessness, and at others blazed with fury, sat chanting a monotonous air at the doors of their *ajoupas*,— a species of hut with conical roofs somewhat resembling our military tents, but thatched with palm or banana leaves. Their black or copper-coloured wives, aided by the negro children, prepared the food for the fighting-men. I could see them stirring up with long forks, ignames, bananas, yams, peas, cocus and maize, and other vegetables indigenous to the country, which were boiling with joints of pork, turtle, and dog in the great boilers stolen from the dwellings of the planters. In the distance, on the out-skirts of the camp, the *griots* and *griotes* formed large circles round the fires, and the wind every now and then brought to my ears strange fragments of their barbaric songs, mingled with notes from their tambourines and guitars. A few videttes posted on the high ground watched over the headquarters of General Biassou,— the only defence of which in case of attack was a circle of wagons filled with plunder and ammunition. These black sentries posted on the summits of the granite pyramids, with which the valley bristled, turned about like the weathercocks in Gothic spires, and with all the strength of their lungs shouted one to the other the cry of " Nada, nada ! " (" Nothing, nothing ! ") which showed that the camp was in full security. Every now and then groups of negroes, inspired by curiosity, collected round me, but all looked upon me with a threatening expression of countenance.

CHAPTER XXV

AT length an escort of negro soldiers, very fairly equipped, arrived. The negro whose property I ap-peared to be unfastened me from the oak to which I was bound, and handed me over to the escort, receiving in exchange a bag full of piastres. As he lay upon the grass counting them with every appearance of delight, I was led away by the sol-diers. My escort wore a uniform of coarse cloth, of a reddish-brown colour, with yellow facings; their head-dress was a Spanish cap called a *montera*, ornamented with a large red cockade. Instead of a cartouche case, they had a species of game-bag slung at their sides. Their arms were a heavy musket, a sabre, and a dagger. I afterwards learned that these men formed the body-guard of Biassou.

After a circuitous route through the rows of *ajoupas* which were scattered all over the place, I came to a cave which Nature had hollowed out in one of those masses of rock

with which the meadow was full. A large curtain of some
material from the looms of Thibet, which the negroes called
katchmir, and which is remarkable less for the brilliancy of
its colouring than for softness of its material, concealed
the interior of the cavern from the vulgar gaze. The entrance was guarded by a double line of negroes, dressed like
those who had escorted me thither.

After the countersign had been exchanged with the sentries
who marched backwards and forwards before the cave, the
commander of the escort raised the curtain sufficiently for
me to enter, and then let it drop behind me. A copper lamp
with six lights, hung by a chain from the roof of the grotto,
cast a flickering light upon the damp walls. Between the
ranks of mulatto soldiers I perceived a coloured man sitting
upon a large block of mahogany, which was partially covered with a carpet made of parrot's feathers. His dress was
of the most absurd kind. A splendid silk girdle, from which
hung a cross of Saint Louis, held up a pair of common blue
trousers, while a waistcoat of white linen which did not meet
the waistband of the trousers completed the strange costume.
He wore high boots, and a round hat with a red cockade, and
epaulets,— one of gold with silver stars, like those worn by
brigadiers; while the other was of red-worsted, with two copper stars (which seemed to have been taken from a pair of
spurs) fixed upon it, evidently to render it more worthy of
its resplendent neighbour. A sabre and a pair of richly
chased pistols lay by his side. Behind him were two white
children dressed in the costume of slaves, bearing large fans
of peacock feathers.

Two squares of crimson velvet, which seemed to have been
stolen from some church, were placed on either side of the
mahogany block. One of these was occupied by the Obi who
had rescued me from the frenzy of the *griotes*. He was seated
with his legs crossed under him, holding in his hand his white
wand, and not moving a muscle: he looked like a porcelain idol
in a Chinese pagoda, but through the holes in his veil I could
see his flashing eyes fixed steadfastly upon mine.

Upon each side of the general were trophies of flags, banners, and pennons of all kinds. Among them I noticed the white flag with the lilies, the tricolour, and the banner of Spain; the others were covered with fancy devices. I also perceived a large standard entirely black. At the end of the grotto, I saw a portrait of the mulatto Ogé who, together with his lieutenant Jean Charanne, had been broken on the wheel the year previous for the crime of rebellion. Twenty of his accomplices, blacks and mulattoes, suffered with him. In this painting Ogé, the son of a butcher at Cap, was represented in the uniform of a lieutenant-colonel, and decorated with the star of Saint Louis and the Order of Merit of the Lion, which last he had purchased from the Prince of Limburg.

The negro general into whose presence I had been introduced was short and of vulgar aspect, while his face showed a strange mixture of cunning and cruelty. After looking at me for some time in silence, with a bitter omen on his face, he said,—

" I am Biassou."

I expected this, but I could not hear it from his mouth, distorted as it was by a cruel smile, without an inward trembling; yet my face remained unchanged, and I made no reply.

" Well," continued he, in his bad French, " have they already empaled you, that you are unable to bend before Biassou, generalissimo of this conquered land, and brigadier of his Most Catholic Majesty?" (The rebel chiefs sometimes affected to be acting for the King of France, sometimes for the Republic, and at others for the King of Spain.)

I crossed my arms upon my chest, and looked him firmly in the face.

He again sneered. "Ho, ho!" said he; "me pareces hombre de buen corazon (" you seem a courageous man "); well, listen to my questions. Were you born in the island?"

5

" No, I am a Frenchman."

My calmness irritated him. " All the better; I see by
your uniform that you are an officer. How old are
you? "

" Twenty."

" When were you twenty? "

To this question, which aroused in me all the recollection
of my misery, I could not at first find words to reply. He
repeated it imperiously.

" The day upon which Leogri was hung," answered I.

An expression of rage passed over his face as he answered,
" It is twenty-three days since Leogri was executed. Frenchman, when you meet him this evening you may tell him from
me that you lived twenty-four days longer than he did. I
will spare you for to-day; I wish you to tell him of the liberty
that his brethren have gained, and what you have seen at the
headquarters of General Jean Biassou."

Then he ordered me to sit down in one corner between two
of his guards, and with a motion of his hand to some of his
men, who wore the uniform of *aides-de-camp*, he said, " Let
the Assembly be sounded, that we may inspect the whole of
our troops; and you, your reverence," he added, turning to
the Obi, " put on your priestly vestments, and perform for
our army the holy sacrament of the Mass."

The Obi rose, bowed profoundly, and whispered a word or
two in the general's ear.

" What," cried the latter, " no altar! but never mind, the
good Giu has no need of a magnificent temple for His worship.
Gideon and Joshua adored Him before masses of rock; let
us do as they did. All that is required is that the hearts
should be true. No altar, you say! why not make one of that
great chest of sugar which we took yesterday from Dubussion's house? "

This suggestion of Biassou was promptly carried into
execution. In an instant the interior of the cave was arranged for a burlesque of the divine ceremony. A pyx and a
monstrance stolen from the parish church of Acul were

promptly produced (the very church in which my nuptials with Marie had been celebrated, and where we had received Heaven's blessing, which had so soon changed to a curse). The stolen chest of sugar was speedily made into an altar and covered with a white cloth, through which, however, the words " Dubussion and Company for Nantes " could be plainly perceived.

When the sacred vessels had been placed on the altar, the Obi perceived that the crucifix was wanting. He drew his dagger, which had a cross handle, and stuck it into the wood of the case in front of the pyx. Then without removing his cap or veil, he threw the cope which had been stolen from the priest of Acul over his shoulders and bare chest, opened the silver clasps of the missal from which the prayers had been read on my ill-fated marriage day, and turning towards Biassou, whose seat was a few paces from the altar, announced to him that all was ready.

On a sign from the general the katchmir curtains were drawn aside, and the insurgent army was seen drawn up in close column before the entrance to the grotto. Biassou removed his hat and knelt before the altar.

" On your knees! " he cried, in a loud voice.

" On your knees! " repeated the commander of the battalions.

The drums were beaten, and all the insurgents fell upon their knees. I alone refused to move, disgusted at this vile profanation about to be enacted under my very eyes; but the two powerful mulattoes who guarded me pulled my seat from under me, and pressed heavily upon my shoulders, so that I fell on my knees, compelled to pay a semblance of respect to this parody of a religious ceremony. The Obi performed his duties with affected solemnity, while the two white pages of Biassou officiated as deacon and sub-deacon. The insurgents, prostrated before the altar, assisted at the ceremony with the greatest enthusiasm, the general setting the example.

At the moment of the exaltation of the host, the Obi raising in his hands the consecrated vessel exclaimed in his creole jargon, "Zoté coné bon Giu; ce li mo fé zoté voer. Blan touyé li: touyé blan yo toute!" ("You see your good God; I am showing Him to you. The white men killed Him: kill all the whites!")

At these words, pronounced in a loud voice, the tones of which had something in them familiar to my ear, all the rebels uttered a loud shout, and clashed their weapons together. Had it not been for Biassou's influence, that hour would have been my last. To such atrocities may men be driven who use the dagger for a cross, and upon whose minds the most trivial event makes a deep and profound impression.

CHAPTER XXVI

AT the termination of the ceremony the Obi bowed respectfully to Biassou; then the general rose and, addressing me in French, said,—

"We are accused of having no religion. You see it is a falsehood, and that we are good Catholics."

I do not know whether he spoke ironically or in good faith. A few moments later he called for a glass bowl filled with grains of black maize; on the top he threw some white maize, then he raised it high in his hand so that all the army might see it.

"Brothers," cried he, "you are the black maize; your enemies are the white maize."

With these words he shook the bowl, and in an instant the white grains had disappeared beneath the black; and, as though inspired, he cried out, "Where are the white now?"

The mountains re-echoed with the shouts with which the illustration of the general was received; and Biassou continuing his harangue, mixed up French, creole dialect, and Spanish alternately: —

"The season for temporizing has passed; for a long time

we have been as patient as the sheep to whose wool the whites compare our hair; let us now be as implacable as the panthers or the tigers of the countries from which they have torn us. Force alone can obtain for us our rights; and everything can be obtained by those who use their force without pity. Saint Loup [Wolf] has two days in the year consecrated to him in the Gregorian calendar, while the Paschal Lamb has but one. Am not I correct, your reverence?"

The Obi bowed in sign of corroboration.

" They have come," continued Biassou,— " these enemies of ours have come as enemies of the regeneration of humanity; these whites, these planters, these men of business, veritable devils vomited from the mouth of hell. They came in the insolence of their pride, in their fine dresses, their uniforms, their feathers, their magnificent arms; they despised us because we were black and naked, in their overbearing haughtiness; they thought that they could drive us before them as easily as these peacock feathers disperse the swarm of sandflies and mosquitoes."

As he uttered these concluding words, he snatched from the hands of his white slaves one of the large fans, and waved it over his head with a thousand eccentric gesticulations. Then he continued: —

" But, my brethren, we burst upon them like flies upon a carcass; they have fallen in their fine uniforms beneath the strokes of our naked arms, which they believed to be without power, ignorant that good wood is the stronger when the bark is stripped off; and now these accursed tyrants tremble, and are filled with fear."

A triumphant yell rose in answer to the general's speech, and all the army repeated, " They are filled with fear!"

" Blacks, Creoles, and Congoes," added Biassou, " vengeance and liberty! Mulattoes, do not be led away by the temptations of the white men! Your fathers serve in their ranks, but your mothers are with us; besides, ' O bermanos de mi alma ' (' O brethren of my soul ') have they ever acted as fathers to you? Have they not rather been cruel masters, and treated you as slaves, because you had the blood of your mothers in your veins? While a miserable cotton garment covered your bodies scorched by the sun, your cruel fathers went about in straw hats and nankeen clothes on work-days, and in cloth and velvet on holidays and feasts. Curses be on their unnatural hearts! But as the holy commandments forbid you to strike your father, abstain from doing so; but in the day of battle what hinders you from turning to your comrade and saying, 'Touyé papa moé, ma touyé quena toué!' ('Kill my father, and I will kill yours!') Vengeance then, my brethren, and liberty for all men! This cry has found an echo in every part of the island; it has roused Tobago and Cuba. It was Bouckmann, a negro from Jamaica, the leader of the twenty-five fugitive slaves of the Blue Mountain, who raised the standard of revolt among us. A glorious victory was the first proof that he gave of his brotherhood with the negroes of St. Domingo. Let us follow his noble example, with an axe in one hand and a torch in the other. No mercy for the whites, no mercy for the planters! let us massacre their families, and destroy their plantations! Do not allow a tree to remain standing on their estates; let us upturn the very earth itself that it may swallow up our white oppressors! Courage then, friends and brethren! we will fight them and sweep them from the face of the earth. We will conquer or die. As victors, we shall enjoy all the pleasures of life; and if we fall, the saints are ready to receive us in heaven, where each warrior will receive a double ration of brandy and a silver piastre each day!"

This warlike discourse, which to you appears perfectly ridiculous, had a tremendous effect on the insurgents. It is true that Biassou's wild gesticulations, the manner in which his voice rose and fell, and the strange sneer which every now and then appeared on his lips, imparted to his speech a strange amount of power and fascination. The skill with which he alluded to those points that would have the greatest weight with the negroes added a degree of force which told well with his audience.

I will not attempt to describe to you the outburst of determined enthusiasm which the harangue of Biassou roused
among the rebels. There arose at once a discordant chorus
of howls, yells, and shouts. Some beat their naked breasts,
others dashed their clubs and sabres together. Many threw
themselves on their knees, and remained in that position as
though in rapt ecstasy. The negresses tore their breasts and
arms with their fish-bone combs. The sounds of drums, tomtoms, guitars, and tambourines were mingled with the discharge of firearms. It was a veritable witches' Sabbath.

Biassou raised his hand, and as if by enchantment the tumult was stilled, and each negro returned to his place in the
ranks in silence. The discipline which Biassou had imposed
upon his equals by the exercise of his power of will struck
me, I may say, with admiration. All the soldiers of the force
seemed to exist only to obey the wishes of their chief, as the
notes of the harpsichord under the fingers of the musician.

CHAPTER XXVII

THE spectacle of another example of the powers of fascination and deception now attracted my attention.
This was the healing of the wounded.

The Obi, who in the army performed the double functions
of healer of souls and bodies, began his inspection of his patients. He had taken off his sacerdotal robes, and was
seated before a large box in which he kept his drugs and
instruments. He used the latter very rarely, but occasionally
drew blood skilfully enough with a lancet made of fish-bone;
but he appeared to me to use the knife, which in his hands
replaced the scalper, rather clumsily. In most cases he contented himself with prescribing orange-flower water, or sarsa-
parilla, and a mouthful of old rum. His favourite remedy,
however, and one which he said was an infallible panacea for
all ills, was composed of three glasses of red wine, in which

was some grated nutmeg and the yolk of an egg boiled hard; he employed this specific for almost every malady. You will understand that his knowledge of medicine was as great a farce as his pretended religion; and it is probable that the small number of cures that he effected would not have secured the confidence of the negroes had he not had recourse to all sorts of mummeries and incantations, and acted as much upon their imaginations as upon their bodies. Thus, he never examined their wounds without performing some mysterious signs; while at other times he skilfully mingled together religion and negro superstition, and would put into their wounds a little *fetish* stone wrapped in a morsel of lint, and the patient would credit the stone with the healing effects of the lint. If any one came to announce to him the death of a patient, he would answer solemnly: " I foresaw it; he was a traitor: in the burning of such and such a house he spared a white man's life; his death was a judgment,"— and the wondering crowd of rebels applauded him as he thus increased their deadly hatred for their adversaries.

This impostor, among other methods, employed one which amused me by its singularity. One of the negro chiefs had been badly wounded in the last action. The Obi examined the wound attentively, dressed it as well as he was able, then, mounting the altar, exclaimed, " All this is nothing." He then tore two or three leaves from the missal, burnt them to ashes, and mingling them with some wine in the sacramental cup, cried to the wounded man, " Drink! this is the true remedy. " The patient, stupidly fixing his eyes on the impostor, drank, while the Obi with raised hands seemed to call down blessings on his head; and it may be the conviction that he was healed which brought about his cure.

CHAPTER XXVIII

ANOTHER scene in which the Obi also played the principal part succeeded to this. The physician had taken the place of the priest, and the sorcerer now replaced the physician.

"Listen, men!" cried the Obi, leaping with incredible agility upon the improvised altar, and sinking down with his legs crossed under his striped petticoat,—"listen. Who will dive into the book of fate? I can foretell the future. 'He estudiado la cienca de los Gitanos' ('I have studied the sciences of the gipsies')." A crowd of mulattoes and negroes hurriedly crowded up to him. "One by one," said the Obi, in that voice which called to my mind some remembrances that I could not quite collect. "If you come all together, altogether you will enter the tomb."

They stopped. Just then a coloured man dressed in a white jacket and trousers, with a bandana handkerchief tied round his head entered the cave. Consternation was depicted on his countenance.

"Well, Rigaud," said the general, "what is it?"

Rigaud, sometimes called General Rigaud, was at the head of the mulatto insurgents at Lagu,—a man who concealed much cunning under an appearance of candour, and cruelty beneath the mask of humanity. I looked upon him with much attention.

"General," whispered Rigaud, but as I was close to them I could catch every word, "on the outskirts of the camp there is a messenger from Jean François who has brought the news that Bouckmann has been killed in a battle with the whites under M. de Touzard, and that his head has been set upon the gates of the town as a trophy."

"Is that all?" asked Biassou, his eyes sparkling with delight at learning of the diminution of the number of chiefs and the consequent increase of his own importance.

"The emissary of Jean François has in addition a message for you."

"That is all right," replied the general; "but get rid of this air of alarm, my good Rigaud."

"But," said Rigaud, "do you not fear the effect that the death of Bouckmann will have on the army?"

"You wish to appear more simple than you are; but you shall see what Biassou will do. Keep the messenger back for a quarter of an hour, and all will go well."

Then he approached the Obi, who during this conversation had been exercising his functions as fortune-teller, questioning the wondering negroes, examining the lines on their hands and foreheads, and distributing more or less good luck according to the size and colour of the piece of money thrown by each negro into a silver-gilt basin which stood on one side. Biassou whispered a few words in his ear, and without making any reply the Obi continued his prophetic observations.

"He," cried the Obi, "who has in the middle of his forehead a little square or triangular figure will make a large fortune without work or toil. The figure of three interlaced *S's* on the forehead is a fatal sign; he who has it will certainly be drowned if he does not carefully avoid water. Four lines from the top of the nose, and turning round two by two towards the eyes, announces that you will be taken prisoner, and for a long time languish in a foreign prison."

Here the Obi paused. "Friends," continued he, "I have observed this sign in the forehead of Bug-Jargal, the brave chief of Morne-Rouge."

These words, which convinced me that Bug-Jargal had been made prisoner, were followed by a cry of grief from a band of negroes who wore short scarlet breeches. They belonged to the band of Morne-Rouge.

Then the Obi began again: "If you have on the right side of the forehead in the line of the moon a mark resembling a fork, do not remain idle, and avoid dissipation of all kinds. A small mark like the Arabic cipher 3 in the line of the sun betokens blows with a stick."

An old negro here interrupted the magician, and dragging himself to his feet begged him to dress his wound. He had been wounded in the face, and one of his eyes almost torn from the socket hung upon his cheek.

The Obi had forgotten him when going through his patients. Directly, however, he saw him he cried out: "Round marks on the right side of the forehead in the line of the moon foretell misfortunes to the sight. My man, let me see your hand."

"Alas, excellent sir," answered the other, "it is my eye that I want you to look at."

"Old man," replied the Obi, crossly, "it is not necessary to see your eye; give me your hand, I say."

The miserable wretch obeyed, moaning, "My eye! my eye!"

"Good," cried the Obi; "if you see on the line of life a spot surrounded by a circle you will lose an eye. There is the mark. You will become blind of an eye."

"I am so already," answered the negro, piteously.

But the Obi had merged the physician in the sorcerer, and thrusting him roughly on one side continued: "Listen, my men.

"If the seven lines on the forehead are slight, twisted, and lightly marked, they announce a short life. He who has between his eyebrows on the line of the moon the figure of two crossed arrows will be killed in battle. If the line of life which intersects the hand has a cross at its junction it foretells death on the scaffold; and here I must tell you, my brethren," said the Obi, interrupting himself, "that one of the bravest defenders of our liberties, Bouckmann, has all these fatal marks."

At these words all the negroes held their breath, and gazed on the impostor with glances of stupid admiration.

"Only," continued the Obi, "I cannot reconcile the two opposing signs, death on the battle-field and also on the scaffold; and yet my science is infallible."

He stopped, and cast a meaning glance at Biassou, who

whispered something to an officer, who at once quitted the cavern.

" A gaping mouth," continued the Obi, turning on his audience a malicious glance, " a slouching carriage, and arms hanging down by the side, announces natural stupidity, emptiness, and want of reasoning powers."

Biassou gave a sneer of delight; at that moment the *aide-de-camp* returned, bringing with him a negro covered with mud and dust, whose feet, wounded by the roots and flints, showed that he had just come off a long journey. This was the messenger whose arrival Rigaud had announced. He held in one hand a letter, and in the other a document sealed with the design of a flaming heart; round it was a monogram, composed of the letters *M* and *N* interlaced, no doubt intended as an emblem of the union of the free mulattoes and the negro slaves. Underneath I could read this motto, " Prejudice conquered; the rod of iron broken; long live the king!" This document was a safe conduct given by Jean François.

The messenger handed his letter to Biassou, who hastily tore it open and perused the contents, then with an appearance of deep grief he exclaimed, " My brothers!" All bowed respectfully.

" My brothers, this is a dispatch to Jean Biassou, generalissimo of the conquered states, Brigadier-General of his Catholic Majesty, from Jean François, Grand Admiral of France, Lieutenant-General of the army of the King of Spain and the Indies. Bouckmann, chief of the hundred and twenty negroes of the Blue Mountain, whose liberty was recognized by the Governor-General of Belle Combe, has fallen in the glorious struggle of liberty and humanity against tyranny and barbarism. This gallant chief has been slain in an action with the white brigands of the infamous Touzard. The monsters have cut off his head, and have announced their intention of exposing it on a scaffold in the main square of the town of Cap. Vengeance!"

A gloomy silence succeeded the reading of this dispatch;

but the Obi leaped on his altar, and waving his white wand, exclaimed in accents of triumph,—

"Solomon, Zerobabel, Eleazar Thaleb, Cardau, Judas Bowtharicht, Avenoes, Albert the Great, Bohabdil, Jean de Hagul, Anna Baratio, Daniel Ogromof, Rachel Flintz, Allornino,— I give you thanks! The science of the spirits has not deceived me. Sons, friends, brothers, boys, children, mothers, all of you listen to me. What was it that I predicted? The marks on the forehead of Bouckmann announced that his life would be a short one, that he would die in battle, and that he would appear on the scaffold. The revelations of my art have turned out true to the letter, and those points which seemed the most obscure are now the most plain. Brethren, wonder and admire!"

The panic of the negroes changed during this discourse to a sort of admiring terror. They listened to the Obi with a species of confidence mingled with fear, while the latter, carried away by his own enthusiasm, walked up and down the sugar-case, which presented plenty of space for his short steps.

A sneer passed over Biassou's face as he addressed the Obi: "Your reverence, since you know what is to come, will you be good enough to tell me the future of Jean Biassou, Brigadier-General?"

The Obi halted on the top of his strange altar, which the credulity of the negroes looked upon as something divine, and answered, "Venga vuestra merced" ("Come, your excellency"). At this moment the Obi was the most important man in the army; the military power bowed to the spiritual.

"Your hand, General," said the Obi, stooping to grasp it. "Empezo" ("I begin"). The line of junction equally marked in its full length promises you riches and happiness; the line of life strongly developed announces a life exempt from ills, and a happy old age. Its narrowness shows your wisdom and your superior talents, as well as the generosity of your heart; and lastly, I see what chiromancers call the luckiest of all signs,— a number of little wrinkles in the shape of a tree with its branches extending upwards; this promises health and wealth; it also prognosticates courage. General, it curves in the direction of the little finger; this is the sign of wholesome severity."

As he said this, the eyes of the Obi glanced at me through the apertures of his veil, and I fancied that I could catch a well-known voice under the habitual gravity of his intonation, as he continued,—

"The line of health, marked with a number of small circles, announces that you will have, for the sake of the cause, to order a number of executions; divided here by a half-moon, it shows that you will be exposed to great danger from ferocious beasts, that is to say from the whites, if you do not exterminate them. The line of fortune surrounded, like the line of life, by little branches rising towards the upper part of the hand, confirms the position of power and supremacy to which you have been called; turning to the right, it is a symbol of your administrative capacity. The fifth line, that of the triangle prolonged to the root of the middle finger, promises you success in all your undertakings. Let me see your fingers: the thumb marked with little lines from the point to the nail shows that you will receive a noble heritage,— that of the glory of the unfortunate Bouckmann, no doubt," added the Obi, in a loud voice. "The slight swelling at the root of the forefinger, lightly marked with lines, promises honours and dignities. The middle finger shows nothing. Your little finger is covered with lines crossing one another; you will vanquish all your enemies, and rise high above your rivals. These lines form the cross of Saint Andrew, a mark of genius and foresight. I also notice the figure of a circle, another token of your arrival at the highest power and dignity. 'Happy the man,' says Eleazar Thaleb, 'who possesses all these signs. Destiny has its choicest gifts in store for him, and his fortunate star announces the talent which will bring him glory.' And now, General, let me look at your forehead. 'He,' says Rachel Flintz, of Bohemia, 'who bears on his forehead, on the line of the sun, a square or a triangular mark, will make a great fortune.' Here is another prediction: ' If the mark is on the right, it refers to an important succession;' that of Bouckmann is, of course, again referred to. The mark in the shape of a horseshoe between the eyebrows, on the line of the moon, means that prompt vengeance will be taken for insult and tyranny. I have this mark as well as you."

The curious manner in which the Obi uttered these words, " I have this mark," attracted my attention.

" The mark of a lion's claw which you have on your left eyelid is only noticeable among men of undoubted courage. But to close this, General Jean Biassou, your forehead shows every sign of the most unexampled success, and on it is a combination of lines which form the letter M, the commencement of the name of the Blessed Virgin. In whatever part of the forehead, and in whatever line of the face, such a sign appears, the signification is the same,— genius, glory, and power. He who bears it will always bring success to whatever cause he embraces, and those under his command will never have to regret any loss. He alone is worth all the soldiers of his army. You, General, are the elect of Fate."

" Thanks, your reverence," said Biassou, preparing to return to his mahogany throne.

" Stay a moment, General," said the Obi, " I forgot one last sign: The line of the sun, which is so strongly marked on your forehead, proves that you understand the way of the world; that you possess the wish to make others happy; that you have much liberality, and like to do things in a magnificent manner."

Biassou at once recognized his forgetfulness, and drawing from his pocket a heavy purse, he threw it into the plate, so as to prove that the line of the sun never lies.

But this miraculous horoscope of the general had produced its effect upon the army. All the insurgents, who since the news of the death of Bouckmann attached greater weight than ever to the words of the Obi, lost their feelings of uneasiness and became violently enthusiastic; and trusting blindly

in their infallible sorcerer and their predestined chief, they
began to shout, "Long live our Obi! long live our general!"

The Obi and Biassou glanced at each other; and I almost
thought I could hear the stifled laugh of the one replied to by
the sardonic chuckle of the other. I do not know how it was,
but this Obi tormented me dreadfully; I had a feeling that I
had seen or heard him before, and I made up my mind to
speak to him.

"Ho, Obi, your reverence, doctor, here!" cried I to him.
He turned sharply round. "There is some one here whose
lot you have not yet cast,— it is mine."

He crossed his arms over the silver sun that covered his
hairy breast, but he made no reply.

I continued: "I would gladly know what you prophesy
with regard to my future, but your worthy comrades have
taken my watch and my purse, and I suppose you will not
give me a specimen of your skill for nothing."

He advanced quickly to me, and muttered hoarsely in my
ear. "You deceive yourself; let me see your hand."

I gave it, looking fixedly at him; his eyes sparkled as he
bent over my hand.

"If the line of life," said he, "is cut by two transverse
lines, it is the sign of immediate death: your life will be a
short one. If the line of health is not in the centre of the
hand, and if the line of life and the line of fortune
are united so as to form an angle, a natural death cannot
be looked for; do not therefore, look for a natural death! If
the bottom of the forefinger has a long line cutting it, a violent death will be the result; prepare yourself for a violent
death!"

There was a ring of pleasure in his sepulchral voice as he
thus announced my death, but I listened to him with contempt and indifference.

"Sorcerer," said I, with a disdainful smile, "you are skilful, for you are speaking of a certainty."

Once more he came closer to me. "You doubt my science," cried he; "listen, then, once more. The severance of

the line of the sun on your forehead shows me that you take an enemy for a friend, and a friend for an enemy."

These words seemed to refer to the treacherous Pierrot whom I loved, but who had betrayed me, and to the faithful Habibrah whom I had hated, and whose blood-stained garments attested to his fidelity and his devotion.

"What do you say?" exclaimed I.

"Listen until the end," continued the Obi. "I spoke of the future; listen to the past. The line of the moon on your forehead is slightly curved; that signifies that your wife has been carried off."

I trembled, and endeavoured to spring from my seat, but my guards held me back.

"You have but little patience," continued the sorcerer; "listen to the end. The little cross that cuts the extremity of that curve shows me all: your wife was carried off on the very night of your nuptials."

"Wretch!" cried I, "you know where she is! Who are you?"

I strove again to free myself, and to tear away his veil; but I had to yield to numbers and to force, and had the mortification of seeing the mysterious Obi move away repeating, "Do you believe me now? Prepare for immediate death."

CHAPTER XXIX

AS if to draw my attention from the perplexity into which I had been thrown by the strange scene that had just passed, a new and more terrible drama succeeded to the farce that had been played between Biassou and the Obi. Biassou had again taken his place upon his mahogany throne, while Rigaud and the Obi were seated on his right and left; the latter, with his arms crossed on his breast, seemed to have given himself up to deep thought. Biassou and Rigaud were chewing tobacco, and an *aide-de-camp* had just asked if he

6

should order a general march past of the forces, when a tumultuous crowd of negroes, with hideous shouts, arrived at
the entrance of the grotto. They had brought with them
three white prisoners, to be judged by Biassou, but what they
desired was easily shown by the cries of " Murte! Murte!"
(" Death, death!") the latter, no doubt emanating from the
English negroes of Bouckmann's band, many of whom had
by this time arrived to join the French and Spanish negroes
of Biassou.

The general with a gesture of his hand commanded silence,
and ordered the three captives to be brought to the entrance
of the grotto. I recognized two of them with considerable
surprise; one was the Citizen General C ———, that philan-
thropist who was in correspondence with all the lovers of the
negro race in different parts of the globe, and who had proposed so cruel a mode of suppressing the insurrection to the
governor. The other was the planter of doubtful origin, who
manifested so great a dislike to the mulattoes, among whom
the whites insisted on classing him. The third appeared to
belong to a section called " poor whites,"— that is to say,
white men who had to work for their living; he wore a
leathern apron, and his sleeves were turned up to his elbows.
All the prisoners had been taken at different times endeavouring to hide themselves in the mountains.

The " poor white " was the first one that was questioned.

" Who are you? " asked Biassou.

" I am Jacques Belin, carpenter to the Hospital of the
Fathers, at Cap."

Surprise and shame struggled for the mastery in the features of the general. " Jacques Belin! " repeated he, biting
his lips.

" Yes," replied the carpenter; " do you not recognize
me? "

" Begin," retorted the general, furiously, " by recognizing
me and saluting me."

" I do not salute *my slave*," replied the carpenter, sturdily.

" Your slave, wretch! " cried the general.

"Yes," replied the carpenter; "yes, I was your first master. You pretend not to recognize me, but remember, Jean Biassou, that I sold you for thirty piastres in the St. Domingo slave-market."

An expression of concentrated rage passed over Biassou's face.

"Well," continued the carpenter, "you appear ashamed of having worked for me; ought not Jean Biassou to feel proud of having belonged to Jacques Belin? Your mother, the old idiot, has often swept out my shop; but at last I sold her to the major domo of the Hospital of the Fathers, and she was so old and decrepit that he would give me only thirty-two livres and six sous for her. There is my history and yours; but it seems as if the negroes and mulattoes are growing proud, and that you have forgotten the time when you served Master Jacques Belin, the carpenter of Cap, on your knees."

Biassou listened to him with that sardonic smile which gave him the appearance of a tiger.

"Good!" said he. Then turning to the negroes who had captured Belin, "Get two trestles, two planks, and a saw, and take this man away. Jacques Belin, carpenter of Cap, thank me, for you shall have a true carpenter's death."

His sardonic laugh too fully explained the horrible punishment that he destined for the pride of his former master; but Jacques Belin did not blench, and turning proudly to Biassou, cried,—

"Yes, I ought to thank you, for I bought you for thirty piastres, and I got work out of you to a much greater amount."

They dragged him away.

CHAPTER XXX

MORE dead than alive, the other two prisoners had witnessed this frightful prologue to their own fate. Their timid and terrified appearance contrasted with the courageous audacity of the carpenter; every limb quivered with affright.

Biassou looked at them one after the other with his foxlike glance, and, as if he took a pleasure in prolonging their agony, began a discussion with Rigaud upon the different kinds of tobacco,— asserting that that of Havana was only good for manufacturing cigars, while for snuff he knew nothing better than the Spanish tobacco, two barrels of which Bouckmann had sent him, being a portion of the plunder of M. Lebattre's stores in the island of Tortue. Then, turning sharply upon the Citizen General C——, he asked him,—

" What do you think? "

This sudden address utterly confounded the timid citizen, and he stammered out, " General, I am entirely of your Excellency's opinion."

" You flatter me," replied Biassou; " I want *your* opinion, not mine. Do you know any tobacco that makes better snuff than that of M. Lebattres? "

" No, my lord," answered C——, whose evident terror greatly amused Biassou.

" ' General,' ' your Excellency,' ' my lord!' you are an aristocrat."

" Oh, no, certainly not," exclaimed the citizen general. " I am a good patriot of '91, and an ardent negrophile."

" ' Negrophile'! " interrupted the general; " pray, what is a ' negrophile' ? "

" It is a friend of the blacks," stammered the citizen.

" It is not enough to be a friend of the blacks; you must also be a friend of the men of colour."

"Men of colour is what I should have said," replied the lover of the blacks, humbly. "I am mixed up with all the most famous partisans of the negroes and the mulattoes —"

Delighted at the opportunity of humiliating a white man, Biassou again interrupted him: "'Negroes and mulattoes'! What do you mean pray? Do you wish to insult me by making use of those terms of contempt invented by the whites? There are only men of colour and blacks here,— do you understand that, Mr. Planter?"

"It was a slip, a bad habit that I picked up in childhood," answered C——. "Pardon me, my lord, I had no wish to offend you."

"Leave off this *my lording* business! I have already told you that I don't like these aristocratic ways."

C—— again endeavoured to excuse himself, and began to stammer out a fresh explanation. "If you knew, citizen —"

"Citizen, indeed!" cried Biassou, in affected anger; "I detest all this Jacobin jargon. Are you by chance a Jacobin? Remember that you are speaking to the generalissimo of the king's troops."

The unhappy partisan of the negro race was dumbfounded, and did not know in what terms to address this man, who equally disdained the titles of "my lord" or "citizen,"— the aristocratic or republican modes of salutation. Biassou, whose anger was only assumed, cruelly enjoyed the predicament in which he had placed C——.

"Alas," at last said the citizen general, "you do not do me justice, noble defender of the unwritten rights of the larger portion of the human race!"

In his perplexity to hit upon an acceptable mode of address to a man who appeared to disdain all titles, he had recourse to one of those sonorous periphrases which the republicans occasionally substituted for the name and title of the persons with whom they were in conversation.

Biassou looked at him steadily and said, "You love the blacks and the men of colour?"

" Do I love them? " exclaimed the citizen C ——. " Why, I correspond with Brissot and —"

Biassou interrupted him with a sardonic laugh. " Ha, ha! I am glad to find in you so trusty a friend to our cause; you must, of course, thoroughly detest those wretched colonists who punished our insurrection by a series of the most cruel executions; and you, of course, think with us that it is not the blacks, but the whites, who are the true rebels, since they are in arms against the laws of nature and humanity? You must execrate such monsters!"

" I do execrate them," answered C——.

" Well," continued Biassou, " what do you think of a man who, in his endeavours to crush the last efforts of the slaves to regain their liberty, placed the heads of fifty black men on each side of the avenue that led to his house? "

C—— grew fearfully pale.

" What do you think of a white man who would propose to surround the town of Cap with a circle of negro heads? "

" Mercy, mercy!" cried the terrified citizen general.

" Am I threatening you? " replied Biassou, coldly. " Let me finish,— a circle of heads that would reach from Fort Picolet to Cape Caracol. What do you think of that? Answer me!"

The words of Biassou, " Do I threaten you," had given a faint ray of hope to C——, for he fancied that the general might have heard of this terrible proposition without knowing the author of it; he therefore replied with all the firmness that he could muster, in order to remove any impression that the idea was his own:—

" I consider such a suggestion an atrocious crime."

Biassou chuckled. " Good! And what punishment should be inflicted on the man who proposed it? "

The unfortunate C —— hesitated.

" What!" cried Biassou, " you hesitate! Are you, or are you not, the friend of the blacks? "

Of the two alternatives the wretched man chose the least threatening one, and seeing no hostile light in Biassou's eyes, he answered in a low voice: "The guilty person deserves death."

"Well answered," replied Biassou, calmly, throwing aside the tobacco that he had been chewing. His assumed air of indifference had completely deceived the unfortunate lover of the negro race, and he made another effort to dissipate any suspicions which might have been engendered against him.

"No one," cried C———, "has a more ardent desire for your success than I. I correspond with Brissot and Pruneau de Pomme-Gouge in France, with Magaw in America, with Peter Paulus in Holland, with the Abbé Tamburini in Italy,—" and he was continuing to unfold the same string of names which he had formerly repeated, but with a different motive, at the council held at M. de Blanchelande's, when Biassou interrupted him.

"What do I care with whom you correspond? Tell me rather where are your granaries and store-houses, for my army has need of supplies. Your plantation is doubtless a rich one, and your business must be lucrative since you correspond with so many merchants."

C——— ventured timidly to remark: "Hero of humanity, they are not merchants, but philosophers, philanthropists, lovers of the race of blacks."

"Then," said Biassou, with a shake of his head, "if you have nothing that can be plundered, what good are you?"

This question afforded a chance of safety of which C——— eagerly availed himself. "Illustrious warrior," exclaimed he, "have you an economist in your army?"

"What is that?" asked the general.

"It is," replied the prisoner, with as much calmness as his fears would permit him to assume, "a most necessary man,— one whom all appreciate, one who follows out and classes in their proper order the respective material resources of an empire, and gives to each its real value, increasing and improving them by combining their sources and results, and pouring them like fertilizing streams into the main river of general utility, which in its turn swells the great sea of public prosperity."

"*Caramba!*" observed Biassou, leaning over towards the Obi. "What the deuce does he mean by all these words strung together like the beads on your rosary?"

The Obi shrugged his shoulders in sign of ignorance and disdain, as citizen C —— continued:—

"If you will permit me to observe, valiant chief of the regenerators of St. Domingo, I have carefully studied the works of the greatest economists of the world,— Turgot, Raynal, and Mirabeau the friend of man. I have put their theories into practice; I thoroughly understand the science indispensable for the government of kingdoms and states —"

"The economist is not economical of his words," observed Rigaud, with his bland and cunning smile.

"But you, eternal talker," cried Biassou, "tell me, have I any kingdoms or states to govern?"

"Not yet perhaps, great man, but they will come; and besides, my knowledge descends to all the useful details which are comprised in the interior economy of an army."

The general again interrupted him: "I have nothing to do with the interior economy of the army; I command it."

"Good!" replied the citizen; "you shall be the commander, I will be the commissary. I have much special knowledge as to the increase of cattle —"

"Do you think we are going to breed cattle?" cried Biassou with his sardonic laugh. "No, my good fellow, we are content with eating them. When cattle become scarce in the French colony I shall cross the line of mountains on the frontier and take the Spanish sheep and oxen from the plains of Cotury, of La Vega, of St. Jago, and from the banks of the Yuna; if necessary I will go as far as the Island of Jamaica, and to the back of the mountain of Cibos, and from the mouths of the Neybe to those of Santo Domingo; besides, I should be glad to punish those infernal Spanish planters for giving up Ogé to the French. You see I am not uneasy as regards provisions, and so have no need of your knowledge."

This open declaration rather disconcerted the poor economist; he made, however, one more effort for safety. "My studies," said he, "have not been limited to the reproduction of cattle; I am acquainted with other special branches of knowledge that may be very useful to you. I can show you the method of manufacturing pitch and working coal mines."

"What do I care for that?" exclaimed Biassou. "When I want charcoal I burn a few leagues of forest."

"I can tell you the proper kinds of wood to use for shipbuilding,— the chicarm and the sabieca for the keels; the yabas for the knees, the medlars for the framework, the hacomas, the gaïacs, the cedars, the acomas —"

"Que te lleven todos los demonios de los diez-y-siete infernos!" ("May the devils of the thirty-seven hells fly away with you!") cried Biassou, boiling over with impatience.

"I beg your pardon, my gracious patron," said the trembling economist, who did not understand Spanish.

"Listen," said Biassou. "I don't want to build vessels; there is only one vacancy that I can offer you, and that is not a very important one. I want a man to wait upon me; and now, Mr. Philosopher, tell me if that will suit you. You will have to serve me on your bended knees; you will prepare my pipe, cook my *calalou* and turtle soup, and you will stand behind me with a fan of peacock or parrot feathers like those two pages. Now, will the situation suit you?"

Citizen C ——, whose only desire was to save his life, bent to the earth with a thousand expressions of joy and gratitude.

"You accept my offer, then?" asked Biassou.

"Can you ask such a question, generous master? Do you think that I should hesitate for a moment in accepting so distinguished a post as that of being in constant attendance on you?"

At this reply the diabolical sneer of Biassou became more

pronounced. He rose up with an air of triumph, crossed his arms on his chest, and thrusting aside with his foot the white man's head who was prostrate on the ground before him, he cried in a loud voice,—

"I am delighted at being able to fathom how far the cowardice of the white man could go; I had already measured the extent of his cruelty. Citizen C——, it is to you that I owe this double experience. I knew all; how could you have been sufficiently besotted to think that I did not? It was you who presided at the executions of June, July, and August; it was you who placed fifty negro heads on each side of your avenue; it was you who proposed to slaughter the five hundred negroes who were confined in irons after the revolt, and to encircle the town of Cap with their heads from Fort Picolet to Cape Caracol. If you could have done it, you would have placed my head among them; and now you think yourself lucky if I will take you as my body-servant. No, no, I have more regard for your honour than you yourself have, and I will not inflict this affront on you; prepare to die!"

At a gesture of Biassou's hand the negroes removed the unhappy lover of the blacks to a position near me, where, overwhelmed by the honour of his position, he fell to the ground without being able to articulate a word.

CHAPTER XXXI

"IT is your turn now," said the general, turning to the last of the prisoners,— the planter who was accused by the white men of having black blood in his veins, and who had on that account sent me a challenge.

A general clamour drowned the reply of the planter. "Muerte! Mort! Touyé!" cried the negroes, grinding their teeth, and shaking their fists at the unhappy captive.

"General," said a mulatto, making himself heard above the uproar, " he is a white man, and he must die."

The miserable planter, by cries and gesticulations, managed to edge in some words. " No, general! no, my brothers! it is an infamous calumny. I am a mulatto like yourselves, of mixed blood; my mother was a negress, like your mothers and sisters."

" He lies!" cried the infuriated negroes; " he is a white man; he has always detested the coloured people."

" Never!" retorted the prisoner; " it is the whites that I detest. I have always said with you, ' Negre cé blan; blan cé negre.' (' The negroes are the masters; the whites are the slaves ')."

" Not at all!" cried the crowd, " not at all! Kill the white man, kill him!"

Still the unhappy wretch kept repeating in heartrending accents, " I am a mulatto, I am one of yourselves."

" Give me a proof," was Biassou's sole reply.

" A proof?" answered the prisoner, wildly; " the proof is that the whites have always despised me."

" That may be true," returned Biassou, " but you are an insolent hound to tell us so."

A young mulatto stepped to the front and addressed the planter in an excited manner. " That the whites despised you is a fact; but, on the other hand, you affected to look down upon the mulattoes among whom they classed you. It has even been reported that you once challenged a white man who called you a half-caste."

A howl of execration arose from the crowd, and the cry of " death " was repeated more loudly than ever; while the planter, casting an appealing glance at me, continued, with tears in his eyes,—

" It is a calumny; my greatest glory and happiness is in belonging to the blacks. I am a mulatto."

" If you really were a mulatto," observed Rigaud, quietly, " you would not make use of such an expression."

" How do I know what I am saying?" asked the panic-stricken wretch. "General, the proof that I am of mixed blood is in the black circle that you see round the bottom of my nails."

Biassou thrust aside the suppliant hand. "I do not possess the knowledge of our chaplain, who can tell what a man is by looking at his hand. But listen to me: my soldiers accuse you — some, of being a white man; others, of being a false brother. If this is the case you ought to die. You, on the other hand, assert that you belong to our race, and that you have never denied it. There is one method by which you can prove your assertion. Take this dagger and stab these two white prisoners!"

As he spoke, with a wave of his hand, Biassou designated the citizen C —— and myself.

The planter drew back from the dagger which, with a devilish smile on his face, Biassou presented to him.

"What!" said the general, "do you hesitate? It is your only chance of proving your assertion to the army that you are not a white, and are one of ourselves. Come, decide at once, for we have no time to lose."

The prisoner's eyes glared wildly; he stretched out his hand towards the dagger, then let his arm fall again, turning away his head, while every limb quivered with emotion.

"Come, come!" cried Biassou, in tones of impatience and anger, "I am in a hurry. Choose: either kill them, or die with them!"

The planter remained motionless, as if he had been turned to stone.

"Good!" said Biassou, turning towards the negroes; "he does not wish to be the executioner, let him be the victim. I can see that he is nothing but a white man; away with him!"

The negroes advanced to seize him. This movement impelled him to immediate choice between giving or receiving death. Extreme cowardice produces a bastard species of courage. Stepping forward, he snatched the dagger that Biassou still held out to him, and without giving himself time to reflect upon what he was about to do, he precipitated himself like a tiger upon citizen C——, who was lying on the ground near me. Then a terrible struggle commenced. The lover of the negro race, who had at the conclusion of his interview with Biassou remained plunged in a state of despair and stupor, had hardly noticed the scene between the general and the planter, so absorbed was he in the thought of his approaching death; but when he saw the man rush upon him, and the steel gleam above his head, the imminence of his danger aroused him at once. He started to his feet, grasped the arm of his would-be murderer, and exclaimed in a voice of terror,—

"Pardon, pardon! What are you doing? What have I done?"

"You must die, sir," said the half-caste, fixing his frenzied eyes upon his victim, and endeavouring to disengage his arm. "Let me do it; I will not hurt you."

"Die by your hand," cried the economist; "but why? Spare me! you wish perhaps to kill me because I used to say that you were a mulatto. But spare my life, and I vow that I will always declare that you are a white man. Yes, you are white; I will say so everywhere, but spare me!"

The unfortunate man had taken the wrong method of suing for mercy.

"Silence, silence!" cried the half-caste, furious at the idea of the danger he was incurring, and fearing that the negroes would hear the assertion.

But the other cried louder than ever that he knew that he was a white man, and of good family. The half-caste made a last effort to impose silence on him; then finding his efforts vain, he thrust aside his arms, and pressed the dagger upon C——'s breast. The unhappy man felt the point of the weapon, and in his despair bit the arm that was driving the dagger home.

"Monster! wretch!" exclaimed he, "you are murdering me!" Then casting a glance of supplication towards Biassou, he cried, "Defend me, avenger of humanity!"

Then the murderer pressed more heavily on the dagger;

a gush of blood bubbled over his fingers, and spattered his face. The knees of the unhappy lover of the negro race bent beneath him, his arms fell by his side, his eyes closed, he uttered a stifled groan, and fell dead.

CHAPTER XXXII

I WAS paralyzed with horror at this scene, in which I every moment expected to play an important part.

The "avenger of humanity" had gazed on the struggle without a lineament of his features changing. When all was over, he turned to his terrified pages. "More tobacco," said he, and began to chew calmly. The Obi and Rigaud were equally impassible, but the negroes appeared terrified at the horrible drama that their general had caused to be enacted before them.

One white man, however, yet remained to be slaughtered; my turn had come. I cast a glance upon the murderer who was about to become my executioner, and a feeling of pity came over me. His lips were violet, his teeth chattered, a convulsive tremor caused every limb to quiver. By a mechanical movement his hand was continually passed over his forehead, as if to obliterate the traces of the blood which had so liberally sprinkled it; he looked with an air of terrified wonder at the bleeding body which lay at his feet, as though he were unable to detach his strained eyeballs from the spectacle of his victim. I waited for the moment when he would resume his task of blood. The position was a strange one: he had already tried to kill me and failed, to prove that he was white; and now he was going to murder me to show that he was black.

"Come," said Biassou, addressing him, "this is good; I am pleased with you, my friend." Then glancing at me, he added, "You need not finish the other one; and now I declare you one of us, and name you executioner to the army."

At these words a negro stepped out of the ranks, and bowing three times to the general, cried out in his jargon, which I will spare you,—

" And I, General? "

" Well, what do you want? " asked Biassou.

" Are you going to do nothing for me, General? " asked the negro " Here you give an important post to this dog of a white, who murders to save his own skin, and to prove that he is one of ourselves. Have you no post to give to me, who am a true black? "

This unexpected request seemed to embarrass Biassou, and Rigaud whispered to him in French,—

" You can't satisfy him; try to elude his request."

" You wish for promotion, then? " asked Biassou of the true black. " Well, I am willing enough to grant it to you. What grade do you wish for? "

" I wish to be an officer."

" An officer, eh? And what are your claims to the epaulet founded on? "

" It was I," answered the negro, emphatically, " who set fire to the house of Lagoscelte in the first days of August last. It was I who murdered M. Clement the planter, and carried the head of his sugar refiner on my pike. I killed ten white women and seven small children, one of whom on the point of a spear served as a standard for Bouckmann's brave blacks. Later on I burnt alive the families of four colonists, whom I had locked up in the strong room of Fort Galifet.

" My father was broken on the wheel at Cap, my brother was hung at Rocrow, and I narrowly escaped being shot. I have burnt three coffee plantations, six indigo estates, and two hundred acres of sugar-cane; I murdered my master, M. Noé, and his mother —"

" Spare us the recital of your services," said Rigaud, whose feigned benevolence was the mask for real cruelty, but who was ferocious with decency, and could not listen to this cynical confession of deeds of violence.

' I could quote many others," continued the negro, proudly, " but you will no doubt consider that these are sufficient to ensure my promotion, and to entitle me to wear a gold epaulet like my comrades there," pointing to the staff of Biassou.

The general affected to reflect for a few minutes, and then gravely addressed the negro. " I am satisfied with your services, and should be pleased to promote you; but you must satisfy me on one point. Do you understand Latin?"

The astonished negro opened his eyes widely. " Eh, General?" said he.

" Yes," repeated Biassou, quickly; " do you understand Latin?"

" La — Latin?" stammered the astonished negro.

" Yes, yes, yes, Latin; do you understand Latin?" said the cunning chief, and unfolding a banner upon which was embroidered the verse from the Psalms, " In exitu Israël de Egypto," he added, " Explain the meaning of these words."

The negro, in complete ignorance of what was meant, remained silent and motionless, fumbling with the waistband of his trousers, while his astonished eyes wandered from the banner to the general, and from the general back again to the banner.

" Come, go on!" exclaimed Biassou, impatiently.

The negro opened and shut his mouth several times, scratched his head, and at last said slowly: " I don't understand it, General."

" How, scoundrel!" cried Biassou; " you wish to become an officer, and you do not understand Latin!"

" But, General —" stammered the puzzled negro.

" Silence!" roared Biassou, whose anger appeared to increase; " I do not know what prevents me from having you shot at once. Did you ever hear such a thing, Rigaud? He wants to be an officer, and does not understand Latin. Well, then, idiot, as you do not understand, I will explain what is written on this banner: *In exitu* —' Every soldier '— *Israël*

—'who does not understand Latin '— *de Egypto* —'cannot be made an officer.' Is not that the translation, reverend sir?'"

The Obi bowed his head in the affirmative, and Biassou continued,—

"This brother of whom you are jealous, and whom I have appointed executioner, understands Latin!" He turned to the new executioner: "You know Latin, do you not? Prove it to this blockhead. What is the meaning of *Dominus vobiscum?*"

The unhappy half-caste roused from his gloomy reverie by the dreaded voice, raised his head; and though his brain was still troubled by the cowardly murder that he had just committed, terror compelled him to be obedient. There was something pitiable in his manner, as his mind went back to his schooldays, and in the midst of his terrible feelings and remorse he repeated, in the tone of a child saying its lesson, "*Dominus vobiscum,*— that means, 'May the Lord be with you.'"

"Et cum spirito tuo," added the mysterious Obi, solemnly.

"Amen," repeated Biassou; then resuming his angry manner, and mingling with his reproaches some Latin phrases to impress the negroes with the superior attainments of their chief, he cried: "Go to the rear rank, *sursum corda!* Never attempt to enter the places of those who know Latin, *orate fratres,* or I will have you hung. *Bonus, bona, bonum!*"

The astonished and terrified negro slunk away, greeted by the hoots and hisses of his comrades, who were indignant at his presumption, and impressed with the deep learning of their general.

Burlesque though this scene was, it inspired me with a very high idea of Biassou's administrative capabilities. He had made ridicule the means of repressing ambitious aspirations, which are always so dangerous to authority in undisciplined bodies, and whose cunning gave me a fuller idea of his mental powers, as well as of the crass ignorance of the negroes under his command.

7

CHAPTER XXXIII

THE breakfast hour had now arrived. The shell of a turtle was placed before Biassou, in which smoked a species of *olla-podrida* seasoned with bacon, in which turtle-flesh took the place of lamb; an enormous carib cabbage floated on the surface of the stew, and in addition, on strips of bark, were dried raisins and water-melons, a loaf of maize bread; a bottle of wine, bound round with tarred string, completed the feast. Biassou took from his pocket a few heads of garlic and rubbed his bread with them; then, without even ordering the bleeding form to be carried away, he began to eat, inviting Rigaud to do the same. There was something terrible in Biassou's appetite.

The Obi did not join their repast; like others in his profession, I could easily understand that he never took anything in public, to induce a belief among the negroes that he lived entirely without food.

During breakfast, Biassou ordered one of his *aides-de-camp* to direct the review of the army to commence, and the different corps began to defile past in fairly good order. The negroes of Morne-Rouge were the first; there were about four thousand of them, divided into companies commanded by chiefs, who were distinguished by their scarlet breeches and sashes. This force was composed of tall and powerful negroes; some of them carried guns, axes, and sabres, but many had no other arms than bows and arrows, and javelins rudely fashioned by themselves. They carried no standard, and moved past in mournful silence. As they marched on, Biassou whispered to Rigaud,—

"When will Blanchelande's and Rouvray's shot and shell free me from these bandits of Morne-Rouge? I hate them; they are nearly all of them Congos, and they only believe in killing in open battle,— following the example of their chief Bug-Jargal, a young fool, who plays at being generous and

magnanimous. You do not know him, Rigaud, and I hope
you never will; for the whites have taken him prisoner, and
they may perhaps rid me of him, as they did of Bouckmann."

" Speaking of Bouckmann," answered Rigaud, " there are
the negroes of Macaya just passing, and I see in their ranks
the negro whom Jean François sent to you with the news of
Bouckmann's death. Do you know that that man might upset
all the prophecies of the Obi, if he were to say that he had
been kept for more than half an hour at the outposts, and
that he had told me the news before you sent for him? "

" Diablo! " answered Biassou, " you are in the right, my
friend; this man's mouth must be shut. Wait a bit."

Then raising his voice he called out " Macaya! " The
leader of the division left the ranks, and approached the
general with the stock of his firelock reversed, in token of
respect.

" Make that man who does not belong to your division
leave his rank and come forward."

Macaya speedily brought the messenger of Jean François
before the general, who at once assumed that appearance of
anger which he knew so well how to simulate.

" Who are you? " cried he.

" General, I am a black."

" Carramba! I can see that well enough; but what is your
name? "

" My name is Vavelan; my patron saint is Sabas, deacon
and martyr, whose feast is on the twentieth day before the
nativity of our Lord."

Biassou interrupted him: " How dare you present yourself
on parade, amidst shining muskets and white cross-belts with
your sword without a sheath, your breeches torn, and your
feet muddy? "

" General," answered the negro, " it is not my fault. I
was dispatched by the Grand Admiral, Jean François, to
bring you the news of the death of the chief of the English
negroes; and if my clothes are torn and my feet bemired, it

is because I have run, without stopping to take breath, to bring you the news as soon as possible; but they detained me at —"

Biassou frowned. "I did not ask you about that, but how you dared to enter the ranks in so unbecoming a dress. Commend your soul to Saint Sabas, your patron, the deacon and martyr, and go and get yourself shot."

And here I had another proof of the ascendency that Biassou exercised over the insurgents. The unfortunate man who was ordered to go and get himself executed did not utter a protest; he bowed his head, crossed his arms on his breast, saluted his pitiless judge three times, and after having knelt to the Obi, who gave him plenary absolution, he left the cavern. A few minutes afterwards a volley of musketry told us that Biassou's commands had been obeyed, and that the negro was no more.

Freed from all sources of uneasiness, the general turned to Rigaud, a gleam of pleasure in his eye, and gave a triumphant chuckle which seemed to say, " Admire me!"

CHAPTER XXXIV

BUT the review still continued. This army, which had presented so curious a spectacle in camp, had a no less extraordinary appearance under arms. Sometimes a horde of almost naked negroes would come along armed with clubs and tomahawks, marching to the notes of a goat's horn like mere savages; then would come regiments of mulattoes, dressed in the English or Spanish manner, well armed and equipped, regulating their pace by the roll of the drum; then a band of negresses and their children carrying forks and spits; then some tag-rag, bent under the weight of an old musket without lock or barrel; then *griotes* with their feathered aprons, *griots* dancing with hideous contortions, and singing incoherent airs to the accompaniment of guitars, tomtoms, and balafos; then would be a procession of priests, or Obi men, of half-castes, quarter-castes, free mulattoes, or wandering hordes of escaped slaves with a proud look of liberty on their faces and shining muskets on their shoulders, dragging in their ranks well-filled wagons, or some artillery taken from the whites which were looked on more as trophies than as military engines, and yelling out at the top of their voices the songs of " Grand-Pré " and " Oua-Nassé." Above the heads of all floated flags, banners, and standards of every form, colour, and device,— white, red, tricolour, with the lilies, with the cap of liberty, bearing inscriptions: " Death to Priests and Nobles ! " " Long live Religion ! " " Liberty and Equality ! " " Long live the King ! " " Viva Espana ! " " No more Tyrants ! " etc.,— a confusion of sentiments which showed that the insurgents were a mere crowd collected together, with ideas as different as were the men who composed it. On passing in their turn before the cave the companies drooped their banners, and Biassou returned the salute. He addressed every band either in praise or censure, and each word that dropped from his mouth was received by his men with fanatical respect or superstitious dread.

The wave of savage soldiery passed away at last. I confess that the sight that had at first afforded some distraction to my feelings finished by wearying me. The sun went down as the last ranks filed away, and his last rays cast a copper-coloured hue upon the granite portals of the cave.

CHAPTER XXXV

B IASSOU seemed to be dreaming. When the review was concluded, his last orders had been given, and the insurgents had retired to the huts, he condescended to address me again.

"Young man," said he, "you have now had the means of judging of my power and genius; the time has now arrived for you to bear the report to Leogri."

"It is not my fault that he has not had it earlier," answered I, coldly.

"You are right," replied Biassou. He then paused, as if to note what the effect would be upon me of what he was going to say, and then added: "But it will depend upon yourself whether you ever carry the message or not."

"What do you mean?" exclaimed I, in astonishment.

"Why," replied he, "that your life depends upon yourself, and that you can save it if you will."

This sudden paroxysm of pity — the first, and no doubt the last, which had ever possessed Biassou — surprised me much, and astonished Obi so greatly that he leaped from the position which he had so long maintained, and placing himself face to face with the general addressed him in angry tones:—

"What are you saying? Have you forgotten your promise? Neither God nor you can dispose of this life, for it belongs to me."

At that instant I thought that I recognized the voice; but it was only a fleeting recollection, and in a moment had passed away.

Biassou got up from his seat without betraying any anger, spoke for a few moments in whispers to the Obi, and pointed to the black flag which I had already remarked; and after a little more conversation the Obi nodded in sign of assent. Both of them then reverted to their former positions.

"Listen to me," said the general, drawing from his pocket the dispatch which Jean François had sent to him. "Things are going ill. Bouckmann has been killed. The whites have slaughtered more than two thousand of our men in the district of Cul-de-Sac. The colonists are continuing to establish and to fortify military posts. By our own folly we have lost the chance of taking Cap, and it will be long before another occasion will present itself. On the eastern side our line of march has been cut by a river, and the whites have defended the passage by a pontoon battery and a fortified camp. On the south side they have planted artillery on the mountainous road called the Haut-du-Cap. The position is, in addition, defended by a strong stockade, at which all the inhabitants have laboured, and in front of it there is a strong *chevaux-de-frise*. Cap, therefore, is beyond our reach. Our ambush in the ravines of Dompte-Mulâtre was a failure; and, to add to all these misfortunes, the Siamese fever has devastated our camps. In consequence, the Grand Admiral (and I agree with him) has decided to treat with the Governor Blanchelande and the Colonial Assembly. Here is the letter that we have addressed to the Assembly on this matter. Listen!"

GENTLEMEN OF THE HOUSE OF DEPUTIES.— In the great misfortunes which have afflicted this great and important colony we have also been enveloped, and there remains nothing for us to say in justification of our conduct. One day you will render us the justice that our conduct merits.

According to us, the King of Spain is a good king, who treats us well, and has testified it to us by rewards; so we shall continue to serve him with zeal and devotion.

We see by the law of Sept. 28, 1791, that the National Assembly and the King have agreed to settle definitely the status of slaves, and the political situation of people of colour. We will defend the decrees of the National Assembly with the last drop of our blood.

It would be most interesting to us if you would declare, by an order sanctioned by your general, as to your intentions regarding the position of the slaves. Knowing that they are the objects of your solicitude through their chiefs, who send you this, they will be satisfied if the relations now broken are once again resumed.

Do not count, gentlemen Deputies, upon our consenting to take up arms for the revolutionary Assemblies. We are the subjects of three kings,— the King of Congo, the born master of all the blacks; the King of France, who represents our fathers; and the King of Spain, who is the representative of our mothers. These three kings are the descendants of those who, conducted by a star, worshipped the Man God. If we were to consent to serve the Assemblies, we might be forced to take up arms and to make war against our brothers, the subjects of those three kings to whom we have sworn fidelity. And, besides, we do not know what is meant by the will of the Nation, seeing that since the world has been in existence we have always executed that of the King. The Prince of France loves us; the King of Spain never ceases to help us. We aid them,— they aid us; it is the cause of humanity;

and, besides, if these kings should fail us we could soon enthrone a king of our own.

Such are our intentions, although we now consent to make peace.

(Signed)   JEAN FRANÇOIS, *General.*
BIASSOU, *Brigadier.*
DESPREZ,
MANZEAU,   *Commissaires,*
TOUSSAINT,   ad hoc.[1]
AUBERT,

"You see," said Biassou, after he had read this piece of negro diplomacy, every word of which has remained imprinted on my memory, "that our intentions are peaceable; but this is what we want you to do: Neither Jean François nor I have been brought up in the schools of the whites, or learned the niceties of their language; we know how to fight, but not how to write. Now, we do not wish that there should be anything in our letter at which our former masters can laugh.

"You seem to have learned these frivolous accomplishments in which we are lacking. Correct any faults you may find in this dispatch, so that it may excite no derision among the whites, and — I will give you your life!"

This proposition of becoming the corrector of Biassou's faults of spelling and composition was too repugnant to my pride for me to hesitate for a moment; and besides, what did I care for life? I declined his offer. He appeared surprised.

"What!" exclaimed he, "you prefer death to scrawling a few marks with a pen on a piece of paper?"

"Yes," replied I.

My determination seemed to embarrass him. After a few moments of thought he again addressed me: "Listen, young fool! I am less obstinate than you are; I give you until to-morrow evening, up to the setting of the sun, when you shall again be brought before me. Think well, then, before you refuse to obey my wishes. Adieu. Let night bring reflection

[1] It is a fact that this ridiculously characteristic letter was sent to the Assembly.

to you; and remember that with us death is not simply death, — much comes before you reach it."

The frightful sardonic grin with which he concluded his last speech too plainly brought to my recollection the awful tortures which it was Biassou's greatest pleasure to inflict upon his prisoners.

"Candi," continued Biassou, "remove the prisoner, and give him in charge to the men of Morne-Rouge. I wish him to live for another day, and perhaps my other soldiers would not have the patience to let him do so."

The mulatto Candi, who commanded the guard, caused my arms to be bound behind my back; a soldier took hold of the end of the cord, and we left the grotto.

CHAPTER XXXVI

WHEN any extraordinary events, unexpected anxieties or catastrophies, intrude themselves suddenly into a life up to that period peaceful and happy, these unexpected emotions interrupt the repose of the soul which lay dreaming in the monotony of prosperity. Misfortune which comes on you in this manner does not seem like an awakening from bliss, but rather like a dream of evil. With the man who has been invariably happy, despair begins with stupor. Unexpected misery is like cramp,— it clasps, and deadens everything. Men, acts, and things at that time pass before us like a fantastic apparition, and move along as if in a dream. Everything in the horizon of our life is changed, both the atmosphere and the perspective; but it still goes on for a long time before our eyes have lost that sort of luminous image of past happiness which follows in its train, and interposes without cessation between it and the sombre present. Then everything that is appears to be unreal and ridiculous, and we can scarcely believe in our own existence, because we find nothing around us that formerly used to compose our life, and we cannot understand how all can have gone away without taking us with it, and why nothing of our life remains to us.

Were this strained position of the soul to continue long, it it would disturb the equilibrium of the brain and become madness,— a state happier perhaps than that which remains, for life then is nothing but a vision of past misfortune, acting like a ghost.

CHAPTER XXXVII

GENTLEMEN, I hardly know why I lay before you my ideas upon such a subject; they are not those which you understand, or can be made to understand. To comprehend them thoroughly, you must have gone through what I have. But such was the state of my mind when the guards of Biassou handed me over to the negroes of Morne-Rouge. I was still in a dream,— it appeared as if one body of phantoms passed me over to another; and without opposing any resistance I permitted them to bind me by the middle to a tree. They then gave me some boiled potatoes, which I ate with the mechanical instinct that God grants to man even in the midst of overwhelming thought.

The darkness had now come on, and my guards took refuge in their huts,— with the exception of half-a-dozen who remained with me, lying before a large fire that they had lighted to preserve themselves from the cold night-air. In a few moments they were all buried in profound sleep.

The state of physical weakness into which I had fallen caused my thoughts to wander in a strange manner. I thought of those calm and peaceful days which but a few weeks ago I had passed with Marie, without being able to foresee any future but one of continued happiness. I compared them with the day that had just expired,— a day in which so many strange events had occurred as almost to make

me wonder whether I was not labouring under some delusion.
I had been three times condemned to death, and still remained
under sentence. I thought of my future, bounded only by
the morrow, and which offered nothing but misfortune and a
death happily near at hand. I seemed to be the victim of
some terrible nightmare. Again and again I asked myself if
all that had happened was real: was I really in the power of
the sanguinary Biassou, and was my Marie lost to me forever?
Could this prisoner, guarded by six savages, bound to a tree,
and condemned to certain death, really be I? In spite of all
my efforts to repel them, the thoughts of Marie would force
themselves upon me. In anguish I thought of her fate; I
strained my bonds in my efforts to break them, and to fly to
her succour, ever hoping that the terrible dream would pass
away, and that Heaven would not permit all the horrors that
I dreaded to fall upon the head of her who had been united
to me in a sacred bond. In my sad preoccupation the thought
of Pierrot returned to me, and rage nearly took away my
senses; the pulses of my temples throbbed nearly to bursting.
I hated him, I cursed him; I despised myself for having ever
had friendship for Pierrot at the same time I had felt love for
Marie; and without caring to seek for the motive which had
urged him to cast himself into the waters of Grande-Riviere,
I wept because he had escaped me. He was dead, and I was
about to die, and all that I regretted was that I had been
unable to wreak my vengeance upon him.

During the state of semi-somnolency into which my weakness had plunged me, these thoughts passed through my brain.
I do not know how long it lasted, but I was aroused by a
man's voice singing distinctly, but at some distance, the old
Spanish song, " Yo que soy contrabandista." Quivering
with emotion I opened my eyes; all was dark around me, the
negroes slept, the fire was dying down. I could hear nothing
more. I fancied that the voice must have been a dream, and
my sleep-laden eyelids closed again. In a second I opened
them; for again I heard the voice singing sadly, but much
nearer, the same song,—

"'Twas on the field of Ocanen
That I fell in their power,
To Cotadilla taken,
Unhappy from that hour."

This time it was not a charm,— it *was* Pierrot's voice. A few moments elapsed; then it rose again through the silence and the gloom, and once more I heard the well-known air of " Yo que soy contrabandista." A dog ran eagerly to greet me, and rolled at my feet in token of welcome; it was Rask! A tall negro stood facing me, and the glimmer of the fire threw his shadow, swelled to colossal proportions, upon the sward. It was Pierrot!

The thirst for vengeance fired my brain; surprise rendered me motionless and dumb. I was not asleep. Could the dead return? If not a dream, it must be an apparition. I turned from him with horror.

When he saw me do this, his head sank upon his breast. " Brother," murmured he, " you promised that you would never doubt me when you heard me sing that song. My brother, have you forgotten your promise? "

Rage restored the power of speech to me. " Monster! " exclaimed I, " do I see you at last? Butcher, murderer of my uncle, ravisher of Marie, dare you call me your brother? Do not venture to approach me! "

I forgot that I was too securely tied to make the slightest movement, and glanced to my left side as though to seek my sword.

My intention did not escape him, and he continued in a sorrowful tone of voice: " No, I will not come near you; you are unhappy and I pity you,— while you have no pity for me, though I am much more wretched than you are."

I shrugged my shoulders; he understood my feelings, and in a half dreamy manner continued,—

" Yes, you have lost much; but, believe me, I have lost more than you have."

But the sound of our conversation had aroused the negro guard. Perceiving a stranger, they leaped to their feet and seized their weapons; but as soon as they recognized the intruder they uttered a cry of surprise and joy, and cast themselves at his feet, striking the ground with their foreheads.

But neither the homage that the negroes rendered to Pierrot, nor the fondlings of Rask, made any impression upon me at the moment. I was boiling over with passion, and maddened at the bonds that restrained me; and at length my fury found words. "Oh, how unhappy I am!" I exclaimed, shedding tears of rage. "I was grieving because I thought that this wretch had committed suicide, and robbed me of my just revenge; and now he is here to mock me, living and breathing under my very eyes, and I am powerless to stab him to the heart! Is there no one to free me from these accursed cords?"

Pierrot turned to the negroes, who were still prostrate before him.

"Comrades," said he, "release the prisoner!"

CHAPTER XXXVIII

HE was promptly obeyed. With the greatest eagerness, my guards cut asunder the ropes that confined me. I rose up free; but I remained motionless, for surprise rooted me to the spot.

"That is not all," said Pierrot; and snatching a dagger from one of the negroes, he handed it to me. "You can now have your wish. Heaven would not be pleased should I dispute your right to dispose of my life. Three times you have preserved it. Strike! it is yours, I say; and if you wish, strike!"

There was no sign of anger or of bitterness in his face; he appeared resigned and mournful. The very vengeance offered to me by the man with whom I had so much longed to stand face to face, prevented my seizing the opportunity. I felt that all my hatred for Pierrot, all my love for Marie, could not induce me to commit a cowardly murder; besides, however damning appearances might be, a voice from the depths of my heart warned me that no criminal, no guilty man, would thus dare to stand before me and brave my vengeance. Shall I confess it to you,— there was a certain imperious fascination about this extraordinary being which conquered me in spite of myself. I pushed aside the dagger he offered to me.

"Wretch!" cried I, "I wish to kill you in fair fight; but I am no assassin. Defend yourself!"

"Defend myself!" replied he, in tones of astonishment, "and against whom?"

"Against me!"

He started back. "Against you! That is the only thing in which I cannot obey you. Look at Rask there: I could easily kill him, for he would let me do it; but as for making him fight me, the thing would be impossible,— he would not understand me if I told him to do so. I do not understand you; in your case I am Rask."

After a short silence, he added: "I see the gleam of hate in your eyes, as you once saw it in mine. I know that you have suffered much; that your uncle has been murdered, your plantations burned, your friends slaughtered. Yes, they have plundered your house, and devastated your inheritance; but it was not I that did these things, it was my people. Listen to me. I one day told you that your people had done me much injury; you said that *you* must not be blamed for the acts of others. What was my reply?"

His face grew brighter as he awaited my reply, evidently expecting that I would embrace him; but fixing an angry gaze upon him, I answered,—

"You disdain all responsibility as to the acts of your people, but you say nothing about what you have yourself done."

"What have I done?" asked he.

I stepped up close to him, and in a voice of thunder I

demanded, "Where is Marie? What have you done with Marie?"

At this question a cloud passed over his face; he seemed momentarily embarrassed. At last he spoke. "Marie!" said he; "yes, you are right. But too many ears listen to us here."

His embarrassment, and the words "You are right," raised the hell of jealousy in my heart; yet still he gazed upon me with a perfectly open countenance, and in a voice trembling with emotion, said,—

"Do not suspect me, I implore you! Besides, I will tell you everything; love me, as I love you, with perfect trust." He paused to mark the effect of his words, and then added tenderly, "May I not again call you brother?"

But I was a prey to my jealous feelings, and his friendly words seemed to me but the deep machinations of a hypocrite, and only served to exasperate me more. "Dare you recall the time when you did so, you monster of ingratitude?" I exclaimed.

He interrupted me, a tear shining in his eye: "it is not I who am ungrateful."

"Well, then," I continued, "tell me what you have done with Marie!"

"Not here, not here!" answered he,—"other ears than ours listen to our words; besides, you would not believe me, and time presses. The day has come, and you must be removed from this. All is at an end. Since you doubt me, far better would it have been for you to take the dagger and finish all; but wait a little before you take what you call your vengeance,— I must first free you. Come with me to Biassou."

His manner, both in speaking and acting, concealed a mystery which I could not understand. In spite of all my prejudices against the man, his voice always made my heart vibrate. In listening to him, a certain hidden power that he possessed subjugated me. I found myself hesitating between vengeance and pity, between the bitterest distrust and the blindest confidence. I followed him.

CHAPTER XXXIX

WE left the camp of the negroes of Morne-Rouge. I could not help thinking it strange to find myself at perfect liberty among a horde of savages, in a spot where the evening before each man had seemed only too ready to shed my blood. Far from seeking to bar our progress, both the negroes and the mulattoes prostrated themselves on all sides, with exclamations of surprise, joy, and respect. I was ignorant what rank Pierrot held in the army of the insurgents; but I remembered the influence that he used to exercise over his companions in slavery, and this appeared to me to account for the respect with which he was now treated.

On our arrival at the guard before the grotto, the mulatto Candi advanced before us with threatening gestures, demanding how we dared approach so near the general's quarters; but when he came close enough to recognize my conductor, he hurriedly removed his gold-laced cap, as though terrified at his own audacity, bowed to the ground, and at once introduced us into Biassou's presence with a thousand apologies, of which Pierrot took no heed.

The respect with which the simple negro soldiers had treated Pierrot excited my surprise very little; but seeing Candi, one of the principal officers of the army, humiliate himself thus before my uncle's slave, made me ask myself who this man could be whose power was illimitable. How much more astonished was I then, when, upon being introduced into the presence of Biassou,— who was alone when we entered, and was quietly enjoying his *calalou*,— he started to his feet, concealing disappointment and surprise under the appearance of profound respect, bowed humbly to my companion, and offered him his mahogany throne.

Pierrot declined it. " No, Jean Biassou," said he. " I have not come to take your place, but simply to ask a favour at your hands."

"Your Highness," answered Biassou, redoubling his obeisances, "you know well that all Jean Biassou has is yours, and that you can dispose as freely of all as you can of Jean Biassou himself."

"I do not ask for so much," replied Pierrot, quickly; "all I ask is the life and liberty of this prisoner," and he pointed to me.

For a moment Biassou appeared embarrassed, but he speedily recovered himself. "Your servant is in despair, your Highness; for you ask of him, to his great regret, more than he can grant. He is not Jean Biassou's prisoner, does not belong to Jean Biassou, and has nothing to do with Jean Biassou."

"What do you mean?" asked Pierrot in severe tones, "by saying that he does not belong to you? Does any one else hold authority here except you?"

"Alas, yes, your Highness."

"Who is it?"

"My army."

The sly and obsequious manner in which Biassou eluded the frank and haughty questions of Pierrot showed, had it depended solely upon himself, that he would gladly have treated his visitor with far less respect than he felt himself now compelled to do.

"What!" exclaimed Pierrot, "your army! And do not you command it?"

Biassou, with every appearance of sincerity, replied, "Does your Highness really think that we can command men who are in insurrection because they will not obey?"

I cared too little for my life to break the silence which I had imposed upon myself, else, having seen the day before the despotic authority that Biassou exercised over his men, I might have contradicted his assertions, and laid bare his duplicity to Pierrot.

"Well, if you have no authority over your men, and if they are your masters what reason can they have for hating your prisoner?"

8

" Bouckmann has been killed by the white troops," answered Biassou, endeavouring to conceal his sardonic smile under a mask of sorrow, " and my men are determined to avenge upon this white man the death of the chief of the Jamaica negroes. They wish to show trophy against trophy, and desire that the head of this young officer should serve as a counterpoise to the head of Bouckmann in the scales in which the good Giu weighs both parties."

" Do you still continue to carry on this horrible system of reprisals? Listen to me, Jean Biassou! it is these cruelties that are the ruin of our just cause. Prisoner as I was in the camp of the whites (from which I have managed to escape), I had not heard of the death of Bouckmann until you told me. It is the just punishment of Heaven for his crimes. I will tell you another piece of news: Jeannot, the negro chief who served as a guide to draw the white troops into the ambush of Dompte-Mulâtre,— Jeannot also is dead. You know — do not interrupt me, Biassou! — you know that he rivalled you and Bouckmann in his atrocities; and pay attention to this,— it was not the thunderbolt of Heaven, nor the bullets of the whites, that struck him; it was Jean François himself who ordered this act of justice to be performed."

Biassou, who had listened with an air of gloomy respect, uttered an exclamation of surprise. At this moment Rigaud entered, bowed respectfully to Pierrot, and whispered in Biassou's ear. The murmur of many voices was heard in the camp.

" Yes," continued Pierrot, " Jean François, who has no fault except a preposterous love of luxury and show; whose carriage with its six horses takes him every day to hear Mass at the Grande-Riviere,— Jean François himself has put a stop to the crimes of Jeannot. In spite of the cowardly entreaties of the brigand, who clung in despair to the knees of the priest of Marmalade who attended him in his last moments, he was shot beneath the very tree upon which he used to hang his living victims upon iron hooks. Think upon this, Biassou. Why these massacres which provoke the whites to reprisals? Why all these juggleries which only tend to excite the passions of our unhappy comrades, already too much exasperated? There is at Trou-Coffi a mulatto impostor, called Romaine the Prophet, who is in command of a fanatical band of negroes; he profanes the holy sacrament of the Mass, he pretends that he is in direct communication with the Virgin, and he urges on his men to murder and pillage in the name of Marie."

There was a more tender inflection in the voice of Pierrot as he uttered this name than even religious respect would have warranted, and I felt annoyed and irritated at it.

"And you," continued he, "you have in your camp some Obi, I hear,— some impostor like this Romaine the Prophet. I well know that having to lead an army composed of so many heterogeneous materials, a common bond is necessary; but can it be found nowhere save in ferocious fanaticism and ridiculous superstition? Believe me, Biassou, the white men are not so cruel as we are. I have seen many planters protect the lives of their slaves. I am not ignorant that in some cases it was not the life of a man, but a sum of money that they desired to save; but at any rate their interest gave them the appearance of a virtue. Do not let us be less merciful than they are, for it is not our interest to be so. Will our cause be more holy and more just because we exterminate the women, slaughter the children, and burn the colonists in their own houses?

"These, however, are every-day occurrences. Answer me, Biassou! must the traces of our progress be always marked by a line of blood and fire?"

He ceased. The fire of his glance, the accent of his voice, gave to his words a force of conviction and authority which it is impossible for me to imitate. Like a fox in the clutches of a lion, Biassou seemed to seek for some means of escape from the power that constrained him.

While Biassou vainly sought for a pretext, the chief of the negroes of Cayer, Rigaud, who the evening before had calmly watched the horrors that had been perpetrated in his presence, seemed to be shocked at the picture that Pierrot had drawn, and exclaimed with a hypocritical affectation of grief, "Great heavens! how terrible is a nation when aroused to fury!"

CHAPTER XL

THE confusion in the camp appeared to increase, to the great uneasiness of Biassou. I heard afterwards that it was caused by the negroes of Morne-Rouge, who hurried from one end of the camp to the other, announcing the return of my liberator, and declaring their intention of supporting him in whatever object he had come to Biassou's camp for. Rigaud had informed the generalissimo of this, and it was the fear of a fatal division in the camp that prompted Biassou to make some sort of concession to the wishes of Pierrot.

"Your Highness," remarked he, with an air of injured innocence, "if we are hard on the whites, you are equally severe upon us. You are wrong in accusing us of being the cause of the torrent, for it is the torrent that drags us away with it. But what can I do at present that will please you?"

"I have already told you, Señor Biassou," answered Pierrot; "let me take this prisoner away with me."

Biassou remained for a few moments silent, as though in deep thought; then putting on an expression of as great frankness as he was able, he answered, "Your Highness, I wish to prove to you that I have every desire to please you. Permit me to have two words in private with the prisoner, and he shall be free to follow you."

"If that is all you ask, I agree," replied Pierrot.

His eyes, which up to that moment had wandered about in a distrustful manner, glistened with delight, and he moved away a few paces to leave us to our conversation.

Biassou drew me on one side into a retired part of the cavern, and said in a low voice, "I can only spare your life upon the condition that I proposed; are you ready to fulfil it? "

He showed me the dispatch of Jean François; to consent appeared to me too humiliating.

" Never! " answered I, firmly.

" Aha! " repeated he, with his sardonic chuckle, " are you always as firm? You have great confidence, then, in your protector. Do you know who he is? "

" I do," answered I, quickly " He is a monster, as you are; only he is a greater hypocrite."

He started back in astonishment, seeking to read in my glance if I spoke seriously. " What! " exclaimed he, " do you not know him then? "

With a disdainful look, I replied: " I only know him as my uncle's slave; and his name is Pierrot."

Again Biassou smiled bitterly. " Aha, that indeed is strange: he asks for your life and liberty, and you say that you only know him for a monster like myself."

" What matters that? " I answered; " if I do gain a little liberty, it is not to save my own life, but to take his."

" What is that you are saying? " asked Biassou. " And yet you seem to speak as you believe; I cannot think you would trifle with your life. There is something beneath all this that I do not understand. You are protected by a man that you hate; he insists upon your life being spared, and you are longing to take his! But it matters little to me; you desire a short spell of freedom,— it is all that I can give you. I will leave you free to follow him; but swear to me, by your honour, that you will return to me and reconstitute yourself my prisoner two hours before the sun sets. You are a Frenchman, and I will trust you."

What shall I say, gentlemen? Life was a burden to me, and I hated the idea of owing it to Pierrot, for every circumstance pointed him out as a just object of my hatred. I could not think for a moment that Biassou (who did not easily permit his prey to escape him) would allow me to go free except upon his own conditions. All I desired was a few hours'

liberty which I could devote to discovering the fate of my beloved before my death. Biassou, relying upon my honour as
a Frenchman, would grant me these, and without hesitation I
pledged it.

"Your Highness," said Biassou, in obsequious tones, "the
white prisoner is at your disposal; you can take him with you,
for he is free to accompany you wherever you wish."

"Thanks, Biassou," replied Pierrot, extending his hand.
"You have rendered me a service which places me entirely at
your disposal. Remain in command of our brethren of
Morne-Rouge until my return."

Then he turned towards me; I never saw so much happiness
in his eyes before. "Since you are free," cried he, "come
with me." And with a strange earnestness he drew me away
with him.

Biassou looked after us with blank astonishment, which
was even perceptible through the respectful leave that he took
of my companion.

CHAPTER XLI

I WAS longing to be alone with Pierrot. His embarrassment when I had questioned him as to the fate of Marie,
the ill-concealed tenderness with which he had dared to pro-
nounce her name, had made those feelings of hatred and
jealousy which had sprung up in my heart take far deeper
root than at the time I saw him bearing away through the
flames of Fort Galifet her whom I could scarcely call my wife.
What did I care for the generous indignation with which he
had reproved the cruelties of Biassou, the trouble which he had
taken to preserve my life, and the curious manner which
marked all his words and actions? What cared I for the
mystery that appeared to envelop him, which brought him living before my eyes when I thought to have witnessed his
death? He proved to be a prisoner of the white troops when

I believed that he lay buried in the depths of Grande-Riviere, — the slave become a king, the prisoner a liberator. Of all these incomprehensible things one was clear,— Marie had been carried off by him; and I had this crime to punish, this outrage to avenge. However strange were the events that had passed under my eyes, they were not sufficient to shake my determination, and I had awaited with impatience for the moment when I could compel my rival to explain all. That moment had at last arrived.

We had passed through crowds of negroes, who cast themselves on the ground as we pursued our way, exclaiming in tones of surprise, " Miraculo! ya no esta prisonero!" (" A miracle! he is no longer a prisoner!"); but whether they referred to Pierrot or to myself I neither knew nor cared. We had gained the outskirts of the camp, and rocks and trees concealed from our view the outposts of Biassou; Rask in high good humour was running in front of us, and Pierrot was following him with rapid strides, when I stopped him.

" Listen to me!" cried I; " it is useless to go any farther: the ears that you dreaded can no longer listen to us. What have you done with Marie? Tell me that!"

Concentrated emotion made my voice tremble. He gazed upon me kindly.

" Always the same question!" said he.

" Yes, always," returned I, furiously; " always! I will put that question to you as you draw your last breath, or as I utter my last sigh. Where is Marie?"

" Can nothing, then, drive away your doubts of my loyalty? But you shall know all soon."

" Soon, monster!" repeated I, " soon! it is now, at this instant, that I want to know all. Where is Marie? Where is Marie? Answer, or stake your life against mine. Defend yourself!"

" I have already told you," answered he, sadly, " that that is impossible; the stream will not struggle against its source, — and my life, which you have three times saved, cannot contend against yours. Besides, even if I wished it, the thing is impossible; we have but one dagger between us."

As he spoke, he drew the weapon from his girdle and offered it to me. " Take it," said he.

I was beside myself with passion. I seized the dagger and placed the point on his breast; he never attempted to move.

" Wretch!" cried I, " do not force me to murder you. I will plunge this blade into your heart if you do not at once tell me where my wife is!"

He replied in his calm way: " You are the master to do as you like; but with clasped hands I emplore you to grant me one hour of life, and to follow me. Can you doubt him who thrice has owed his life to you, and whom you once called *brother?* Listen: if in one hour from this time you still doubt me, you shall be at perfect liberty to kill me. That will be time enough; you see that I do not attempt to resist you. I conjure you in the name of Marie,— of your wife," he added slowly, as though the victim of some painful recollection,— " give me but another hour, I beg of you, not for my sake, but for yours."

There was so much pathos in his entreaties that an inner feeling warned me to grant his request, and I yielded to that secret ascendency which he exercised over me, but which at that time I should have blushed to confess.

" Well," said I, slowly, " I will grant you one hour, and I am ready to follow you;" and as I spoke I handed him his dagger.

" No," answered he, " keep it; you still distrust me, but let us lose no time."

CHAPTER XLII

AGAIN we started. Rask, who during our conversation had shown frequent signs of impatience to renew his journey, bounded joyously before us. We plunged into a virgin forest, and after half an hour's walking came out on a grassy opening in the wood. On one side was a waterfall dashing over rugged rocks, while the primeval trees of the forest surrounded it on all sides. Among the rocks was a cave, the grey face of which was shrouded by a mass of climbing plants. Rask ran towards it barking; but at a sign from Pierrot he became silent, and the latter taking me by the hand led me without a word to the entrance of the cave.

A woman with her back towards the light was seated on a mat; at the sound of our steps she turned. My friends, it was Marie! She wore the same white dress which she had worn on the day of our marriage, and the wreath of orange blossoms was still on her head. She recognized me in a moment, and with a cry of joy threw herself into my arms. I was speechless with surprise and emotion. At her cry an old woman carrying a child in her arms hurried from an inner chamber formed in the depth of the cave; she was Marie's nurse, and she carried my uncle's youngest child.

Pierrot hastened to bring some water from the neighbouring spring, and threw a few drops in Marie's face, who was overcome by emotion; she speedily recovered, and opening her eyes exclaimed,—

" Leopold! my Leopold! "

" Marie! " cried I, and my words were stifled in a kiss.

" Not before me, for pity's sake! " cried a voice, in accents of agony.

We looked around, it came from Pierrot. The sight of our endearments appeared to inflict terrible torture on him; his bosom heaved, a cold perspiration bedewed his forehead, and every limb quivered. Suddenly he hid his face in his hands and fled from the grotto, repeating in tones of anguish,—

"Not before me! not before me!"

Marie half raised herself in my arms, and following his retreating form with her eyes, exclaimed, "Leopold, our happiness seems to trouble him; can it be that he loves me?"

The exclamation of the slave had shown that he was my rival, but Marie's speech proved that he was my trusty friend.

"Marie," answered I, as the wildest happiness mingled with the deepest regret filled my heart, "Marie, were you ignorant of it?"

"Until this moment I was," answered she, a blush over-spreading her beautiful features. "Does he really love me, for he never let me know it?"

I clasped her to my bosom, in all the madness of happiness. "I have recovered both wife and friend! How happy am I, but how guilty, for I doubted him!"

"What!" cried Marie, in surprise, "had you doubts of Pierrot? Oh, you have indeed been in fault. Twice has he saved my life, and perhaps more than life," she added, casting down her eyes. "Without him the alligator would have devoured me; without him the negroes — It was Pierrot who rescued me from their hands when they were about to send me to rejoin my unhappy father."

She broke off her speech with a flood of tears.

"And why," asked I, "did not Pierrot send you to Cap, to your husband?"

"He tried to do so," replied she, "but it was impossible. Compelled as he was to conceal me both from the whites and the blacks, his position was a most difficult one; and then, too, he was ignorant where you were. Some said that they had seen you killed, but Pierrot assured me that this was not the case; and a something convinced me that he spoke the truth, for I felt that had you been dead I should have died at the same time."

" Then, Pierrot brought you here? " asked I.

" Yes, my Leopold; this solitary cave is known only to him. At the same time that he rescued me, he saved all that re-mained alive of our family, my little brother and my old nurse,— and hid us here. The place is very nice, and now that the war has destroyed our house and ruined us, I should like to live here with you. Pierrot supplied all our wants. He used to come very often; he wore a plume of red feathers on his head.

" He used to console me by talking of you, and always as sured me that we should meet again; but for the past three days I have not seen him, and I was beginning to be uneasy, when to-day he came back with you. He had been seeking for you, had he not? "

" Yes," replied I.

" But if so, how can he be in love with me? Are you sure of it? "

" Quite," answered I. " It was he who was about to stab me beneath your window, and spared me lest it should afflict you; it was he who sang the love songs at the pavilion by the river."

" Then he is your rival," exclaimed Marie, with naïve surprise; " and the wicked man with the wild marigolds is Pierrot! I can hardly believe that: he was so respectful and humble to me, much more so than when he was our slave. It is true that sometimes he looked at me in a strange manner, but I attributed his sadness to our misfortunes. If you could only know with what tenderness he spoke of you, my Leopold! His friendship made him speak of you as much as my love did."

These explanations of Marie enchanted and yet grieved me. I felt how cruelly I had treated the noble-hearted Pierrot, and I felt all the force of his gentle reproach, " It is not I who am ungrateful."

At this instant Pierrot returned. His face was dark and gloomy, and he looked like a martyr returning from the place of torture, but yet retaining an air of triumph. He came towards me, and pointing to the dagger in my belt said, " The hour has passed ! "

" Hour ! what hour ? " asked I.

" The one you granted me; it was necessary for me to have so much time allowed me in which to bring you here. Then I conjured you to spare my life; now I supplicate you to take it away."

The most tender feelings of the heart — love, gratitude and friendship — united themselves together to torture me. Unable to say a word, but sobbing bitterly, I cast myself at the feet of the slave.   He raised me up in haste.

" What are you doing ? " cried he.

" I pay you the homage that is your due; but I am no longer worthy of friendship such as yours.   Can your friendship be pushed so far as to forgive me my ingratitude ? "

For a time his expression remained stern; he appeared to be undergoing a violent mental contest.   He took a step towards me, then drew back, and seemed on the point of speaking; but no words passed his lips.   The struggle was a short one, he opened his arms to embrace me, saying,—

" May I *now* call you brother ? "

My only reply was to cast myself on his breast.   After a short pause he added,—

" You were always kind, but misfortune had rendered you unjust."

" I have found my brother once again," said I.   " I am unfortunate no longer, but I have been very guilty."

" Guilty, brother ?   I also have been guilty, and more so than you; you are no longer unhappy, but I shall be so forever ! "

CHAPTER XLIII

THE expression of pleasure which the renewal of our friendship had traced on his features faded away, and an appearance of deep grief once more pervaded them.

"Listen," said he coldly. "My father was the King of Kakongo. Each day he sat at the door of his hut and dispensed justice among his subjects. After every judgment, according to the custom of the kings his ancestors, he drank a full goblet of palm wine. We were happy and powerful. But the Europeans came to our country; it was from them that I learned the accomplishments which you appeared to be surprised at my possessing. Our principal acquaintance among the Europeans was a Spanish captain; he promised my father territories far greater than those he now ruled over, treasure, and white women. My father believed him, and gathering his family together, followed him. Brother, he sold us as slaves!"

The breast of the negro rose and fell, as he strove to restrain himself; his eyes shot forth sparks of fire; and without seeming to know what he did, he broke in his powerful grasp a fancy medlar-tree that stood beside him.

"The master of Kakongo in his turn had a master and his son toiled as a slave in the furrows of St. Domingo. They tore the young lion from his father that they might the more easily tame him; they separated the wife from the husband, and the little children from the mother who nursed them, and from the father who used to bathe them in the torrents of their native land. In their place they found cruel masters and a sleeping place shared with the dogs!"

He was silent, though his lips moved as though he were still continuing his narrative; after a moment's pause he seized me roughly by the arm, and continued: "Brother, do you understand? I have been sold to different masters like a beast of burden. Do you remember the punishment of Ogé?

It was on that day that I saw my father after a long separation: *he was on the wheel!* "

I shuddered; he went on: —

" My wife was outraged by white men, and she died calling for revenge. I must tell you I was guilty towards her, for I loved another; but let that pass by. All my people urged me to deliver and avenge them; Rask brought me their messages. I could do nothing for them, I was fast in your uncle's prison. The day upon which you obtained my release, I hurried off to save my children from the power of a cruel master. Upon the very day that I arrived, the last of the grandchildren of the King of Kakongo had expired under the blows of the white man; he had followed the others! "

He interrupted his recital, and coldly asked me: " Brother, what would you have done? "

This frightful tale froze me with horror. I replied by a threatening gesture. He understood me, and with a bitter smile he continued: —

" The slaves rose against their master, and punished the murder of my children. They chose me for their chief. You know the frightful excesses that were perpetrated by the insurgents. I heard that your uncle's slaves were on the point of rising. I arrived at Acul on the night upon which the insurrection broke out. You were away. Your uncle had been murdered in his bed, and the negroes had already set fire to the plantation. Not being able to restrain them (for in destroying your uncle's property they thought that they were avenging my injuries), I determined to save the survivors of his family. I entered the fort by the breach that I had made. I entrusted your wife's nurse to a faithful negro. I had more trouble in saving your Marie; she had hurried to the burning portion of the fort to save the youngest of her brothers, the sole survivor of the massacre. The insurgents surrounded her, and were about to kill her. I burst upon them, and ordered them to leave her to my vengeance; they obeyed me, and retired. I took your wife in my arms; I intrusted the child to Rask,— and I bore them both away to this cavern, of which I alone knew the existence and the access. Brother, such was my crime!"

More than ever overwhelmed with gratitude and remorse, I would again have thrown myself at his feet, but he stopped me.

"Come," said he, "take your wife and let us leave this, all of us."

In wonder I asked him whither he wished to conduct us.

"To the camp of the whites," answered he. "This retreat is no longer safe. To-morrow at break of day the camp of Biassou will be attacked, and the forest will assuredly be set on fire. Besides, I have no time to lose. Ten lives are in jeopardy until my return. We *can* hasten because you are free; we *must* hasten because I am not."

These words increased my surprise, and I pressed him for an explanation.

"Have you not heard that Bug-Jargal is a prisoner?" replied he, impatiently.

"Yes; but what has Bug-Jargal to do with you?"

In his turn he seemed astonished, and then in a grave voice he answered: "*I am Bug-Jargal.*"

CHAPTER XLIV

I HAD thought that nothing that related to this extraordinary man could have surprised me. I had experienced some feelings of astonishment in finding the slave Pierrot transformed into an African king; but my admiration reached its height when from his own confession I learned that he was the courageous and magnanimous Bug-Jargal, the chief of the insurgents of Morne-Rouge; and I now understood the respectful demeanour shown by all the rebels, even by Biassou, to Bug-Jargal, the King of Kakongo. He did not notice the impression that his last words had made upon me.

"They told me," continued he. "that you were a prisoner in Biassou's camp, and I hastened to deliver you."

"But you told me just now that you too were a prisoner."

He glanced inquisitively at me, as though seeking my reason for putting this natural question. "Listen," answered he. "This morning I was a prisoner in the hands of your friends; but I heard a report that Biassou had announced his intention of executing, before sunset to-day, a young prisoner named Leopold d'Auverney. They doubled my guards, and I was informed that my execution would immediately follow yours, and that in the event of escape ten of my comrades would suffer in my stead. So you see that I had no time to lose."

I still detained him. "You made your escape then?" asked I.

"How else could I have been here? It was necessary to save you. Did I not owe you my life? Come, let us set out; we are an hour's march from the camp of the whites, and about the same distance from that of Biassou. See, the shadows of the cocoanut-trees are lengthening, and their round tops look on the pass like the egg of the giant condor. In three hours the sun will have set. Come, brother, time waits for no man."

In three hours the sun will have set! These words froze my blood, like an apparition from the tomb. They recalled to my mind the fatal promise which bound me to Biassou. Alas! in the rapture of seeing Marie again, I had not thought of our approaching eternal separation. I had been overwhelmed with my happiness; a flood of joyful emotions had swept away my memory, and in the midst of my delight I had forgotten that the inexorable finger of death was beckoning to me. But the words of my friend recalled everything to my mind. *In three hours the sun will have set!* It would take an hour to reach Biassou's camp. There could be no faltering with my duty. The villain had my word, and it would never do to give him the chance of despising what he seemed still to put trust in,— the word of a Frenchman; better far to die. The alternative was a terrible one, and I confess that I hesitated for a moment before I chose the right course. Can you blame me, gentlemen?

CHAPTER XLV

WITH a deep sigh, I placed one hand in that of Bug-Jargal, and the other in that of Marie, who gazed with anxiety on the sadness that had overspread my features.

" Bug-Jargal," said I, struggling with emotion, " I intrust to you the only being in the world that I love more than you,— my Marie. Return to the camp without me, for I may not follow you."

" Great heavens! " exclaimed Marie, hardly able to breathe from her terror and anxiety, " what new misfortune is this? "

Bug-Jargal trembled, and a look of mingled sorrow and surprise passed over his face. " Brother, what is this that you say? "

The terror that had seized upon Marie at the thought of the coming misfortune, which her love for me had almost caused her to divine, made me determine to spare her the dreadful truth for the moment. I placed my mouth to Bug-Jargal's ear, and whispered in hurried accents: " I am a prisoner. I swore to Biassou that two hours before sunset I would once more place myself in his hands; in fact, I have sworn to return to my death! "

Filled with rage, in a loud voice he exclaimed: " The monster! This then was his motive for a secret interview with you: it was to bind you with this fatal promise. I ought to have distrusted the wretch. Why did I not foresee that there must be some treachery lurking in the request, for he is a mulatto, not a black."

" What is this — what treachery — what promise? " said Marie in an agony of terror. " And who is Biassou? "

9

"Silence, silence," repeated I, in a low voice to Bug-Jargal; "do not let us alarm Marie."

"Good," answered he; "but why did you give such a pledge,— how could you consent?"

"I thought that you had deceived me, and that Marie was lost to me forever. What was life to me then?"

"But a simple promise cannot bind you to a brigand like that."

"I gave my word of honour."

He did not seem to understand me. "Your word of honour," repeated he; "but what is that? You did not drink out of the same cup; you have not broken a ring together, or a branch of the red-blossomed maple?"

"No, we have done none of these things."

"Well, then, what binds you to him?"

"My honour!"

"I cannot understand you; nothing pledges you to Biassou; come with us!"

"I cannot, my brother, for I am bound by my promise."

"No, you are not bound," cried he, angrily. "Sister, add your prayers to mine, and entreat your husband not to leave you. He wishes to return to the negro camp from which I have rescued him, on the plea that he has promised to place his life in Biassou's hands."

"What have you done?" cried I.

It was too late to stay the effects of the generous impulse that had prompted him to endeavour to save the life of his rival by the help of her he loved. Marie cast herself into my arms with a cry of anguish, her hands clasped my neck, and she hung upon my breast speechless and breathless.

"Oh, my Leopold, what does he say?" murmured she, at last. "Is he not deceiving me? It is not immediately after our reunion that you must quit me again. Answer me quickly, or I shall die. You have no right to throw away your life, for you have given it to me. You would not leave me, never to see me again!"

" Marie," answered I, " we shall meet again, but it will be in another place."

" In another place! Where? " she asked, in faltering accents.

" In heaven," I answered; for to this angel I could not lie.

Again she fainted, but this time it was from grief. I raised her up, and placed her in the arms of Bug-Jargal, whose eyes were full of tears.

" Nothing can keep you back, then," said he. " I will add nothing to my entreaties; this sight ought to be enough. How can you resist Marie? For one word such as she has spoken to you I would have sacrificed the world; and you cannot even give up death for her! "

" Honour binds me," answered I, sadly. " Farewell, Bug-Jargal! farewell, brother! I leave her to you."

He grasped my hand, overwhelmed with grief, and appeared hardly to understand me. " Brother," said he, " in the camp of the whites there are some of your relatives; I will give her over to them. For my part, I cannot accept your legacy."

He pointed to a rocky crag which towered high above the adjacent country. " Do you see that rock? " asked he; " when the signal of your death shall float from it, it will promptly be answered by the volley that announces mine."

Hardly understanding his last words, I embraced him, pressed a kiss upon the pale lips of Marie, who was slowly recovering under the attentions of her nurse, and fled precipitately, fearing that another look or word would shake my resolution.

CHAPTER XLVI

I RUSHED headlong, and plunged into the depths of the forest, following the tracks that we had left but a short time before, not daring to cast a glance behind me. To stifle the grief which oppressed my heart, I dashed, without a moment's pause, through the thickets, past hill and plain, until I reached the crest of a rock from which I could see the camp of Biassou, with its lines of wagons and huts swarming with life, and looking in the distance like a vast ant-hill. Then I halted, for I felt that I had reached the end of my journey and my life at the same time. Fatigue and emotion had weakened my physical powers, and I leaned against a tree to save myself from falling, and allowed my eyes to wander over the plain, which was to be my place of execution.

Up to this moment I had imagined that I had drained the cup of bitterness and gall to the dregs; but I had not until then tasted the most cruel of all misfortunes,— that of being constrained by powerful moral force to voluntarily renounce life when it appeared most sweet. Some hours before, I cared not for the world; extreme despair is a simulation of death which makes the reality more earnestly desired. Marie had been restored to me, my dead happiness had been resuscitated, my past had become my future, and all my overshadowed hopes had beamed forth more gloriously than ever; and again had a new life,— a life of youth and love and enchantment,— shone gloriously upon the horizon. I was ready to enter upon this life; everything invited me to it; no material obstacle, no hindrance, was apparent. I was free, I was happy, and yet — I was about to die. I had made but one step into paradise, and a hidden duty compelled me to retrace it, and to enter upon a path the goal of which was death!

Death has but few terrors for the crushed and broken

spirit; but how heavy and icy is his hand when it grasps the heart which has just begun to live and revel in the joys of life! I felt that I had emerged from the tomb, and had for a moment enjoyed the greatest delights of life, love, friendship, and liberty; and now the door of the sepulchre was again opened, and an unseen force compelled me once more to enter it forever.

CHAPTER XLVII

WHEN the first bitter pang of grief had passed, a kind of fury took possession of me; and I entered the valley with a rapid step, for I felt the necessity of shortening the period of suspense. When I presented myself at the negro outpost, the sergeant in command at first refused to permit me to pass. It seemed strange that I should be obliged to have recourse to entreaties to enable me to effect my object. At last two of them seized me by the arms and led me into Biassou's presence.

As I entered the grotto he was engaged in examining the springs of various instruments of torture with which he was surrounded. At the noise my guard made in introducing me he turned his head, but my presence did not seem to surprise him.

"Do you see these?" asked he, displaying the horrible engines which lay before him.

I remained calm and impassive, for I knew the cruel nature of the "hero of humanity," and I was determined to endure to the end without blenching.

"Leogri was lucky in being only hung, was he not?" asked he with his sardonic sneer.

I gazed upon him with cold disdain, but I made no reply.

"Tell his reverence the chaplain that the prisoner has returned," said he to an *aide-de-camp*.

During the absence of the negro, we both remained silent,

but I could see that he watched me narrowly. Just then Rigaud entered; he seemed agitated, and whispered a few words to the general.

"Summon the chiefs of the different bands," said Biassou calmly.

A quarter of an hour afterwards, the different chiefs in their strange equipments were assembled in the grotto. Biassou rose.

"Listen to me, friends and comrades! The whites will attack us here at daybreak; our position is a bad one, and we must quit it. At sunset we will march to the Spanish frontier. Macaya, you and your negroes will form the advanced guards. Padrejan, see that the guns taken at Pralato are spiked; we cannot take them into the mountains. The brave men of Croix-des-Bouquets will follow Macaya; Toussaint will come next with the blacks from Léogane and Trose. If the *griots* or the *griotes* make any disturbance, I will hand them over to the executioner of the army. Lieutenant-Colonel Cloud will distribute the English muskets that were disembarked at Cape Cabron, and will lead the half-breeds through the by-ways of the Vista. Slaughter any prisoners that may remain, notch the bullets, and poison the arrows. Let three tons of arsenic be thrown into the wells; the colonists will take it for sugar, and drink without distrust. Block up the roads to the plain with rocks, line the hedges with marksmen, and set fire to the forest. Rigaud, you will remain with me; Candi, summon my body-guard. The negroes of Morne-Rouge will form the rear-guard, and will not evacuate the camp until sunrise."

He leaned over to Rigaud, and whispered hoarsely: "They are Bug-Jargal's men; if they are killed, all the better. 'Muerta la tropa, murte el gefe!' ('If the men die, the chief will die.')

"Go, my brethren," he added, rising, "you will receive instructions from Candi."

The chiefs left the grotto.

"General," remarked Rigaud, "we ought to send that dispatch of Jean François; affairs are going badly, and it would stop the advance of the whites."

Biassou drew it hastily from his pocket. " I agree with you; but there are so many faults, both in grammar and spelling, that they will laugh at it."

He presented the paper to me. " For the last time, will you save your life? My kindness gives you a last chance. Help me to correct this letter, and to re-write it in proper official style."

I shook my head.

" Do you mean no? " asked he.

" I do," I replied.

" Reflect," he answered, with a sinister glance at the instruments of torture.

" It is because I have reflected that I refuse," replied I. " You are alarmed for the safety of yourself and your men, and you count upon this letter to delay the just vengeance of the whites. I do not desire to retain a life which may perhaps have saved yours. Let my execution commence."

" Ha, boy!" exclaimed Biassou, touching the instruments of torture with his foot, " you are growing familiar with these, are you? I am sorry, but I have not the time to try them on you; our position is a dangerous one, and we must get out of it as soon as we can. And so you refuse to act as my secretary? Well, you are right; for it would not after all have saved your miserable life, which, by the way, I have promised to his reverence my chaplain. Do you think that I would permit any one to live who holds the secrets of Biassou? "

He turned to the Obi, who just then entered. " Good father, is your guard ready? "

The latter made a sign in the affirmative.

" Have you taken it from among the negroes of Morne-Rouge, for they are the only ones who are not occupied in preparations for departure? "

Again the Obi bowed his head.

Then Biassou pointed out to me the black flag which I

had before remarked in a corner of the grotto. " That will show your friends when the time comes to give your place to your lieutenant. But I have no more time to lose; I must be off. By the way, you have been for a little excursion; how did you like the neighbourhood? "

" I noticed that there were enough trees upon which to hang you and all your band."

" Ah," retorted he, with his hideous laugh, " there is one place that you have not seen, but with which the good father will make you acquainted. Adieu, my young captain, and give my compliments to Leogri."

He bade me farewell with the chuckle that reminded me of the hiss of the rattlesnake, and turned his back as the negroes dragged me away. The veiled Obi followed us, his rosary in his hand.

CHAPTER XLVIII

I WALKED between my guards without offering any resistance, which would indeed have been hopeless. We ascended the shoulder of a hill on the western side of the plain, and then my escort sat down for a brief period of repose. As we did so, I cast a last lingering look at the setting sun, which would never rise again for me on this earth.

When my guards rose to their feet, I followed their example, and we descended into a little dell, the beauty of which under any other circumstances would have filled me with admiration. A mountain stream ran through the bottom of the dell, which by its refreshing coolness produced a thick and luxuriant growth of vegetation, and fell into one of those dark-blue lakes with which the hills of St. Domingo abound. How often in happier days have I sat and dreamed on the borders of these beautiful lakes, in the twilight hour, when beneath the influence of the moon their deep azure changed into a sheet of silver, or when the reflections of the stars sowed the surface with a thousand golden spangles! How lovely this valley appeared to me! There were magnificent plane-trees of gigantic growth, closely grown thickets of *mauritias*, a kind of palm, which allows no other vegetation to flourish beneath its shade; date-trees and magnolias with the goblet-shaped flowers. The tall catalpa, with its polished and exquisitely chiselled blossoms, stood out in relief against the golden buds of the ebony-trees; the Canadian maple mingled its yellow flowers with the blue aureolas of that species of the wild honeysuckle which the negroes call "coali;" thick curtains of luxurious creepers concealed the bare sides of the rocks, while from the virgin soil rose a soft perfume, such as the first man may have inhaled amidst Eden's groves.

We continued our way along a footpath traced on the brink of the torrent. I was surprised to notice that this path closed abruptly at the foot of a tall peak, in which was a natural archway, from which flowed a rapid torrent. A dull roar of falling waters, and an impetuous wind issued from this natural tunnel. The negroes who escorted me took a path to the left which led into a cavern, and seemed to be the bed of a torrent that had long been dried up. Overhead I could see the rugged roof, half hidden by masses of vegetation, and the same sound of falling waters filled the whole of the vault.

As I took the first step into the cavern, the Obi came to my side, and whispered in a hoarse voice, " Listen to what I have to predict: only one of us two shall leave by this path and issue again from the entrance of the cave."

I disdained to make any reply, and we advanced further into the gloom. The noise became louder, and drowned the sound of our footfalls. I fancied that there must be a waterfall near, and I was not deceived. After moving through the darkness for nearly ten minutes, we found ourselves on a kind of internal platform caused by the central formation of the mountain. The larger portion of this platform, which was of a semicircular shape, was inundated by a torrent which burst from the interior of the mountain with a terrible din. Above this subterranean hall the roof rose into the shape of a dome, covered with moss of a yellowish hue. A large opening was formed in the dome, through which the daylight penetrated; and the sides of the crevice were fringed with green trees, gilded just now by the last rays of the setting sun. At the northern extremity of the platform the torrent fell with a frightful noise into a deep abyss, over which appeared to float, without being able to illuminate its depths, a feeble portion of the light which came through the aperture in the roof.

Over this terrible precipice hung the trunk of an old tree, whose topmost branches were filled with the foam of the waterfall, and whose knotty roots pierced through the rock two or three feet below the brink. This tree, whose top and roots were both swept by the torrent, hung over the abyss like a skeleton arm, and was so destitute of foliage that I could not distinguish its species. It had a strange and weird appearance; the humidity which saturated its roots prevented it from dying, while the force of the cataract tore off its new shoots, and only left it with the branches that had strength to resist the force of the water.

CHAPTER XLIX

IN this terrible spot the negroes came to a halt, and I knew that my hour had come. It was in this abyss, then, that was to be sunk all my hopes in this world. The image of the happiness which but a few hours before I had voluntarily renounced brought to my heart a feeling of regret, almost one of remorse. To pray for mercy was unworthy of me, but I could not refrain from giving utterance to my regrets.

"Friends," said I to the negroes who surrounded me, " it

is a sad thing to die at twenty years of age, full of life and strength, when one is loved by one whom in your turn you adore, and when you leave behind you eyes that will ever weep for your untimely end."

A mocking burst of laughter hailed my expression of regret. It came from the little Obi. This species of evil spirit, this living mystery, approached me roughly.

"Ha, ha, ha! you regret life then, *Labadosea Dios!* My only fear was that death would have no terrors for you."

It was the same voice, the same laugh that had so often before baffled my conjectures. "Wretch!" exclaimed I, "who are you?"

"You are going to learn," replied he, in a voice of concentrated passion; and thrusting aside the silver sun that half concealed his brown chest, he exclaimed, "Look!"

I bent forward. Two names were written in white letters on the hairy chest of the Obi, showing but too clearly the hideous and ineffaceable brand of the heated iron. One of these names was Effingham; the other was that of my uncle and myself, D'Auverney! I was struck dumb with surprise.

"Well, Leopold d'Auverney," asked the Obi, "does not your name tell you mine?"

"No," answered I, astonished to hear the man name me, and seeking to re-collect my thoughts. "These two names were only to be found thus united upon the chest of my uncle's fool. But the poor dwarf is dead; and besides that, he was devotedly attached to us. You cannot be Habibrah."

"No other!" shrieked he; and casting aside the blood stained cap, he raised his veil and showed me the hideous features of the household fool. But a threatening and sinister expression had usurped the half imbecile smile which was formerly eternally imprinted on his features.

"Great God!" exclaimed I, overwhelmed with surprise, "do all the dead, then, come back to life? It *is* Habibrah, my uncle's fool!"

"His fool, and also his murderer."

I recoiled from him in horror. " His murderer, wretch! Was it thus that you repaid his kindness —"

He interrupted me. " His kindness! rather say his insults."

" What! " I again cried, " was it you, villain, who struck the fatal blow? "

" It was," he replied, with a terrible expression upon his face. " I plunged my knife so deeply into his heart that he had hardly time to cast aside sleep before death claimed him. He cried out feebly, ' Habibrah, come to me!' *but I was with him already!* "

The cold-blooded manner in which he narrated the murder disgusted me. " Wretch! cowardly assassin! You forgot, then, all his kindness; that you ate at his table, and slept at the foot of his bed —"

" Like a dog! " interrupted Habibrah, roughly, " *como un perro.* I thought too much of what you call his kindness, but which I looked upon as insults. I took vengeance upon him, and I will do the same upon you. Listen: do you think that because I am a mulatto and a deformed dwarf that I am not a man? Ah, I have a soul stronger, deeper, and bolder than the one that I am about to set free from your girlish frame. I was given to your uncle as if I had been a pet monkey. I was his butt; I amused him, while he despised me. He loved me, do you say? Yes, forsooth; I had a place in his heart between his dog and his parrot; but I found a better place there with my dagger."

I shuddered.

" Yes," continued the dwarf, " it was I, I that did it all. Look me well in the face, Leopold d'Auverney: you have often laughed at me, now you shall tremble before me. And you dare to speak of your uncle's liking for me,— a liking that carried degradation with it. If I entered the room, a shout of contemptuous laughter was my greeting; my appearance, my deformities, my features, my costume,— all furnished food for laughter to your accursed uncle and his accursed friends, while I was not allowed even to remain silent;

it was necessary for me to join in the very laughter that was levelled at me! I foam with rage when I think of it. Answer me: do you think that after such humiliations I could feel anything but the deadliest hatred for the creature that inflicted them upon me? Do you not think that they were a thousand times harder to endure than the toil in the burning sun, the fetters, and the whip of the driver, which were the lot of the other slaves? Do you not think that they would cause ardent, implacable, and eternal hatred to spring up in the heart of man as lasting as the accursed brand which degrades my chest? Has not the vengeance that I have taken for my sufferings been short and insufficient. Why could I not make my tyrant suffer something of what I endured for so many years? Why could he not before his death know the bitterness of wounded pride, and feel what burning traces the tears of shame leave upon a face condemned to wear a perpetual smile? Alas! it is too hard to have waited so long for the hour of vengeance, and then only to find it in a dagger thrust! Had he but known the hand that struck him, it would have been something; but I was too eager to hear his dying groan, and I drove the knife too quickly home: he died without having recognized me, and my eagerness balked my vengeance. This time, however, it shall be more complete. You see me, do you not? Though in point of fact you may be unable to recognize me in my new character. You have always been in the habit of seeing me laughing and joyous; but now nothing prevents me from letting my true nature appear on my face, and I do not greatly resemble my former self. You only knew my mask; look now upon my real face!"

At that moment his appearance was truly terrible. "Monster!" exclaimed I, "you deceive yourself; there is more of buffoonery than heroism in your face even now, and nothing in your heart but cruelty."

"Do not speak of cruelty," retorted he, "think of your uncle —"

"Wretch!" returned I, "if he were cruel, it was at your instigation. You, to pretend to pity the position of the poor slaves! Why, then, did you not exert all your influence to make their master treat them less harshly? Why did you never intercede in their favour?"

"I would not have done so for the world. Would I ever attempt to hinder a white man from blackening his soul by an act of cruelty? No, no! I urged him to inflict more and more punishment upon his slaves, so as to hurry on the revolt, and thus draw down a surer vengeance upon the heads of our oppressors. In seeming to injure my brethren I was serving them."

I was thunderstruck at such a cunning act of diplomacy carried out by such a man.

"Well," continued the dwarf, "do you believe now that I had the brain to conceive and the hand to execute? What do you think of Habibrah the buffoon? What do you think of your uncle's ' fool ' ? "

"Finish what you have begun so well," replied I. "Let me die, but let there be no more delay."

"And suppose I wish for delay? Suppose that it does my heart good to watch you in the plunder of suspense? You see Biassou owed me my share in the last plunder. When I saw you in our camp I asked for your life as my share, and he granted it willingly; and now you are mine, I am amusing myself with you. Soon you will follow the stream of the cataract into the abyss beneath; but before doing so, let me tell you that I have discovered the spot where your wife is concealed, and it was I that advised Biassou to set the forest on fire; the work, I imagine, is already begun. Thus your family will be swept from the face of the earth. Your uncle fell, by steel, you will perish by water, and your Marie by fire! "

"Villain! villain!" I exclaimed, and I made an effort to seize him by the throat, but a wave of his hand summoned my guards.

"Bind him!" cried he; "he precipitates his hour of doom! "

In dead silence the negroes began to bind me with the

cords that they had carried with them. Suddenly I fancied that I heard the distant barking of a dog, but this sound might be only an illusion caused by the noise of the cascade.

The negroes had finished binding me, and placed me on the brink of the abyss into which I was so soon to be hurled. The dwarf, with folded arms, gazed upon the scene with a sinister expression of joy. I lifted my eyes to the opening in the roof so as to avoid the triumphant expression of malice painted on his countenance, and to take one last look at the blue sky. At that instant the barking was more distinctly heard, and the enormous head of Rask appeared at the opening. I trembled.

The dwarf exclaimed, " Finish with him!" and the negroes, who had not noticed the dog, raised me in their arms to hurl me into the hell of waters which roared and foamed beneath me.

CHAPTER L

" COMRADES!" cried a voice of thunder.

All looked at the spot from whence the sound proceeded. Bug-Jargal was standing on the edge of the opening, a crimson plume floating on his head.

" Comrades," repeated he, " stay your hands! "

The negroes prostrated themselves upon the earth in token of submission.

" I am Bug-Jargal! " continued he.

The negroes struck the earth with their heads, uttering cries the meaning of which I could not comprehend.

" Unbind the prisoner! " commanded the chief.

But now the dwarf appeared to recover from the stupor into which the sudden appearance of Bug-Jargal had thrown him, and he seized by the arm the negro who was preparing to cut the cords that bound me. " What is the meaning of this? What are you doing? " cried he.

Then, raising his voice, he addressed Bug-Jargal: " Chief of Morne-Rouge," cried he, " what are you doing here? "

" I have come to command my own men," was the reply.

" Yes," answered the dwarf, in tones of concentrated passion, " these negroes do certainly belong to your band; but," added he, raising his voice again, " by what right do you interfere with my prisoner? "

The chief answered, " I am Bug-Jargal!" and again the negroes struck the ground with their foreheads.

" Bug-Jargal," continued Habibrah, " cannot contravene the orders of Biassou. This white man was given to me by Biassou; I desire his death, and die he shall. Obey me," he added, turning to the negroes, " and hurl him into the abyss!"

At the well-known voice of the Obi the negroes rose to their feet and took a step towards me. I thought all was lost.

" Unbind the prisoner!" cried Bug-Jargal again.

In an instant I was free. My surprise was equalled by the fury of the Obi. He attempted to throw himself upon me. The negroes interfered; then he burst out into imprecations and threats.

" Demonios! rabia! inferno de mi alma! How, wretches, you refuse to obey me? Do you not recognize my voice? Why did I lose time in talking to this accursed one? I ought to have had him hurled without delay to the fishes of the gulf. By wishing to make my vengeance more complete I have lost it altogether. *Orabia de Satan.* Listen to me: if you do not obey me, and hurl him into the abyss, I will curse you; your hair shall grow white, the mosquitoes and sand-flies shall eat you up alive; your legs and your arms shall bend like reeds; your breath shall burn your throat like red hot-sand; you shall die young, and after your death your spirit shall be compelled to turn a millstone as big as a mountain, in the moon where it is always cold!"

The scene was a strange one. I was the only one of my colour in a damp and gloomy cavern surrounded by negroes with the aspect of demons, balanced as it were upon the edge of a bottomless gulf, and every now and then threatened by a deformed dwarf, by a hideous sorcerer upon whose striped garments and pointed cap the fading light shone faintly, yet protected by a tall negro who was standing at the only point from which daylight could be seen. It appeared to me almost that I was at the gates of hell, awaiting the conflict between my good and evil angels, to result in the salvation or the destruction of my soul. The negroes appeared to be terrified at the threats of the Obi, and he endeavoured to profit by their indecision.

"I desire the death of the white man, and he *shall* die; obey me!"

Bug-Jargal replied solemnly: "He shall live! I am Bug-Jargal; my father was the King of Kakongo who dispensed justice at the gate of his palace."

Again the negroes cast themselves upon the ground.

The chief continued: "Brethren, go and tell Biassou not to unfurl the black banner upon the mountain-top which should announce to the whites the signal of this man's death, for he was the saviour of Bug-Jargal's life, and Bug-Jargal wills that he should live."

They rose up. Bug-Jargal threw his red plume on the ground before them. The chief of the guard picked it up with every show of respect, and they left the cavern without a word. The Obi, with a glance of rage, followed them down the subterranean avenue.

I will not attempt to describe my feelings at that moment. I fixed my eyes, wet with tears, upon Pierrot, who gazed upon me with a singular expression of love and tenderness.

"God be praised," said he, "you are saved! Brother, go back by the road by which you entered; you will meet me again in the valley."

He waved his hand to me and disappeared from my sight.
10

CHAPTER LI

EAGER to arrive at the appointed meeting-place, and to learn by what fortunate means my saviour had been enabled to make his appearance at so opportune a moment, I prepared to leave the cavern in which my nerves had been so severely tried; but as I prepared to enter the subterranean passage an unexpected obstacle presented itself in my path. It was Habibrah!

The revengeful Obi had not in reality followed the negroes as I had believed, but had concealed himself behind a rocky projection of the cave, waiting for a propitious moment for his vengeance; and this moment had come. He laughed bitterly as he showed himself. A dagger, the same that he was in the habit of using for a crucifix, shone in his right hand. At the sight of it I recoiled a step.

"Ha, accursed one! did you think to escape me? But the fool is not such a fool after all! I have you, and this time there shall be no delay. Your friend Bug-Jargal shall not wait for you long,— you shall soon be at the meeting-place; but it will be the wave of the cataract that shall bear you there."

As he spoke he dashed at me with uplifted weapon.

"Monster!" cried I, retreating to the platform, "just now you were only an executioner; now you are a murderer."

"I am an avenger!" returned he, grinding his teeth.

I was on the edge of the precipice; he endeavoured to hurl me over with a blow of his dagger. I avoided it. His foot slipped on the treacherous moss which covered the rocks, and he rolled into the slope polished and rounded by the constant flow of water.

"A thousand devils!" roared he.

He had fallen into the abyss. I have already mentioned that the roots of the old tree projected through the crevices of the rocks, a little below the edge of the precipice. In his fall the dwarf struck against these, and his striped petticoat caught in them; he grasped at them as a last hope of safety, and clung to them with all the energy of despair. His pointed bonnet fell from his head; to maintain his position he had to let go his dagger, and the two together disappeared in the depths of the abyss.

Habibrah, suspended over the terrible gulf, strove vainly to regain the platform, but his short arms could not reach the rocky edge, and he broke his nails in useless efforts to obtain a hold on the muddy surface of the rocks which sloped down into the terrible abyss. He howled with rage. The slightest push on my part would have been sufficient to hurl him to destruction; but such an act would have been one of cowardice, and I made no movement. This moderation on my part seemed to surprise him. Thanking Heaven for its mercies, I determined to abandon him to his fate, and was about to leave the cave, when, in a voice broken with fear, and which appeared to come from the depths of the abyss, he addressed me.

" Master," cried he, " master, do not go, for pity's sake! Do not, in the name of Heaven, leave a guilty creature to perish whom it is in your power to save! Alas! my strength is failing me; the roots bend and slip through my fingers; the weight of my body drags me down: I must let go, or my arms will break! Alas! master, the fearful gulf boils and seethes beneath me! *Nombre santo de Dios!* Have you no pity for the poor fool? He has been very guilty, but prove that the white men are better than the mulattoes, the masters than the slaves, by saving him!"

I approached the brink of the precipice, and the feeble light that broke through the aperture in the roof showed me on the repulsive features of the dwarf an expression which I had never noticed before,— that of prayer and supplication.

" Señor Leopold," continued he, encouraged by the movement of pity that I showed, " can you see a fellow-creature in so terrible a position of peril, without stretching out a hand to save him? Give me your hand, master; with very slight assistance from you I can save myself: I only ask for a little help. Help me then, and my gratitude shall be as great as my crimes!"

I interrupted him. "Unhappy wretch, do not recall them to my memory."

"It is because I repent of them that I do so. Oh, be generous to me! O heavens, my hand relaxes its grasp, and I fall! *Ay desdichado!* Your hand, your hand! in the name of the mother who bore you, give me your hand!"

I cannot describe the tone of agony in which he pleaded for help. In this moment of peril I forgot all; he was no longer an enemy, a traitor, and an assassin, but an unhappy fellow-creature, whom a slight exertion upon my part could rescue from a frightful death. He implored me in heart-rending accents. Reproaches would have been fruitless and out of place. The necessity for help was urgent and immediate.

I stooped, knelt down on the brink of the precipice, and grasping the trunk of the tree with one hand, I extended the other to Habibrah.

As soon as it was within his reach, he grasped it with both his hands, and hung on to it with all his strength. Far from attempting to aid me in my efforts to draw him up, I felt that he was exerting all his powers to draw me down with him into the abyss. If it had not been for the assistance afforded to me by the trunk of the tree, I must infallibly have been dragged over by the violent and unexpected jerk that the wretched man gave me.

"Villain!" cried I, "what are you doing?"

"Avenging myself!" answered he, with a peal of devilish laughter. "Aha, madman! have I got you in my clutches once more? You have of your own free-will placed yourself again in my power, and I hold you tight. You were saved and I was lost; and yet you of your own accord place your head between the jaws of the alligator, because it wept after having roared. I can bear death, since it will give me revenge. You are caught in the trap, *amigo*, and I shall take a companion with me to feed the fishes of the lake."

" Ah, traitor! " cried I, struggling with all my strength, " is it thus that you serve me when I was trying to save you? "

" Yes," hissed he. " I know that we could have saved ourselves together, but I would rather that we should die at the same moment. I had rather compass your death than save my life. Come down! "

As he spoke, his brown muscular hands renewed their grasp upon mine with unexpected strength; his eyes blazed, his mouth foamed. The strength, the departure of which he had before so piteously bewailed, had returned to him increased a thousandfold by the hope of revenge. His feet were planted like two perpendicular levers on a ledge of rock, and he struggled like a tiger against the root which, entangled in his clothes, supported him in spite of himself; for he was endeavouring with all his might to shake himself free, so as to bring all his weight to bear on me, and to drag me more quickly into the yawning gulf below. In his rage he endeavoured to bite me, while his hideous features were rendered more terrible by their expression of satanic frenzy. He looked like the demon of the cave seeking to drag down his victim to his abode of gloom and darkness.

One of my knees, by good fortune, was planted in a groove of the rock, and my arm was wound round the trunk of the tree, and I strove against the efforts of the dwarf with all the strength that the feeling of self-preservation could give me at such a moment. Every now and then I drew a long breath, and shouted " Bug-Jargal! " with all the force of my lungs. But the roar of the cascade and the distance that he must be off gave me but faint hopes of my voice reaching him.

The dwarf, who had not anticipated so vigorous a resistance on my part, redoubled his efforts. I began to grow weak, though in reality the struggle had not taken so long as the narration of it. A violent pain paralyzed my arm, my sight grew dim, bright sparks flashed before my eyes and a buzzing sound filled my ears. I heard the creaking of the root as it bent, mingled with the laugh of the monster, and the abyss seemed to rise up towards me as though eager to engulf its prey. But before I gave up all hope I made a last effort, and collecting together my exhausted forces, I once again shouted, " Bug-Jargal! "

A loud bark replied to me; it was Rask who thus answered my appeal for help. I glanced upwards: Bug-Jargal and his dog were gazing at me from the orifice in the roof. He saw my danger at once. " Hold on! " cried he.

Habibrah, fearing that I might yet be saved, foamed with rage; and crying, " Come down there! come down! " he renewed the attack with almost supernatural vigour.

At this moment, weakened by the long struggle, my arm lost its hold of the tree. All seemed over with me, when I felt myself seized from behind. It was Rask! At a sign from his master he had leaped down on the platform, and seized me by the skirts of my uniform with his powerful teeth.

This unlooked-for aid saved me. Habibrah had exhausted all his strength in a last convulsive effort; while I put forth all mine, and succeeded in withdrawing my hand from his cramped and swollen fingers. The root, which had been for some time yielding, now parted suddenly; Rask gave me a violent pull backwards, and the wretched dwarf disappeared in the foam of the cascade, hurling a curse at me which was swallowed up with him in the whirl of waters.

Such was the terrible end of my uncle's fool.

CHAPTER LII

THE excitement of the last few hours, the terrible struggle and its awful conclusion, had utterly exhausted me; and I lay where I had fallen, almost deprived of sense or power of motion. The voice of Bug-Jargal restored me to myself.

" Brother," cried he, " hasten to leave this place. In half an hour the sun will have set; I will meet you in the valley. Follow Rask."

The words of my friend restored hope, strength, and courage to me. I rose to my feet. The great dog ran rapidly down the subterranean passage; I followed him, his bark guiding me through the darkness. After a time I saw a streak of light, and in a few minutes I gained the entrance, and breathed more freely as I passed through the archway. As I left the damp and gloomy vault behind me, I recalled to my mind the prediction of the dwarf, and its fatal fulfilment, " One only of us shall return by this road! " His attempt had failed, but the prophecy had been carried out.

CHAPTER LIII

BUG-JARGAL was waiting for me in the valley. I threw myself into his arms; but I had so many questions to put to him that I could not find words in which to express them.

" Listen to me," said he. " Your wife, my sister, is in safety in the camp of the white men; I handed her over to a relative of yours who was in command of the outposts, and I wished again to constitute myself a prisoner, lest they should execute the ten prisoners whose lives were security for my re-appearance. But your relative told me to return, and, if possible, to prevent your execution; and that the ten negroes should not be executed until Biassou should announce the fact by displaying a black flag on one of the highest peaks of the mountains. Then I returned to do my best. Rask led me to where you were; thanks be to Heaven, I arrived in time! You will live, and so shall I."

He extended his hand to me, adding, " Brother, are you satisfied? "

I again clasped him to my breast; I entreated him not to leave me again, but to remain with the white troops, and I promised him to exert all my influence to procure him a commission in the colonial army.

But he interrupted me with an angry air. "Brother," asked he, "do I propose to you to join *my* army?"

I kept silence, for I felt that I had been guilty of a folly; then he added in a tone of affected gaiety,—

"Come, let us hurry to the camp to reassure your wife."

This proposal was what I most ardently desired; we started at once. The negro knew the way, and took the lead; Rask followed us.

Here D'Auverney stopped suddenly, and cast a gloomy look around him; perspiration in large beads covered his forehead; he concealed his face with his hands. Rask looked at him with an air of uneasiness.

"Yes, you may well look at me like that," murmured he.

An instant afterwards he rose from his seat in a state of violent agitation, and followed by the sergeant and the dog, rushed hurriedly from the tent.

CHAPTER LIV

"I WILL lay a bet," said Henri, "that we are nearing the end of the drama; and I should really feel sorry if anything happened to Bug-Jargal, for he was truly a famous fellow."

Paschal removed from his lips the mouth of his wicker-covered flask, and said, "I would give twelve dozen of port to have seen the cocoa-nut cup that he emptied at a draught."

Alfred, who was gently humming the air of a love-song, interrupted himself by asking Henri to tie his aguilettes; then he added: "The negro interests me very much, but I have not dared to ask D'Auverney if he knew the air of ' Beautiful Padilla.' "

" What a villain that Biassou was! " continued Paschal; " but for all that he knew the value of a Frenchman's word! There are, however, people more pitiless than Biassou,— my creditors, for instance."

" But what do you think of D'Auverney's story? " asked Henri.

" *Ma foi*," answered Alfred, " I have not paid much attention to it; but I certainly had expected something more interesting from D'Auverney's lips; and then I want to know the air to which Bug-Jargal sang his songs. In fact, I must admit that the story has bored me a little."

" You are right," returned Paschal, the *aide-de-camp*. " Had I not had my pipe and my bottle, I should have passed but a dreary evening. Besides, there was a lot of absurdities in it: how can we believe, for instance, that that little thief of a sorcerer (I forget his name) would have drowned himself for the sake of destroying his enemy? "

Henri interrupted him with a smile. " You cannot understand any one taking to water, can you, Captain Paschal? But what struck me more than anything was, that every time D'Auverney mentioned the name of Bug-Jargal, his lame dog lifted up his head."

The sound of the sentry carrying arms warned them of D'Auverney's return. All remained silent. He walked up and down the tent for a few moments with folded arms, without a word.

Old Sergeant Thaddeus, who had returned with his captain, bent over Rask and furtively caressed him, hoping by that means to conceal his countenance, which was full of anxiety, from the eyes of his officer. At length, after making a strong effort, D'Auverney continued his narrative.

CHAPTER LV

RASK followed us. The highest rock in the valley was not yet lighted by the rays of the sun; a glimmer of light touched it for an instant, and then passed away.

The negro trembled, and grasped my hand firmly. " Listen," said he.

A dull sound like the discharge of a piece of artillery was heard, and was repeated by the echoes of the valleys.

" It is the signal," said the negro in a gloomy voice. " It was a cannon shot, was it not? "

I nodded in sign of the affirmative.

In two bounds he sprang to the top of a lofty rock; I followed him. He crossed his arms and smiled sadly. " Do you see that? " asked he.

I looked in the direction to which he pointed, and on the lofty peak to which he had drawn my attention during our last interview with Marie, and which was now glowing in the rays of the setting sun, I saw a huge black flag, its folds flapping idly in the breeze.

[At this point of his recital D'Auverney again paused.]

I learned afterwards that Biassou, in a hurry to leave his ground, had ordered the flag to be hoisted without waiting for the return of the negroes who had been despatched to assist at my execution.

Bug-Jargal was still in the same position, his arms folded, and his eyes eagerly fixed upon the fatal signal. Suddenly he started, and seemed about to descend from his post of observation. " Great heavens! my unfortunate comrades! " cried he. " Did you hear the gun? "

I made no reply.

" It was the signal, my brother. They are leading them now to the place of execution."

His head fell upon his breast; after a short pause, he said: "Go, brother, and rejoin your wife; Rask will guide you to her;" and he whistled an African air, which Rask appeared to recognize, for he wagged his tail, and seemed ready to set out.

Bug-Jargal grasped my hand, and strove to smile; but his features were contracted, and his look was ghastly. "Farewell forever!" cried he, and dashed into the thicket by which we were surrounded.

I remained motionless; the little that I understood of the position made me fear the worst.

Rask, on seeing his master disappear, advanced to the edge of the rock, and raising his head uttered a plaintive howl. Then he turned to me; his tail was between his legs and his eyes were moist. He looked at me with an air of inquietude, and turned to the spot from which his master had disappeared, and barked several times. I understood him, and shared his fears. Suddenly he dashed off in pursuit of his master, and I should soon have lost sight of him had he not every now and then halted to give me time to come up to him. In this manner we passed through many a valley and leafy glade; we climbed hills and crossed streams. At last —

D'Auverney's voice failed him, an expression of despair covered his face, and he could not find words to continue his narrative. "Continue it, Thaddeus," said he, "for I can go on no further."

The old sergeant was not less distressed than his captain, but he made an effort to obey him.

"With your permission, gentlemen," said he, "and since it is your wish, Captain, I must tell you, gentlemen, that Bug-Jargal (otherwise called Pierrot) was a tall negro, very strong, very gentle, and the bravest man in the world,— except you, Captain, if you please. But I was terribly prejudiced against him,— for which I will never pardon myself, though you, Captain, have forgiven me,— so much so, that when we heard that your execution had been fixed for the evening of the second day I flew into a furious rage with the poor fellow, and felt a fiendish pleasure in informing him that his death would pay for yours, or that if he escaped ten of his men would be shot by way of reprisal. He said nothing upon hearing this, but an hour afterwards he made his escape through a great hole which he pierced in the wall of his prison."

[D'Auverney made a movement of impatience, and Thaddeus continued.]

" Well, when we saw the great black flag hoisted on the mountain, and as the negro had not returned,— a fact which surprised none of us,— our officers ordered the signal gun to be fired, and I was directed to conduct the ten negroes to the place of execution, which was a spot we call the Devil's Mouth, about — but it does not matter how far it was from the camp. Well, as you can imagine, we did not take them there to set them at liberty. I had them bound, as is the custom, and paraded my firing party, when who should burst upon us but the tall negro. He was out of breath with the speed that he had made.

" ' Good evening, Thaddeus,' said he. ' I am in time.'

" No, gentlemen, he did not utter another word, but hastened to unbind his comrades. I stood there in stupefaction. Then (with your permission, Captain) there was a good deal of generous argument between the other negroes and himself, which might have lasted longer, but — well, it is no good hiding the fact, it was I that stopped it. At any rate he took their place. Then the great dog came, poor Rask! He leaped at my throat: he ought to have held me longer, but Pierrot made a sign to him, and the poor brute released me; but he could not be prevented from taking his place at his master's feet. Then, believing that you were dead, Captain — well, I was in a fine rage. I gave the word; Bug-Jargal fell, and a bullet broke the dog's foot.

" Since that time, gentlemen," continued the sergeant,

sadly, " Rask has been lame. Then I heard groans in the adjacent wood; I reached it, and found you: a stray bullet had hit you as you were running forward to save the tall negro. Yes, Captain, you were wounded, but Bug-Jargal was dead!

" We carried you back to the camp; you were not dangerously wounded, and the doctors soon cured you; but I believe Madame Marie's nursing had a good deal to do with it."

The sergeant stopped in his story, and D'Auverney, in a solemn voice, added: " Bug-Jargal was dead!"

Thaddeus bowed his head. " Yes," said he, " he spared my life, and I — killed him."

EPILOGUE

THE reader, in general, is seldom satisfied with the con- clusion of a narrative unless it enters into every detail in winding up the story. For this reason the minutest re- searches have been made into the facts having reference to the concluding details of the last scenes of Leopold d'Auver- ney's life, as well as those of his sergeant and the dog Rask.

The reader is already aware that the captain's feelings of melancholy arose partly from the death of Bug-Jargal, other- wise called Pierrot; but he is not acquainted with the fact that those feelings were terribly increased by the loss of his beloved Marie,— who, after having been preserved from the horrors that attended the taking of Fort Galifet, perished in the burning of Cap, which took place some weeks later.

The fate of Leopold d'Auverney may be briefly recapitu- lated. A great victory had been won by the Republic forces against one of those united European armies which so often struggled vainly against our soldiers; and the General of Di- vision, who was in command of the entire force, was seated in his tent drawing up, from the reports of his staff, the bulletin which was to be sent to the National Convention concerning the victory of the day before. As he was thus occupied, an *aide-de-camp* announced to him the arrival of a Representa- tive of the People, who demanded an audience. The general loathed these ambassadors of the guillotine, who were sent by the party of the Mountain to humiliate the military offi- cers, and too often to demand the heads of the most gallant of the men who had fought bravely for the Republic,— look- ing upon them as chartered informers charged with the hate- ful mission of spying upon glory. But it would have been dangerous for him to refuse to admit him, especially after

158

such a victory as had resulted to the arms of the Republic. The gory idol which France had then set up almost invariably demanded victims of the highest lineage; and the executioners of the Place de la Révolution were delighted if they could at the same time cause a head and a coronet to fall,— were it one of thorns, like that of Louis XVI.; of flowers, like those of the girls of Verdun; or of laurels like those of Custine or of André Chénier. The general, therefore, gave immediate orders that the Representative of the People should be introduced to his presence.

After a few clumsy congratulations regarding the recent victory, the Representative of the People came up close to the general, and muttered in a suppressed voice: "But this is not all, Citizen General; it is not enough to destroy the foreign enemy,— those nearer home must be also crushed."

"What do you mean, Citizen Representative?" asked the astonished general.

"There is in your division," answered the emissary of the Convention, in an unpleasant manner, "a captain named Leopold d'Auverney, who is serving in the Thirty-second Brigade; do you know him, General?"

"Know him! certainly I do," replied the general; "only as you came in I was reading the report of the adjutant-general which refers to him. The Thirty-second Brigade had in him an excellent officer, and I was about to recommend him for promotion."

"What, Citizen General!" interposed the representative, harshly, "were you thinking of promoting him?"

"Such was most certainly my intention, citizen."

"Victory has blinded you, General," cried the representative, imperiously; "take care what you say or do. If you cherish serpents who are the enemies of the people, take care that the people do not crush you and the serpents at the same moment. This Leopold d'Auverney is an aristocrat, a hater of the revolution, a royalist, a Girondin! Public justice demands his head, and he must be given up to me on the spot."

"I cannot do so," replied the general, coldly.

" How! you cannot do so? " shouted the representative, whose rage was redoubled at this opposition. " Are you ignorant, General, of the extent of my power? I, in the name of the Republic, command you, and you have no option but to obey. Listen to me: in consideration of your recent success, I will read you the report which has been handed in regarding this D'Auverney, and which I shall send with him to the Public Prosecutor: ' Leopold Auverney (formerly known as D'Auverney), captain in the Thirty-second Brigade, is convicted of having, at a meeting of conspirators, narrated an anti-revolutionary tale, conducing to the ridicule of the true principles of Equality and Liberty, and exalting the worn-out superstitions known under the names of *royalty* and *religion;* convicted, secondly, of having used expressions deservedly forbidden by all good republicans, to describe certain recent events, notably those referring to the negroes of St. Domingo; convicted, thirdly, of having made use of the expression *Monsieur* instead of *Citizen* during the whole of his narrative; and, by the said narrative, of having endeavoured to bring into contempt the Republic one and indivisible, and also to propagate the infamous doctrines of the Girondins.' Death is the punishment for these crimes, and I demand his body. Do you hesitate, General, to hand this traitor over to me, to meet the well-merited punishment of his crimes? "

" Citizen," answered the general, with dignity, " this enemy of his country has given his life for her. As a contrast to your report, listen to an extract from mine: ' Leopold d'Auverney, captain in the Thirty-second Brigade, has contributed largely to the success that our arms have obtained. A formidable earthwork had been erected by the allies; it was the key to their position, and it was absolutely necessary to carry it at the point of the bayonet. It was an almost impregnable position, and the death of the stormers who led the attack was almost inevitable. Captain d'Auverney volunteered to lead the forlorn hope; he carried the earthwork, but was shot down at the moment of victory. Sergeant

Thaddeus of the Thirty-second, and a large dog were found dead within a few paces of him.' It was my intention to propose that the National Convention should pass a vote that Captain Leopold d'Auverney had merited the thanks of his country. You see, Citizen Representative," continued the general, calmly, " that our duties differ slightly. We both send a report to the Convention. The same name appears in each list: you denounce him as a traitor, I hold him up to posterity as a hero; you devote him to ignominy, I to glory; you would erect a scaffold for him, while I propose a statue in his honour. He is fortunate in having, by death in action, escaped the infamy you proposed for him. He whose death you desired is dead; he has not waited for you."

Furious at seeing his conspiracy disappear with the conspirator, the Representative muttered, " Dead, is he? More's the pity ! "

The general caught his words, and in indignant tones exclaimed: " There is still something left for you, Citizen Representative. Go seek for the body of Captain d'Auverney among the ruins of the redoubt. Who can tell if the bullets of the enemy may not have spared his head for his country's guillotine? "

THE END.

Lightning Source UK Ltd.
Milton Keynes UK
UKOW04n1547081113

220664UK00004BA/37/A